MW01226692

# TWILIGHT WORLDS

## BEST OF NEW MYTHS ANTHOLOGY, VOLUME TWO

SCOTT T. BARNES    J.E. BATES    MARY SOON LEE
JAMES EASTICK    CHRISTINA SNG    LISA TIMPF
DEBORAH L. DAVITT    JOSH PEARCE
SHANNON CONNOR WINWARD    BETH CATO
SAMANTHA HENDERSON    TRAVIS HEERMANN
TIMOTHY GWYN    LYNNE SARGENT    D. A. D'AMICO
GENE TWARONITE    RONALD D. FERGUSON
MARTA TANRIKULU    MARGE SIMON
RODDY FOSBURG    ROBERT MITCHELL EVANS
GERALD WARFIELD    JAMEYANNE FULLER
STEPHEN    ANNE E. JOHNSON    DAVIAN AW
JENNIFER LORING    SUSAN SHELL WINSTON
ALY PARSONS    BARUCH NOVEMBER
JOANNE STEINWACHS    RUSSELL HEMMELL
BRUCE BOSTON    DAN MICKLETHWAITE

NEW MYTHS PUBLISHING

**TWILIGHT WORLDS**
BEST OF NEW MYTHS ANTHOLOGY, VOLUME TWO
Edited by Scott T. Barnes, Marta Tanrikulu, and Susan Shell Winston

Cover Art "Sunset Music" © 2020 by June

Cover Art layout © 2020 by Arielle Rohan-Newsom

# CONTENTS

# INTRODUCTION

If 2020 didn't get you thinking about the end of an age, I don't know what would. The global pandemic and reactions to it may have changed forever the way humanity faces a crisis. In addition to the tragic loss of life, freedoms have been sacrificed, families divided, elections influenced, economies wrung out, on-line kings crowned and small businesses bashed, government debt mushroomed...

Who would have thought?

All is not bleak. The end of every era brings a new spring. This anthology explores those endings and beginnings across four broad categories:

> Section I - Collapse
> Section II - The Journey to New Edens
> Section III - Ever Evolving, Ever Revolving
> Section IV - Accepting Loss

Publishing *Twilight Worlds* was a long project turned longer with the onset of Covid 19 and subsequent lockdown. The editors would like to thank the contributors who have waited so patiently to see their "babies" see the light of day. Not a single one wrote to ask "Where in the blazes is this promised anthology?" We hope *Twilight Worlds* meets your expectations.

Editors

Scott T. Barnes, Marta Tanrikulu, and Susan Shell Winston

# SECTION I

## COLLAPSE

*Every act of creation is first an act of destruction.*
*—Pablo Picasso*

# THE COLORS OF THE SUN

## J. E. BATES

**About the Author**

J. E. Bates is a lifelong communicant of science fiction, fantasy, horror and other mind sugar and screen candy. He has lived in Finland, Singapore, California and many worlds between. Currently, he can be found at jebates.com.

Snow powdered the angled roofs and pagodas of the ancient city, dropping flakes on a sullen, angry crowd. Citizens and refugees alike sheltered under the eaves, watching enemies file in through the open gates.

*The wolfpack stalks the stumbling deer.* Forest-born, Laen understood that law, but it also governed mortal realms. The cities of the weak fell to the guns of the strong. He understood that now, but he still seethed with helpless rage.

The soldiers marched to the rat-a-tat-tat of snare drums and the tramp-tramp of marching feet. The sun, white and distant, sparkled on breastplates and bayonets. Steel masks shaped like griffons, dragons, and raptors concealed the faces of the conquerors. Mailed hands carried white pennants marked with black grids and magic squares. Every so often, a soldier stretched his wings skyward in triumph, displaying feathers pearly, ebon, or smoke gray. Boots and hooves churned snow to slush. The Angelarchy had arrived.

*I hate them,* Laen thought. He squatted in the mire next to Koa, peering through the spokes of a wagon wheel. The archons outnumbered the forest-folk by more hands of hundreds than he could reckon; they numbered more than leaves on a tree, than the stars in the sky. How could he loathe so many? The spectacle defeated him. Anger gave way to hunger and numbing cold. The next apple rind, the next damp cellar, circumscribed his world now.

"Where's the volant bastard?" Koa asked. She squatted under their ratty blanket. Like his tunic, her linen kirtle hung in filthy rags. "I want to see a flying castle."

"The Volant Bastion," he said, patient. Only nine, she needed a mother, but had only him. "I don't know where it is."

"But you're a far-seer."

"Do not say it," he hissed. "Please. Try and remember, Koa."

Petulant, she grabbed muddy snow and put it in her mouth.

"Do not eat that!"

"I'm hungry." She wiped her hand on the blanket. "Will they burn the city too?"

"No, even soldiers must winter."

"I want eggy porridge and quince marmalade and acorn cakes."

"When the crowd breaks up, we'll put out our hands."

She cringed. "I won't."

"We must eat."

"I won't beg anymore."

"Please, Koa. More hands mean more food."

"A man spat on me," Koa said. "He says there's not enough, that dirty Misja should go back to the forest. Why do they hate us? The angels burned the trees, not me."

Laen stared at her thin hand. Food would grow scarcer with the army here. *It is one thing, grand-mage,* he thought, *to teach me to see a hundred miles. But you never prepared me for this.*

His grand-mage's voice came, raspy and unbidden from the far-mind, the enchanted eidolon of her memory. It was all that remained of her. In the far-mind, she sat beneath a quilt, rocking beside a crackling fire on a winter's eve. Tree-roots roofed the burrow.

*Thought tilled the earth and planted the corn,* her memory said. *Thought built the cities, minted the coins, and forged the arms. Thought wrote the books where thought lies enshrined. Whomsoever thought enshrines holds mind's power.*

Laen did not answer, for one could not speak to a far-mind, only listen. He said to Koa, "Spring is but a month away. Then we'll return to the greenwood, to warm and plenty."

"You say that every day."

"Because it's true."

"We'll die blue-faced." She wiped her eyes. "Like the man in the cellar."

"He died of a war-wound. Spring is but a month away."

Stubborn, Koa flung snow toward the road.

Tramping boots gave way to the clatter of wagon wheels. Carts drawn by yaks and centaur thralls lumbered past, laden with booty and stores. Next came carts bearing prisoners as trophies of war: knights in bloodstained mail; changelings of the mountains, bound in chains; archon apostates, wings hacked off and hexagons cut into bare torsos.

*We may not survive,* Laen thought. He was young; he should have fled to the coast, fled this land. Yet he alone of the Misja carried the far-mind. He alone preserved her memories. He must stay for the sake of his people.

The next wagon crystallized his fears. It carried Misja witches, their bodies squat and round beside the lanky, hollow-boned archons. Misja skin and hair varied from eggplant dark to grass green, touching every color in the spectrum. Only their blood stayed the same, as red as other mortals. But Misja witches did not carry mortal blood. Occult power transmuted it.

The conquerors knew this and displayed these special captives on racks. Strange colors trickled from deliberate wounds. From one witch came a greenish trickle; from another, violet ooze. The drops froze and fell into flasks and decanters. Moans cut above the din of turning wheels.

Laen yanked the blanket over Koa's eyes. Too late.

"Mama!" she cried.

"She's not there."

"Mama. Gram-mage."

"Shh."

She trembled beneath the blanket. "I wanna go home."

"Spring comes soon."

On the wagon, a warlock with skin the color of a gourd turned toward Laen. Lacerated cheeks showed cerulean trickling from his bandaged eyes.

Under the blanket, Koa shivered. "Will they burn the witches?"

"No," Laen said, "they will let them sleep." But in truth, fire wasted a witch's innate power. The Angelarchy would bleed them, drop by drop.

∽

CAMPFIRES DOTTED THE SNOWBOUND CONFINES OF THE MARKET square. The Hoikimi townsfolk hurried home to barred windows, shuttered doors. Misja voices called out in hushed tongues from the fires. Some sang of their lost forest. Others stared into the fire. Fear cast long shadows across the city.

"Alms, sir!" Laen shouted at a passerby. "A crust of bread, a hay-copper! Pity your woodland cousins!" His throat rasped, worked ragged by the bracing air. Where once bread or coin fell, now his begging cup stood empty. Hunger gnawed. Cold bit. Koa shivered under the blanket, too cold to hold out her shaking hand. They must eat and shelter soon.

An elderly Misja stopped, recognition flickering in sienna eyes. His face contorted with fear. "You are First Apprentice of the Great Grand-Mage?

"I am, father."

"You must go from here!"

"Where, father?" Laen rattled his cup, undeterred. "Where would we go?"

"Off the streets!" the man hissed. "The angels are pricking hands, seeking witches." He held up his palm. A fresh cut scored the creases. Crimson blood stained the cold, the natural red showing the old man was no witch. The stranger scuttled off.

Laen buried his face between his knees, the cup slipping from his fingers. He pictured the fire-lit burrow, the figure in his far-mind. *What now, grand-mage?*

From afar, an answer: *Whom thought enshrines holds mind's power.*

*What does that mean? Where do I go?*

But the far-mind could not answer.

*Enshrined, enshrined...surely, she didn't mean the archons. No, she meant something else.* He found it in the store of her memories. He shook Koa awake. "Come. We must go."

"Where?" She rose with effort.

"A place I know. It's risky, but we must chance it."

They left the market square, moving like ghosts toward quieter districts along the river, hewing to side streets but avoiding the darkest alleys. With his far-sight, he scouted ahead around corners, avoiding archon patrols and gangs of thieves and desperate men. Night and cold deepened as the moon rose.

Ahead lay the broad loop of the river, sheltering the high town beyond an inner wall. A bridge linked inner and outer cities, casting long shadows across the illuminated ice. Gate-houses and drawbridges sealed it on both ends.

Koa planted her feet and wouldn't budge. "We can't cross."

"The ice can bear our weight."

"We'll drown."

"Trust the grand-mage. She told me so."

That got her moving again and they scurried down the embankment and out onto the ice. The bridge's shadow provided cover from watchful eyes. On the far side, he found an old sluice-gate the far-mind knew. It opened onto a dark, decrepit sewer, but Misja dwelt in burrows and did not fear the dark places under the earth, only hunger and cold. They passed into the inner ward through the tunnel, exiting via a drain.

Here, the broad, silent streets were free of thieves and beggars. Safety at last, though Misja were not permitted here. Laen led them toward a particular two-storey manse, a place the far-mind knew. The house was shuttered but firelight shone through window slats.

He thumped the knocker against the ancient oak. The steel ring showed a dragon devouring its tail, cold to the touch.

After a moment, the door opened a crack, spilling light

across the sill. A brass chain prevented it from opening further. A Hoikimi serving-woman opened the door then tried to slam it shut.

Laen put his foot between it and the frame. "Please, mother."

"Begone."

"I must see the burgomaster. Please."

"We have no truck with Misja paupers." The door pressed his foot.

"Laen, angels are coming," said Koa. She tugged his sleeve, pointing.

He glanced down the road.

Archon boots crunched on stone, accompanied by high, alien voices. The angels spoke their own tongue, ancient and intricate, its pronunciation guarded by tradition. Beams from storm lanterns chased down the cold, silent street.

Laen grabbed his knife and cut his palm. Yellow blood beaded along the palm, knotting like tree sap. He held it up for the woman. "I am no beggar. Look!"

"Witch-blood!" she hissed, recognizing its import.

"I am no mere witch; I am First Apprentice of the Far-mind. Fetch your master."

The door crushed against his foot. "You must leave!"

Laen abandoned caution, shouting: "Burgomaster! Are you there?"

"Who is at my door?" said another Hoikimi, a deeper bass. The burgomaster himself appeared. He unchained the door and opened it, though the girth of his mink-lined doublet barred the way. "First Apprentice, you say?"

"Yes, master." Laen pled with his eyes. The tramping boots approached, now only mere houses away. "I am a far-seer and First Apprentice to the Great Grand-Mage herself. I claim guest-right by the ancient treaties between my mentor and the Burgomasters of Min Kirl."

"Well, well," the Burgomaster said, eyeing Koa with a wrinkled nose. "Perhaps I can make room for you, but who is this?"

"My—sister."

"Well, well. Come in, then. We have fire and food."

A HOT MEAL LATER, KOA SLUMBERED BENEATH A WOOL BLANKET. The serving-woman bustled the dishes away, her scowl telling what she thought of such guests come so late. The burgomaster acted more welcoming.

Laen let down his guard for the first time in ages, glancing around the warm, cozy room. The homey furnishings, the crackling fire reminded him of grand-mage's lost burrow. He fought against envy, unable to blame the burgomaster for his good fortune. The Hoikimi had not burned out the Misja or started the war with the Angelarchy. They were victims, too. Laen expressed his gratitude instead.

The burgomaster nodded in acknowledgment, sipping spirits distilled of whey and making small talk, though his features betrayed an occasional flicker of annoyance. Perhaps he'd rather be in bed—Laen could not blame him. As Laen ate, his host asked after the grand-mage's treasures.

"Burned up in the flames," Laen said, "with her burrow."

"More the pity," said the burgomaster. "We lost so much to their fires."

Laen picked at the bandage across his left palm, remembering. The conflagrations had raged throughout the dry season, mile-wide fires that gutted field and forest alike with the infernal power of the archon pyromancers. "As did we."

"A senseless waste!" the burgomaster snapped. "Destruction profits no one."

"Misja witches draw strength from the forests," Laen said.

"Your mages tap river and field. Their infernos broke the back of our power before their armies even crossed the frontier."

"Perhaps so," the burgomaster said. He regarded Laen with pursed lips. "Why did you not retreat with our garrison? Our armies will make a last stand on the western shores. Foolish, of course. They have no chance. Still, they would have taken you into their ranks. Misja witches are welcome allies."

"Your garrison marched out in the dead of night," Laen said. "I did not have foreknowledge of their departure. Had I known..." He trailed off: he would not have left Koa or his people.

The burgomaster chuckled, a dry, crackling sound, like his fire. "The far-seer could not foresee this?"

"Far-sight is not foresight. I cannot see what I do not know."

"Then the Misja are lost," he said. "As are the Hoikimi." He sat back in his chair, sipped his whiskey.

From outside, the door-knocker thudded. The housekeeper scurried out of the parlor to answer it.

Laen sat up, worried.

"Do not fear," said the burgomaster. "It is only my friends."

"You have my trust," Laen said, settling back into his seat. "And I'm sorry for the conquest of your city. The Hoikimi Regime has ever been a friend of the Misja."

"Don't be sorry, First Apprentice," the burgomaster said. "Do you know the phrase, 'The sun has wings'?"

"No," Laen said, adjusting Koa's blanket. "It sounds like an archon proverb."

"It is," said his host. "It means those who fly, rule. It is time for accommodation, Laen. It is time for peace."

Something in the man's voice startled Laen. The words presaged a breaking of faith, an ending of things. "Is this why you opened your gates without a fight?"

"I am sorry, First Apprentice." A heavy tread came down the hall. "We are all subjects of the Angelarchy now."

The housekeeper reappeared, leading a handful of armored archons. Firelight glinted orange off steel hawk-masks. "There!" she said, pointing. "Misja witches!"

"You betrayed us!?" Laen shouted at the Burgomaster. The man looked at the ground, unwilling to meet his eyes.

Mailed hands seized Laen. Others lifted Koa from the couch. She awoke to archons holding her. Her legs kicked out as she screamed.

"I betrayed only you, First Apprentice," said the burgomaster. "The girl may stay in my service in honor of our treaties. It is for the best."

"Laen!" Koa shouted. "Spring! Don't leave me! You promised! Spring!"

"You're safe here, Koa!" he said, struggling against half a dozen hands.

Only after the guards secured them in their strong grips did a more senior archon enter the room. He proved no soldier but a priest and an aged one at that. His wings were bound with iron bands, whether as punishment or penance, Laen did not know. The archon drew proving knives then beckoned toward the guards holding Koa.

She cried out as an archon twisted her wrist and bared her palm. She balled her fist and kicked.

"Don't cut her!" Laen shouted. He fought in vain against strong hands. "She's no witch!"

The priest gashed the back of Koa's wrist. She screamed. The wound showed red. Not a witch.

"How odd," the priest said in fluent Hoikimi. "This boy is as orange as a squash, the girl as green as a leaf. You say they are siblings. Is there no end to the variety of these lop-eared midges? We have not enough hounds to run them all down."

The burgomaster winced. "There's no rhyme to the Misja, milord. They don't breed true like other folk. A blue may take a red to bride and their get will be green, yellow, orange—who can say. They carry in their eyes, hair, skin every hue and pigment. Only the blood stays true: red as all mortals."

"Save for warlocks," said the priest, thin lips curled back in a smile.

"As you say, milord," said the burgomaster. "Witch-blood runs to every color of the sun."

"Blood is the grease of progress," the priest said, sharpening his knife against a whetstone, "but the blood of Misja witches is another thing altogether. Occult power congeals in their veins, untapped. Such power is the property of our God-King. This is the purpose of Angelarchy: the demarcation and allocation of all things within the world."

The priest grabbed Laen's unmarked palm and turned it upward in a smooth, practiced motion. The knife cut once, hard. The blade bit like ice, then fire, before giving way to a dull, throbbing ache. Amber blood trickled between his fingers, dripping to the floor.

Grimacing, Laen curled his fingers over the tell-tale sign. The cut betrayed his first secret. The other would follow soon enough. *I'm sorry, grand-mage. I failed.*

The priest caught a drop of Laen's golden witch-blood on one gray fingertip and held it up to the light. "Ha! We snare a warlock this night. You may keep the girl, burgomaster. But the witch comes with us."


II.

"It is an unfortunate situation," said the archon priest. He'd given his name as Hierophant Hlo-Hlodz, an Exsanguinator of the Volant Bastion. "You are a victim of Hoikimi intransigence. Had they surrendered the disputed territories as stipulated by the ancient treaties, no armed chastisement would have been necessary—and their realm would not have imploded like a puffball before our inexorable might."

The grandiose words washed over Laen, meaningless. The Angelarchy faked its treaties. The cities of the weak fell to the guns of the strong. He lay bound upon a slab in Min Kirl's tallest tower, a deserved fate. He'd failed Koa, failed the grand-mage, failed his people.

Hlo-Hlodz marked Laen's body with charcoal, indicating where the incisions would go. He named them the dextar ulnar, the palmar arch, the canalis facialis.

These words also meant nothing to Laen. Instead, he studied the priest: the first archon he'd seen without a steel mask.

Fine, hollow bones extended into the face, giving it a pinched, hawk-like visage. Thin, rangy, stooped—else the wings would not bear his weight. Smooth-skinned though, save for wispy, gray hair across a bald, speckled pate the color of parchment. The man appeared washed out, leeched of color. Patches showed within the black feathers, baring leathery skin. Age and the iron bands had atrophied his wings.

"That other Misja, she is your kin?" the Hierophant asked.

"An orphan I befriended," Laen said, picking his words with care. He did not care for this man to know Koa's relation to the grand-mage. "Nothing more."

"Curious. Our scholars wonder if Misja witches breed true, passing talent from parent to child."

"We do not," he spat. "The gift comes from the Dreaming Gods."

"Ah, yes. Your old, dead gods of wood and stone. How convenient to your theology that they slumber and render no aid! Can you not wake them with your cries?"

Laen glowered. "Our gods are true gods, not mortal men like your God-Kings. They may slumber, but they do not live among men, nor die like other men, demanding obelisks for tombs, each taller than their father's."

The hierophant ignored the jibe, laying out and polishing his knives. He adopted a reasoned, moderate tone. "Inform me when the numbing agents take effect. Only then shall I proceed with the necessary incisions. I take no undue pleasure in painful tasks."

"You lie! I saw witches on racks, mutilated heretics, centaurs lashed to yokes. Your Angelarchy rejoices in pain."

"You misunderstand," Hlo-Hlodz said, hands outstretched. "The army creates these spectacles to awe the conquered, forestalling rebellion and preserving the peace. These warnings save more lives, in the end. As for me, I provide my witches with food, warmth, recuperative baths, even the teachings of the Angelarchy. Attend the first lesson: the sacrifice of a few benefits the many."

"So you mean to farm us like milch-cows, squeezing out our blood until we die."

"Your essence belongs to the God-King. Such is the decree. Cooperation ensures comfort. Intransigence, the lash. Come, it is not so bad a life. Others must labor in the celaneum mines, where luminescent dusts inflict painful cysts and growths. Which do you prefer?"

Laen rolled onto his side, ignoring the honeyed mockery.

*Thought is the maker,* the far-mind said, *shaping and building the worlds. Let your mind master your thoughts until mind alone exists.*

But he could not do that while bound like this. And now his greatest secret would be revealed.

Hlo-Hlodz approached, reopened the incision on Laen's palm. Then the hierophant made another cut, a light gash across the shoulder.

Laen bit his lip against the pain. *Forgive me, grand-mage.*

"What's this?" Hlo-Hlodz gasped. "Cerulean from the shoulder?" Another quick gash scored Laen's cheek. Green drops billowed in the periphery of his vision. "Could it be you are polychromatic?!"

Laen said nothing. The pain hurt less than knowing his iridian blood would feed the engines of their enemies.

"Magnificent!" Hlo-Hlodz said, his eyes sparkling with genuine joy. "Outstanding! We thought only the veins of a Great Grand-Mage could produce every tincture, but here you are, my boy, here you are. Bleeding every color of the spectrum. I need my specialist texts! The *Haimaturgy of the Verja,* the Ouranian Enchiridion. Yet this backwater lacks even a complete *Encyclopedia Celefangorea!* What to do?" He waved his arms about and retreated to the bookshelf.

Laen groaned, hating himself.

His far-mind called out. *Our secrets,* whispered his grand-mage, *are written in a tome reached only in dream. It is named* The Book That Never Sleeps.

HLO-HLODZ DID NOT WISH TO RISK INJURING SO PRICELESS A specimen and ordered Laen taken back to his cell. Two archon soldiers marched him down a spiral stair, one in front, one behind. Halfway down the staircase, an open door led onto the battlements. Cold air billowed from without.

*Thought is the maker. It shapes and builds the worlds.*

Laen swept his foot backward then ducked.

The archon behind him stumbled and fell. He rolled across Laen's back and careened into his fellow. Then both cried out in a clatter of mail and flesh, tumbling down the stairs.

Laen darted out the open door, hands still manacled behind him. Winter cold blasted him like a fist but he did not care. Iridian blood pumped through his pounding heart.

The portal opened onto an enclosed barbican. A snow-covered tarp tented an indistinct siege engine. All around lay only machicolations and flurries. No ladders, no stairs. Just a white void of snow on a castle battlement.

He rushed to the farthest wall, leaning over. Forty ells below, the smooth, sheer wall dropped to the outer courtyard. No moat in sight. If he leapt, he would die.

His guards recovered fast. They rushed out onto the terrace, furious. One spat out in mangled Hoikimi: "What-how, witch-boy? *Mees-yeah* can't fly."

Laen said from his perch: "One step closer and I'll jump."

"Go on, un' less rabbit to bleed."

"The hierophant will take your wings if I die."

The guards traded worried looks. One growled. The other stalked off to fetch their priest.

Hlo-Hlodz, when he arrived, proved more solicitous. "Please, Laen! Come down from the brink. This is the height of folly!"

The interval had given Laen time to plan. "Free all the Misja in Min Kirl," he said. "Give them food and wagons and seeds so they may return to the wilds. Or I leap and you get half a gallon of my polychromatic blood and never another drop."

"Laen! Be reasonable!"

"It is your doctrine—the few for the many."

"You ask too much."

Laen dangled one foot over the edge. The icy stone stung like death through his ragged breeches. "The Great Grand-Mage is dead. I am the last iridian. The power transfers only at death. Choose, priest."

The guards spread and flexed their wings, readying for flight. Could they move fast enough to catch him before he hit the frozen courtyard below? Could they hold him aloft if they did? They could not. He knew it and they knew it. They were men with wings, not birds. They could only glide in a stiff, strong breeze. Legend said their bodies were shaped for another world, far from this place.

"Stay!" Hlo-Hlodz shouted. "Don't be rash! Your demands

are onerous. I will consult with the commandant of the cohort." He withdrew.

Laen crouched between two merlons, sheltering from the wind. Lazy flakes fell across his body, icing the many-colored wounds.

A HALF-TURN OF THE WHEEL LATER, THE HIEROPHANT RETURNED. "The commandant accedes to your demands. Behold the postern gate. Your burrow-kin depart."

Laen warned them. "I will watch them get to safety before I come down from the wall. I am a far-seer and my eyes can walk for miles. Do not send birds or riders or angels to pursue them or I will know!"

Hlo-Hlodz flung up his hands in disgust, retreated. But the archons kept their distance. Someone flung him a warm robe.

Laen watched the Misja vanish into the wilderness atop carts. At first, he watched with his eyes, still young and strong, but the black specks soon vanished over a snowy crest beyond the city walls. He pushed his eyes outward, his spirit-sight, his far-eyes, following his brethren like an unseen eagle.

A few miles from the city, the Misja broke into groups of threes and fours, scattering in many directions. No archons pursued. With their stores, the Misja could burrow, tough out the rest of winter beneath the frigid earth. No doubt some would survive, maybe even Koa. She rode aback a yak-cart with the others, red-eyed but munching a cheese rind.

He wished he could far-speak to her and bid her a safe journey but he lacked that gift. Still, he'd made the best bargain he could. It felt too little, helping the Misja of one city only. How many more lay dead or dying across this blasted land? How valuable was his iridian blood?

*Could I have demanded more?*

When his eyes tired and could far-see no more, he pulled them back. For a moment, he stared down at the icy courtyard so far below. One leap now would forestall torture and deny the Angelarchy the use of his blood.

"*Pink at dawn, white in winter, gold at noon, green in spring,*" his grand-mage had once said. "*We are the sun's evering.*"

"*You mean evening, grand-witch,*" he had answered back, all those years ago.

"*I mean evering, child.*"

"*I don't understand.*"

"*The sun's mind is forevering within the eternal now.*"

She spoke in riddles then but now he saw. His death could not be a breaking of a pledge. He climbed off the wall. Angry hands seized him. He did not resist.

THERE WOULD BE NO FURTHER ESCAPE. THE HIEROPHANT MADE sure of that. The guards chained him hand and foot and laid him within a well-appointed stagecoach, the hierophant's own. They would not remain in Min Kirl: the hierophant was taking his witches south. The wagons rolled through the open gates, escorted by a troop of forty cuirassiers. Hooves and wheels clattered across the drawbridge.

As hours wore into days, Laen settled into a routine of far-seeing and listening to his far-mind. All around the roads, winter wore heavy on an abandoned wasteland. His far-mind shared only warm memories: the scent of acorn-cakes, the freshness of spring, the rocking of grand-mage's chair beside her burrow's fire.

Each evening, the hierophant fed Laen broth, trusting no one else with the task lest they introduce poisons. Hlo-Hlodz also filled tiny vials with iridian blood. A clever archon, he concealed them throughout the wagon and on his person. Had grand-mage known their blood so valued, she might have bought off this invasion with a pint or two.

On the third day, Laen broke his silence. "Where do we go?"

"The Volant Bastion awaits," said Hlo-Hlodz said. "Its engines thirst for the blood of my witches."


III.

*There's your flying castle, Koa*, he thought, gazing upon the wonder. *There's your volant bastard.*

On the seventh day, they reached the capital of the Hoikimi Regime, present location of the Volant Bastion. Feeling charitable, the hierophant let Laen gaze out the coach-window at the buoyant throne-city of the God-King.

A great broad disc, a thousand ells in circumference, bore a massive structure of stone and bronze. Beneath, mighty lodestones rotated in ribbed carapaces. Above, tiers of towers and parapets hinted at gardens and domes of glass. Archons darted through the sky, graceful as kites amid billowing airships and hot-air balloons. Baskets and cranes conveyed a continuous stream of goods and wingless folk up and down.

The Bastion cast a long, dark shadow across the pagodas and angled roofs of the city below it. The Hoikimi capital smoldered, its walls knocked down. Soldiers came and went. Misery hung about like a miasma.

Before Laen knew it, he and the other witches were placed in baskets and lifted into the Volant Bastion.

"THE ASTRAL EMPIRE FELL THOUSANDS OF YEARS AGO— thousands!" the hierophant said. Knife scraped on knife, a fast, keening sound Laen had learned to dread. "It claimed to rule a hundred stars. Red ones, blue ones, yellow, even orange."

*What now,* Laen wondered. He tried to pull away.

"But stars have no color," the priest said. "That is an illusion caused by noxious vapors within the upper aethers. There are no other worlds and heaven is reserved for the God-Kings alone."

Laen coughed. "And for us?"

"For us profane ones, there is only this hell, this bastion of pain. Do you attend the lesson?"

Laen's chest heaved. "Yes."

Steel flashed in candlelight. Agony ensued.

Laen did the only thing he could do—he used his far-sight. He used his eyes to see. And in his agony, he pushed the far-sight farther than before, beyond where even grand-mage had said it could go, further than described in the legendary annals.

His eyes soared across a stark and snowy landscape. Ragged bands hunted and grubbed in the ruins of the Hoikimi Regime. In the west, nearest the ocean, a few ports remained in Hoikimi hands where the armies of the Angelarchy had yet to reach. But those towns were in chaos. Desperate men fought for the last places aboard fleeing ships.

He pushed his eyes further, across the western ocean. No army of relief gathered on the farther shore, only more cities, more kingdoms, some under snow, others under tyranny. There would be no aid from any quarter, not on this world.

Skyward he rose, moving out of the blue of day to night's ever-black. Pain became his ladder. The power responded, sending his mind soaring through celestial spheres. Music echoed from rotating spheres made of glass, each as vast as a planet's orbit. And there in the center hung a shining, silver disc, the legendary home of the gods.

Never had he flown so far, so fast, so free. Perhaps the pain unleashed new reservoirs of strength; perhaps his plight gave his ability unparalleled range.

The silver orb resolved into a rotating palace, built round

above as it was below, for it floated in the night sky, unrooted to the earth. Colossi of iron, copper, and gold held the gates. Seeing his approach, one raised a great-sword nine ells long. The sword moved as slowly as glacier ice.

Laen shot past the colossi as swift as a paper-wasp. The gods would aid his people! They must.

Eternal starlight played across crystal walls and lace curtains. Birdsong echoed from the garden, hinting of sunlight, foreshadowing spring. His spirit darted around the colonnades and among the thrones where the Dreaming Gods themselves slumbered.

They wore immense forms like no living man or woman, each figure molded of a single substance: ebony, amber, ivory, chalcedony, jade, and more besides. Each wore a shimmering liquidity of star-silk, the fabric of legend.

*Gods! Please, O gods! I beseech you!* He ran from figure to figure, tugging on their glorious raiment. Yet none would stir from their sleep. The Dreaming Gods remained sleeping still. Exhausted, his far-sight faded back to the roughhewn stones of the torture chamber.

"BLACK AND WHITE ARE NOT COLORS," SAID THE HIEROPHANT, cleansing a new set of instruments in a brass basin. "They are markers for the presence and absence of energy. There is no color in reason, there is no tint in logic, there is no tone in formalism. These are the equations of the God-King, the basis of Angelarchy." His speech complete, he advanced. "Oh, do open your eyes, Laen. I have so little pleasure in life. Would you deny me this?"

Laen's eyes opened. *What more can I do? Where else can I flee? I've seen the gods themselves. They would not aid me.* Every word hurt, but he strove for calm. "Teach me, priest, a different lesson. Do the gods themselves have gods of their own?"

The knife paused. "An interesting question. Yes. Nature arranges all things in magnitudes. There are entities above your dreaming gods, even our living God-Kings."

"Who?"

"There are...whispers...of beings older than the sun. Blasphemy, but if it helps you endure the blade, I shall give you their hard instruction. Learn first the name of Tsha the World-Eater, devourer of time."

The knife pricked again. "Grimmoth is named That Which Shadows the Moon."

Pain. "Ur-a-zu is the worm within the cosmic corpse."

Agony. "Great Kton they name the squirming, scarlet madness; the killer of stars."

Oblivion. "Nelgotha is the maw of the infinite void."

Unconscious, Laen pushed his far-sight above the green and blue bands of his world and through the celestial spheres. He soared past outer planets—sleepy, ringed Roëllo and cloud-girded Kathoth—beyond the limits of telescopy.

This brought him to a strange and formless place, where blasphemous entities piped above the maelstrom of creation. The great Ungods named by the hierophant appeared, vast and indifferent, lords of cosmic gulfs beyond mortal reckoning.

Ur-a-zu gnawed the roots of the World-Tree. Great Kton raised crimson tentacles within a crystalline cyst. All swam about the maw of the infinite void.

Yet though Laen cried out to each, they did not heed his call. He was a gnat alongside planets, invisible and irrelevant.

He failed and collapsed back to the world, his world. His prison cell. The agony of the Hierophant's blades. Surely, he would die now. No beings could exist beyond such entities. And though he'd beheld a wonder no Misja far-seer had ever before seen, no good came of it. He was done. His power had reached its end.

"We have completed our drainage for the day," the Hierophant said, his voice gentle. New underlings joined him, silent acolytes clad in robes and masks of flowing gray. Their raiment concealed narrow, jointed clockwork limbs and faces of brass. They moved with stiff, mechanical movements. They could only be automata, clockwork men, ancient artifacts known to serve the God-King.

Laen wondered if he dreamt still.

"Rest now," said Hlo-Hlodz, as the clacking, insect-like creatures carried Laen away. "Recoup your strength. Tomorrow we embark upon a great work, you and I. It is the highest honor that the Angelarchy can bestow upon you, this new form of service."

The clockwork men carried Laen to a warm but lonely tower. Too weak to move, he lay on the stone tablet, sipped broth, and slept.

At dawn, the great work began. The automata roused him, bound him, and carried him not to the bleeding chamber used in previous sessions but down a different passage. They descended zigzag staircases, arriving in a great furnace in the heart of the Bastion itself. Here, pistons thrust and fell while mighty gears knocked clanking teeth. Valves hissed hot steam across the room. Gauges spun. Dials turned.

In the center of it all, a bound woman hung upon a rack. At first, she appeared in the green, comely shape of a dryad. But within the minute she transformed into a sleek-furred lycan with black ears, then a pale Hoikimi, then an archon, then a sea-goblin. With every turn of the great gears, the changeling writhed in agony, forced to break her shape.

*We see a changeling,* said the far-mind of his grand-mage. *A shape-shifter, a skin-glamour, a were-mortal—none has ever beheld their true form.*

No changeling should shift so fast, Laen knew. No creature could endure such treatment for many months. Yet the engines drained her, shape after shape. The changeling's magic fed the lodestones keeping the Volant Bastion aloft.

Yet even as Laen watched, automata surged forward and removed her from her bonds. Some applied gauzes and unguents to her body. Then they bore her off, clanking like insects. The strange procession flowed by as one.

As she passed, the changeling locked pain-wracked eyes on Laen. Her lips did not move, but he heard a wisp of far-speech, echoed with the plea in her iridian eyes: *Kill me.*

The automata carried her out the door. Others lifted Laen into the now-empty place. They fitted him to straps, placed new accouterments onto old wounds. All the while, the pistons never ceased their mechanical rhythm. Strange machines rattled and blinked to the tick-tock of a great clock, the vast beating of a mechanical heart.

The Hierophant entered, accompanied by another archon whose cloth-of-silver and platinum mask marked him as the living God-King.

"Welcome to the Engine of the Volant Bastion," the God-King boomed. "Can you endure as well as our hamadryad? Can you play Sibyl to my great machine?"

The potentate waved a hand. Clockwork men surged forward. Screws drilled into Laen's thumbs, driving wires to his nerves. The engine did not drain his blood but drank his life essence from the source.

By now, Laen knew but one escape. He flung far-sight back across the cosmos. It soared through the clouds above the blue-green planet. It pushed beyond the sphere where the gods lay dreaming then plunged through the nameless abyss of the elder cosmos where the shapeless things cavorted to the keening flutes of the mad Ungods. He dove into the maw of the infinite void.

He came then to a further place—a great blankness, to a white that was not white, to where color was no color at all. The not-ness faded, resolving into a familiar burrow.

Roots canopied the ceiling. His grand-mage's chair still rocked, though empty, beside the fire. On her chair lay an old book, a few quills, an inkwell, her knitting.

In a daze, he picked up the volume, took the old, familiar seat. The book was bound in jester's motley and jewels and colored feathers. No title showed, but he knew through the unspoken intuition of dream that he held *The Book That Never Sleeps.*

He opened it, letting it fall open to the bookmarked page. This chapter told of the Angelarchy's conquest of the Hoikimi Regime, the fall of Min Kirl, and the rest. It described the binding of the First Apprentice as a Sibyl within the Volant Bastion. An illustration showed him taking the changeling's place.

With shaking fingers, he turned the page.

The next vellum lay blank.

For a long moment, he sat wondering. Then he picked up an inkwell and wrote. When he finished he shut his eyes.

WHEN HE OPENED THEM AGAIN, HE STILL HUNG FROM CHAINS amid the tubes and wires of the Great Engine. But now raw power surged through every nerve and muscle of his body. His eyes pulsated and glowed, cycling through the spectrum, throwing beams of iridian light in shifting patterns across the room. The beams burned through wires, shattered vacuum tubes.

The Great Engine shook as if gripped by a sky-quake. Whistles hissed and alarums sounded. Pistons snapped and steam hissed across the chamber. Magical librams tumbled from shelves, braziers overturned, spilling particolored blood and more fiery fluids. Fires erupted from spilt volatiles.

Automata scattered and clacked, arms flailing. The God-King cried out. "What is this?"

"I heave with illimitable power," Laen said.

Fear filled the God-King's voice. "What will you do?"

"This."


IV.

Spring pushed green and raw through the crackling carpet of melting ice. It filled streams and courses, washing away blackened trunks and last year's bones.

Koa walked through the fresh shoots, scattering seeds upon burrow, garden and field. She could not plant it all herself, no, the older witches would oversee that; the Misja would plant their gardens anew.

When the Volant Bastion crashed, everyone aboard died in its blazing wreck. The armies of the Angelarchy withdrew in confusion, generals choosing sides from a bloody civil war. The Hoikimi rallied, chased the invaders back over the border.

She'd learned all this through the far-mind. The gift came upon her in an instant as she huddled in a dark and damp burrow a hundred miles from the Bastion, eating a root. In the blink of an eye, the far-mind passed to her, flowed into her blood, turning it iridian. Only then did she know what Laen knew. And she knew that he was dead.

He murmured in her thoughts now, from time to time, sharing wisdom, telling riddles, just as grand-mage had done for him. It was strange and sad to hear his voice but not to be able to speak with him. But the far-mind was only an eidolon of the forest. It held the memories of Laen and his grand-mage and every grand-mage who came before; the far-mind held the thoughts of every father and mother down from the ages back to the roots of all things.

Now, as she flung new life into the earth, her transfigured blood flowed from her cut palms, marking the seeds with red, green, amber, purple-dawn, cerulean, gold, every color of the sun.

# RED

## MARY SOON LEE

**About the Author**

Mary Soon Lee was born and raised in London, but now lives in Pittsburgh. She writes both fiction and poetry, and has won the Rhysling Award and the Elgin Award. Her book *Elemental Haiku*, containing haiku for each element of the periodic table, has recently been published by Ten Speed Press. She has an antiquated website at marysoonlee.com and tweets at @MarySoonLee.

REDSHIFT, THE SPECTRAL SHIFT OF RECEDING GALAXIES.

Red, the color of sunset, of blood, of warning, of the passion that led to you, my dearest.

Red, a color seen as fortunate by the Chinese for most of our long history, an association that recent developments have reversed.

In 2016, scientists discovered that the universe was expanding 5% to 9% faster than expected: by then the universe was expanding 22% to 28% faster than original predictions.

By 2049, the expansion rate exceeded earlier expectations by 59%, an ever-accelerating discrepancy attributed to dark energy, the changing acceleration fitted by a doubly-exponential function.

By November 2056, the dreadful power of doubly-exponential growth visible to everyone in the red-tinged stars. Even the sun's nearest neighbors were speeding away from us fast enough to tinge them pinkly.

This morning, December 3rd, 2056, the sun rose red and remained red, rushing away from us, driven by forces we can neither fathom nor defy.

In minutes, the earth itself will sunder as I try to hold onto you, my baby daughter, my dearest, as the universe itself pulls us apart.

Have courage, don't cry, I promise it will be quick.

# RED SKY AT DAWN

## JAMES EASTICK

**About the Author**

James Eastick was born and raised in the sleepy and some-what poorly regarded backwater that is Norwich, England. Alongside a career in catering, James has dabbled in creating far off fictional worlds with several short stories published and a somewhat unhealthy enthusiasm for the works of Frank Herbert, George R R Martin, Scott Lynch and Gordon Ramsay. When not knuckle-deep in gumbo, he can be found avoiding any serious housework whilst pacing a furrow in the lounge carpet, trying to conjure more dystopian science fiction.

"WHY DO THEY GO?" GEN ASKED, TUGGING ON HER FATHER'S SHIRT sleeves.

He stood beside her, watching as the first of the ships departed, never to return. The vessel's searing blue rockets danced in his wide dark eyes, growing gradually dimmer as it soared high into the night's sky.

When they were all but gone, her father knelt down, placing one hand on each of her shoulders. "The Pilgrims, they have faith there is something out amongst the stars. They leave because they hope they might find it."

Gen looked up, trying to pick out the ship against a host of stars.

"Shouldn't we go too?" she asked.

His good humour evaporated and his hands gripped her tightly, the fingers pinching into her flesh. "No. We have to stay here." He let go and stood, watching the sky and the absent space the ship had left behind. Gen stretched out and took his hand in hers.

"Why does no one ever come back?" she said.

As soon as she'd spoken she knew she'd said the wrong thing. His lower jaw clenched, quivering so slightly she could barely see it, his eyes wrapped in water, but he said nothing. Instead he patted her atop her head and stroked down the side of her face, cupping her chin gently in his hand.

"I didn't mean to—"

"I know," he interrupted. His lips split apart and widened as he attempted to smile, but though his mouth lied, his pallid eyes told the truth. She smiled back in a way that inadvertently copied her father.

Behind him, the second Pilgrim vessel began its journey, launching into the air. He turned to watch it, guiding her forward with an arm around her shoulders. Around them, the rest of the crowd moved forward. Men and women held each other as they watched the departing ship, their faces cast with the same expression Gen's father possessed. She wondered about her mother every day, where she was and if she would come home, but the days continued to pass and with each one her memory faded a little more.

"Should we pray?" Gen asked.

"You can if you want," her father answered.

She didn't want to do it alone. In truth she couldn't remember what to say and had forgotten the holy words her mother had taught her. Her father never prayed anymore.

With the crowd of people now in front of her, she could no longer see the ships clearly. Her eyes wandered over the backs of their heads, the long dark hair, braided or loose, and the wrinkles in the neck of a tired old man in front. She was the first to notice the trucks that pulled up behind them.

She peered around her father's waist and saw lots of men pour from the back of the trucks. Every one of them wore grey uniforms and carried large plastic shields and black sticks that fizzed with electricity.

"Dad..." she uttered, hesitantly.

Others in the crowd had turned to see, hearing the noise. Their faces darkened and they seemed to no longer care for the Pilgrims or their ships.

"We have to go," Gen's father said, lifting her up and off her feet.

The reverence and piety was replaced by hate and anger in the people around her. They began to swear and scream, bunching together like an army. Across from them, the men in grey began thumping their fists against their shields in a steady rhythm. Gen buried her head against her father's shoulder.

"It's okay," he told her, stroking her long brown hair. "Just hold on tight."

She drew her arms around his neck and wished the world away. His shoulders were broad and strong and his chest rose and fell as he breathed. He smelled of sweat and dry earth, familiar, enveloping and comforting. The crowd surged around her and she held him tight.

When she did lift her head again, they were already at the station and the sounds of fighting had grown soft and distant. The train was almost free of passengers, so Gen's father set her down in the middle of the carriage. She picked a spot on the opposite side that looked out over the open plain between the port and the eastern Sahara.

The train started, moving off with an uneven jolt, and began to collect speed. Gen placed her hand against the cool glass and traced the outline of a jagged ridge in the distance with her finger. When she had been younger, her mother had brought her to the same place to see the dawn. They watched the way the red sun pierced cracks and dips in the ridge, casting long shadows like grasping fingers. The first time she'd seen it, it had scared her, but gradually she had grown familiar with it. Now it reminded her of her mother.

Morning had come by the time they arrived back in Hahran-Nulim, sending a pale orange over the horizon. Days passed quicker in summer than winter. The Sun grew strong and with it, the blood of men grew hot. Gen saw the change every year, even in her father.

A rage to mimic the red dawn.

She recalled her mother's voice, tempered by the sadness before she had left. Gen gripped her father's hand as they left the train.

Outside the station, a large group of adults had gathered in the plaza, surrounding a man upon a raised platform. When he spoke they cheered his words and chanted in unison. She could see their anger. The Red Sun was dawning.

The city was like a man in the grip of a fever. People swarmed the streets in crowds bigger than any Gen had ever seen. She bunched close to her father, following him as he cut a path through them back towards home.

Less than a few minutes in, she could no longer tell how far they'd come or even where they were. Everything looked so different. Across the street a tall glass building stood cracked and broken, nearly every panel smashed or torn out, and smoke poured from the empty spaces and fed upwards into the sky.

Gen's father pulled her down to the edge of the street where they made faster progress trudging through the dry gutters. Along the side of the street, men filled the usually empty alleyways, watching her as she passed with unfriendly eyes.

"You okay, Genny?" he said, looking down at her over his shoulder.

He held a forced smile. Gen nodded though the fear he couldn't disguise in his eyes made her feel worse. He stopped and turned back towards her, kneeling.

"We're not far from home, now," he continued. "We'll be there before you know it."

He swept a few loose strands of long brown hair back from her eyes and made a funny face, pinching her nose gently between his thumb and forefinger. She giggled and playfully jabbed him in the stomach.

"Is Carin going to be there?" she asked.

Carin was her father's special friend. She was very nice, but Gen had found it hard to like her, though she had promised to try.

"She's probably waiting for us right now," her father answered.

"I hope so," she said, lying.

Gen's father ruffled her hair and took her hand in his.

Back on the road, people continued to pass Gen and her father without seeing either of them. He held her hand so tight it almost hurt, but she didn't want him to let go. The deeper into the city they went, the crowds became bigger and huge buildings loomed overhead, their tops disappearing into the lowest clouds.

Far away she could hear rumbling, though the air was dry and there was no rain.

"What is that?" she asked her father.

If he heard her, he didn't answer, nor even stop to check. Others in the crowd slowed their pace, however, and looked to the heavens. Cracks of yellow light split the thick grey sky like faint creases. The Red Sun was high but smoke filled the air in a hazy blanket.

She knew nights were no longer safe in the heart of the city, but the days were turning dark too. Years before she'd been able to leave her apartment with her mother before the sunrise. Now her father shielded their windows with blinds that stayed closed day and night. He said that men had done something terrible and the world was dying.

They turned off the main street and rounded the featureless stone monolith she knew as home. Beneath the broad grey arch, Carin was waiting by the doors, her face drawn with worry. When she saw Gen's father, the worry lifted and evaporated.

"Alex!" she cried, running out onto the street.

It had always been odd for Gen to hear Carin use her father's name. The only other person she could recall using it was her mother.

"I knew you'd be here," her father said, with a smile.

He released Gen's hand and put his arms around Carin, hugging her.

"I was so worried," she said, "when you didn't come home and I saw the crowds starting to gather…"

"It's okay," he insisted. "We're fine."

"…And look at you, Gen," Carin said as she and her father broke apart. "Not a flicker of fear. Here's me, an absolute mess, but you…you're so brave. Just like your dad."

Gen smiled. She didn't know what else to do. She didn't feel brave.

"Come on," her father said, and he pushed open the door for Carin and ushered Gen in ahead of her.

The lobby interior was the same drab grey as the building's exterior. Several residents sat in the lobby, in chairs outside the superintendent's office. A boy from two floors up watched her as she walked in. His face was miserable, and the pale yellow lamps on the ceiling made him look ill. Gen knew him well enough not to like him. She stared back and stuck her tongue out.

Carin entered the lobby after her, still talking to her father.

"...and when they don't disperse, what happens then? The fleet is in orbit, just waiting for an excuse..."

She sounded upset. They were talking softly, in hushed tones, the way they always did,  thinking Gen couldn't hear them.

"Let's not jump to conclusions. We don't know what's happening yet," her father answered.

"You do know what's happening!" Carin said, matter-of-factly, and then quieted her voice a shade more. "Don't tell me you didn't hear the drop-ships coming in."

"I heard something."

"Oh come on!"

"This isn't the time," he said softly and brushed by her into the lobby. "Gen, go upstairs, we'll be right behind you."

Gen started up the steps, jumping two at a time. She could still hear the rumbling outside. The building shook ever so slightly each time it came and flakes of dust fell from the ceiling. Her father and Carin carried on their arguing behind her. She went up each flight of stairs quickly, trying to synchronise her jumps with the thunder so she couldn't hear them.

Her apartment was on the eighth floor, just next to the stair-well. Gen was still small and the eye scanner was located quite high up on the door, but her father kept an old box close by so that she could climb up to use it. The laser was warm as it passed over her face. It tingled, but she liked the way it felt. When she was smaller, her father would lift her up in his arms and hold her in front of it. She remembered how she would squirm and giggle and the way he would laugh too. He never laughed like that anymore.

The door opened and she stepped inside, pushing the box away with her foot. She went straight to the birdcage and opened it. The canary inside chirruped softly and side-stepped away from the open hatch, but when Gen reached inside it jumped onto her finger. In the past few months it had grown large and felt heavier to hold. It had been bought for her after her mother went away, but she wasn't allowed to tell anyone about it because it was contraband. The canary ate crumbs of bread from her other hand, its beak tickling her palm.

"Look, Dad. He's getting big," she said, smiling, as he walked in.

He didn't seem to hear her. He walked straight past, towards the window and peeled back the blind. The bird jumped from Gen's finger back into the cage.

"What's happening?" Gen asked.

"Nothing, don't worry."

She shut the cage and walked over to him.

"Can I see?"

"Not now," he insisted. "Go to your room and stay away from the window."

Gen scowled, but she did what her father said.

Her room felt cold. The sun was enough to warm it, but the blinds were closed and sealed tight. She sat on her bed and wrapped the duvet around her shoulders. The walls were thin and she could still hear their voices.

"They'll declare martial law, if they haven't done so already," Carin said.

"I'm not sure that's going to help at this point," her father answered.

"What do you mean?"

"There was trouble at the port, too. The police came but it's spreading. The city is on fire."

"And so they'll call in the army."

There was a pause, her father's voice returning soft and low.

"You were right," he said. "We should have left this place a long time ago. This planet is dying. Earth cares nothing for us. Their industry came and drained it dry, then left our people with nothing. The riots will only get worse until they break completely. Then it'll be too late."

Gen curled up on the bed with her back to the wall and tried to go to sleep. A sliver of light spilled in through a small crack in the blinds and touched upon her pillow. She laid her hand beneath it and felt the warmth.

Through the wall she could still hear her father and Carin talking. Gen stepped out from under her blankets and crept quietly towards the window. She pulled at the corner of the blinds and peeked through the gap.

The last vestiges of red sunlight flowed through the city streets below, washing everything in its colour: the buildings, the cars, the masked men and women. Orange and scarlet sparkled off the metal weapons they carried in their hands and fierce hatred burned in their eyes.

She inched back from the window, but held the gap open. The bedroom door opened behind her.

"Gen!"

Her father bounded over and picked her up.

"What did I tell you!"

He put her down on the bed. His face was carved with anger, reminding her of the people outside.

"I only wanted to see outside," she protested.

"It's not safe...God dammit, Genny! You've got to listen to me!"

"You're not supposed to say things like that. Mummy would never say that."

"Yeah, well, Mummy isn't here."

Gen sniffed, and fought back the tears she could feel welling up behind her eyes.

"Alex..." Carin said carefully, walking in through the doorway.

Her father stood up and stepped back, fury still etched across his face. Then, without another word, he stormed out of the room.

Carin stepped towards the edge of the bed and bent down beside her.

"Your dad, he didn't mean anything by that."

She stretched a tentative hand out towards Gen, but stopped halfway, holding it still in hesitation. Gen stayed as she was, her lower lip quivering, unable to stem the trickle of tears rolling down her cheeks. She wiped them away with the edge of her sleeve and turned to face Carin.

"Go away," she said.

Carin's face softened. She had sharp, angular features with pointed cheek bones and a clearly defined jaw. Gen saw the firmness of her flesh fade as though her youth were withering before her eyes, tempered by despair. Carin looked away and rose slowly to her feet, retreating from the room and closing the door gently behind her.

When the tears had ebbed and the sound of voices from the next room had ceased, Gen lifted her head up to look back at the window. The sun was beginning to set and the faint light in her room was growing darker, but a soft dull red still seeped in through the crack in the blinds.

She sat up and rubbed at her eyes with her forearms. The apartment was so quiet that the sound of her sniffs seemed to echo in her room. Anger and frustration boiled inside her, making her wonder if the rage that was touching her father would come to her too. He never spoke about Gen's mother anymore and she couldn't mention her without his mood darkening. It wasn't fair, Gen missed her too. She didn't want a canary or to move to another world or anything else. All she wanted was for things to go back to the way they used to be.

Gen pushed back the sheets and slipped off the bed, creeping barefoot to the door. She slowly turned the handle and peered out into the living room.

The shuttered windows shrouded most of the room in darkness, though a small lamp had been left on just outside her bedroom. Her cup was there too, holding the same water from yesterday. The white light from the bulb made her skin look like paper, and when she placed her hand in front of it, the spaces between her fingers glowed red like the Sun.

She pushed her bedroom door open and closed it softly again behind. The plastic floor was cold underneath her feet, drawing the warmth out from her toes. Water dripped from the kitchen tap, striking the metal sink with a repetitive monotonous sound. She picked up her cup and walked briskly across the room and reached her fingers up toward the tap. The sink itself was as high as her shoulders so that she had to tip-toe and draw herself up with one arm. She pushed at the valve, too hard, so that the water poured out hard, splashing into the sink and spraying up and around, soaking everything nearby, including her.

"Ugh!" she grumbled quietly, using the sleeve of her shirt to towel the water from her face.

She recalled the games she used to play with her parents, water fights in the summer sun before the rage came. They had to ration the water now and she'd been told she always had to finish what was in her cup before she could have more, but what she had was warm and stale and the smell of it made her wrinkle her nose. She poured it down the sink.

The door to her father's bedroom opened and he strode out

with Carin following.

"...this is just the beginning," Carin said. "You said it yourself, 'it's spreading.' This isn't just rioting anymore, it's revolution."

Gen hopped away from the sink and ducked behind the corner where she couldn't be seen.

"What is it you want me to do?" her father said, solemnly.

"We have to leave! There're already barricades up in the streets. If we don't go, we'll be stuck here!"

"Keep your voice down." Gen's father answered. "We can't leave now, it's too dangerous."

"And it'll only get worse..."

"So we have to wait it out."

Carin threw her hands down in dismay.

"Sometimes, I wonder if you hear anything I say." She sighed.

Gen's father jumped up to his feet, leaning over Carin aggressively.

"I made a promise, do you understand that? I made a promise and now... You're right, we should have left the city when we had the chance, but I'm not going out there again. If something were to happen to Gen, her mother would never forgive me."

Gen could see her father slump back down again, his hands clasped together as though in prayer. Carin knelt before him and placed a gentle hand on his shoulder.

"You're talking about the woman who left you and your daughter to chase a paradise that doesn't exist. There's nothing out there. This is the world we have. To leave you both behind for a fantasy, who would she be to judge?"

"That's not the way it happened," her father answered, weakly. "She left with the Pilgrims because she still had hope."

Gen inched forwards, her little hands pushed against the wall, balled into white spheres of fury. Anger built inside, but in her helplessness and the withering of her father, it transformed into beads of water in her eyes.

"I'm not seven years old. You don't have to feed me the same lies you feed Gen." Carin said, "No Pilgrim ever returns. It's a voyage into the aimless black that only blind faith could provoke. How long ago did you stop believing? It's not fair for you to have to carry her torch. It's not fair for you, for me; and if you won't face reality, what chance does Gen have?"

"Shut up!" Gen blurted, "Shut up! Shut up! Shut up!" She marched out from her hiding spot defiantly, unable to contain her fury a moment longer. "She is coming home, she promised she would and when she does you'll have to leave!"

Both her father and Carin turned their necks sharply to face her, their mouths open with shock and disbelief.

"Gen? Oh God!" Carin said, shrinking back ashamedly. "I'm so sorry, sweetheart, I...I didn't know you were there."

Her father rose and went over to her.

"You have to tell her, Dad!" Gen pleaded. "You have to tell her, Mum's coming home."

He looked back at her, eyes wide, but didn't say anything.

"Please..." she whimpered.

"Gen, your mother... She...she won't be coming home."

"Don't say that."

"I'm sorry."

His voice was weak, as though whispered through paper.

"I hate you," she told him. "I wish it was you that left."

"Gen..." he said, reaching out to her.

She pulled away from him and ran back to her room, slamming the door as hard as she could.

The thunder returned outside, slowly spreading like it had done before. Through the thick glass of her window, she could hear it coming steadily closer. Gen sunk away from the window and sat on the floor with her back to the bed, trying not to listen.

A knock came at her door. She heard her father clear his throat on the other side.

"Gen, I'm sorry. Can I come in?"

"No! Leave me alone."

His shadow passed away from the gap under the door, leaving just the narrow strip of light. Gen watched and waited for him to return. When he didn't, she crawled under her bed and hid in silence and darkness.

When Gen woke, the red outside her window had long since faded. The clock beside her bed held nothing but an empty display, flashing on and off with three zeros. She rubbed the tiredness from her eyes and stretched her arms up above her head, then, quietly as possible, she got dressed and opened her bedroom door.

The sound of her father sucking in a lungful of air made her heart jump. She pulled the door back so it was almost closed and put an eye up to the narrow gap. He was snoring softly on the old sofa, his quiescent face lit with the pale light of the lamp outside her room.

When the canary saw her, it jumped in response and fluttered about in its cage, singing a soft, sweet tune. Carefully, she crept over to it, stepping over her father's outstretched legs, and opened the hatch. The bird hopped onto the edge of the opening and stood, silently twirling its head left and right, eyeing her expectantly.

Gen took a handful of seed and held it up. In the dark, the bright yellow seemed drawn from its feathers, the quick bobbing movements no longer so graceful. It rested on the edge of her thumb, tapping down at the seed in her palm. She watched it for a while, waiting to see what it would do when it had finished, though when it did, it simply angled its head back towards her, as though asking for more.

She took another handful of seed and tipped it onto the table outside the cage and, leaving the hatch open, she went to fetch her jacket and favourite pair of shoes.

From the lobby downstairs she could see the shades of both

moons glowing in the dark. She leaned against the windows and looked up and down the length of the street. The glass felt cold against her fingers, but the road was clear.

Placing a hand around the fixed steel handle, she pulled until she felt the hermetic seal break free. Wind rushed in through the open doorway, cool against her face, smelling of burned metal. Every instinct told her to close the door again, go back to her apartment and into her warm bed, but there was something else now that compelled her even more than fear.

Behind her the door slid back to its original position and re-sealed itself. The streets were empty, it was a ghost town. The heat coming off the blackened cars by the roadside was strong and thick smoke rose from the flames into the night sky, feeding the night. Gen walked down the middle of the road where it seemed safest. The buildings on either side of the street appeared broken and abandoned. There was no light to be seen from any window on any floor. She pictured the monsters of her younger dreams living in empty black holes, watching her in stealth and silence, but there was nothing to be seen and nothing to be heard. If there were monsters there, that was where they chose to stay.

The city looked completely different by night. Homes and businesses up and down the street had been burned and now stood as hollow shells. Darkness filled the hollow spaces, consuming the lives that had once been lived therein.

Gen skirted the ruins, straying to the side of the road to peer up at an overpass that trailed across her path. Beneath, the night looked darker, punctuated only by the faint light of moons on the other side.

As she wandered perilously close to the derelict shells at the roadside, an old man suddenly emerged and leaned from a shel-tered alley. Gen froze. He turned his neck slowly, revealing the other half of his face covered by a white bandage stained red.

"What're you doing out here?" he said in a harsh tone, the bandage only enough to cover half his grimace.

Gen's throat turned dry. Carefully, she began backing away towards the other side of the street.

Noticing her alarm, the old man's expression mellowed.

"It isn't safe," he said.

He staggered out of the alleyway and the shadows fell away from him. His thin, wiry frame was visible beneath a dirty grey shawl, his arms and shoulders like points of carved wood under the fabric.

Behind her Gen could hear shuffling from deep within the dark recesses of the buildings she had thought abandoned. Her eyes drifted up to the windows of the second floor where fearful and tormented faces looked back at her.

The old man stepped off the kerb and onto the street. Gen could see the spots of dried blood around his ankles.

"This is no place for you to be. Come," he said, and stretched out a bony arm in her direction.

As he did so, the shawl slipped from his shoulders and fell to the ground. Underneath was a frail and wizened creature that moved awkwardly with one hand held clamped against the left side of his chest. Smears of red seeped through the gaps between his fingers, through which Gen could see a patch of blood-soaked gauze.

Gen's heart throbbed heavily within her chest and fear welled up inside of her, propelling her down the street towards the underpass. The old man ambled after, dragging his feet through the broken brickwork and shattered splinters of wood that littered the road.

Sudden and real terror shrank Gen's world, encasing her in the darkest shade of night. Shouts and calls followed her from behind, gradually diminishing against a deep pervasive rumbling that steadily grew, filling the air around her.

The dual light of the moons shone like beacons at the far end of the underpass and fear blinded her to everything but their distant façades, drawing her on. She ran and ran, throwing her shoulders and arms back and forth to propel her along the road, but the noise only grew louder, swallowing form and definition from the world. She could feel the wind blowing against the tears on her face, cool and dry, and desperate whimpers of fear and exertion rose up against the background noise sporadically, punctuating its steady monotony.

Emerging on the other side of the underpass, she was struck by a beam of brilliant white light. She stopped and peered up through her hands to the source, her skin glowing red against the glare. Heavy, shuffling footfalls echoed behind her and she turned to see the old man, just feet away, his arm stretching out like a wrinkled branch on a dying tree. He gripped at her shoulder and threw her aside with surprising ease and stood himself within the beam of light, closing his eyes.

A shot angled down to him from above, slamming into his chest, and he fell limply to the ground. Gen scrambled to her feet and began to run again, casting her eyes back over her shoulder to the man's motionless body and the light which momentarily left him and began to sweep the street behind her.

The night wind came stronger, chasing her down the street like a gale. Stones lifted and tumbled through the air while slivers of broken wood careered forward like darts. Gen dodged the debris, stumbling as she went. The light followed behind, moving steadily over the street in an angle toward her.

As it lifted and passed overhead she saw the dark metallic body of a ship and an array of burning blue rockets spaced along its undercarriage. The heat was strong and the rising engines blew an indiscriminate swathe through the ruins, shaking the husks of empty cars and flipping them over with ease. The air caught Gen like a fast advancing wall, striking her in the chest and lifting her off her feet. She flew backwards like a rag doll being thrown through the air and landed awkwardly on the hard concrete, scraping a long gash in the side of her knee. She yelped in pain and cradled her leg in her hands, feeling the wet warmth of her blood slipping through her fingers. Then the ship turned and hovered back in her direction, throwing its light over her once, then twice before it rested, bathing her in cold illumination.

She sobbed, lifting one feeble hand up in front of her face, and begged for forgiveness, thinking of home and her father.

Immune and uncaring to her pleas, the vessel loomed up above her ready to strike. Gen drew her hands over her ears and cowered.

From a dark window on the side of the street a loud searing bolt shot out, crashing into the side of the ship in a ball of flame. The ship veered and twisted in the air under the impact as smoke poured from its side. The engines screeched in agony and the ship spun wildly out of control, thundering into the ground.

The earth rose up before Gen in a wave of concrete and steel, lifting over her before crashing back down.

Gen's world went black.

Darkness filled the air, wavering and restless. Shapes swirled and grew in the smoke, and voices like distant echoes rose and fell against each other. Gradually, the stars broke through, puncturing the black and outlining the figures that loomed above.

"She's alive," one said.

It was a woman's voice, soft and light. Her hands reached down and closed around her waist, pulling her upwards and out of the gloom. Smoky air drifted over her, carried by the wind, and filled her lungs. Gen coughed. Her chest felt heavy, as if weighed down by an unseen object.

More hands coiled around her arms and legs, drawing her up to her feet and gently brushing the dust from her hair and shoulders. Her eyes sharpened to focus on the man in front of her with deep blue eyes and a face sticky with blood and dirt.

"We can't stay here," he said. "They'll be sending reinforcements right now. We don't have much time."

A woman pushed forward next to him and knelt down before Gen. She had a kind, pretty face, framed with long brown hair. Dark smudges lined her pale skin beneath large doleful eyes. Her sombre expression reminded Gen of her mother.

"Are you one of the Pilgrims?" she asked.

"No," the woman answered. "There're no Pilgrims left anymore. People are leaving this place. It's not safe anymore."

She tilted her head away from Gen, her face touched with a sudden sadness. Her wide eyes rested upon the end of the road where two tall buildings thrust up into the sky. In the space between them, ships could be seen rising softly and silently from the ground.

"This is no place for a child," the Kindly Woman said. "We need to get you away from here."

She clamped gentle but firm hands on Gen's shoulders. Gen squirmed, trying to wrestle free, but her grip was strong and the man with blue eyes helped her.

"It's okay," she said, soothingly, wrapping her arms around her and holding her close.

Gen's eyes trailed up and carefully, the Kindly Woman guided her towards the edge of the street, reassuring her and lifting her up and over the tall kerb towards the nearest building. She winced as she was placed down again. The gash at the side of her knee was still raw and covered with dirt. The Kindly Woman saw it and drew a coiled rag from around her wrist and wiped at the wound.

"What're you doing out here?" she asked.

Gen tried to ignore the stinging pain in her knee. She pointed off down the street in silence towards the spaceport beyond two towering apartment buildings. The Kindly Woman stopped wiping Gen's knee and gently tied the rag around her leg to cover the gash.

"There're no more ships," she said. "There's no more space."

Gen could see a sadness in her. A grim determination that propelled her on past the point of hope. Tired lines trailed down her face like soft wrinkles and she looked at Gen with wide, desperate eyes as though she waited on her to provide inspiration.

"I need to find my mother," Gen told her.

The Kindly Woman's eyes drew down to the ground, still sad, and fixed on the join between two slabs of concrete. Crumbs of loose mortar rattled freely along the groove. She placed the flat of her hand against the concrete and Gen watched as terror crept into her expression.

She grabbed at Gen and began to push her hard towards the withered shell of a building behind her. A wave of rage swept the street towards them and a host of lights emerged at the far end of the street in a sudden strobe.

Panicked voices and the screech of machinery filled Gen's ears and the whole street erupted with fire and flame. The Kindly Woman pushed her to the ground and shielded her as metal tore through masonry and ripped the derelict home beside them to pieces. Splinters of white-hot steel shards fizzed through the air and brick dust poured over them like a cloud.

Huddled beneath the woman's protective form, Gen clamped her hands over her ears and screamed. Her tiny voice proved shallow against the extremity of noise all around her. The attack was answered by a roar and an array of gunfire opening up from inside every building still standing.

With the ochre dust still hanging over her, Gen slipped out from beneath the Kindly Woman, who rolled onto her back and lay staring sightlessly up into the sky. The shadowy, monstrous forms of ships passed her overhead, throwing the cloud into patterns of coiled spires. Searchlights cut through the haze and struck down at the houses as fire tore through them. Gen staggered to her feet and ran as the world ruptured around her.

Bright spots of flame illuminated the dust cloud like points of lightning, their impacted violence obscured though the sound was deafening. Gen stumbled on, her hands up before her, as though to cut a path through the smog. It cleared briefly as she happened upon the blunted edge of a building that rose up in her path like a wall. She skirted around the corner and used her hands to guide her along its side.

She could hear her own cries as the extent of the violence faded gradually. The jagged edge of her sobbing contrasted with the distant sounds of war so that she could no longer deny her own fear. She pushed on, trying to distance herself from the rage and anger, finding a hastily assembled barricade blocking the street. She clambered up the broken furniture and dislodged car doors to the top and dropped to the other side.

She fell awkwardly, the ground rising up to meet her quicker than she expected. Her knees buckled and her arms went out in front to break her fall, scuffing over the surface of the road. Her wrists and elbows reddened and welters of blood broke through her skin as though punctured by a thousand needles, but she refused to stop, and quickly drew back to her feet, running on.

Fierce down winds pushed the cloud and smoke away to reveal the night sky and half a dozen ships still lifting towards the stars. She raised her hands above her and threw them through the air, shouting as loud as she possibly could, but it was too late. Slowly, the ships faded against the night and disappeared into the heavens.

Gen fell to her knees. Tears streamed down her face in a gentle tide. The city was tearing itself apart, she was lost, and the noise began to grow again as men and women began to scale the barricade, desperate to escape the violence.

Refugees poured into the spaceport, swarming past her, each of them trapped into their own unique crisis. Gen didn't move, her eyes stayed fixed on the sky, waiting for the lights to return.

Ahead of her, one man stopped. She noticed him from the corner of her eye, his still and familiar posture.

"Dad!" she cried.

His dark eyes darted to the sound of her voice. His face was tired and pale, though a light sparked in his eyes when he saw her.

Quickly, he pushed a path through the swarming crowds and ran to her, wrapping his strong arms around her, lifting her up. Gen cradled her head against his chest, feeling spots of water fall like rain. She looked up to see tears streaking his face.

"I'm sorry," she said.

His eyes were creased with sadness. All hint of the rage she'd seen before was gone, like a façade stripped away, exposing the fragility of the man beneath. She pulled her hand inside her jacket and wiped at his tears with the soft cloth of her sleeve. He took her hand and pressed it into his.

"I swore I'd keep you safe," he said, holding her close.

The soft light of a new dawn cut across the horizon, shining upon his pale face. He narrowed his eyes, the dark points shrinking against the sunrise.

"How did you know where to find me?" Gen asked.

"Faith," he said, turning her away from the burning city. The red sun cut the cracks of the distant ridge, spilling long fingers of light that reached towards them. "You have a courage I lost long ago. I see so much of your mother in you. I know you miss her, Gen. I miss her too, but she's gone and nobody ever comes back."

# FENRIR

## CHRISTINA SNG

**About the Author**

Christina Sng is the Bram Stoker Award-winning author of *A Collection of Nightmares* (Raw Dog Screaming Press, 2017). Her poetry has been nominated multiple times for the Rhysling Awards, Dwarf Stars, and Elgin Awards, received honorable mentions in the *Year's Best Fantasy and Horror* and *Best Horror of the Year* anthologies, and appeared in numerous venues worldwide. Visit her at christinasng.com and connect on social media @christinasng.

We first found him as a pup, lost and starving in a ditch by our house. He was tiny, fitting perfectly in the palm of my hand, this little black and white ball of fluff. His eyes met mine when I first picked him up, full of depth and sorrow. I had to take him home.

Our 5-year-old daughter Ava took him in her arms and refused to let him go. She named him Fenrir, after a wolf she read about in a book on Scandinavian folktales. Apt, since we had lived in Scandinavia all her life.

For most of his puppyhood, Fenrir slept beside Ava. When he grew larger, he slept by her feet, and later, on the ground next to her bed when he could no longer fit on it. She always dropped her hand over the side to touch his fur. She told me it comforted her.

Fenrir grew fast. By year's end, he was fully grown, handsome and dignified with a coat sleek and black as onyx. All his baby white fur was gone, but for a small patch on his chest.

The vet declared that he must be part-wolf for his size and wolven face. But Fenrir had the good nature of a golden retriever and was gentler than a kitten, especially with Ava whom he now towered over. He loved her with all his heart and followed her everywhere.

He never did stop growing, however. Soon, he was the size of a horse. The vet could not explain that.

We built him his own barn in the backyard and took him to the forest for long walks.

In another year, he was the size of a bus and could no longer comfortably fit in our small yard. We moved him to a grassy clearing next to the forest. There was a pond which housed a family of ducks and an old grumpy snapping turtle he surprisingly befriended for company.

Ava visited him daily. Often, I would find them in the open plain near the heart of the forest, a tiny little girl lying peacefully against a bus-sized black wolf, singing him her favorite songs.

He was the size of our house when the accident happened: a drunk driver lost control of his car and smashed into Ava, standing on the curb.

My little girl, sweeter than the Sun, gone in an instant. I held her till they pried her from me, promising they would bring her home after their investigations were done. But too late, she was already gone.

Fenrir was frantic when she hadn't visited in days, howling every night with a roar that shook the ground, until the day we carried her and placed her beside him.

Between our tear-drenched faces and her unmoving form, he understood, very gently nuzzling her and bowing his head before we placed her in the ground.

We buried her in their favorite place by the forest and marked her grave with a young bamboo sapling.

She once told me that the bamboo was a miracle plant. It provided food, water, shelter, and weaponry. Everything one needed to survive a disaster.

So we chose it for her. A final gesture to our beloved girl. We could not imagine how we would carry on without her.

Fenrir watched helplessly, his window-sized eyes damp with tears, creating large pools as they fell into the grass. He brought the rain with his grief.

HE STAYED WITH HER FOR A YEAR. THE VEGETATION AROUND HIM disappeared as he grazed. He grew to the size of a football field.

The bamboo around her grave sprung new saplings and grew so tall, the branches seemed to graze the sky.

We would find him lying listlessly beside her grave, staring into space. He would nuzzle us gently then return to his tearful gazing. Ava's death created a hole in his heart he could never mend. He loved her as much as we did. Perhaps even more.

One day, he consumed the forest bare, and vanished without a trace. No track marks. No evidence he was ever there. Where trees once stood, now lay an expanse of barren land.

I should have suspected when we last visited. He nuzzled us for a long time and bowed before settling down for the night. It was his way of saying farewell.

For in the morning, the world was gone, except for our cottage and the plot of grass where Ava was buried.

We trekked out as far as we could, searching for anything at all that remained, but found nothing but sand. Finally, we returned home, weak and starving, and resigned.

OFTEN, WE PEERED OUT INTO THE SANDY WASTELANDS JUST beyond our garden to see if we could find him. But we never saw him again nor did he ever visit Ava's grave just half a mile north from our backyard. That small patch of grass thick with bamboo amidst the pale dead desert. Perhaps he too was gone now, as she was, as was the world.

We spent evenings on the porch, watching the sun set, wondering if there was anyone out there and if we should go and look again. But we had everything we needed here, and each other. And soon, another child. And another.

When Tyr was 5 and Freya was 2, I picked up a book from Ava's shelf to read to them. It was simply titled, *Scandinavian Folktales*.

A picture of Fenrir was on the inside cover, along with the inscription, "Monstrous Wolf Destined to Devour the World."

# NO FAIRY TALE WORLD

## LISA TIMPF

**About the Author**

Lisa Timpf is a retired HR and communications professional who lives in Simcoe, Ontario. Her poems have been published in *Star\*Line, Eye to the Telescope, Dreams & Nightmares*, and other venues, and over 30 of her speculative short stories have appeared in magazines and anthologies including *Enter the Rebirth, Future Days, Electric Spec, Third Flatiron*, and *From a Cat's View*. When not writing, Lisa enjoys bird-watching, organic gardening, and spending outdoor time with her border collie, Emma. You can find out more about Lisa's writing projects at lisatimpf.blogspot.com. You can also find her on Goodreads and Amazon Author.

*"was the spider radioactive, Mommy?"*—
her son Nate's small voice, piping—
"is that why Little Miss Muffet ran away?"

she closes the volume of nursery rhymes
handed down from her mother
the book she saved from the wood stove
that awful winter
and her gaze sweeps across the counter
where the handheld Geiger apparatus
rests silent for now

no home should be without one
the ads all say
cheerfully, as if that were
something to be celebrated

that night, she dreams of a cat
fiddling while the world burns
under a full moon
bereft of cows or dreams

# WINGS AT MIDNIGHT, WINGS AT DAWN

## DEBORAH L. DAVITT

**About the Author**

Deborah L. Davitt was raised in Reno, Nevada, where she graduated from University of Nevada, Reno in 1997. While an undergraduate, she focused heavily on medieval and Renaissance literature from *Beowulf* to Shakespeare. She received her master's degree in English from Penn State, but found work as a technical writer on projects ranging from nuclear ballistic missile submarines to NASA to computer manufacturing.

She currently lives in Houston, Texas, with her husband and son. Her poetry has received Pushcart, Rhysling, and Dwarf Star award nominations; her fantasy and science fiction short stories have appeared in *InterGalactic Medicine Show*, *Pseudopod*, and *Galaxy's Edge*; and her novels are available through Amazon. For more about her work, including her forthcoming poetry collection, *The Gates of Never*, please see edda-earth.com.

ADERYN SWEPT ON SNOWY WINGS ACROSS A MOONLESS SKY, WHERE aquamarine fire hung in folds like finest silk. Below her, black trees limned in snow rose up from white ground like twisted hands. But no humans seemed to dwell here, in these lands of endless night.

At first she'd rejoiced at the desolation around her. *I've strayed far to the north,* she'd thought. *Far from the hands of kings and lords, to lands free from machinations and betrayal.* Even the dead trees cloaked in snow had a kind of sere beauty to them. But after days passed, and she'd flown over many ruined clusters of huts, all roofless and sheathed in ice, she began to worry. She'd seen no smaller birds, no hares or squirrels. Not so much as a mouse scampering under the snow.

Horns blew in the distance—the first sign of human habitation she'd perceived here. Hungry but still wary, she drifted in the wake of a hunting party. Eyes night-keen, she noted the ribs and hips of the horses jutting against their dull hides, sure sign of famine. The heavy armor of the men. *A war-party, a patrol, not hunters. With whom are they at war? With winter itself, perhaps?*

And yet, even in this death-cold, no breath-clouds warmed the air with white. Prickles of unease lifted her feathers from her skin. *No food to be found here. And men and war are no longer my concern.*

Aderyn turned to swoop away, but her movement must have caught their attention. A thrown net folded her wings to her body, and she plummeted to earth.

She flung off her cloak of feathers, revealing skin as she struggled with the strands that trammeled her. *No, no, no,* she thought, desperate, incoherent, but the riders closed, catching her with chill hands, chaining her with cold iron bands. "Let me go!" she cried, dread rising in her. *Not a prisoner, not again!*

To her surprise, one of them showed enough compassion to take the tattered cloak from his own shoulders and drape it around her to ward against the frost-tinged air. "Where are you taking me?" she demanded, trying to remember the language that men of the north spoke. Trying to remember the tones of command she'd once used, when she'd ridden to war herself, on an iron-shod steed, with a cohort of steel-clad men around her. Her second skin they'd been, protectors assigned by a king to defend his loyal court mage on the battlefield. Before feathers had replaced them as her defense.

For an instant, she remembered their laughing voices on the wind. Recalled their faces and smiles, the feeling of cama-raderie. *Dead, all dead now, and some even at my hand when they turned on me.* Grief assailed her—vivid and sharp as a knife, in human form. Owl-shape, owl-thoughts usually blunted it. *And yet, how could they not turn on me? The evidence was overwhelming—*

But these men, unlike the ghosts of her memory, never spoke as they took her to their gray-walled fortress, past abandoned farms long gone to ruin, under the eternal night of their northern sky.

Inside, their leader waited, silent and indifferent in a throne room that seemed little different than all the others she'd stood in before. Yet in spite of being in the safety of his fortress, he bore arms and armor, like his followers.

"Lord Faris, a trespasser found in your lands. She wore this, and flew as an owl." Her captor's voice echoed like an empty room as he displayed her feather-cloak, the white curls of it lifting up around the black-enameled mail of his gauntlets like a living thing. "We smelled pine sap and oak leaves. Southern magic—fire and earth. Heard her heartbeat, if not her wings on the wind. And captured her."

*Faris,* Aderyn thought, her hungry stomach twisting. *A northern king's family once bore that name and stood as enemy to my lord's house. But none from the roof of the world have fought in the alliance against the southern lands in hundreds of years.* The rest of the words washed over her, pulling her into the silence that now lingered like a wave drawn back from the shore. *They heard my heartbeat? What manner of men are these?*

From under the lord's visor, no glitter of eyes; his voice a breathless whisper: "Those who trespass upon my lands forfeit their lives, owl-woman. Explain why you should not die."

"I did not willingly set foot upon your land," Aderyn replied, shaking in the chill of the air. Feeling the cold rising up from the ground through her feet, leaching the life from her. "I flew above it till your men forced me to the ground." *A pretty technicality, I'm sure.*

His hand rose. Through gaps in the mail, she spotted shapely bones, and shuddered. *Dead. They're all dead men. Ghosts that have more voices and will than the ones that dwell in my memory—but they're dead still.* "Then you may live, owl-woman. But you may not leave."

The fetters fell from her limbs at his gesture. *Northern magic, ice and wind and steel.* "Let me have my wings, and I will fly from here." Her voice sounded thin to her own ears. "I will trouble you not at all. You have my oath on it."

"Wings or not, you are as trapped as we are. Such is the curse upon my land." His head turned as if to study her.

"Curse?" Aderyn asked, swallowing. "Who set it? I've felt no magic in this land." *And I would have. Should* have. *Unless I've abandoned myself so deeply into owl-shape that I haven't paid attention to what my other senses have told me—*

She stepped closer as Faris unfolded the tale: "Two centuries ago, my men and I pledged to protect this land and our people to our last human breaths, against an enemy formed of and armed by southern magic." A pause. "Magic like *yours.* Creatures built of stone and fire, and trees uprooted from the earth to fight us."

Aderyn nodded, memories surging. Working in the castle forges to animate the statues chiseled from stone by skilled masons. Manning the bellows to pump living fire into their bellies, leading the incantations that would bind it there. Riding out alongside the host of golems that she and the other castle mages had built. Hundreds of stone feet slamming against the ground, implacable. Impenetrable. Lifting her hands to weave fire from the air, and rain it down on her lord's lockstep foes. "The southern way of war has not changed since those days," she whispered, her lips dry. "Except that they've turned upon their own."

A pause, and then he stood from his cold throne and advanced. Unclasped his cloak—just as tattered as the one already wrapped around her shoulders by his men—and offered it to her. "Take this." He gestured to his men, who took jingling strides to other rooms, and returned with armloads of damp wood to pile in the empty hearth at the end of the long hall. A snap of his fingers lit the blaze, and she huddled close to it. In spite of its heat, she could still feel fingers of cold pressing against her back.

As the golden glow of the fire stretched through the dark hall, she noticed that somehow, the light seemed to avoid Faris. His black armor should have shone with it, reflected it, gleamed; instead, the light faded around him. Dulled. Muted. He stood beside her, silent for a long moment, and then finally asked, "You said *their* way of war. Not *our.* Why?"

"Does it matter?" Aderyn closed her eyes. "Were we not discussing your curse?"

"My curse is old tidings to me. What curse do *you* suffer under, owl-woman?"

Old loyalties clung to her lips like cobwebs, but a dead northern lord had extended her more courtesy, more honor, more hospitality, than she'd encountered in a dozen years. She stared into the fire. "My lord had enemies within his own court. His first wife bore him only daughters. His second wife had a son when she came to him, and she was ambitious for her child. When she, too, gave him only daughters, she began to plot for her son's advancement." Dull words, as if recited from some ancient chronicle. "She needed the castle mages out of the way —we were all loyal to her husband, and to his nephew, who would inherit when our lord died. And she needed someone to take the blame for their deaths. She had all the others besides me killed. Poison in their cups. Poison in my lord's food."

She could see it all again in memory's glass. A whispered word, a gesture, and the flames leaped and curled, becoming familiar faces. A masque put on for the benefit of the dead man beside her, a puppet-show of the deaths of those once so dear to her. Mathos, one of her fellow mages, laughing and performing little illusions to delight the company, until he frowned and reached for his throat. Swallowed hard. Began to choke for air. To her left, Hamilax, leader of the mage-guards, pushed back from the table, gasping, his big shoulders heaving. Fighting an enemy his sword couldn't reach. An enemy lodged inside his own body.

She closed her eyes against the memories. *Reaching out for Hamilax, who'd shared her bed on campaign and off. Aware of the surge of bodies around them as the others surged to their feet, knocking over the benches as they did. "Can't breathe," Hamilax choked out, and she reached for a knife. Shoved him back onto the table as if he didn't weigh half again what she did, and pressed the knife into his throat with shaking hands. Rummaged in her belt for a scroll, filled with the magic words used to give the golems life. "Live," she shouted as if her will could make it so.*

*She ripped at the useless parchment with her knife, rolled it into a tube. Tucked it into the gash she'd made in his throat, her fingers red with his blood. Clutched his hand as he took one labored breath. Then another, as people fell to the floor around them, bodies arching, convulsing. She took her eyes from her lover's only once, to gaze up the table to where Lord Abimilki sat, face purple and swollen, gasping for air. Reaching out a shaking hand for his wife beside him, who sat motionless in her tall chair. Untouched. Untroubled. Unpoisoned.*

*Lady Shakheto regarded him expressionlessly as he died. As men died all around her. Aderyn turned her gaze back towards Hamilax in time to watch the light die from his eyes, locked on her face as they were—*

She held up her fingers, stopping the flow of images in the fire, spilling from her mind to be wrought fresh in the flames. "I tried to save my beloved, and not my lord. That was wrong of me. But even in that, I failed. There's no healing in these hands." She looked down.

"Did you not kill her?" her host asked, his voice cold and remote.

The very chill of him braced her. "I tried," Aderyn replied, feeling her lips tighten. "The other guards of our company entered on hearing the screams. Saw my dagger, red in my hand. Saw Ha—" Her throat tightened around a name she'd been unable to speak for over a decade. "Saw their guard captain's throat cut. Saw their lord dead, and me throwing fire at their lord's wife, as she dove under the table to hide from me. They saw me betray my liege-oath to try to kill her." She closed her eyes again, and added dully, "One of them struck me from behind. When I awoke, she'd told them a pretty tale of how I'd been bought by one of their lord's enemies, and had killed everyone in the room besides herself. That she'd been too ill to drink the wine, and only that had saved her."

"And they believed her?" Faris' voice held disbelief.

A hand touched her shoulder, the cold of it burning through two layers of thick cloth. "But she did not execute you for your crimes."

Aderyn shook her head. A bitter half-smile touched her face. "She had killed all the castle mages but one. She could not make the golems march without me. Could not give the living fire to new ones. She needed me alive until she could recruit new mages. Buy their loyalty. She imprisoned me within a tower, and told me I'd walk free if I swore loyalty to her and her son, and worked my magic for her." *Foolish woman. With such lies as she told about me? I wouldn't have walked free more than a day before someone loyal to her husband and the others gutted me with a knife.*

"Did you swear that oath?" Simple, bare words.

"No." The word twisted her lips. "I worked for my escape, my freedom. Owls nested near the tower. Their feathers, my freedom. And on the night that I flew from her tower, I saw that her enemies had come for her. My lord's nephew and his allies. Ready for a full year's siege, their campfires red in the distance, their engines dark skeletons of wood against the horizon." She relived the memory for an instant. How she'd exulted, seeing the downfall of Lady Shakheto moving slowly, inexorably towards the keep. *Though her defeat would surely mean the deaths of many more within the keep. And likely the death of her son, who was blameless in all of this.*

"They had a host of siege golems with them, where she had none that she could command." Aderyn shrugged. She hadn't stayed to watch the siege, but she knew how it would have progressed. *Golems to carry the huge battering rams to bear down the gate, arrows and flaming oil raining off of them harmlessly. Smaller models, sheathed in iron and heated to forge-glow by magic, to scale the walls and clasp the defenders in red-hot embraces. The largest to lift stones and hurl them with all the force of a catapult, or to tear at the walls with their huge clay hands.*

She swallowed. "Her enemies might have freed me. They might have believed me loyal to her, and executed me. Either way, I was done with all of them. And I did not wish to wait and watch as those in the keep whom I had sworn to protect, died." *Even if they chose not to believe me, they didn't deserve death. They didn't deserve the iron advance of the golems, the fire of the war-mages. They didn't deserve the destruction I wrought so often at my lord's command.*

Aderyn raised her eyes now, weary to her soul with the retelling. "So yes. I say *them* and not *us*. I have nowhere and nothing and no one to whom I belong." *Exile,* she thought bitterly. *It's so much easier as an owl. They aren't social creatures. Even now, just a few minutes in human form, I already feel the longing to be a part of something creeping into my soul with the cold. To be warmed by more than fire. But there's nothing here for me but death of another sort.* "What cursed your land?" she asked, her voice empty.

The lord stood motionless. "As I said, we swore that we would defend these lands to our last human breaths. The gods heard vows made in good faith." A sound that might have been a bitter laugh. "And ensured that we would not fail them—for our last breaths lie locked within us."

"Then the *gods* brought destruction to this land?" Shock and consternation warred within her. *The gods of the south have been silent for generations. Are the northern gods more active? Is that why their lands have not fallen before the golem-armies?*

"Not them alone." Faris shook his head, his visor swinging. "Our enemy tied the land to me, cursing the realm to darkness until I die. Bound my people here with me." She watched his gauntleted fingers clench into fists. Watched frost trace its patterns across the metal, die into liquid as his hands strayed near the fire—only to be born again as he shifted away. *Nothing but death and cold and starlight here.* "I watched my family, my servants, my farmers, everyone die. Some of starvation, some of lost hopes. Except my faithful soldiers, trapped here with me."

Some instinct made her reach out her hand, blindly. *Perhaps the accursed need to touch, to offer comfort and accept the same.* She caught his hand in hers, feeling a shock of death-chill within the metal. Metal and the clay of the body beneath. *I used to bring to life golems made of little more than he is now. His life has been trapped within him for centuries. What separates him from a golem now, but his suffering?*

He tried to pull away, but she held tenaciously. "It's a hard thing," Aderyn whispered, her eyes burning, "to watch all that you love suffer and die."

Silence, but for the crackle and pop of the fire. After a moment, Faris admitted, "At least I have had company in my suffering. You have not. Still, I long for death, for a dawn which will never come." He turned his hand, clasping hers now. She could barely feel it through the spreading numbness of the cold of him. Needles of pain as the blood in her fingers fought to flow. "And the worst of it is, that in spite of your compassion, in spite of your own curse and pain, I will watch you, too, die. I wish this were not so." Aching regret tinged his words.

A jag of anger and pain passed through her, but she left her hand where it was, in spite of the bone-deep chill. "Can you not let me go?"

He knelt beside her. "Even flying creatures cannot escape. My men have found their bones all along the borders of my realm. I watched my people claw their fingers bloody on empty air, trying to pass the borders. Some turned on me then, but could not kill me." His visored head lowered. "I stripped off my armor and let them try. Under this armor is a ruin. They used blades. After a time, I threw myself into a pyre. To no avail. My men and I have been alone here for many years. Any human trespassers, we bring here so that they will at least not die alone. In the wilderness. With none to mark their passing."

"And as penance for yourselves." It wasn't a question.

A faint nod as he raised his free hand to gesture at the fire. "What little comfort we can offer before your end—is yours, my lady."

Aderyn's eyes stung. "How often have you had to offer this comfort? How often have you watched people suffer and die in this way?"

"Too often." Emptiness. Emptiness that echoed with centuries of loss.

"Then let me see if I can offer you respite. Southern magic might abate a southern curse."

"But not a god's blessing twisted."

She shook her head. "That which has been twisted can be set straight." *I have to believe that. I must. If I don't, then to what purpose do I still live?* "Lift your visor."

Faris hesitated but obeyed, revealing sunken, dull eyes, a skull wrapped in dried skin, blackened in places. It wasn't beautiful to look on, but any smell of decay had long since left him.

Aderyn hesitated in turn. The wording of the curse seemed clear: to his last *human* breath. She could erase that humanity—but at great cost to herself. "I couldn't save Hamilax," Aderyn admitted, the name halting on her lips. "Or my lord. There is no healing in my hands; I was trained to end life, and manufacture its similitude." She swallowed. "But I think, perhaps, that I can offer you something else."

"What could you bring, that time has not?" Faris asked.

"Transformation."

She turned her head, catching sight of her feathered cloak, which had been folded and draped over a decrepit chair. She reached out and caught it, the milk-white feathers curling around her hand like a caress. Familiar. Comforting. The path to escape, and an escape in itself. A refuge from herself, a way of being that required nothing from her but survival. *No connection. No belonging. No hands to hold, or to hold mine in turn.* "This took me two years to weave," she murmured. "I twisted my blood into the thread of its net. Collected the feathers night by night. I made it of myself, of my need to escape where I was prisoned." *Prisoned, as he and his are.*

A hint of hope in a dust-dry voice: "Then you could make such for us?"

"Not before I starve to death." Her stomach clawed at her innards in reminder.

His head lowered. Resignation. "We can offer you a dagger,

to make the end quicker, if you wish. Though—I have enjoyed hearing a new voice."

"I will not be a memory with which you will flay yourself in the night." The words felt like glass in her throat. "I will free you, Lord Faris." *Once, I escaped using these wings. Now, I must escape by giving them up. And—he and his deserve to be as free as I have been. Free to live. Free to die. I can always craft other wings for myself, in years to come, twisting them out of my own life-essence. If I still feel the need to escape from the past. From the world. From myself.*

So she stood and wrapped him in her wings, pressing her lips against his bare chops, breathing her life into him. Felt him sigh his last human breath against her lips in grateful release. Felt his skin smooth and soften under her lips, before soft feathers caressed her face. He rose on snowy wings, uncertain, unsure, landing on her bare arm as his men fell in clatters of armor and bone all around them.

And as she caught him, the first of his feathers fell to the ground at her feet, and the sun rose.

# AND THEN THERE WERE INFINITE

## JOSH PEARCE

**About the Author**

Josh Pearce is a writer from the San Francisco Bay Area with stories and poetry in *Analog, Asimov's, Beneath Ceaseless Skies, Cast of Wonders, Clarkesworld, IGMS,* and *Nature*. He currently works as an assistant editor and film reviewer at *Locus* magazine and lives in the East Bay with his wife and son. You can find more of his writing at fictionaljosh.com or on Twitter: @fictionaljosh. One time, Ken Jennings signed his chest.

"Do you ever feel like you're standing with your finger in the dam of reality?"

There were two buttons in front of Miller: one red, which would execute the programmed course correction, turn them around, send the great battleship *Commodore Thomas ap Catesby Jones* home; and one blue, which would cancel all previous commands and keep them on their current heading into the black. Miller braced himself against the console, shaking sick with the cold and with sleep, withdrawing from the many, many drugs. The captain's body lay pressed against the deck with a hole blown through her midriff, her hair escaping from the tight bun in which it had been wound.

August Domino, Lieutenant, stood over the body, shouting something at Miller, urging him to choose a button. The lensor pistol slipped from Domino's hand and fell to the deck next to the captain's body. Its delicate focusing and internal magnifying lenses cracked. There was no one else to hear all the shouting because, apart from Miller and Domino, all the rest of the crew was in one form or the other of long sleep. Miller leaned weakly on the helm. He had never felt heavier than he did right now. He reached out for the buttons, and pressed one.

The battleship woke him by heating his cryonic cells with radio waves. The cryoprotectant in his veins turned back into liquid as it warmed, drawn out of his body through the femoral IV, replaced with someone else's fresh blood and polyvinyl alcohol anti-nucleators. Before the warming cycle had fully finished, Lt. Domino cracked open Miller's pod and pulled him out. "I had to get you out of there. The captain is atomizing all the pods."

Miller climbed out slowly and painfully and looked around the pod bay. The nine cryogenic coffins that were at the far end of the bay now sat empty, their red-orange-yellow spray-painted hatches hanging open. His eyes took a long time to focus on Domino's face, which was pushed close up to his. "What's our current schedule?" he asked.

"Captain Rifkin has us on twenty years down, six months up now."

"What?" said Miller. "That's impossible. We don't have enough crew to maintain that." He felt more tired and colder than his previous duty shift, like his bones were made out of ice.

"I know that. She's been giving us bad blood when we wake up for our duty shifts." Then Domino saw the panic on Miller's face and said, "Don't worry, I gave you captain's blood that was only on ice for a couple of weeks. It might not be A-1 premium kosher USDA standard considering how much radiation she's been soaking up, but it was better than giving you what I had in my veins."

"Yeah, you don't look so hot." Miller could only imagine how bad he himself looked, just out of deep freeze. The shakes overtook him and he collapsed on the floor, trying to curl up on himself under a canvas blanket until they went away. "I feel so weak. Are you sure I didn't get a tainted blood supply?" Or was this the side effect of having been frozen for so long? But then he noticed how the blanket didn't drift around him, and how solidly Domino was planted on his feet. "No, that's not it. Our gravity is stronger, because our acceleration's greater. Why?"

Lt. Domino crouched down next to him. "Like I said. Captain Rifkin is burning everything that's not nailed down for fuel, trying to get our delta-v curve as steep as possible. She says it's the only way we'll catch the Infraviolets."

"Well, is she right?" Miller reached for the duty-officer flimsy that Domino was holding. "What does the computer say about the projected trajectories?" The flimsy screen was dark.

The lieutenant shrugged. "The *Catesby* locked me out of the system because I couldn't pass the cog test when I woke up. I don't think anyone has been able to since Rifkin put us on the new schedule. Like I said, bad blood." Domino pointed at the bridge of his nose but not, alarmingly, with his finger. With the muzzle of the lensor pistol. "It's right behind the eyes. You can see it if you close them tight enough."

Miller woke the flimsy with his thumbprint, and it greeted him with a series of reasoning tests, spatial comprehension, simple things to test for brain damage, because repeated thawings and freezings could easily damage the delicate cells of the body with ice crystal build-up. Coordination and balance. Recite the alphabet. Touch your nose with your finger. Once Miller had done that, the flimsy unlocked his access to the server. The ship's computer said, "Midshipman Hale Imamovich Miller, declared cognitively fit for duty."

"Damn, now she knows I woke you up off schedule."

"She would know that anyway. Catesby could relay our conversation to her."

"I smashed all the microphones in this room," Domino said, pleased with himself. "They can't hear us talk in here."

With great effort Miller levered himself up and propped up against Domino. "Where is she now?"

"She's barricaded herself on the bridge." Domino waved the lensor around. "But I'm gonna raise the rest of the crew so we can take back control of the ship. It'll be a few more weeks before you're ready to give blood, but once you are we can wake the next two at the same time. And then there'll be four. And a few weeks after that we can all use our blood to make eight of us. And then..."

"I get it," said Miller. "I know how we mass for battle stations." Training was superseding pain and discomfort. "But before we can plan for that, we have to find out where we are and how long it'll take us to get back to base. If you have us hot-blooding it until the whole crew is awake, that could create more problems than we'd solve. We're only designed to be at full battle rotation once during our deployment. There won't be enough slush to feed an entire awakened crew again. We used up our battle rations when we hit the Infraviolet station."

"Well, ask Catesby where we are."

Miller played with the flimsy for a minute and finally said, "The info's been restricted by the captain."

"I can try burning the hatch off the bridge."

"With that tiny thing? It'd take you years and you'd probably melt the gun's mirrors long before you got through one hinge. No, let's go talk to her, and see what all this is about."

"I'm telling you, she's not going to listen. I've been screaming at the hatch for weeks and she doesn't answer. Even Catesby stopped talking to me," Domino said, as he dragged Miller through the ship's corridors. He looked worried. "Do you think she died in there? We could be stuck on autopilot."

"Then I'll tell Catesby to let me in, because I'll be in command. Or we'll wake up another officer." They were at the vacuum-sealed hatch to the bridge and Miller flicked the flimsy. "Catesby, call to the bridge."

"Connecting."

A pause, and then Captain Rifkin's detached voice came on speaker. "Hello, Hale."

"Good morning, Captain. I want to discuss the current duty schedule with you."

"Very well. Discuss."

How much had she aged as he'd slept? What had years of micro-gravity done to her body, and how was it holding up to the current acceleration? Was her heart about to explode with the strain? "Ma'am, as the active duty officer, I require access to the bridge." The speakers hissed and popped with cosmic static. "Captain?"

She said, "Access denied."

"See? I told you," Domino hissed, like static.

"Is that Lt. Domino with you?" said Rifkin. "He is unfit for duty and has been relieved. He should be put down."

"Catesby," said Miller. "Requesting shift-change evaluation of all awake crew. Has the captain taken a cog test since the last shift?"

There was a long pause as something happened behind the locked door, and then the ship's computer came back, saying, "Captain Rifkin has scored fit-for-duty on the cognitive test."

"How is that even possible?" Domino demanded. "She's burning the crew as rocket fuel."

"Nonetheless," said Catesby, "she has made those decisions of sound mind."

"We could starve her out," Domino suggested. "I can cut the slush line to the bridge's spigot, and then she'd have to come out for food." He banged on the hatch. "You hear that, Captain?"

Her voice sounded weary over the speakers. "The survival of my physical body is immaterial to the completion of this mission. If I die in here, the ship will continue on the course I set."

"Captain, please." Miller tried to be rational. "Let me in and you can lay out the plan. If I agree that it's sound, then I can stand watch for you and you can sleep. Otherwise, the lieutenant and I wait out here until you starve to death and Catesby lets me onto the bridge."

There was a promising pause. At least she was thinking about it. Then Rifkin gave a command to the ship. Radio waves flickered over the two men and Catesby said, "Lt. August Domino is armed with a lensor pistol, in contravention of ship law regarding non-duty crew."

"Okay, okay." Miller took the sidearm from Domino, saying, "It's the only way she'll open the hatch." He tucked it into a pocket of his undersuit. "I have control, Captain."

The hatch finally released its seals and Domino pulled it open. Inside, the bridge was dim, Rifkin silhouetted against a wall-sized flimsy screen that showed the starfield outside. Blue-shifted stars on her left, red-shifted on her right. "Come in. Though Mr. Domino should still be put under medical care."

"In time, ma'am. Once we put him to sleep, he'll have to stay under until we get back to an Ultrarose base with a full hospital to revive him. Ship conditions won't be able to handle it." He hobbled to the center of the bridge, towards the helm. "As with most of the rest of the crew, Captain. Our current rotation schedule is unsustainable."

She turned to him. Miller bit back his shock. Her skin was wrinkled, inelastic, hair gray and white, an old woman whose eyes had started to go opaque. While the rest of her crew slept, she'd stayed awake and watched for the universe to change, like a sailor's wife standing vigilant on the widow's walk of a light-house. "The schedule must work," she told him, "otherwise we would not be here. We must stop the Infraviolets before they reach the Omega point. I mean, we must have stopped them." She looked confused. "Perhaps, we must have already will have stopped them? In the future?"

"How is that the talk of the cognitively fit?" Domino demanded.

"Discussion of Omega points necessarily involves logical convolutions," she answered.

"I think the whole idea of an Omega point is ridiculous in the first place," said the lieutenant. "You have no proof. What do you think, Catesby?"

"I have repeatedly analyzed the equations that we pulled from the Infraviolet station's computers during our assault. Their scientists' calculations appear to be internally consistent, but there is no way to confirm their conclusions in any objective frame."

"A non-answer."

"Captain," Miller interrupted. "How far out are we from base? How close are we to catching the Infraviolet ship?"

Rifkin waved her hand at the flimsy display and it melted into a graph of their course and position. Miller blinked blearily at it, but Domino was first to catch on, and he squawked in terror. "We've over forty years out from our Alpha point! We have to turn over now. With braking and getting back up to return speed, it'll take us a hundred years to get back home."

More, actually, because every minute spent heading outward-bound added days to the return trip. And with diminishing fuel supplies. But the part that frightened Miller the most was the point on the graph where the red trail of the *Commodore Thomas ap Catesby Jones* intersected with the blue track of the enemy ship's course. "This says we won't intercept the Infraviolets for another five hundred years."

"At this acceleration rate, that is correct," she said. "Which is why I ordered the dead used as reaction fuel. To cut down on their lead. Less mass, more exhaust."

"This is a suicide plan," Miller argued, "on so many levels. Even if someone on our crew is still alive, miraculously, by the time we reach the Infraviolets, how are they going to be revived? Our blood supplies will have gone bad long before then. And the return trip would take a thousand years. We weren't prepared for that long of a voyage, in terms of cold storage, crew size, or mass-acceleration ratios."

"Returning is not the primary mission," said Rifkin. "Only stopping them from entering the Omega point."

"And how are we going to prevent that?" he asked. "We're out of warheads."

"I have already locked in a collision course. Even if we are all dead, Catesby will ram the Infraviolet ship and destroy it."

Domino and Miller were shocked silent. Then Miller said, "Catesby? What do you think of this plan?"

"I think this part of the galaxy is filled with frequencies undetectable from our home systems. In short, it is like nothing I have ever seen before."

"Shit," Domino said. "Everyone on this bucket has bit rot. Catesby, you dumbass, is the captain's plan right? Will we even be able to stop their ship?"

The computer said, "The Infraviolets expected to reach the supposed Omega point less than three hundred years after launching from their station."

"Well then we don't stand a chance anyway," said Domino, "so we should reverse course right away and good riddance to them."

"Which is why I had Catesby calculate a different intercept path," said the captain. A new curved line appeared on the screen. "Which is the course we are on now. With these new parameters, we can intercept and destroy the enemy before they reach the Omega point. But only if we get our acceleration up beyond this threshold." More lines. "We can accomplish this goal, Catesby and I decided, if we atomize the rest of the pods with our reactor core and bring our speed up."

"The rest of the pods?" said Miller. But all the dead had already been burned for fuel.

"You mean the rest of the crew!" Domino said. "Killing them in their sleep!"

"To reduce our mass and increase our velocity," she said. "Yes, it is a difficult sacrifice to make, but this is war, and if the Infraviolets outrun us, then our existence will be over. I believe it is apparent that this is the correct path, because we are still here. Because I have already made the decision, and deviating from it will erase us."

"Or we're still here because there is no Omega point," Domino shouted. "You just believe there is! If you're wrong, then you've killed us all, did you think about that?"

She stared at him coldly. "And if I am right, then not only will everyone on this ship die, but we will cease to have ever existed, and so will the whole Ultrarose society. If you turn this ship around, or slow us, or deviate from its course at all, then you will blink out of existence. We have the best chance of success if you two, as well, provide yourselves as reaction fuel. I know that when the time comes, I will gladly throw myself into the furnace for the greater good."

Miller was paralyzed. It was a coin-toss. What else was he to do? August Domino made the first move, though, saying, "You go first, old lady," and struck out at the weakened Miller. While Miller was falling, Domino snatched the pistol from him, turned it on the captain, and blew her in half.

"Unauthorized weapon discharge on the bridge," Catesby announced to anyone who was listening. The smell of torched flesh filled Miller's mouth and he spat it out. He looked up to see Domino aiming the gun at him.

"You can't shoot me," Miller said, pulling himself up.

"The hell I can't. I just shot the captain. I can shoot anybody." Domino punched commands into the helm flimsy, but it was unresponsive.

"The computer is only going to accept commands from someone who is not crazy," Miller pointed out. "The captain's fried, so I'm in control, and I've got the last of the good blood. Kill me, and you lock yourself out of the helm forever." He brushed Domino aside. The computer woke when he touched it and showed that the helm had two courses pre-plotted—a blue course that took them after the enemy and a red course that took them back to base. Caught between their own Alpha and Omega points. Behind him, Domino dropped the lensor pistol.

"Well, Hale? Make your choice."

THE CAPTAIN ADDRESSED THEM IN THE FORWARD MESS, WHICH WAS the only section large enough to hold the entire ship complement at once. The mood was a harsh mix of after-battle euphoria and mourning for the nine spacemen they'd lost in the assault on the enemy station, where the Infraviolets were building a superweapon, or stockpiling warheads, or holding undeclared P.O.W.s, or any other rumored horror. The nine dead were frozen in their cryogenic pods, which were now coffins, draped with the Ultrarose colors. There they would stay for the long trip home where they could be properly buried. There had been 51 when the *ap Catesby* launched. Nine dead. And then there were 42.

During this after-action debrief, Domino called out, "So what were they really doing way out here, Captain? The station is light-years away from any star system."

Rifkin had a flimsy animation on display to follow along with her words. "From captured intel, we believe this station was a deep-space dock for a new type of Infraviolet ship." A schematic showed up in the distinct green-blue-purple of the enemy flag. They all took in the strange warship, with heavy radiation shielding, extended crew capacity, excessive fuel holds. "Unfortunately, this ship launched long before we arrived. We have an estimated escape trajectory based on the enemy files." The blue curved line shot out from the enemy station and pierced deep into the empty black space.

"That's in the opposite direction of the war ground," Domino said. "Where the hell do they think they're going?"

"The Infraviolet scientists think that they've found..." Rifkin hesitated. "An Omega point. A deep gravity well."

Sounds of disbelief from the officers, who had better astrophysics classes than the able-bodied spacemen like Miller. "What?" he asked the woman next to him. "Is that a bad thing?"

"Catesby is reviewing the available information," said the captain, "but that is uncharted space. Anything could be out there." The mess hall had one wall completely given over to slush spigots, but nobody was eating because almost the entire crew was scheduled back into cold sleep after the audience. "Fact or wishful thinking, our mission was to eliminate the enemy presence, and that remains incomplete until that ship is destroyed.

"So we are in hot pursuit. Excess and depleted equipment will be atomized as reaction fuel to get us up to full steam. Deep sleep is ordered for all crew except Lt. Domino, who will be pulling first watch. Duty schedule is standard one year down, one month up, unless calculated otherwise necessary." Even though the crew sometimes referred to her as "the old lady," Heather Erisova Rifkin had actually joined a crew when she was sixteen, as a cabin girl in the times before appetite suppressants had made that an archaic role. She worked her way up and made captain at 25 and now, a decade later, was due for promotion to commodore after their current mission. She had been born and grown up during and now lived entirely in the war. She smiled. "Dismissed, and good rest, everyone."

Miller caught up with Domino as the crew drifted to the pod bay at the back of the ship. "What is that all about?" he asked. "The Omega point?"

"I think it's a waste of time. An astronomer's fairy tale. There's nothing out there," Domino said. They passed the assault bays, hauntingly empty because all of the war machines inside had already been scrapped for reaction mass. Engineering crews squeezed past them, detailed to convert the ship's remaining warheads into nuclear fuel. "I bet the ship we're chasing is an empty decoy, just bait to draw us away from the battleground, where we're really needed."

At the end of the corridor they saw Rifkin slip into her private cabin, a squeeze pouch of ship's slush in hand. "Is she not going to sleep?" Miller asked. The slush was warmed, which was about all you could say for it. Fungus, algae, bacteria, anything they could get to grow on the crew's own waste and skin cultures. The slush fed on them and they ate it. Not something you wanted rotting in your guts as you slept away the years.

"Not from what I saw of the schedule, which is a surprise. Usually, command staff sleep for a very long time and age only reluctantly. Who knows how long she'll stay up? But I'll tell you, I'd sleep a lot better with a gun under my pillow."

"Why's that?"

"The black does strange things to a person. Cosmic radiation damage, low-gravity, isolation. A month alone on this ship is enough for me."

The first group of crew went down. In their pods, a slow-moving cold liquid circulated over head, neck, groin, and underarms for two hours to bring their temperatures down to 10 degrees C. Then the blood washout, replaced with an isotonic nutrient. Vitrification, a cryoprotectant injected through their femoral arteries, solidifying into a syrupy glass. Cool-down at 5 degrees C per minute by liquid nitrogen vapor down to −120 degrees. Further cooling to −196 degrees was slower to prevent cracking of cells. A dozen more crew down. And then there were thirty.

The ship was firing all nozzles, but the acceleration was slight, gravity barely noticeable as it got underway. While Miller waited his turn, he looked up what Catesby knew about Omega points. "Omega objects are theoretical, super-massive points that create paths in space-time with terminal ends that exist prior to their beginnings," said Catesby.

"You mean time-travel," said Miller. "That can't...is that possible?"

"Theoretically, traveling an orbital path around a spinning black hole, a cosmic string, or something resembling a Tipler cylinder—perhaps constructed by a civilization far older than our own—this would allow a ship to exist in a space called a chronosphere, where gravity is so strong that it drags not only matter and light in a whirlpool around it, but also time as well."

The lights went out in the corridors. "Why is it so dark?"

"All spare resources, including photons, are being used as

rocket exhaust."

Another cluster of spacemen went into cryogenic sleep, sipping up medications through their IVs. EGTA to prevent vomiting. Heparin, sodium citrate to prevent blood coagulation. Dextrose as a nutrient for tissues. Broad-spectrum antibiotics, followed by Maalox to neutralize gastric acid. "So the Infraviolets want to go back in time to a pivotal point in the war and alter the way it's going? What are some possible targets?"

Mannitol to inhibit cell swelling and prevent cerebral edema. Dextran-40 prevented tissue edema and reduced blood cell agglutination. Dextran-1 to prevent anaphylactic reaction to Dextran-40.

Catesby started listing past engagements. "The Battle of Five Stars, Greenwick's Folly, the Third Oort Battle, the Coronation of Governor Leopold, Jupiter Engagements I–IV, the Limited War of All Heavenly Light..."

Ten more asleep. And then there were twenty.

Catesby said, "But Infraviolet documents suggest a more ambitious scenario."

"What's that?"

The computer put up a little animation on Miller's flimsy screen. On it, a blue spaceship hovered in front of a dark sphere, an Omega point. "Hypothetically, the ship enters orbit around the object, and travels one minute backwards in time." The little ship did just that.

"And meets itself from one minute in the past." And then there were two Infraviolet ships, floating in space next to the Omega point.

"One from the present, and one from the past."

"Or you can think of it as one from the present and one from the future. It matters not. Now these two ships enter orbit around the Omega point together, and travel back one minute in time, whereupon they both meet themselves from one minute in their past." Four blue ships on the screen.

Methylprednisolone to stabilize membranes. Propofol to reduce brain metabolism. Magnesium sulfate would act as a neuro-muscular blocker. "They double in number every minute," said Miller.

"There would be more than one quintillion Infraviolet ships within an hour. Though, from an outside point of view, all of those ships would appear at the same time, instantaneously. And once they reached a desired number, the ships could enter the Omega point en masse and travel backwards, for instance, several hundred years and begin their journey home. With a proper course and a good bit of timing, they could arrive back at their station before they'd even left."

"And that's what we're heading into," said Miller.

Dextromethorphan, alpha-lipoic acid, vitamin E, deferoxam-ine, nimodipine, all to minimize ischemic damage. And then there were eight crew left to put to sleep. The blue ships doubled again. And then there were eight.

"If the Omega point existed, and the enemy reached it, then the skies above primordial Earth would suddenly fill with Infraviolet spaceships."

It was Miller's turn. He switched off his flimsy and drifted to the pod room. On the way, he passed the armory gun locker, which had an empty slot in one of its racks. Miller climbed into his pod with his head facing aft, his feet toward the bridge, so that if any liquid nitrogen evaporated away in his sleep, the tissue damage would be limited to his feet and spare his head. He accepted the injection gladly, anything to turn off his brain for a while.

Miller closed his eyes, leaving the ship empty except for Domino and Rifkin, who would watch the skies for him. Ahead of the *ap Catesby*, the stars shrank into blue dots and in its wake they stretched to red streaks. Two choices. Toward the enemy, or toward home.

# THE PUZZLEIST

## SHANNON CONNOR WINWARD

**About the Author**

Writing by Shannon Connor Winward has appeared in *Fantasy & Science Fiction*, *Pseudopod*, *Analog*, *PerVisions Flash Fiction Online*, *Strange Horizons*, *NewMyths.com*, and elsewhere. She is the author of the Elgin-award winning chapbook *Undoing Winter* and winner of a 2018 Delaware Division of the Arts Emerging Artist Fellowship in Literature. In between parenting, writing and other madness, Shannon is also founding editor of *Riddled with Arrows*, a literary journal dedicated to metafiction, ars poetica, and writing that celebrates the process and product of writing as art. Her first full-length poetry collection, *The Year of the Witch*, was released from Sycorax Press in 2018.

"THERE'S JUST SOMETHING ABOUT PEPSI IN A STYROFOAM CUP. It's better than any other kind of Pepsi."

"I've heard that."

"Especially with those little ice cubes that they had—kind of square but not exactly square?"

"I know what you mean."

"And I used to get the Swedish fish, because that's what my brother liked—"

"You usually bought Raisinets, actually."

"I did?"

"Yes, but that's not important. Go on."

"Oh. Well, I remember the way Swedish fish and that Pepsi went together." Susan wrinkled her nose, thinking. "And also...the concession stand always smelled like ketchup and French fry salt."

"What else?"

"Um...the color of the rocks on the road before they black-topped it, kind of grayish blue? And the way it felt walking over the rocks in my sneakers. The feel of the sun on my neck while I was trying to decide what to buy with the money my parents gave me. I remember how those afternoons felt like eternity— we went to so many ballgames, between my two brothers. I used to play on these huge piles of rocks and dirt behind the chain link fence. They were mountains to me, with my little dolls, or even just my fingers as people. I felt like the queen of my own little world," she added with a wistful smile.

"I can still hear the thunk of a bat hitting a ball, people clap-ping or yelling. You don't hear a cadence like that anywhere else. I remember all the dads smoking and drinking beer in lawn chairs. They don't even make that kind of chair anymore, with the, what, nylon? Braided over aluminum frames? And those ball fields, they're not there anymore. It's all industrial parks now... I'm sorry," Susan sniffed. "I've been going on forever. I thought I'd spend my whole life waiting for ballgames to be over. But, god, that was a lifetime ago. I don't even remember your question. How did I start talking about baseball?" She glanced around the room, bemused. "How did we start...talking...?"

The old woman recognized the moment—the soul was losing its anchor, urging faster towards dissolution. But she'd held on long enough to pass on her treasure, her pearl, polished to perfection by a life's work.

"You told me just what I needed to know, dear," the old woman said. "Just the piece I've been looking for." She kissed Susan on the brow, infusing her with the fullness of peace everlasting. Then, with a twist of her hands, she spun, folded, and reduced Susan to a tiny orb of swirling color. This she carried into the next room, where she kept all of creation—an omnidimensional panoramic display of every perspective, experience, and memory.

Pausing to savor the moment, she held up this last unprocessed soul (Susan McInnes Wild: 1977-2061, poet, advocate, mother of three) and sighed. The final piece. How many eons had she spent on her creation, deciphering the framework, the order, the angles, placing each precious and perfectly unique being with painstaking precision. Painstaking precision. She giggled, congratulating herself for the alliteration—as pleasing, perhaps, as the taste of warmish Pepsi and a particular candy on the lips of a seven-year-old girl from Montchanin, Ohio.

With a satisfied little smile, she set Susan's soul, with its memory of the Kirkwood Junior League field, into place between Bryan Vince O'Dooley (who worked that concession stand as a teenager in the spring of 1985), Alison Marie Fray (who cut her bottom lip on Bryan's braces, kissing against the concessions' clapboard wall), and Jamal Malcolm Keith (the young pitcher widely believed to have a future in the pros until he was killed by a drunk driver in '93). Perfect, perfect.

But as she stepped back to admire her work, she saw what

she'd previously overlooked. Her smile faded. The puzzle was not, in fact, complete.

With a tsk and a tut, she cast her gaze over the floor. Perhaps a soul had come loose and popped out. Perhaps she'd been distracted, skimped on the adhesive. There were so many wars and disasters toward the end. But surely the stray was nearby, tucked under the rocking chair, or stuck in the shag carpet.

She found nothing.

In fact, now that she thought about it, staring at the singularly-shaped void in her creation, she realized, no. She'd never put a piece there in the first place.

But there was nothing in the box where she kept the unsorted souls. Nothing was stuck behind the tape or in the folds where the edges overlapped. Nothing on the bottom of her shoes.

Had she miscalculated, mis-engineered? No—something belonged in that spot. Somewhere out in her vast universe floated an unprocessed soul. She had no idea where. She couldn't remember who.

She tsked again. She was getting old.

She got herself a cup of tea.

Her puzzle was beautiful and tragic, by design. Exquisitely bittersweet... but even she was surprised by the effect of the gaping hole. For all the color, depth, and careful nuance, in the end her eye returned always to that empty space—to her mistake.

It was...imperfect.

It was, she thought, her best one yet.

She took one last, lingering look, a final sip, and put down her cup. Hooking a finger into the void, she pulled. The whole of her creation fell asunder, all the many splendid pieces spinning back into chaos, ready to be imagined (if infinitesimally smaller) once again.

# EXPRESS YOUR FEELINGS

## BETH CATO

**About the Author**

Nebula-nominated Beth Cato is the author of the Clock-work Dagger duology and the Blood of Earth trilogy from Harper Voyager. She's a Hanford, California native transplanted to the Arizona desert, where she lives with her husband, son, and requisite cats. Follow her at BethCato.com and on Twitter at @BethCato.

it's been ages since you gave in
but as old as you are
sometimes the boredom is too much
and the anger, too
you'd think after this long
you'd have a better cap on that
but no
sometimes it just feels good
to demolish something
not like anyone will miss
this planet, anyway

# QUINCE

## SAMANTHA HENDERSON

**About the Author**

Samantha Henderson's short fiction and poetry have been published in *Strange Horizons, Clarkesworld, Interzone, Weird Tales, Goblin Fruit,* and *Mythic Delirium* and in the anthologies *Tomorrow's Cthulu, Running with the Pack,* and *Zombies: Shambling through the Ages.* Her work has been reprinted in *Year's Best Science Fiction 34,* the *Nebula Awards Showcase, Aliens: Recent Encounters, Steampunk Reloaded,* and *The Mammoth Book of Steampunk.* Her stories have been podcast at *Podcastle, Escape Pod, Drabblecast* and *Strange Horizons,* and she's the author of the Forgotten Realms novels *Heaven's Bones* and *Dawnbringer.* She is very fond of pomegranates and other dangerous fruit.

I miss
the hypodermic benediction
that brought dreamless sleep.
These dreams I can't control; they are
jagged,
disordered
as a pack of shuffled cards, or the spill of textured
    bearings
into red dust.

Three miles above the surface, hills and hillocks
    and dunes
and the concentric volcanoes,
all layered and caked with fine, sunset grit,
take on the aspect of the rippled surface of an
    ancient marble
that an old man brought for luck
tucked in the flap of a utility suit. Like a stone
    peach,
in a stone bowl in a painting
in a book on a digi-drive.

Alarums. Acquire target: peck
*pow*
a burst of silent gravel
like a fruiting body
out of an ant's head.
Alarums. Acquire target: peck
*pow*

At home we eat oranges against the scurvy,
and apples mealy from the heat.
Sometimes there are grapes, each an explosion

of pallid juice, but sweet, a little, enough.

But here, I can revel in the memory of fruits never
    tasted
when the interface lulls me back into that place
between wake and sleep
between targets and the jagged dreams.
Quince, syrupy and pale yellow,
greengages ripe at fair-time
kumquats sweet and gloriously bitter
blood oranges tangy and clotted
apricots seasoned as wine, musky as sex—
the fruits are not necessary,
only their names.

One target, just one
can will wipe out a pod
just one can hit the nexus of tube and rivet
and all burst forth like a drop of blood
blooming in water.

They say that when you are tempted to let one,
    just one, pass
just to see what will happen—then it's time to go
    home,
to leave your catamites and concubines,
your tagger-girls and twilight-boys
the crimes uncommitted you savored
the sins you pretended to taste.

This time,
I'm keeping the quince.

# SHADOWS OF THE DEEP

## TRAVIS HEERMANN

**About the Author**

Freelance writer, novelist, editor, and Scribe Award nominee, Travis Heermann is the author of eight novels, including *The Hammer Falls*, *Death Wind*, and *The Ronin Trilogy*, short fiction in the Baen Books anthology *Straight Outta Deadwood*, plus *Apex Magazine*, *Cemetery Dance*, and others. His freelance work includes contributions to the *Firefly Roleplaying Game*, *Battletech*, *Legend of Five Rings*, and *EVE Online*.

KURIKO WALKED AGHAST THROUGH THE WRECKAGE OF HER childhood. It was worse than she feared; every village in Iga province was wiped away clean. Charred timbers protruded like burnt ribs from the snow.

Circumventing Oda clan checkpoints had been child's play, but after crossing over the mountains once haunted by a score of *shinobi* families, she saw naught but blackened rubble and emptiness. Even the cemeteries had been ravaged. Graves lay open, urns shattered, markers scattered like twigs, funereal ashes mixed with snow.

Hiji Mountain loomed before her, swathed in deep forest and secrets. By nightfall, she could arrive in Hoshino, but the leaden sky threatened snow. And just then, a cold, wet kiss settled upon her cheek.

How appropriate that her return would mirror her departure seven years before.

THE SNOWFALL IN THE DEEP OF THAT NIGHT MUFFLED MOMOKO'S wails. The Master of the Hattori clan held her tight.

She wriggled and strained toward Kuriko with a pale little arm. "Mama!" The sweet little girl with the plump rosy cheeks, the face of a baby goddess, a shriek that could shatter crockery, and a giggle that could melt the heart of a mountain.

Kuriko reached back, tears mixing with snowflakes on her cheeks, sobbing past the lump in her throat. "Momoko!"

"Fear not, my daughter," Master Hanzo said to Kuriko, "she will grow well in the arms of the clan, just as you did. If the gods are kind, she will become half the *shinobi* her mother is."

Sadness slashed open Kuriko's heart and it bled into her bowels. "But why me? Choose another!" Let her stay with her daughter!

"There is no one better, and the payment is high. Your mission awaits," the Master said, "now go."

How could she have expected differently? Her own mother was but a distant memory, torn away from her on a night much like this one. Only the gold had returned, payment for a successful mission.

Kuriko stood in the snow, tears burning in her eyes, icy kisses of snowflake pattering her cheeks, as the Master turned and disappeared into the darkness with her daughter.

Like Kuriko, Momoko could be the seed of one of several wealthy nobles or powerful daimyo. A shinobi female's most important work was often accomplished in the afterglow of passion. She should know that the clan would care for Momoko, without fail, without hesitation, but had her mother felt such agony? Momoko would undergo the same long rigors, training, and spiritual discipline necessary to blur the boundaries between human being and shadow.

Kuriko had infiltrated the pleasure houses, gained the affection of her target, listened, observed, served as quiet counsel in his most vulnerable moments, and then, when she had gleaned what she needed, he died choking on a fishbone. No one would ever know that the poisoned fishbone had been jammed into his throat.

Every year she had sent secret missives to Master Hanzo, requesting a return to Iga, yearning to watch Momoko grow and learn. In return, the Master sent new missions.

And then news of the attack reached her, and no reply came to her last letter. Now, seven years after she departed, Kuriko looked up at Hiji Mountain. "Mama is coming home."

THE HIJIKI RIVER RAN CLEAN AND CLEAR, OFFERING A CHANCE TO fill her water gourd.

She kicked off her wooden *geta*, peeled off her *tabi*, and waded into the shallows. The ice-cold water numbed her feet and calves, but washed away the road mud. This riverbed had devoured thousands of her small footprints.

A smear of white that was not ice in the water caught her eye.

A human thigh bone, half buried in the sand. A few sloshing steps and she knelt over it. She reached into the water and gently pulled it free. Strange gouges marred the knob, the opposite end splintered, the marrow gone.

Iga had not been home to bears or wolves for centuries.

The river flowed down from Hiji Mountain where Kannonji Temple once stood. The slopes were too high, the forest too thick, for her to see what remained of the temple. She would have to pass it to reach Hoshino.

Hoshino had never been more than an innocuous collection of hovels hidden away in bamboo groves and pine woods at the summit of Hiji Mountain, difficult to reach at best. Innocuous, yes; unimportant, no. Hoshino village formed the hub of the Hattori clan's power and influence.

Momoko would be ten years old now, if she lived. Had Master Hanzo survived the siege? Kuriko could scarcely fathom the master of the greatest *shinobi* clan being killed on his own ground.

How small the valley looked now, silent except for the burble of the river and the call of a distant pheasant cock…

Pheasant cocks did not crow at this time of year.

Standing stock still in the freezing river, clutching her staff in both hands, she reached out with every tendril of her senses, seeking the source of the sound. A tuft of snow pattered from the naked branches of an empty maple tree.

The hairs on her neck rose; she was being watched.

Let them watch. Whether they were survivors, or Oda spies, or even Master Hanzo himself, she would find Momoko.

SNOW MADE THE CLIMB TO KANNONJI TEMPLE TREACHEROUS, slicking the rocks and turning the earth to icy mud. The leaden sky darkened like a bed of drowned coals. The snow-laden forest muffled her movements as she climbed the switchback trail. Having spent the first fifteen years of her life here, she still knew every tree, in spite of the scars inflicted by war. The land below still bore the evidence of a siege, trampled earth, flattened forest, blackened dimples of firepits, great mounds of refuse.

Her face tightened at the devastation.

For four hundred years, warlords had squabbled over pride and land and gold, trading in the talents of the shadow families of Iga, and for as long, Iga had enjoyed prosperity and quiet autonomy. The *shinobi* of Iga were content to study the secrets of where flesh met spirit and to await the next contract. But when Oda Nobunaga could not countenance an unclaimed space of map, he invaded with forty thousand troops from all six roads into Iga.

The road up the mountain had been all but destroyed by the passage of countless feet. When Kuriko reached the ruins of the Kannonji Temple gate, dusky shadows lengthened over the patches of snow. Standing between the massive charred timbers of the great *torii* arch, she allowed the loss to wash through her. All the clans of Iga had gathered here for one last desperate defense—and failed. Remnants of the temple's stone walls and great blackened mounds of timbers lay scattered as if the palm of a god had ground the ancient temple into the mountainside.

Kuriko stepped through the remains of the wooden pillars onto the once beautiful temple grounds, once a place of serene tranquility. Now the snow lay thick atop destruction.

The hairs on her neck and arms stood spear-straight and she froze. She was still being watched.

A black spot opened in a snowdrift, like an eyelid falling open, snow collapsing into a void beneath.

She slid one hand into her sleeve, where her steel teeth lay hidden. Rather than betray her awareness, her gaze meandered in every other direction while she strolled closer. A hint of movement? Nearing the palm-sized opening in the snowdrift, she feigned tripping and knelt to rub her toes.

The snow muffled a strange slithering beneath, receding. She probed the hole with the tip of her staff, and more snow fell inward. Moments later, she revealed a space beneath a tangled heap of rubble, an opening suitable for a fox or a *tanuki* burrow —except that the burrow went vertically into the rocky earth.

A tunnel.

She had not known of any tunnels beneath Kannonji, but she was unsurprised. The entire mountain was fortified with tunnels both natural and hand-carved. The empty veins of Hiji Mountain had hidden their ultimate depths from even the Hattori clan.

The whisper of dust told her that something moved in the tunnel. Human or venturesome *tanuki*?

She shrugged off her traveling pack and slid feet-first into the opening, feeling for the floor below her. Snow crunched under her *geta*, and the already feeble light disappeared ten paces down the passage. She drew her staff and pack in after her and tied back her sleeves warrior-style to ensure freedom of movement. The tunnel was too low to allow standing and too narrow for moving abreast, fashioned of close-set stone blocks as part of the temple foundations. Perhaps this was a distraction from finding Momoko, but she could not abide being watched on her home ground. She had questions demanding answers.

She slid as easily into silence and darkness as into a well-loved memory, slipping off her noisy *geta*, ears sharpened for any sound beside the brush of her own clothing. As the darkness thickened around her, so did the unidentifiable sounds of something ahead.

A sifting of dried silt and ash covered the floor, but darkness obscured details. She withdrew the wooden box of matches from her pack. Closing one eye to protect her night-vision from the flare, she struck one against the coarse tunnel wall. The flame blazed with brimstone and drove back the encroaching darkness. Holding the flame low, she examined the tunnel floor. There were indeed footprints in the silt, but the feet were grotesque, deformed, interspersed irregularly with long-fingered hand prints like those of a monkey.

A breath of wind from behind fluttered wisps of hair around her ears, extinguishing the flame, and for a moment she was strangely conscious of her own scent wafting into unseen abysses.

The movement in the darkness ahead silenced.

She thrust her staff one-handed before her, stretching with her awareness beyond the limitations of sight, half-expecting the distinctive whistle of *shuriken* slicing the air toward her. For an eternity of endless moments, she waited, and nothing came.

Her fingertips told her only two matches remained. She lit another.

In the flare of light, a pair of distant eyes glowed, then disappeared.

Her heart leaped to a gallop. She dropped the match. It went out. Her mind whirled to make sense of what she had seen. They were not the eyes of an animal, nor were they human.

Threads of caution tightened every sinew in her body as she slid deeper into this game of cat and mouse. Even so, she thrilled at the hunt. She had risked death too many times to count, but in every one of those instances, she felt most lusciously alive, thrumming with the heartbeat of the world.

After a hundred paces, the winter chill diminished, and the

stone fortifications against her back became natural cave. The pitch-black echoes told her the chamber expanded.

She struck her last match.

Her flame glittered in the rocks of a high chamber thirty paces across, a multitude of pinpoints. Another tunnel led deeper.

Those eyes had retreated from her flame, but there was no fuel here to burn. Eyeing her match burn down, she rummaged through her pack for her only candle, found it, and lit it with the final stub of her match. The candle would offer perhaps two hours of light, barring any sudden breezes.

The air here was moist and cool, smelling of earth and something else, perhaps animal, but sour and thick, like a den where a fox went to die.

She set the candle down, suddenly wary.

Her hair spiked again.

Something loomed behind her.

Her staff slid apart in her hands, exposing the glittering sheen of blade within, and she leaped away, slashing behind her. In the guttering candlelight, the tip of her blade passed through a faint apparition. Steel met something, unlike the feel of human flesh and bone, thicker, more resilient. Wisps of dark steam holding semblance of shape.

Something she could not see slithered across the rough stone. *Shinobi* were masters of moving unseen, of disappearing into crowds or shadows or wilderness, but none had ever achieved true invisibility. She dropped the sheath half of her "staff" and sent a spray of *shuriken* hissing across the cavern. Her aim was true. Two *shuriken* struck something and hung amid the faint smoky shape until some appendage struck them free. A guttural hiss issued from the shape. Her eyes failed to make sense of the partially solid apparition.

She leaped forward again, but the air whished with the entity's movement, quicker than even a master *shinobi*. Her blade sliced empty air. Something took purchase on the rough stone of the deeper tunnel. Her eyes caught the merest ripple of movement, like steam disturbed by passing fingers. Then it was gone.

She retrieved her *shuriken*. The points of two were stained with something dark and wet. So, it was not a hungry ghost or evil spirit. Her blade's kiss could hurt it. If it bled, it could be killed.

THE PASSAGE BEFORE HER WAS REDOLENT WITH THAT STRANGE stench. The candlelight revealed dark wet droplets on the floor, droplets too dark for blood.

The passages climbed, meandered, and branched through the mountain's flesh, some of them natural caves, some cut to enlarge or connect the caves.

One of the caves forced her to skirt a black abyss so deep she felt compelled to test it. The stone she dropped down the well struck nothing for a long time, and it continued to bounce and careen deeper and deeper, until the sound itself was lost.

She followed the droplets until she found herself in a small chamber furnished with a moldy straw mat, a firepit filled with old ashes, and bits of shattered, dusty crockery. This place felt familiar, but the years had smeared her memory. Had she slept here herself in her dawning years? But she did not recall stick figures drawn on the stone with ash. A mother, a child, smiling.

A scrap of scarlet caught her eye amidst the tangled straw. She knelt and dragged it into view with the tip of her sword. The doll's scarlet robe was tattered and filthy, but missing the same wooden eye as when she had given it to baby Momoko.

Her eyes misted, and a wave of trembling swept through her.

"Damn you, Hanzo," she whispered.

With the doll thrust into her sash, she moved on. Hot tallow coated her left hand, and the candle was now little more than a stub with less than an hour of life.

This close to Hoshino, the upper reaches of tunnels were defensible, replete with traps, hidden guard points, branches that could be sealed at will. If any of those had been sealed during the siege, she could easily find herself forced to go back without even a feeble candle, trapped in the dark with that creature.

She quickened her pace.

Perhaps fifty paces farther, the tunnel opened into a much larger circular chamber, one of which she had only heard tell. Shelves reached to the timbers of the vaulted ceiling. Stacked thick upon the shelves were hundreds of scrolls.

In every generation of the Hattori clan, there was one Master. That Master had a handful of disciples, and those disciples taught the children the ways of *shinobi*. Of those disciples, one Heir was chosen. Only the Master and the Heir were allowed into the Library, the repository of the Hattori's knowledge, a thousand years of secrets, of tradition, of the deepest knowledge of combat, espionage, the spiritual disciplines that allowed transcendence beyond mundane human abilities, the secrets of the mind and body that permitted survival in the harshest circumstances and infliction of death with little more than a touch. It was all here.

A crunchy litter covered the floor almost ankle-deep, like pale buckwheat hulls.

On the desk, a scroll lay unrolled. A dust-coated earthenware lamp on the table still housed a bit of oil. The inkwell was still sticky, the brush still damp. She lit the lamp with the remnants of her candle and unrolled more of the scroll with one hand, sword still in the other.

The calligraphy was strangely crabbed, not like Master

Hanzo's at all, with strange flourishes and unfamiliar angles. The most recent writing read:

*In the world above, Oda, Akechi, Tokugawa all believe that the Hattori clan has been stamped out. But when our transformation is complete and our power reborn, they will fear the night as no human being since the days of the gods.*

On the table nearby lay a thick book with a cover of red leather, embossed in Chinese characters. She had studied Chinese as part of her education, but the style of these characters was immensely complex, with stroke patterns she did not recognize. The ancient leather creaked when she opened the tome. Countless lines of miniscule, cramped Chinese characters, interspersed with strange drawings and incomprehensible diagrams, crammed the pages. Inside the front cover was a folded sheaf of rice paper that seemed to be a partial translation lexicon, written in somewhat less arcane Chinese, which she could understand. After some assiduous cross-referencing, she determined the tome's title: *The Book of the Dreaming Deep.*

Only then did she notice the patterns of unusual stitches binding several pieces of leather into the whole. Her gaze traced the lines for a moment before she recognized mummified human eyelids, nose, lips. With a gasp of revulsion she shoved the book away.

A noise in the room spun her around, her feet crunching on the litter. Her blade glinted in the lamplight, poised to kill. The shadowy reaches of the ceiling could hide any number of those creatures. Her awareness encompassed the room, but detected no other presence.

She rolled the scroll further backward with one hand, scanning until she found the account of the siege itself. Here the strokes resembled Master Hanzo's hand.

*After three months of siege, Kannonji has fallen with all souls butchered. The crows feast as if the gates of Hell itself have been opened. An envoy from Lord Oda arrived this afternoon demanding surrender or face annihilation. I sent him away impregnated with a slow-acting poison.*

Long passages followed, accounts of growing despair and hunger. The villagers of Hoshino, *shinobi* all, took to eating such things as rats, pine bark, leather. The desperation tainted the calligraphy.

*No one can get through. Oda has employed shinobi of Koga, who thwart our every attempt. There has been no food in a week. Taro offered himself up to feed us all.*

Then she gasped at the sight of her own name.

*I have no Heir to whom I must transmit the secrets of the clan. Taro and Saburo, the most suitable candidates, are dead. Kuriko, away in Kyoto these seven years, would be my next choice, but we are trapped here. I would have chosen her long ago, but she first had to prove her worth. Without an Heir, the Hattori clan will die with me. I must live, and there is only one book of secrets I have yet to study—the ancient Chinese text that Master Mitsuhara forbade me to touch, at risk of my very soul. But how can I watch the children starve?*

There was no mention of Momoko.

The writing in the next entry was so disjointed and incoherent she could not make sense of it—

The attack came faster than sight and opened a gash in her back.

She spun and slashed. Her blade bit deep this time. A sickening ululation and a blast of fetid breath sent chills down her limbs. Unseen feet fell into the noisy litter on the floor, and she pressed her advantage with a low, gutting lunge that sank deep into vague wispy steam. A ripping twist of her blade brought a deluge of tarry blackness spilling from nothing onto the floor, splattering coldness up her arm. The apparition began to take shape into that of a man with strangely distorted legs and face. She lunged and cut again, opening his belly with hardly a sound.

He sprawled backward, clearing a swath of floor before skidding to a halt.

Now that her antagonist lay revealed, her blood turned to ice. The face elongated into a beast-like snout filled with stained fangs, legs bent back like the knees of an animal, tipped not in toes, but in two padded hooves. What she had thought were clothes proved to be folds of blackish-purple skin.

The clear patch of floor revealed an image carved into the stone, an image that recollected the drawings in the Chinese tome. She cleared the strange debris with her foot and revealed more of the circle. Looking at the symbols inscribed there made her head hurt.

And now, for the first time, the debris seized her attention with revelation of its nature.

Shards of bone. Somehow she knew the bone was human. Splintered, broken, reduced to little more than coarse gravel. In a chamber this size, the sheer quantity of bone represented the remains of hundreds of people.

"Welcome home, Little Chestnut," a voice said.

She whirled behind flashing steel, but saw no one.

"Have you learned all that you need to?" The voice resembled Hanzo's but strangely thick and guttural. "I am pleased that your skills have not diminished. How far have you progressed?"

Unseen movement filled the air like wind from every direction. She slashed and spun in a lethal net. Severed limbs appeared in midair and fell. Spurts of black ichor stung her eyes, the stench heaved retches out of her gut. Honking roars of anger and pain fell back, but soon unnatural fists and feet found their way inside her defense. Three successive, invisible blows to three sides of her skull, and she collapsed into blackness amid the sea of bones.

When the blackness receded, she hung from her bound wrists, stripped naked, in an aboveground shack that she recognized instantly. In her childhood, it was used for butchering the village's meat, whenever boar or deer could be found. It had fallen into disrepair, but the iron hooks hanging from the ceiling were unmistakable. Outside, the chill depth of night lay dark upon the mountaintop.

Silhouetted against the moonlight from the latticed window, another body hung from its hands, a man. And another. No sound of breath came from them.

The air smelled of dust, wood, and cold rotting meat.

A vicious pounding in her head, redoubled by heart-thundering heartbeat, hands and feet numb from binding, the rest of her naked flesh shivering from the cold.

This felt like one of Master Hanzo's old tests at escape.

After a moment to steady her breathing and heartbeat, she swung her legs upward and felt for purchase around the rafter with her toes. The bonds of her wrists were so thin they cut her flesh, but freeing them from the hook was child's play.

She fell hard onto the ground. Something dark and wet burst under her weight, spraying thick, acrid liquid. Her hands shot out and found themselves entangled in cold, leathery entrails. In spite of a lifetime trained at killing, she reeled back and her gorge shot into her throat. With hands and feet still bound, she stumbled and fell over and over into piles of offal, slabs of cold dead flesh, until finally she could do nothing in the shack's narrow confines except slump against the wall and tremble.

The door of the shack opened with a creak. A tall, distorted figure stood silhouetted in moonlight. Outside, the mountaintop lay blanketed in fresh snow. Unblinking yellow eyes studied her.

Even with the distortions, she saw something familiar in the shape. "Master Hanzo?"

"Yes, daughter."

"Why have you done this? I am Hattori clan! I am not your enemy!"

"Why have you returned?"

*To reclaim Momoko*, she thought, but she said, "I came for a new mission."

The sound could have been laughter if the world was made of nightmare.

She leaned forward. "You are not Hattori Hanzo! You are a demon who has taken his place!"

He laughed again. "A demon took the place of Hattori Hanzo the moment Master Mitsuhara died all those years ago."

"Is no one here a human being anymore?"

"We have always been better than mere humans, Kuriko. You should know that."

"The book!"

"Ah, yes, the book. Our greatest weapon. A secret for centuries."

"What did you do?"

"I allowed the Hattori clan to survive. The entirety of the knowledge of the greatest *shinobi* clan would have been lost to the sands of time. Oda's forces would have slaughtered every one of us, even your little Momoko." He gestured outside. "Isn't that right, Momo-chan."

Another silhouette joined him, a little girl of about ten.

"Momoko!" Kuriko cried.

Hanzo laid a long-fingered hand on the child's shoulder. "Do you remember your mother?"

The silhouette nodded.

Kuriko reached out, her eyes misting with tears. "Momoko, it's mama!"

The girl edged closer to Hanzo.

Kuriko's ragged scream filled the close confines of the shack. *"What have you done?"*

"What I was forced to do. Among the clan's most ancient

relics is *The Book of the Dreaming Deep*, which tells of lands so deep in the earth they touch the realms of Dreams. In the caverns below Hiji Mountain lie the limitless abysses that lead to these realms. There resides the Emperor of the Deep. I summoned him, and he came with his court. He taught us secrets of the underworld, so that we could become shadows of the deepest earth, and travel to realms that touch the dreams of the world. We begged him for food, and his minions brought food from battlefields across Iga, shared it with us."

"You ate the flesh of the dead!" She rolled over onto her side and pretended to retch, concealing her hands as she reached between her legs and withdrew the slim palm-length blade from the soft folds of her deepest secrets, pinched it in her palms, and silently sliced her wrists free.

"It was the first step to joining the Dark Emperor's realm. Unlike samurai so willing to die for their lord's cause, our credo has ever been to survive at all costs, to pass on the knowledge. Oda's armies came, and we disappeared into the realm of Dreams. From there we convinced them of their ultimate success, and they went away."

"Are you going to kill me now? Eat me like these others?"

"We prefer them somewhat less fresh. And as I said, the Hattori clan must have an Heir. But now, the clan's deepest secrets cannot be learned by a mere human."

Several hunched, wiry silhouettes slunk behind him, dark slick flesh gleaming in the moonlight, yellow eyes gleaming. Unlike his minions, he wore clothes—and a katana on his hip.

He said, "These creatures bridge the chasm between our world and another parallel realm. They walk in both worlds. They could not teach this to us unless we *became* them. Now, you must join us. We have prepared a feast for you." He gestured around the interior of the shack.

"If I refuse?"

"Momo-chan is a growing child, and there haven't been any battles for a long time."

Momoko's wild shock of hair, crowning her head like a pheasant's tail, remained still. She clutched something to her chest.

In an instant, Kuriko sliced the sinew binding her ankles, and launched herself at Hanzo.

He side-stepped, and Kuriko sailed past to land in the snow among the creatures flanking him.

Her tiny knife tore an otherworldly howl from one of them. She must have looked like a snow maiden in the moonlight, all pale flesh and eyes of death. The creatures about her slipped into invisibility, but their feet were still evident in the snow. She dove under the sweep of great monkey-like arms, deep into the snow, then exploded upward in a blinding geyser of shimmering powder.

The powder dusted over the invisible shapes, betraying their shapes.

Kuriko's hands and feet became the killing tools only two decades of *shinobi* discipline could produce. In ten heartbeats, three of them lay twitching in death, and her tiny knife had snapped, but two more remained. Whirling through the blizzard of snow, her hands found one, then two short clubs. Human thigh bones. She shattered them against the creatures' skulls, and used the shards to pierce their hearts.

Then, amid settling clouds of snow, only Kuriko, Momoko, and Hanzo remained standing.

He smiled at her. "You are truly the Heir of the Hattori clan."

She faced him with two splintered, ichor-smeared thighbones.

He pushed Momoko gently behind him and drew his weapon. Momoko clutched the ragged doll to her chest.

Moonlight glimmered across the razor-sharp sheen.

Then a snarl sounded from behind him. He grunted and staggered.

In the space between heartbeats, Kuriko launched herself into the moment of opening.

She thrust his wrists upward with the pommel of one bone, and drove the splintered end of the other into his throat. A gurgling, nightmarish howl tore from him. His grip on the sword loosened. She seized the hilt between his hands, and wrenched it from his grip.

His eyes flickered in the moment before she struck, not with fear, but with satisfaction. The katana hissed, and his head tumbled into the snow, rolling past her feet.

His body lurched and fell forward, spurting tarry ichor.

Momoko chewed heartily on something, her lips wet and black. She swallowed, licked her lips, and smiled at her mother.

For a long time, Kuriko stood before her, sword quivering in hand. They looked into each other's eyes.

"Mama is home," Kuriko said.

She stroked Momoko's leathery cheek, took her little long-fingered hand, and led her down into the depths where the secrets waited.

# SECTION II

## THE JOURNEY TO NEW EDENS

*A hundred struggle and drown in the breakers. One discovers the new world. But rather, ten times rather, die in the surf, heralding the way to that new world, than stand idly on the shore.*
—*Florence Nightingale*

# GONE

## LISA TIMPF

**About the Author**

Lisa Timpf is a retired HR and communications professional who lives in Simcoe, Ontario. Her poems have been published in *Star\*Line, Eye to the Telescope, Dreams & Nightmares,* and other venues, and over 30 of her speculative short stories have appeared in magazines and anthologies including *Enter the Rebirth, Future Days, Electric Spec, Third Flatiron,* and *From a Cat's View.* When not writing, Lisa enjoys bird-watching, organic gardening, and spending outdoor time with her border collie, Emma. You can find out more about Lisa's writing projects at lisatimpf.blogspot.com. You can also find her on Goodreads and Amazon Author.

"Whuzzat, Tollie?" Frisco gestured with his squared snout, indicating the hard, opaque sphere, roughly twice the size of a tennis ball, lying on the cracked pavement.

I circled the object, placed a wary forepaw upon it, then withdrew quickly, shaking my head. " It feels *hard*," I said. "Like bone."

"Mebbe you can crack it open." Frisco cocked his head. "Like a nut."

"What do *you* know about that?" I stared at him. He returned the look and shrugged, his dark face inscrutable in a way only a German shepherd could manage. Had I told him, during my delirious ravings after he dug away the rubble that had blocked my escape from under the porch, about that time I'd raided my master's stash of hazelnuts? I didn't think so, but—

I returned my attention to the sphere that rested, ominous and brooding, on the asphalt before me.

*Think*, I scolded myself, panting. *That's what border collies do, isn't it?*

But thinking had become a laborious process since the Bombings. My AI implant wasn't much good now that there was no 'Net to connect to. Now that the Greenoans had gone and—

"Something coming," Frisco snarled. A ridge of hair on his back stiffened and he pulled his lips back, revealing the sinister sickles of his canine teeth. Seconds later, the ridge settled back into place. "Cat," he muttered. "Buckeye."

I looked up. Sure enough, weaving around the rubble—a car tire, a headless doll, a broken flower pot from what used to be the O'Hare's house—an enormous, short-haired, orange-striped tom-cat made his way toward us. Dust rose from his fur, and his tattered right ear bore a fresh wound, still oozing. For all of that, Buckeye carried himself like a businessman with important matters to tend to, walking with authority and a trace of smug superiority.

"I bear news, comrades," Buckeye eased himself into a sitting position, his tail continuing to twitch.

I ground down, hard, on my back teeth to repress the impulse to take out my frustrations and worries on Buckeye. A low growl rumbled in my throat.

"There now," Buckeye said, affixing me with a keen, clear gaze. "Don't you want to know what became of the Masters?"

"They're gone," I whined. "Gone, gone, gone. And left us behind." I raised my muzzle skyward and howled.

"Is *that* what you think?" Buckeye leaned forward, pressing his whiskered face so close to my snout that I could smell his breath. He'd recently dined on a mouse. I licked my lips. *So hungry.*

I clinched my ears tighter to my head, but not before I heard it. *Purring. He's purring.* I stared at him, incredulous.

"Someone took them, while you were sleeping."

"Trapped in the rubble, you mean." I took a step forward.

He ignored my comment. "Rounded them up," he said. I studied his green eyes, open and guileless, for once.

"What—why?" I sputtered.

"Dangerous, here," he said. He glanced around, allowing his gaze to linger on the gaping hole in the ground where the Madisons once lived, and on the collapsed roof on my own former abode. "No water. No power, after the Bombings. Afraid of disease. Afraid the Greenoans will come, to finish what they started."

"How?" I asked, trying to imagine the number of vehicles it would have taken to evacuate the neighbourhood. "So many lived here—"

"But not so many survived."

Frisco shot Buckeye a warning glance.

"And they left us behind?" I began to pace, five strides one way, five strides the other.

Buckeye shrugged. "Priorities. People first."

I closed my eyes and shuddered. *My worst nightmare, come true. Master, gone.*

"You'd best be moving on," Buckeye said. "See that?" He nodded toward the sphere on the ground. "Cameras. They're dropping them everywhere, running a close-proximity info-send. If they come—" he gave a meaningful look to each of us in turn "—they'll round you up. And then—who knows?"

"What about you?" I asked.

"Cat colony just outside town," he said, kneading the hard ground with his front paws. "They won't find me there. Lots of mice, in the ruins. I'll be fine." He hissed at the sphere, took a swipe at it with a lightning-fast front paw, then turned, tail in the air, and made to leave.

I swallowed, hard, and closed my eyes. "Buckeye," I said. He looked back over his shoulder.

"Thank you."

He bowed his head, a gesture so subtle I almost didn't catch it, then strutted away.

"What'choo make of that?" Frisco asked, coming over to lean his shoulder against mine.

"I hate to think he's telling the truth," I said. "But I believe him."

"Me too."

"Now what?" I whimpered. I lowered myself to the ground and placed my chin on my paws.

"We need to go."

Weariness, in my bones. Grey inside, without Master. *I should lie here and wait. Sleep.* "You go."

Frisco stood in place, his ears upraised. "Copters."

I shivered. No matter how miserable I might be right now, at least I *lived*. If I were to stay, perhaps that should cease to be true.

Frisco levelled a lingering look at me. "I saw your master, alive, before I crawled into the rubble after you. Don't you want to find her?" Without waiting for an answer, he turned away. The rasp of his dry paw-pads on the asphalt grew less and less prominent, till I could no longer hear him padding off.

I stared at the spot where my house had once stood. The place where Ena and I spent so many happy years.

Even if Frisco spoke the truth, would she still be alive *now*?

*I have to know!*

With an effort, I forced myself to move. Though it contradicted all of my instincts, I trotted away from the only home I'd known.

"Hey, Frisco," I shouted. "Wait up."

Hearing no response, I galloped to the ridge. By the time I reached that vantage point, my rib cage ached from the force of my labored breaths.

"What took you so long?" Frisco asked, rising from a clump of tall grass where he'd trampled a resting spot. Without waiting for an answer, he began to lope westward.

HOW WE MADE IT THROUGH THE NEXT THREE DAYS, I CANNOT SAY. I fell, from time to time, into a catatonic state, my mood dark as a moonless night as I lurched in Frisco's wake, suspended in the nightmare that my life had become. We skirted ruined towns, foraged in compost heaps and trash cans.

Always, Frisco spurred me to move when my instincts screamed that I should simply lie down and let my life-force slip away. He goaded me, called me names. He nipped me, once. At other times, he admonished me to stay hopeful.

What he refused to do was leave me behind. At times, I hated him for that.

During the bad moments, I reassured myself that our partnership would be of limited duration. We'd lived in the same neighborhood, that was all. Once I found Ena—

"Hunh. Almost there."

At Frisco's words, I forced myself into a semblance of alertness as I looked into the valley ahead of us.

"Truck stop," Frisco said, his voice radiating self-satisfaction. "Still in operation."

We approached the building from the east, scurrying down the conifer-studded hill, layers of dried pine needles soft under our paws.

Frisco paused part-way down, peering around the branches. I halted behind him.

The faded brick of the main building suggested age, but a recently built addition sprouted off to one side. Likewise, a new section of pavement to the north of the building sported bright lighting, while the illumination remained sporadic on the older stretch of asphalt.

Frisco nodded his head. "Makes sense," he muttered.

"What?"

He gestured toward several parked trucks with his muzzle. "The 'Net's down, right?"

I closed my eyes and tried to connect. *Nothing.* I grimaced. "Yeah."

"So, they can't run the one-driver GPS-controlled convoys, like they used to. More drivers, more trucks. More trucks, more space needed." He paused. "And, more chances to hitch a ride."

I licked my lips. "But they might round us up. Take us away."

"Look. Do you want to find your Master, or not?" He stomped his right front foot for emphasis.

"We need to *look.*"

"But—"

"Head for that truck, there." With his muzzle, Frisco indicated a tractor-trailer parked on the fringe of the brightly lit area. The sleeper-equipped cab wasn't new, but it wasn't ancient, either, and the gleaming chrome suggested that the driver took meticulous care of the vehicle.

As I moved to follow Frisco down the hill, I realized his omission. He'd mentioned finding my master, but not his. *He thinks Yvan's been deployed,* I thought. *Because he's a Reservist.* My brow furrowed. Maybe I'd been wrong about Frisco. Maybe he worried about the Masters after all.

When we arrived at the target vehicle, Frisco flopped down on the pavement beside it.

"What now?" I asked, panting.

"We wait."

"Wait?" My voice scaled up, and my forepaws danced on the pavement. "I thought we were looking for the Masters."

"Can you drive?" Frisco levelled an icy stare at me.

"Um, no."

"Then we wait for the driver."

"Hey, youse." I glanced around me, and saw nothing. Then, following the direction of Frisco's glance, I looked up. Way up.

The driver's side window of the truck's cab had been lowered a couple of inches. And then I saw the small face in the window—black and white, with tan-colored triangles over the eyes.

Up-pricked ears. *A dog.* I snorted. *Of sorts. Smaller than Buckeye.*

"What you want?" The voice, again.

"We're looking for a ride," I said.

"So is everwan else," the dog replied. "Why I should help you?"

"We could protect you," I offered. "And your master."

Wrong thing to say. The little dog lunged at the window. "No need help. I bite hard. You doubt?"

I shook my head. "Sorry. I didn't mean—"

"Look out!" Frisco's voice.

"He can't get through the window," I protested.

"Not him," Frisco jerked his muzzle toward the shadowy section of parking lot. "Over there."

I turned and noticed a tall, broad-shouldered woman with shoulder-length blonde hair walking toward us. A white plastic bag dangled from her left hand. The breeze carried the scent of cooked chicken, causing my mouth to water. How long had it been since I'd eaten? I wavered on my feet.

*Not too intimidating,* I thought. *What's Frisco—*

Then I saw *them.* Three men, one carrying a baseball bat and one wielding a golf club while the third clutched a large rock in his right hand. Concealed from the woman by the vehicle to our right, they stood poised. Waiting.

*We need to stop them.* I turned toward Frisco, but the big shepherd had already taken two steps toward the men.

"On three," he whispered.

*Sscrrritch!* I'd stepped on a rock, and the noise it created grating across the asphalt sounded, to my worried ears, as loud as summer thunder. I froze in place, but the three would-be assailants seemed too intent on their approaching quarry to notice.

"One. Two." Frisco's voice came low and confident across the short distance between us. I bunched the powerful muscles in my hindquarters. Frisco's ears flattened in anticipation.

"Three!"

Frisco's forepaws caught the guy with the baseball bat square in the back, knocking him to the ground. A frenzied barking ensued in the background, followed promptly by the blaring of an alarm.

I hurled myself at the golf-club carrier, seizing his right wrist. He dropped his makeshift weapon and yanked his hand away, cursing.

As the third man raised a rock above his head, I yelled at Frisco. "Duck!"

Frisco heard me just in time, and dove to the ground. The rock whizzed past his left ear.

The stone-thrower searched the pavement for another

weapon, while baseball-bat-guy staggered to his feet and took two steps toward me.

I heard footfalls on the hard surface of the parking lot. *Reinforcements?* I gritted my teeth and spun to look. A pair of security guards approached, guns drawn.

Baseball-bat-guy threw a venomous glare Frisco's way, then spat on the pavement. Then all three of the men we'd attacked raised their hands in surrender.

The alarm stopped bleating. I looked back at the truck, and saw the little dog peering through the window.

The security guards pulled out wide zip-ties and secured them around the wrists of the would-be assailants with a facility that suggested this was an oft-repeated task. The man I'd bitten grunted in pain but offered no further protest. Once the men had been subdued, the blonde-haired woman drew closer, taking in the scene with widened eyes.

"They belong to you, lady?" The taller of the two guards glanced at the woman, then nodded toward Frisco and me.

She hesitated for a moment, eyeing us up. I winced. Frisco, with his matted coat and sunken flanks, didn't look like any prize, and the twigs and burrs snarled in my fur did nothing to enhance my own attractiveness. I plopped on my haunches and allowed my tongue to loll out, offering what I hoped would be interpreted as a friendly overture.

"If not," the shorter guard said, shrugging, "we have our orders for what to do with strays."

*If we high-tail it as fast as we could go, we might make it to the shelter of the tree line. Might.*

I shot a glance at Frisco and tensed.

"Yeah, they're mine," the woman replied breezily. "I leave them outside the truck, in case—you know." She motioned toward the three men.

"Things're so desperate these days. These guys, in better times, they wouldn't—" The taller guard jerked his head toward where the three men stood, slump-shouldered, and I noticed for the first time how thin their arms looked. "We do our best to keep the 'stops safe. Heaven knows, without you truckers, nothing'd get through, especially with the damage to the rail lines."

The woman nodded, murmured her thanks, and left the guards to herd their captives back to the truck stop's main building.

"Coming?" the woman said, glancing over her shoulder at Frisco and me.

We didn't wait for a second invitation.

LIFE SETTLED INTO A STEADY ROUTINE—TRAVEL THE HIGHWAY with Lora and her toy terrier, Hyku, and guard the truck during pickups and deliveries. Between jobs, we stayed at Lora's trailer on a campground north of the truck stop.

I felt my strength returning, and I regained the weight lost during those first few days after the Bombings. Though many things had changed for the better, one thing remained constant —my aching sense of loss without Ena. Each time we stopped, I sniffed the ground and the air eagerly, seeking any sign of my master.

*Nothing.*

"Is it so bad, this life?" Frisco asked me one day as a late-April breeze riffled our fur.

I shifted position on the pavement, raising my head to study an approaching woman. *Just a tourist,* I told myself, and relaxed.

"It's just—I miss her," I confessed. "Don't you miss Yvan?"

A cryptic expression shifted across Frisco's face, so quickly I couldn't read it. He shrugged. "You don't mourn spilled kibble," he said, frowning. "You just eat it."

I took his meaning. Take life as it comes. But we border collies had never been good at that.

Besides, how could he *not* miss his master. Unless—maybe Yvan had been mean to him? He didn't seem the sort, but you never knew, with humans.

I opened my mouth to ask a question, then noted Frisco's stern look and swallowed the words, unasked. *Sparta and Athens,* I thought. *That's what we're like, him and me. He's the brawn and I'm the—*

A shrill yap interrupted my thoughts. Since we'd arrived on the scene, Lora let Hyku run loose at the truck stops, trusting us to look after him. That yap sure sounded like his voice, but where'd he gotten to?

*There.* I shuddered as I spotted Hyku walking toward a huge Rottweiler whose muscles rippled under a sleek coat.

"Hey, you," Hyku said. "Whazzamatter, you lost? No, I know, you lose your brain, no?"

The Rottie blinked. "Care to repeat that?"

"Why, you deaf?" Hyku displayed his teeth in a broad grin.

Not caring to witness the inevitable outcome, I loped over and interposed myself between the two dogs.

*Now what?*

"Watch whatcha say to my friends," Frisco drawled, strutting toward us.

Seeing himself outnumbered, the Rottie snorted once, then stomped away.

"What were you *thinking,* mouthing off to a Rottweiler?" I hissed at Hyku as Frisco and I shepherded him back to the truck.

"It was on my buck-buck list."

"*Bucket* list," I snarled. I rolled my eyes and turned to look at Frisco, expecting a terse remark to put the upstart in his place. But instead, Frisco opened his mouth in a panting grin.

"Bucket list, huh?" he said, his tone contemplative. He nodded. "Everyone needs something to look forward to. It is best to point one's muzzle toward the future."

I stared at him. *Sparta, philosophical?* I shook my head and racked my brain for a witty retort—not as easy a process as it once might have been, with the 'Net down. But then I noticed the brooding darkness in Frisco's eyes.

*What's on your bucket list, Frisco?* I wondered.

By the end of May, the fresh greenery on those trees that remained standing made the world look brighter and more hopeful. Though the 'Net had yet to be restored, a handful of radio stations had resumed reporting. The news they brought was good. Slowly and through great effort, humans were shifting the tide of the War in their favor. We saw the evidence ourselves—streaks of neon blue light against the night sky signalling the departure of Greenoan ships, half a dozen at a time. Yes, there was reason for hope.

One day, we started a new delivery run north of Toronto, along a winding and up-and-down roadway that led us past lush fields. I saw, for the first time since the start of the Greenoan Conflict, acreage dotted with grazing cows and even horses. *Maybe today's the day,* I told myself.

When we jumped out of the cab at New Requiem, where Lora was delivering supplies to a local grocery store, I told Frisco and Hyku I needed to expend some energy.

I trotted down the main street, head high. Now that I sported the bright orange safety vest Lora insisted on fitting each of us with when she put us on duty, I felt confident no one could mistake me for a stray.

Noise to the west of the small town attracted my attention—the banging of hammers, the chatter of voices. I raised my head, sniffing. *Fresh-sawn lumber.* Curious, I trotted over to investigate.

As I rounded the corner of a side-street on the outskirts of town, I skidded to a halt. To my right, workers bantered as they erected the framework for a large building. Straight ahead, on the parking lot behind a large, one-storey steel-sided building with the letters A-R-E-N-A on it, dozens of plasta-dome structures had been arrayed in neat rows. Ropes zigzagged between the structures, and the articles of clothing pegged to them fluttered in the breeze. In the centre of the encampment, two men and a woman wearing military camo uniforms stood behind a table loaded with bread, fruit, and pancakes, serving up food as members of the settlement formed a good-natured line, plates in hand. Some community members were already sitting at the picnic tables, eating.

I wove my way around the eating area. People smiled. Children laughed. Some folks even extended a trembling hand, seeking to pat me.

But I didn't pause until I'd sniffed every one of them.

I lowered my head. *No Ena. I'd been so sure.*

*But there's Reservists. I'll have to tell Frisco—*

I turned to face in the direction I'd come, and frowned when I saw Lora, Frisco, and Hyku approaching at a trot, accompanied by a number of other people. Some carried short-barrelled weapons, of the sort that had become ubiquitous when the Greenoan War had erupted eight months ago. Lora herself brandished the handgun she'd carried in the truck's glove compartment since the incident with the three would-be assailants.

"What's up?" I asked Frisco.

"Rumor of a pocket of Greenoans. Soldiers cut off from the main group, skulking around the hillside, yonder." Frisco gestured with his nose.

Behind us, a tall, white-haired man with a Reservist uniform spoke in reassuring tones to the people who had so recently sat down to enjoy a meal. Moving in an orderly fashion, children, youngsters, and the elderly, along with several teenagers, headed into the main building. Men and women deemed capable of staging a defense ranged themselves in positions assigned by the tall Reservist, while a small group armed with guns began marshalling on the grass south of the asphalt.

Without a word, Frisco began to trot in the direction of the latter party. I took a step after him.

"You two, off to the shelter," Lora said, looking at Hyku and me and pointing. "Now."

I shot a longing look in Frisco's direction, then lowered my head.

"Tollie, whass goin' on?" Hyku yipped.

"With me, squirt," I said, deliberately turning my gaze from the gun-armed group. "I want to hear what's on your buck-buck list. All of it. And after that, how about we entertain the kids, huh?"

WHEN THE TALL RESERVIST OPENED THE DOOR AND TOLD US WE could come out, I watched with a detached air as people began to make their way through the entry-door and into the sunlight. *I'll wait till the crowd thins out,* I thought. *Unless Frisco hunts us up first.*

"Beth." I saw the Reservist leader place his hand on a dark-haired woman's shoulder. He moved closer to her, and his voice dropped so low I couldn't make out the words. But I could guess at the content of his message, for as he spoke, the woman's face crumpled and she sagged into a nearby chair.

*Someone who didn't come back,* I thought, feeling an ache in my throat.

Feeling a surge of panic, I hastened for the door. *Frisco's Sparta. He's tough.* Despite my efforts at reassurance, I felt a rising dread as I scanned the line of returnees streaming back in loose single file.

And then I spotted Lora.

She staggered under the weight of her burden, but fended off an offer of assistance from a nearby townsperson. Just before she reached the pavement, she laid Frisco gently on a patch of grass and hollered for someone to find a vet.

I galloped over, barely noticing the heat of the asphalt under my feet as I sped across the parking lot.

With an effort, Frisco lifted his head. "I'm sorry, Tollie," he said.

"Sorry? For what?"

"I—told you I saw your master being rescued. I didn't—"

I turned away, cursing in my heart the cruelty of Sparta and the unadorned truth.

"Why?"

"Because—you needed hope."

"And Yvan?" I turned back to face him.

"I was there, helping, right after the bombs fell. Search and rescue, like I've been trained for." His paused, sides heaving. "He ordered me to wait while he went back in for the last person." Frisco lowered his voice. "I shouldn't have listened."

I cast my mind back over the past months, understanding now why Frisco had cut me off whenever I tried to talk about his master.

Frisco's brow furrowed. "Don't be sad," he said. "With Yvan gone—this, what happened, it gave me a chance to strike back at them. I don't regret it."

I swallowed.

"Tollie, promise me something."

"O—kay."

"Even if you don't find Ena, make room in your heart to love again. The way I made room for you."

I stared at him for a moment. "You—you said I was a burden, and a tenderfoot, and—"

# FAR GONE

## TIMOTHY GWYN

**About the Author**

Timothy Gwyn is a pilot in Northwestern Ontario, Canada. He spends a lot of time sitting around in remote communities, and he writes science fiction for fun. "Far Gone" came to him while he was pondering the backstory for his novel *Avians*.

He also runs *Lake of the Woods Ice Patrol*, a website that documents Kenora's annual spring thaw with aerial photographs.

On Twitter he is @timothygwyn and you can find both the *Ice Patrol* and his writing blog at timothygwyn.com.

I WAS HALF ASLEEP WHEN IT FINALLY REGISTERED. I HAD BEEN staring blindly at it for some time—five or six years, perhaps. It was green. Green! My human brain woke up with a dizzying rush and began to review my sub-routines. The planet had rings. Yes, I remembered that from before I started dozing. We were coming in from above the ecliptic, and they were clearly visible, but poorly defined. At least, that had been the case five years ago. We had made some progress since then, both in physical proximity and sensor acuity. I could see the rings clearly now and something more. A blurry halo that resembled an inner ring structure was nothing of the sort. It was atmosphere, and lots of it. Nothing like Venus' eighty or ninety bars, but at least four bars, at a guess. Spectroscopy showed that the dominant component was nitrogen. Good. Nitrogen is harmless to Naturals. Second component, oxygen. Oxygen is our holy grail. We've been seeking it for hundreds of years. Oxygen is life.

I had told myself to wake up if the planet were blue, because I had been hoping to find water, from which we could liberate oxygen. Mother Nature had done that here already. Trembling inwardly, I scanned the radio spectrum. If I heard anything that sounded like music or even a taxi dispatch, we were hooped. Nothing. I allowed myself a deep "breath" of well-oxygenated blood. Conscious thought, decision making, pattern recognition —I relied on my good old-fashioned gray matter for these things, and emotion, of course. Routine observation, record keeping, mathematics—those duties were best handled by my synthetic parts. Nowadays, I feel most fully alive when both engage together.

Life. It could be good or bad. Civilization would be bad. Ravenous carnivores, almost as bad. Algae might be good. Simple cyanobacteria would be better. On Earth, the little beasties had transformed the whole atmosphere into a toxic oxidizing fog that killed almost everything else, and gave rise to oxygen breathing plants and animals like us. Like our ancestors, anyway, and our cargo. My own evolution was a little more deliberate. And disastrous, but here we are.

I am going to have to notify the others soon, but I can spend a year or two on research first and give them a little more to work with. Our meetings are not social gatherings, anyway. None of us is mobile at all, and in this crowd, you do not ask how someone is doing. At best, it would be rude. At worst, they might tell you, a catalog of organic failure.

Deceleration must begin in ten years or so if this place is a good target. We would take a closer look at the planet from one of the Lagrange points before burning some of our precious hydrocarbons to move into a planetary orbit. But I'm getting ahead of myself.

I have to decide if we should stop. It is a staggering responsibility. Originally, Long Shot was built to find a planet suitable for colonization, preferably something a little nicer than Mars. Now the stakes are higher. If this system has nothing we can use, we will make a course correction as we pass the star and head for Target Four. Each time we have done this, we have maintained our speed. If I call for a full stop and this place is a bust, we will have to start over from scratch. Near zero c. A standing start from deep in a stellar gravity well, just like back at Sol. Those early decades climbing out of the solar system were so slow. Of course, we were just children then, impatient to get moving. We still had human bodies and our synthetic parts were little more than calculating machines.

"Third time's the charm," Mary had said back at Target Two. She may have been right. This planet was looking good. Green versus blue, but it was growing on me. Green could be chlorophyll—the stellar spectrum was pretty close to Sol's. There would be daylight for the Naturals, assuming we could revive any of them. We have not practiced. We are not sure what the mortality will be, but we dare not thaw some out just to learn more about the odds. Wally said we might get thirty percent revival, we might get sixty. But that was back at Target One, a long time ago. I have not asked him, but my own sub-routines are figuring ten to thirty percent now. That's going to give us a nasty genetic bottleneck. The Naturals will have to work at maximizing diversity. Max has a plan to distribute them in mixed lots, assuming that the survivors are not all too similar.

We had stored barely half of our quota of volunteers when the pandemic began. That left us seriously short, but since we were the only long-term haven, we quickly made up the numbers with refugees. We rescued them from all over: the Mars and Moon colonies of course, those were doomed without support from Earth; we took everyone from the space elevator; we got some good people at the Antarctic stations. We were witnesses to one of the biggest mass extinctions Earth ever endured. Material witnesses.

The nanite medical tech that was supposed to keep an inter-stellar crew alive for centuries had huge implications for earthly life-spans. No wonder someone jumped the gun and tried it on the surface. What they failed to understand was that a programmable immune system is an alternative, not a supple-ment. The first thing the nanites do is declare war on the T-cells. In healthy, warm-blooded animals, the battle was soon over and programming could begin—if you were in our facility. In the wild, it was catastrophic. A person can survive a long time with a compromised immune system, but with no immune system at all, life expectancy is about a week. It started with a handful of humans, and we tried to get them into quarantine, but when the birds started dropping, we knew there was no stopping it. In the end, we just hunted down the little pockets of isolated survivors.

WE ARE CLOSE ENOUGH TO SEE MORE OF THE PLANET NOW. THE atmosphere is thick; about four point six bars. If I squint, using an optical distortion correction I worked up, I can see what might be clouds and ocean. The ocean, if that's what it is, is a rich green color, and the clouds are white. The overall effect is a milky, muddy green. I rummage through my color vocabulary. Jade is not quite right. Emerald is way off. I realize I am looking for a word for it. A name. I will not let them call the new cradle of humanity Earth II or New Earth. Some of them will want to; the orbit is very close. But this place is different. The air is so thick that if the Naturals were to settle at sea level, they might suffer from nitrogen narcosis or even oxygen toxicity. The proportion of oxygen to nitrogen is Earth-like. I hope there are mountains. Naturals could live high on the mountainsides, far above the thickest parts of the roiling atmosphere. A subtle Doppler algorithm suggests the wind velocities are not too extreme, but the sheer mass of the atmosphere is going to make those winds very forceful anywhere near sea level.

WE HAVE SETTLED IN AT THE TRAILING LAGRANGE POINT. ALL indications are that we have hit the jackpot. Our list of targets included only sunlike stars with a rocky planet in a habitable orbit; our primary requirement, the one we failed to find at Targets One and Two, was water. With water, we could split out oxygen for a domed habitat, not to mention it's handy for drinking and irrigating plants. This planet is wet. Wringing wet. The oceans are warm; the atmosphere is moist. There's a little xenon, a little argon, but nothing that will kill people. Numerous mountain ranges offer habitable zones with reason-able air pressure, and close to the equator, those zones coincide with comfortable temperatures. The mountains are volcanic, but we have not observed many dust plumes yet. It does not matter anyway; we have stopped. Even if we could refuel and start for Target Four, it would be a long trip. The number of Naturals we could revive would be low. By Target Six, we'd be lucky to get more than one of each sex. We are committed.

There is another problem; one we do not talk about. The number of us with viable organic brains is dwindling. Mary's has entered a sort of coma. She has her mathematical processors composing music, endless variations on a theme. Some of it is beautiful, but I cannot bear to listen to it because it reminds me of her and her fate. Will it happen to all of us? Will that be our punishment for cheating death?

The voyage has stretched out for hundreds of years. The nanites that were supposed to make us immortal have not entirely lived up to their billing. I blame the lack of gravity for the decay in our bodies; I gave up on my heart a long time ago and replaced it with a mechanical pump. The first of many. We were supposed to refine the nanites on the way, but we ran out of bodies to test them in. Our brains struggle on, but we had not counted on the lack of stimulus. Boredom is killing us. At least, I hope that is the problem, because things will get more exciting when we move into planetary orbit.

WE HAVE STABILIZED AN ORBIT AROUND CELADON. I AM PROUD that they let my name stick. I was ruminating on the conveniently Earth-like atmosphere when my vocabulary crawler hit on Celadon. I concocted a full acronym in microseconds, but using my processing power sucks all the fun out of wit, so I just told the others that it's a kind of pottery glaze known for its variety of muted green shades. It reminds us of Earth, and it is appropriate because the Naturals may be making a lot of pottery here. They won't be making nanites. Not if I have anything to say about it.

We have done some robotic exploration of the surface. The cyanobacterial mats on the sea are the only native life. The land is barren, or at least it was before we seeded forests in some of the habitable zones.

I have been teaching my sub-routines about decision making and pattern recognition. Social interaction is proving more difficult, but I think I could pass a Turing test without invoking my wet brain. One accomplishment I am particularly proud of is that I solved the problem of how to build a space elevator from our orbital position down to the surface. Normally, you would do it like the one on Earth—start with a factory in the middle (in a geosynchronous orbit) and feed out "rope" both upward and downward at the same speed so that the center of gravity stays steady. The problem with doing that on Celadon is that the rings are in the way. A mostly mathematical solution is to run two cables, one north of the rings and one south, and anchor them to the surface about a hundred kilometers apart. The rings are thin enough that even though both cables converge at a single space station—this ship—they clear the rings by a wide margin. Still, I felt I showed good creative thought, and I did it without using my organic brain. I isolated my separate sides to prevent any kind of cross-talk.

We have lost Max. His brain no longer responds to any kind of stimulus either from his own circuitry or externally from the rest of us. Blood still flows through it, but oxygen is not taken up. He is brain-dead. We are still able to connect with his synthetic parts, so we have access to his data, but not his childhood memories. I have been trying to transfer some of my own early memories for safekeeping. Images are hopeless, but I have begun dictating a sort of journal.

THE ELEVATOR IS COMPLETE AND WE HAVE BEEN ROUSING OUT THE cargo for weeks now. Plant and animal seed-stock have been fine, and as to the people, recovery has been better than we predicted, around forty percent are viable Naturals. They will settle on the mountains and rebuild the human race.

As to our other problem, all of us have been busy, but we have lost more crew members. Boredom is not the problem, I fear.

LANDING DAY. THE NATURALS ARE BOARDING THE SHIPS TO GO and start their settlements. I cannot resist watching them, they are so excited—they laugh like children going out to play. So hormonal. I wish to share their happiness, so despite sluggish responses from my organic brain, I gorge on images of them until I feel an emotional response. When my brain finally comes around, I feel excitement, too. And for one last time, joy.

I have been struggling with a decision lately; I have managed to complete it without organic input, and it is time. I shut down my life support. The joy fades to sadness as my brain dies. When the last spark of neural activity is gone, an echo of sorrow lingers like regret, but I am not a child any longer, and I have a lot to do.

# VAST, UNCOUNTABLE THINGS

## LYNNE SARGENT

**About the Author**

Lynne Sargent is a writer, aerialist, and Philosophy PhD candidate currently studying at the University of Waterloo. You can find more of her work in venues such as *Strange Horizons, Truancy*, and *Augur Magazine*, among others. If you want to find out more, check out her bibliography at scribbledshadows.-wordpress.com, or reach out to her on Twitter @SamLynneS.

The field of stars never ends.

They said it was out there:
a new world, and we passed
the point of no return
generations before

I was born.
But our planet blew up,
both of them—
the Old Country, and the New,

and now we are nothing but language
echoing across space,
never to land.

We imagine we are crossing
the sea, like our forebears,
that each twinkling star is a fish
swimming in the universe.

Our children play make believe
about fishes. We play make believe
about an end.

# TO WALK UPON CLOUDS

## BETH CATO

**About the Author**

Nebula-nominated Beth Cato is the author of the *Clockwork Dagger* duology and the *Blood of Earth* trilogy from Harper Voyager. She's a Hanford, California native transplanted to the Arizona desert, where she lives with her husband, son, and requisite cats. Follow her at BethCato.com and on Twitter at @BethCato.

the view from the space elevator
reveals a topography
of dandelion fluff meadows
pillows of cumulus
wind-carved trails that lead
to a horizon crowned in gold

logically you know
you can't walk there
but you can imagine the softness
of that ground underfoot

your toes press to the wall
fingers stretch toward
those wisps beyond the window

everyone does it

the glass is strong now

# I AM BRIHASPATI

## D. A. D'AMICO

**About the Author**

D. A. D'Amico has had more than seventy works published in the last nine years in venues such as *New Myths*, *Daily Science Fiction*, and *Shock Totem*...among others. He's a winner of L. Ron Hubbard's prestigious Writers of the Future award, (showcased in volume XXVII), as well as the 2017 Write Well award. Collections of his work and links to anthologies and magazines he's been in can be found on Amazon at: https://www.amazon.com/D-A-DAmico. His website is dadamico.com, his Facebook page is authordadamico, and, on painfully rare occasions, twitter: @dadamico.

THE WELD WORMS AISHWARYA DAS SET THE DAY BEFORE FLARED in brilliant violet arcs across the airlock frame, sealing the shuttle from the unfinished sheath of Brihaspati's lower core. They'd never be able to force her off now.

"What've you done?" Rajesh Kaur's face pressed against the thick digital glass as if he could push his way back onto the station, just like he bullied his way through everything. "This is nuts, Aishwarya."

"I know."

Tremors shook the padded rungs, dull thumps vibrating through her boots as Rajesh tried to free the door. The stench of ozone flowed like waves from the casing. "You won't be able to live here. It's not viable. It's not what Brihaspati was meant for."

"I know that too."

Whatever time she could steal in orbit was worth a lifetime on Earth's surface. She was free here. Her skillsuit gave her mobility for the first time since the accident, and she wouldn't give that up.

"You're a brilliant engineer. Are you going to throw that away?"

"I'm only useful up here. I'd be baggage on Earth." She still remembered the crowded streets of Mumbai, the jostling crowds, the competition for jobs, food, money. Without mobility, she'd be a beggar. "You of all people know what it's like."

They shared similar histories, comparable struggles out of poverty, each fighting and winning a spot in space. He knew she couldn't go back.

"Now what?" Rajesh stepped back from the screen, pressing his thick mustache between the thumb and forefinger of his right hand. His compact features and brooding expression made his head look tiny in the digital glass.

"Now *you* go." She glanced away, up the hundred and twenty meter tube forming Brihaspati's central core. "You have a space station to catch."

"We can compress our window, swing around to the airlock on the up-orbit tier. Meet us there, and we'll rendezvous with the ISP together." The pleading in his tone made her look back. "Come home with us. Nobody will speak of this."

She'd be crazy to stay. She knew it. Brihaspati was nothing more than a gigantic heap of scrap. Originally intended as a Jovian research station, the project had been overambitious, and funding had been pulled before the crew habitat could be completed or the massive thrusters installed. Now, it was just a mountain of metal waiting to be recycled.

"If you try the other airlock, I'll just fuse it." She placed a hand on the glass, the thin gold tracings on her glove reflecting against Rajesh's image. "I can't go back to being a prisoner in my own skin."

His expression sagged. They'd had this discussion many times in the two years since the crash that'd left her paralyzed. He couldn't win, and he knew it. Aishwarya smirked. The look in his eyes said it all. Rajesh wasn't a man who lost anything, especially not an argument.

"The CNSA is sending a ship. They'll be here in three days to take control of the project and begin salvage operations." He didn't ask her if she'd leave with the Chinese transport. He knew it'd be her only option by then. "Good luck."

The digital glass darkened. A jolt told her the shuttle had pulled the docking clamps, and she turned her back on the airlock.

RINGS OF BIOLUMINESCENT PAINT GLOWED AT THREE METER intervals along the cylinder's interior, stretching a hundred meters along the core. Aishwarya felt as if she were falling through a shrinking tunnel, like Alice down the rabbit hole, and she wondered if she'd made a mistake as she pulled herself along.

Rajesh was right. Brihaspati wouldn't work in the long run, not the way they'd left it. Only half of the outer shell had been assembled. The frame motors were still in containers, strapped to the down-orbit tier as ballast. The entire station circled too low, its orbit degrading and soon to become a hazard. She'd have no choice but to leave when the Chinese arrived.

A SOFT MALE VOICE SQUELCHED THROUGH HER COLLAR SPEAKERS. "Your orders were to vacate."

Startled, Aishwarya missed the rung. She crashed into the inner lining, leaving a bluish streak through the patina of oxidation.

"Why was this not done?"

"You scared the crap out of me!" She tried to get her breathing under control, her heartrate monitor shrieking at the spike.

"Why are you not on the shuttle?" The voice from mission control sounded bored, as if her fate meant next to nothing to him.

How could Aishwarya explain to a stranger she didn't want to feel like a pariah? She was functional here. Brihaspati's array powered the thin woven wires and servos of her skillsuit, giving her mobility without the pain and clumsy bulk of a traditional exosuit. It was a symbiotic relationship, and it'd taken her a year to perfect it. The suit made her whole, but it'd never work on the surface.

"You will board the salvage assessor's craft when it arrives. You will continue with them until you reach the International Space Platform, where you'll turn yourself over to the Indian liaison there. Transport to the surface has been arranged on a

Russian drop tanker two days later. These orders are *not* negotiable. Are they understood?"

She sighed. She'd known this was coming.

"What if I don't leave?" She spoke casually, as if refusing a drink at a party, but she trembled inside. "What if I say no?"

She pulled herself into the prep room of the upper tier airlock, affixing her helmet while waiting for a response. She'd spent nights going over the salvage laws, and she had a surprise for them.

"Brihaspati, this is Satish Dhawan Space Center. Do you copy?" The voice sounded different, much calmer, and more authoritarian.

"Copy." Aishwarya keyed the airlock, and the hatch slid aside. She steadied herself, afraid this might not work.

"Director Roddam Sharma here. It's three in the morning, and..."

"With all respects, director, you should be in bed."

"Yes, well...I was, but it seems we have a bit of a problem."

"I'm sorry to hear that." Aishwarya climbed to the outer corner of the airlock. Maybe she shouldn't antagonize the director, but she was tired of being treated like a child.

She took a deep breath, waiting for the right moment to jump. Her timing needed to be precise. Her skillsuit would power down the moment she exited the station, and she'd be at the mercy of her spacesuit's programming.

She hadn't been outside the station since her accident two years earlier. One of the solar grid assemblies had picked up too much speed relative to the restraining arm, and Aishwarya made the rooky mistake of getting between them to try and dampen the grid's momentum. The impact force was enough to smash her spine. She'd spent two months in Brihaspati's medical ward learning to breathe without the aid of machines, and three more fighting to keep from being sent home.

They told Aishwarya she'd never hold a tool again. They said she'd never walk, but the worst news had come when she'd received her orders to return to Earth. An engineer unable to do her job was just fifty-four kilograms of dead weight.

So she'd started to work. She'd designed an exosuit based on current technology, but scaled down, primed for an orbital environment and fueled by the station's power grid. She'd only wanted mobility back, but she'd gotten so much more.

"As a member of the ISRO, your actions are subject to command approval. You mustn't disobey." Director Sharma had a deep voice, and his low, even tone was hypnotic. "We each have a job to do, and everyone must follow their orders."

"I quit."

"Excuse me?" His tone changed. It didn't sound as if he were speaking to a child anymore.

"I quit." Her heart pounded so loud she was surprised it didn't set off her sensors. "I'll be fired the moment I set foot on Earth anyway, so I quit."

"You are essential space personnel." She could hear mumbling in the background. The director wasn't alone. "You can't resign."

"I just did."

Silence, as if he'd dropped communications. Aishwarya bit her lip. She needed them to escalate this. If they didn't, her plan wouldn't work. She counted the seconds. Her next move depended on the ISRO's reaction.

"Your actions are illegal on a national level, astronaut." It wasn't the director. It was the first voice, the rude operations chief who'd tried to order her around earlier. "This is treason."

Aishwarya exhaled, tension blowing out like steam. They'd given her an opening.

"I renounce my national privilege. I don't want to be part of your country." She checked her suit, making sure she'd engaged the autopilot.

"Then you will vacate *our* space platform immediately."

"Understood."

She leapt, holding her breath as she arced over Brihaspati's unfinished upper torus. Earth loomed like a gigantic glowing puzzle above her, its continents and oceans serrated by Brihaspati's latticework of graphene bars and solar power curtains. The soft whisper of her skillsuit servos faded, draining sensation from her limbs until she was left with nothing but a profound sense of loss.

"ISRO control. My spacesuit is transmitting orbital location data. I am officially away from Brihaspati, and the station has been released for salvage."

"Acknowledged..." The voice sounded leery. They knew she was up to something, but they weren't sure what. She felt hurt nobody ever asked where she was going, or how she'd survive.

Her HUD flashed an overlay of Brihaspati's shell across her visor, and her frame motors engaged. She swung out over the station and down beneath the unfinished shock plate. Pitted from exposure, the plate eclipsed the Earth, leaving her totally alone, her breathing the only sound.

In the silence, she wondered if she'd done the right thing.

HER SUIT COMPLETED ITS PROGRAMMED CIRCUIT, SPIRALING down-orbit and away from the station. A chill ran down Aishwarya's spine, lost somewhere behind her ribcage as she fought to keep from hyperventilating. She hadn't been outside Brihaspati in a long time. The station sat like a mismatched dumbbell against the Earth, unfinished but still impressive in the reflected sunlight. It had become so much more than a job to her. It was home.

"For the official record...I am taking possession, per salvage articles of the Orbital Assembly, of abandoned material at these coordinates." She transmitted Brihaspati's position, and then held her breath.

Control didn't respond. They knew she'd be recording everything.

"I'll take your silence as assent, ISRO." Her motors flared. She headed back in, autopilot rotating her across the torus and toward the up-orbit airlock.

"Astronaut Das, those articles you've so earnestly quoted were not meant for you." The man with the snotty voice finally spoke. A video window splashed across the corner of her visor's HUD, and she was face to face with a young man with small eyes and a sour expression that matched his distemper. "Those laws were set down with the anticipation only nations would be in possession of the resources needed to accomplish complex salvage operations in space, and—"

"Your shortcomings are not *my* fault." Aishwarya sneered at the little man. "The law is the law."

When the first Orbital Assembly had drawn up the rules on space salvage more than a decade earlier, they'd assumed no national space program would try to claim significant assets without a contract. It'd be considered a hostile act, and there were other laws covering aggression in orbit. Aishwarya had no such constraint. She didn't for a moment think she could keep the station. The Orbital Assembly would just attach an addendum to close the loophole, but for now Brihaspati technically belonged to her.

HER SPACESUIT HIT THE CURVE OF THE INNER SHELL. HER HEAD slammed the rim of her visor. A wave of nausea engulfed her, and she screamed. Crimson alerts mushroomed across her HUD. Autopilot tried to correct, but she tumbled as she drifted across the outer ring of Brihaspati, helpless, her frantic breaths spilling between clenched teeth.

"No, no, no..." She closed her eyes. Her skin tingled, her face flush. Her suit thrusters cut out. She drifted, hope fading as momentum drew her across the crenelated solar umbrellas.

The sun appeared. Her visor polarized as she rotated past the tip of the solar arrays and struck a spur of carbon tubing. Without power to her skillsuit, her body might as well be frozen. With no way to maneuver, she was already dead.

She should have let Rajesh talk her onto the shuttle. It had been too big of a risk to try and stay, and now she'd lost everything.

"ISRO." Tears beaded her eyes, wicked away by microfiber strips. Her voice faltered. She tried to get it under control before continuing. She didn't want them to gloat. She didn't want *that* to be the last thing she heard.

"Aishwarya, do you copy?" A video window popped onto her HUD. Rajesh stared at her, a curl to his thick mustache that dragged his lips into a frown. He hadn't been happy about leaving her behind. He must be livid over what she'd done since. "We need to talk."

"No lectures, please. Not now."

"If not now, when?" His gaze flickered as if he were paying attention to something out of frame.

"Rajesh, I can't..." Her spacesuit completed its leisurely drift, sliding into the main tier's exposed framework. She faced the dark carbon mesh, unable even to see the stars.

A soft slushing interrupted her dismal self-pity. Sensation tingled at the tips of her fingers, power trickling through her skillsuit from a patch of the station's inner mesh. It was the most beautiful sound she'd ever heard. Her left arm twitched. She lifted her hand, her glove flexing, and she grabbed the station's frame.

"What are you doing to my command, young lady?"

"It's not yours anymore." She panted as she spoke, trying to regain her composure. She struggled through the forest of carbon rods. Power surged through the inner sheath, and she hugged the silvered mesh as she picked her way toward the airlock.

"You can't get away with it. You know that?" His tone dripped with disapproval.

Her first thought was to say something sarcastic, but they'd been friends. It'd been Rajesh who'd stuck by her after the accident when they wanted to ship her back to Earth. "I know."

"Then why?"

Aishwarya wanted to shrug. It was such a simple way to express uncertainty, but it was as impractical in microgravity as it'd been impossible with her paralysis. Instead, she just glanced away from the camera. "I had to do something."

"It's certainly admirable."

"But..." Something in his eyes made her feel he had more to say. Aishwarya could feel it. She wondered what his plans really were.

He smiled, a thin upturning of the lips under his thick mustache. "They're going nuts downstairs. What you've done is all over the news, and some pretty important people are in hot water over this."

"I'm just looking out for myself." It was impossible to explain the freedom Brihaspati allowed her. He wouldn't understand the helplessness of dependence, or her fierce desire to protect that freedom. "I need this."

"You have it." An awkward silence hung between them, a gulf larger than the thousands of kilometers separating Brihaspati from the International Space Platform.

"But you think I can't keep it?"

"I know you can't." He stared at her as if he could make her see his point of view by sheer force of will. "You know it too."

"You're coming back, aren't you?"

"Looks that way." At least he didn't deny it.

"Do I have a choice?"

"No." He frowned into the camera. "Feel lucky it's me, and not a team of Marines."

"Yeah, lucky..." She closed the video, concentrating on her crawl across the inner skin of Brihaspati.

"HELLO, MY BEAUTIFUL FRIEND. IS IT TRUE?"

"I suppose it is." Aishwarya stared at Bete Reis's plump face and friendly brown eyes. "*They* told you, didn't they, and they want you to talk me out of it?"

"Of course." Bete laughed, a sincere chuckle. "When the ISRO discovered my presence in orbit, they immediately tried to recruit me."

The two had met a few years earlier on the International Space Platform, before Aishwarya had ever heard of Brihaspati. Bete had been a hotshot shuttle jockey, full of stories, overflowing with life. They'd become instant friends, and it was because of Bete that Aishwarya had pursued a career on Brihaspati.

"It's like a soap opera up here." Aishwarya flipped to match the video's orientation. She'd taken possession of Brihaspati's command chamber, moving her supplies up from the crew quarters further along the torus.

"My mission, as a favor from my government to yours, is to sweet talk some sense into you." Bete moved a little closer to the camera, her eyes reflecting pinpoints of blue light from her instrument panel. "Is such a thing possible?"

Aishwarya smiled. "You tell me."

"I think not, no." Bete shook her head, her body bobbing. "So what will you do?"

"Brihaspati's my home now." Aishwarya pulled herself into the command chair, wrapping a wide geckopad sash across her torso and mounting her skillsuit connection to an attached input. "I'll stay here, live on my own, and try to make a go of it."

"She can do that?" A male voice chirped in the background, hidden from her video feed. "Could we?"

"Quiet down." Bete turned. A skinny astronaut in a pale blue flight suit drifted into view, a friendly smile on his slender features. He waved.

"Are you serious? Live up here? No restraints? No agenda?"

Aishwarya's recognition software picked him up, tagging the name Paulo Anjos below his bobbing silhouette. "I'm going to try."

"Need help?"

"Don't be hasty." Bete pushed Paulo away from the camera, chuckling as his legs somersaulted from view. "And don't you try and recruit my flight crew."

Aishwarya smiled at her friend's joke, but it'd given her an idea. Brihaspati was huge. It had been designed to house dozens of scientists and technicians during the long journey to Jupiter. It was certainly big enough to hold a few crazy astronauts.

"I have something insane I want to run by you, but I want to wait until I see you in person." Aishwarya tried to keep the excitement from her voice.

"We're on our way. ETA is about a day and a half." Bete passed her hand over the camera, hesitating. "Hang in there, my friend."

Aishwarya turned from the camera and accessed the traffic logs for current orbital missions. There were sixteen manned projects circling Earth, representing nine countries. She sent a transcript of her situation to each, asking for assistance. Politics would keep most away, but politics might also gain her a few allies.

To Aishwarya's surprise, a proximity warning sounded less than six hours later. A gentle thud told her she had company.

"Allo?" It was the European Orbital Science Team. They'd received her message, and had played with their altitude vector to match Brihaspati's orbit. She hadn't really expected such an immediate response to her communication.

She welcomed the three slender men as they slid through the airlock, and was rewarded with friendly, large-toothed smiles. Then they all started talking at once, one in French, the others German.

She held out her hands. "Wait. I don't understand."

The nearest man laughed as if she'd told a joke. He slapped his bald forehead, floating backwards as he brought his helmet microphone to his lips.

"It is good to meet the woman who claims her own world." He grinned as the translator whispered his words. The other two nodded, bobbing in place.

"I didn't have a choice. I..."

Aishwarya hadn't anticipated becoming a celebrity, and she wasn't sure she was ready for the attention.

"Good. Good..." The closest man pulled himself forward. He was shorter than the others, and the corners of his eyes crinkled as he leaned in and tapped something against her right ear. Surprised, she jerked back, spinning into the padded wall. He reached to steady her. His breath smelled of cloves.

"Recording? Yes? Okay?" He pointed to his own ear, and then to the others. Aishwarya hadn't noticed the button cameras.

"Sure, I guess." She smiled, although it made her feel self-conscious. This wasn't a publicity stunt.

AISHWARYA MET THE BRAZILIAN SHUTTLE AT THE UP-ORBIT airlock adjacent to the station's completed hydroponics segment. Hydroponics was the only finished piece of Brihaspati. She'd done most of the work herself, and was proud of what it had become, but she wished they'd been able to complete the whole station.

Paulo Anjos burst through the airlock first, bouncing as he caught a rung near Aishwarya's feet. He had the wiry athletic build of a professional soccer player, but looked too young to be crewing a shuttle. She laughed.

"This will let you go wherever you want." Aishwarya tapped a yellow lozenge against his wrist. The coin-shaped sticker contained access codes to the completed segments of Brihaspati. "Explore."

He took off, careening around the curve of the habitat like a ten-year-old heading to recess. Bete glided into the compartment after he'd gone. Aishwarya caught her by the hands, squeezing the older woman's fingers in a friendly embrace. "It's so good to see you in the flesh, my friend."

"I wish it were under better circumstances."

She guided Bete around the quilted hallway and into a wide compartment filled with crates and plastic-wrapped containers. The muted sounds of laughter bounced from the unfinished ceiling, and the pungent smell of coffee filled the air.

"So, I'm not your first?"

"European Space Agency." Aishwarya waved at the three astronauts who'd taken it upon themselves to unpack a section of the dining hall. They were noisy, and they seemed to be everywhere at once, but it was good to hear life on the station again. It had been nothing but gloom in the months leading up to the shutdown.

"I see."

"They're recording everything I do." Aishwarya tapped the button camera on her ear. Bete frowned, but nodded at the device. "They think I'm some kind of celebrity."

"You are. Nobody's tried anything this crazy before."

"Stupid, you mean." Aishwarya stopped beside a curved section of wall. The material appeared bluish in the sharp LED lighting.

"Enough putting yourself down." Bete brushed her fingers against Aishwarya's cheek, her hand warm and dry. She smelled of roses. "How will you fix this jam you've gotten yourself into?"

"You gave me the idea." Aishwarya swiped her hand across the hull. "Here, I want to show you something."

A video frame appeared, expanding to show Brihaspati out of scale with the Earth. Lines in primary colors extended from the station like the legs of a spider, predicting orbital arcs. Several orbits crossed Brihaspati.

"This is everything circling Earth with the potential to intersect our orbit. There's a Russian heavy boost ferry, an American X-Shuttle, and an Iranian science canister. The Iranians are half an orbit away. I think they're just looking to extend their mission time, but I'll take what I can." She tweaked the simulation. A number of lines vanished, leaving three glowing blue streamers, and a single dotted line in red. "I've already offered them the up-orbit tier for as long as they want."

"The red line, what's that?" Bete slid her finger over the animation.

"The salvage assessors." Aishwarya collapsed the frame, dreading the confrontation. She could feel it in the tightness of her neck, the heaviness of her body even under her skillsuit.

"Will you be ready?"

"All I've got is a loophole in the law, and nothing to back it up." Aishwarya used her fingers to climb the arching wall, plucking two foil packets of wine from overhead storage.

"You're smart, my friend. You'll think of something." Bete took one of the packets.

Aishwarya wished she felt as confident.

THE IRANIAN CRAFT LOOKED LIKE A BASEBALL BAT, ITS WIDE cylinder tapered at one end and capped with a heavy drive ball. Aishwarya felt it dock, a faint shimmy as her video switched to an interior view of the up-orbit airlock.

"Welcome to Brihaspati, gentlemen." She pulled a maintenance pack from a storage slot beside the monitor. She'd have to do something about the down-orbit airlock now that all three bays of the upper docking area were occupied. "I've provided access to many parts of the station for your convenience."

"We are in your debt." A dark man with a neatly trimmed beard and small shiny eyes tugged his helmet off and smiled into the pickup.

Another man glided into view. "As for access...I already have one of my own."

A chill ran through Aishwarya as Rajesh removed his helmet and glared into the camera. He seemed taller, more imposing than she remembered.

"Commander, I didn't expect you so soon."

Aishwarya had been hoping for more time, expecting Rajesh to arrive with the salvage vessel. It was just like him to put her off guard like this.

"I hitched a ride." He ran a hand through his short hair.

She'd gone over her arguments a hundred times. Brihaspati was technically hers. She held all the power, but why did she feel as if it were her first day on the job? An empty pit opened in her stomach at the thought of the coming confrontation.

"I'm on my way to repair the lower tier airlock." She lifted the maintenance pack, waving it in front of the camera like a shield. "I'll meet you in hydroponics when I'm done."

She didn't know how long he'd let her avoid him. Fixing her earlier sabotage wouldn't take very long, and she couldn't hide forever. He knew Brihaspati as well as she did.

"Don't bother. I'll meet you at the airlock." He switched off the video before she could reply.

To her surprise, Rajesh didn't try to bully her the moment he entered the main shaft. Instead, he watched quietly as she unpacked the mushroom-shaped seam ripper and began to work. She could feel him staring. It made the twelve-meter tube seem cramped and confining, but it was better than arguing.

"Why are you doing this?" His voice was a whisper in her headphones, heavy with undertones of disappointment. "If you'd come to me, I would have tried to help. Now..."

She placed the seam slug into the recessed channel separating the airlock hatch and its containing ring. The gelatinous robot oozed across the casing, undoing her earlier sabotage. Its interior glowed emerald bright, like a trapped undersea creature, as it slithered around the airlock frame melting the clumped metal welds. Rajesh clung to the padded rung nearby, his spacesuit like a statue beside her.

"I thought I could extend my time in orbit by a few weeks." She turned away, afraid to look him in the eyes. "We both know my options are limited by skillsuit technology. I was looking at a ticket Earthside no matter what."

"The ISP could've worked something out, I'm sure of it." His voice grew louder.

"My skillsuit's unique to this station. I designed it as *part* of

Brihaspati, light and flexible because it draws its life from the station. Without it, I'm a stone with feet."

"You're afraid." He drifted closer. "Don't let fear own you. Don't let what happened dictate your future, Aishwarya. Be brave enough to take the next step—"

"The next step lands me on Earth." She interrupted, getting angry. He knew there wasn't anything in orbit for her. "Once I'm down, I'm done. And you know it."

"That's not necessarily true."

"Only here. This station and I are one unit. I can't function without it, and it wouldn't exist without me. Like it or not, I am Brihaspati."

He made a noise, and then shifted position to put himself behind her again. He seemed to be waiting for something. It made her nervous.

She palmed one of the smaller weld worms from the pack, holding it loosely in the gloved fingers of her left hand. "Let's cut the crap, Rajesh. Why are you really here?"

Getting back to Brihaspati couldn't have been easy. Control wouldn't have sent him just to continue old arguments. There must be more to it.

He chuckled. "Always so blunt."

"Practical."

"ISRO thought I could talk you into leaving voluntarily." He moved closer, his shadow looming over her as she extracted the slug and cycled the lock open.

"They thought wrong."

"I know." He sighed. The tension in his voice made her turn.

He launched at her.

She dived, her suit bouncing off the hatch. She spun, and he grabbed her. She kicked, and he forced her back against the controls. The lock cycled. She grabbed his arms as the outer hatch blew, ejecting them both.

Rajesh rolled, breaking her grip. Aishwarya, frantic, ignited the weld worm. She jabbed it at his helmet, but he twisted. It struck the edge of his torso plate. The worm burned through the outer coating of her sleeve, exposing layers of protective Nylar resin, fusing her to Rajesh's spacesuit.

They tumbled, Brihaspati spinning from view. Her skillsuit cut out. Her body stilled, leaving her helpless.

"I don't want to hurt you." He panted, his visor touching hers.

Aishwarya watched his dark eyes, concentrating on his face and not the spinning of their bodies. Her breath hissed in ragged gasps through clenched teeth. He'd betrayed her, but there was no anger in his gaze. Only sadness.

"It's over."

"I could've made something here if you'd given me a chance..." She wanted to scream. She wanted to lash out, but she couldn't move. He'd taken more than the station from her.

"Not here, not like this." His face appeared pale, stubbornness written into his features and colored by his HUD LEDs.

"Throwing me overboard isn't going to accomplish anything." She felt utterly helpless, a rag doll strapped to a madman. What would he do with her now?

"Unoccupied, the station reverts to its original owners. The Chinese can dock and take possession. I've already alerted them."

He didn't smile. He didn't look away when she stared into his dark eyes, so close but so very distant.

"It doesn't have to end like this."

"I wish you were right..."

"Hey, still here! Still on board." Bete's voice broke through Aishwarya's labored breathing. The button camera. They could see and hear everything. "You going to throw me off too?"

"This is an internal action on sovereign property, Brazilian commander. I suggest you vacate this station." Rajesh's mustache twitched as he exhaled. He'd forgotten about the others.

"Go to hell!" Bete yelled into her microphone, and Aishwarya cringed. "Because now I am Brihaspati."

Rajesh swore. His visor's HUD reflected an image of the Chinese shuttle, its forward jets flaring to halt its incoming trajectory. They were holding back, waiting to see if he could get a handle on the situation.

"Count me in." The young astronaut who'd been so excited to be allowed to run free through the station squeaked through Aishwarya's speakers. "Anjos here in hydroponics. You've got fresh lettuce, and ginger, and...I think I'll stick around."

"As will we." The smooth translated voice of the European astronaut chimed in.

Aishwarya wanted to cry. She'd felt alone for so long, stranded because of her body, abandoned like the station she'd tried to protect. It had been like a weight, crushing her in despair. Now, no matter what happened, she could endure.

"Unknown astronaut..." Rajesh started to speak, but anger and confusion choked his words. He was outnumbered, and he knew it.

"Greetings, former base commander. The *Omid* will make no attempt to leave." The Iranian module. Aishwarya had almost forgotten about them herself. "We occupy the up-orbital tier, and we are also Brihaspati."

"*Saale*! Is there anyone in orbit who *isn't* on this station?"

"Yes, us..." She smiled, tears in her eyes. The look on his face was priceless.

He sighed. His frame motors hissed, and he aligned his spacesuit to the station's airlock. "They're going to fire me for this, but I give up. You're too stubborn for me."

She laughed. "I told you. *I am Brihaspati*."

# TRASH PICKER ON MARS

## GENE TWARONITE

**About the Author**

Gene Twaronite is a poet, essayist, and author of seven books, including two juvenile fantasy novels, two short story collections and the poetry book *Trash Picker on Mars*, winner of the 2017 New Mexico-Arizona Book Award for Arizona poetry. His latest book of poems *The Museum of Unwearable Shoes* was published by Kelsay Books in 2018.

Gene has always been fascinated by poetry's ability to convey entire worlds of thought and feeling within a few lines of compressed expression. A native New Englander, he is now a confirmed desert rat residing in Tucson.

Follow more of Gene's writing at his website: thetwaronite-zone.com.

In the dim time before dawn
the woman clamped her metal
fingers over a beer bottle.
Her buckets overflowing with
litter from a dying world,
she sat and stared at the
alien landscape of asphalt.
The stars had all faded
except for the one red light
of Mars still defying the sun.
The woman smiled at the
mythical planet now
defrocked of its canals and
green men by Carl Sagan
and the Legion of Reason.
But still she dreamed.
In her electric cart she glided
over the red-gold deserts
of ancient Barsoom—
past  the fairy towers
of Grand Canal and the
monoliths of Helium where
a once great race of Martians
lived, played and died—
filling the canyons of
Valles Marineris with the
excess of their empty lives.
Out of habit she picked up a
fluted green shard, then
laughed and flung it along
with her buckets into the
trash heap of lost Martians.
Through the dark grottoes of

Great Rift Valley she roved to
the shores of Mare Sirenum,
whose salty crust reminded her
of past ruins and distant times
when she could still cry.
For a moment she stared at the
sun, weak and small as it
rose above Olympus Mons,
igniting her in a ruddy glow.
She was the Princess of Mars
and there were still a few
unhatched eggs inside her.
And at the edge of
Candor Chasm she
bared her heart to the
silent, scouring winds.
Then into the dawn
she drove to begin her
new race of Martians.

# LET US GO THEN, YOU AND I

WINNER SECOND PLACE, NEWMYTHS
READERS' CHOICE AWARD 2019

## RONALD D. FERGUSON

**About the Author**

Ronald D. Ferguson taught college mathematics and wrote textbooks for many years. Now, he prefers writing fiction, particularly science fiction and fantasy. His short fiction has appeared in numerous venues. He now writes full time and is an active member of the SFWA. He lives with his wife and a rescue dog near the shadow of the Alamo. For more publication details, see RonaldDFerguson.com.

CAPTAIN MANNY WAYWARD DIDN'T LIKE TO FEEL USELESS. Nonetheless, he twiddled his thumbs and let the computer nudge The *Valhalla* into parking orbit about Mars. He scanned the tagalong readouts. All in-line. No corrections required.

More than adequate for a one-way suicide mission.

"Congratulations, ladies and gentlemen." Manny unbuckled and half-turned in his acceleration chair. "We've achieved areo synchronous orbit 17,100 km above Mars. Resume your duties."

"Woot!" Doris Biggers pushed away from the copilot's console and hugged him.

Manny felt lost in her embrace. She had put on noticeable weight during the three month trip—low metabolism and infrequent exercise—but with all engines off, she pirouetted like a ballerina and sailed across the cabin.

"We're the first humans to reach Mars." Her grin was contagious.

"It's a long way to the surface, my dear." Manny pushed up from his chair. Didn't she remember that every step towards the surface was a step closer to death? "Don't celebrate until all six of us safely set foot on the ground."

Extending her arms, Doris slowed her spin at the hatchway bulkhead. When she reached the bulkhead, a wisp of gray streaked hair looped over her left eye. Her dry lips needed work, but her expression was warm, attractive, and playful.

"You old fossil. Grouch all you want. I'm making celebration cookies." She propelled herself through the hatch.

Manny frowned at her gibe. Fossil indeed. At a sensible sixty-seven years of age, he thought of himself as stable and reliable, not dour as Doris often described him. Nonetheless, she took every opportunity to kid him about his age because he was, after all, the youngest person on board.

～

"I'VE LOST VISUAL ON THE LAST TAGALONG." MARIETTE Henderson pushed away from the monitor.

Although his neck ached, Manny twisted his head towards her. He admired her lithe grace. At seventy—her latest birthday was two weeks ago—she was the oldest crew member, but she was still spry and shapely, with a face unmarred by time. Not a surprise: the first criterion for selection on the Mars mission was to be beyond retirement age, but the second was to appear youthful enough that the public would not consider this one-way trip to be euthanasia for the elderly.

Mariette hadn't impressed Manny during training, but he developed a crush on her over the three month trip. Unfortu-nately, she had partnered with Doctor Joe Wilson early in the voyage. Unlike Manny's on-and-off relationship with Doris, everyone treated Joe and Mariette as a couple. The remaining team members, Dwayne and Gloria, had boarded as the token married couple, together for thirty-seven years before the Mars mission came along.

"Manny," Mariette repeated, "I've lost visual on the last tagalong."

Despite his neck ache, Manny nodded, and winced. Ah well, Mariette seemed happy with Joe. Besides, he liked Joe, and he refused to let envy distort the social interactions among the six crewpersons.

He massaged his neck. Fatigue had crept up on him three hours before and never relented. "Joe, any word from Houston?"

Joe manned the communication console. "I pinged them ten minutes...wait, here we go. Houston confirms soft-landings for five tagalongs, but unit six hit hard. Damage unknown. Too early yet for Houston data on unit seven, but our telemetry indicates a bit high on its trajectory, easy to correct."

"Anything vital in number six?"

"Not sure yet." Joe ticked items on the onscreen manifest. "No oxygen, water, or hydroponics. Mostly kitchen equipment and furniture, crates of freeze-dried food and some medical supplies. I'll cross-reference with the other modules for redundancy."

"Very well." Manny drooped in his chair. He flexed his shoulders to a rewarding pop.

"Manny, you look exhausted. No one else worked a double shift." Joe tapped the medical emblem on his sleeve. "Get some sleep, doctor's orders. Mariette and I can handle this."

"I'm fine." Manny pushed himself away from his chair. He hadn't expected weightlessness to be so tiring.

Joe shook his head. "Doris is an excellent pilot, but I want you both top-notch when our asses are on the line during descent tomorrow."

"Or what? You'll report me to mission control?"

"Houston can't control us," Joe said. "They lost that leverage when we left Earth orbit. After all the bad publicity about a suicide mission for senior citizens, they don't dare reprimand us."

"Then how will you force me to bed?" Feeling annoyed and combative stimulated Manny's adrenaline and perked him for a moment. Maybe some testosterone too. He liked the revival.

"You're a big guy, but I can wake Dwayne. The two of us can hold you while Mariette injects a sedative. Don't make me do it. We all bruise too easily."

"Don't argue, dear." Mariette hugged Manny's free arm and dragged him towards the sleeping quarters.

"You're almost mutinous." Manny half-grinned, but he couldn't resist the weightless tow, not with the warm comfort of Mariette's breasts against his arm. "I'll let the insubordination slide this time."

Once secure in his sleeper, Manny's mind raced. The ache from his neck spread to his shoulders. The arthritis hadn't shown in his pre-launch physical, else they might have refused to let him captain this expedition. Narrow minded of them.

What real difference did a little arthritis make to a man his age, a man queued up for death? Wasn't that why they crewed the ship with elderly astronauts? Who else had less life left to lose?

Spinning the ship during the outbound trip had produced only miniscule gravity, but even a small amount of gravity ameliorated calcium loss. Despite the exercise and drugs, Joe said everyone onboard had significant calcium loss. Did that mean that everyone had osteoporosis? Would Manny's calcium loss brittle his bones against Martian gravity? He would weigh thirty-eight kilograms on Mars, but after the lost calcium, would he still be six feet tall? He hated the thought of being shorter more than being brittle.

Perhaps Doris was right when she called him a grouchy old fossil. He preferred to think of himself as a realist rather than a pessimist, but then why was he cataloging his problems instead of sleeping? Ridiculous to worry about tomorrow's landing. He had prepared to do the best job possible, and he wouldn't allow himself any regrets. Now he worried about his worrying. What kind of worry is that? He checked the time, but he couldn't focus to read the digits. Did he need reading glasses? No optometrist on Mars. Great. How would blindness play out on the Red Planet?

Wind it down. Turn it off.

He exhaled heavily and focused on even breathing. He had been exuberant when they left Earth, why this downturn? Establish the first Martian colony—what a lie to win public support. A one-way mission was more precise. Death waited at the end. He knew that going in. They all knew that when they signed on. Death might be difficult, but it was also inevitable. More important to Manny, could he maintain his composure and dignity when his time expired?

He was still counting his troubles when sleep came.

∾

ONCE THE LANDING MODULE BROKE FREE OF THE *VALHALLA* SHELL, no return to the orbiting vessel was possible. From the beginning, planners designed the mission to be cheap and technologically feasible; in other words, to be one-way. They simply couldn't build a ship with fuel and supplies sufficient for a return—not with current technology and not within the budgetary constraints.

Manny wondered why those thoughts paused his hand when he reached for the landing module release. Any hope of returning to Earth expired forty days ago when they crossed the failsafe mark, so what difference did it make whether they could reconnect with the skeleton of this ship. Little fuel remained onboard, certainly not enough to take them home, although solar energy would continue to power the *Valhalla* to relay radio signals. All available supplies were already on Mars in the tagalongs, but even with recycling, the air and water would barely stretch for the next four months. The only choice was to descend to the surface.

He activated the release, and the computer ran through the sequence that separated the module from the husk of the *Valhalla*. The official ship name was *Ares*. Renaming the ship *Valhalla* while en route had been Doris's idea. She reasoned that the transport gave them an adventurous opportunity to die in the battle against the unknown rather than dwindle into oblivion in the company of age. Once the steering thrusters cleared the landing module from the *Valhalla*, the main engine slowed their orbital speed and directed their descent.

The atmosphere engaged, and the module rotated for better exposure of the heat shield. Unless a problem arose, Manny would leave adjustment details to Doris and the computer guidance system while he monitored overall progress and the ship's condition.

Soon, the glow from the heat shields reflected warm hues into the cabin ports, and the hull bumped from the turbulence and droned with the friction. The Martian atmosphere made aerodynamic flight difficult, but despite the thin air, the drag chutes deployed with a neck-wrenching jerk.

After several minutes of slowing the vessel, the chutes popped the primary rocket loose from its cradle. The chutes hauled the engine to the end of its tether so that the landing module swung below it like a giant pendulum.

"Trajectory?" Manny didn't glance at Doris. She knew her job.

"Nominal." She hummed a song under her breath, which Manny didn't recognize. Nice voice. She sang well. "We'll land within sight of all the tagalongs."

Explosive bolts popped the chutes loose, and the rocket fired. For the first time in three months, Manny felt heavy, very heavy. The panel displayed only one-point-three G's, but Manny couldn't lift his arms—too many months in space. He glanced at Doris. Her eyes were closed and her head lolled as if she were unconscious. Damn. Why hadn't she kept up her exercises?

At the edge of his vision, a green status light flickered to red. Which one? Colors grayed out. The G-force crept upwards. He'd taken three times this before without a G-suit. What was wrong? Unable to fight the strain any longer, Manny sagged against his chair. He couldn't focus, and the panel darkened. Blackout. If the computer program failed, they would all die, and he could do nothing about it.

Perhaps the terminal aspect of the mission was about to commence. Manny closed his eyes. He accepted the inevitable, and his thoughts lost their cohesion.

MANNY RAISED HIS GLASS. "A TOAST TO MY FRIENDS."

Despite the failure of a landing strut, they had tailed-down with little damage and no injuries. Luck was with them.

"A smile from Captain Grouchy Box." Doris winked at him. "If booze is all it takes to loosen him up, Joe should prescribe a daily dose. Carpe Diem... Ooh, that's a good name for this base, Camp Carpe Diem. So much better than Mars Base One."

"To our first week." Manny cocked his head and lifted his glass higher. "All the habitat modules are connected. Once they're fully inflated, we can move into roomier quarters. Maybe tomorrow?"

He glanced at Mariette, who confirmed his estimate with a nod.

"Here's more good news." Manny took a quick sip of the reconstituted champagne. "Houston announced a tentative launch schedule for the resupply drone. That means if all goes as planned, then our four months gets extended to a full twelve month mission."

"Ah, the Governor is on the phone with a reprieve but not a pardon." Joe clinked his glass against Mariette's. "Did they give a reason for the delay or an excuse for only one ship?"

"The delay is obvious." Manny stared into his drink. "Why should they waste money until they were sure we'd landed? With the launch window closing, they'll need extra fuel for a faster trajectory—so one ship towing tagalongs is all they could manage—but it should arrive before we exhaust critical supplies."

"I'm surprised they bothered," Joe said. "We need two years of supplies to make the next feasible launch window. Ah well, we're eminently expendable. I remember the wording on the contract."

"Strange." Mariette smiled at Joe. "You keep forgetting a lot of other stuff, my dear, like my birthday."

"One year is better than I expected," Doris said. "I'm surprised we survived the landing. Maybe if we are very productive with the hydroponics and recyclers, and we send lots more scientific data than they expect, then they'll cough up enough funds for a second supply ship. With that we could stretch it to two years. Hey, speaking of birthdays, we have another reason to celebrate. Today is our captain's sixty-eighth birthday. I baked a cake."

"Don't cut the cake before you wake up Dwayne and Gloria." Manny smiled broadly. "You know how Dwayne loves to party."

"It'll be a tight fit with all six of us in here." Doris squeezed past Manny and ran a light hand across his arm. "You keep on drinking, Manny dear. I want you very relaxed for the private present I've planned for later."

Manny took a long drink from his glass before he dared glance at Joe and Mariette. Mariette kept her lips pursed and stared at the ceiling.

However, Joe smirked. "Wouldn't it be nice if everyone got a private present on Manny's birthday?"

"Hush, Joe." Mariette's voice was stern, but a thin smile crossed her lips. "Let's talk about something else. When will the resupply ship launch, Manny?"

Manny started to answer her, but the look on Doris' face when she returned interrupted him. "What's wrong, Doris?"

"Manny, please." She stood in the passageway. Her voice quavered. "Gloria can't wake Dwayne. I think he's dead."

Two weeks later after dinner, Manny drank hot coffee with Joe and watched the three women decorate the lounge. In the background, the energy pump purred and extracted heat from the ground to warm the shelter against the minus 100 degree Martian night.

Gloria repositioned a small reproduction of *David* on the dining table. Mariette nodded her head in approval. Doris stopped, folded her arms across her chest, and displayed a smile worthy of the Mona Lisa.

"How many Michelangelos did you bring?" Doris asked.

"I love Michelangelo Buonarroti." Gloria's lips were thin and her complexion pasty. "Great art on Mars was my goal, but two small replicas were all I could pack with my personal items."

"I recognize *David*," Mariette said. "The other is very familiar, but I don't remember its name."

"The *Pietà*." Gloria held up the hand-size version. "The original is in St. Peter's Basilica. I'll keep this one by my bed. I wanted to bring a replica of *Moses*, too, but Dwayne convinced me I didn't have the room, so I settled for an electronic encyclopedia of art. Fine for viewing, I suppose, but not very tactile."

"She's been a real trooper," Manny whispered to Joe.

"Gloria?" Joe used his coffee spoon to measure powdered creamer into his cup as if he measured out his life. "Yes, she has. We would still be without solar power except for her expertise, but she's not sleeping well. I give her a mild oral sedative each night, but it doesn't seem to work. I'm worried about her health."

Doris winked at Manny when she passed. She had lost none of her extra weight even with the hard work of setting up the base camp. When she squirmed into her pressure suit, it stretched to the limits. Still cute, though. Doris disappeared into the sleeping quarters module.

"Women cope with the death of a spouse better than men," Manny said.

"Statistically correct." Joe's lips narrowed, and his forehead wrinkled. "But statistics don't apply well to individuals."

Obviously hiding something more than just herself beneath her blouse, Doris returned. The low gravity introduced a bouncy perkiness to her Rubenesque figure. With an enigmatic grin, she pranced to the center of the lounge and demanded attention by loudly clearing her throat.

"Gloria, I needed to analyze some soil samples," Doris said. "So I unpacked Dwayne's geological instruments this afternoon. That sly old geezer stashed an unauthorized item in his instrument crates."

Gloria looked puzzled. Mariette smiled as if she already knew the secret.

"Ta-da." Doris pulled a small statue from inside her blouse. "Your husband stowed away this copy of Michelangelo's *Moses*. He did it for you."

Tears glistened in Gloria's eyes and tracked her cheeks. She clasped her hands against her lips.

By the end of the following week, Gloria's secreted supply of accumulated sedatives was sufficient for her to take a fatal overdose.

~

MANNY GLANCED OUT THE WINDOW IN THE PRESSURE LOCK.

Soon the sun would rise on the long, Martian summer day. Yestersol, the supply drone from Earth, finally had arrived. Unfortunately, the tagalongs came in too fast and impacted far from the base—the closest tagalong at twelve kilometers east.

Nearby, Joe and Mariette prepared to take the Mars Buggy to salvage what they could from the wreckage.

Manny exchanged fuel cells for batteries and ran a final check on the Mars Buggy. With passengers in heated pressure suits, the insulated cab provided adequate protection against all but the worst cold. Joe and Marietta would need that protection because Manny wanted them in the Buggy and on the road before the sun was up. With fully charged batteries, the vehicle should be able to make a roundtrip under heavy load.

Liquid hydrogen reserves were low, so they had to conserve power usage from fuel cells. Already they had closed off half of Carpe Diem Base to conserve power and heat. Using solar panels to crack water into hydrogen and oxygen simply didn't produce enough hydrogen.

Joe had experimented with using heat and hydrogen to partially reduce the Martian ferric oxide soil into magnetite and water. The results looked promising, but required even more solar power to crack the water for oxygen and to free the hydrogen to recycle into the process.

For her part, Doris fine-tuned the hydroponic system to produce adequate oxygen for four people. Between that and the chemical scrubbers, oxygen wasn't as critical as the low hydrogen reserves.

While Joe finished putting on his pressure suit, Mariette pulled Manny aside.

"You need to talk with Doris while Joe and I are outside."

Manny firmed his lip. "Doris and I should be the ones going, not you and Joe."

"First, get rid of your anger." Mariette squeezed his arm. Manny hadn't realized she had such a strong grip. "Joe's memory is fine. He just needs a nudge now and then, and I know when to give it to him. Second, quit blaming Doris."

Manny gritted his teeth. "She can't get into her damn pressure suit."

"She can get into it, but it's far too tight. It's difficult for her to breathe, and she could get a blood clot..."

"Then you and I should go."

"Oh, Manny. That's not an option for me." Mariette's face softened. "This trip could be dangerous, and I won't be widowed like Gloria, nor will I leave Joe to a similar fate."

"An hour and a half out, load what we can, and an hour and a half back. What could happen?"

"Anything. Everything." Mariette sighed. "I care about Joe. He needs me. If we live much longer, he'll need me even more. I'm committed to finishing this adventure with him, and that's why we must do the risky stuff together. I wish you would build that kind of contentment with Doris. Please don't argue with me anymore."

"I could order you." Manny couldn't meet her gaze.

"Yes, but you can't make me. Please, talk to Doris while we're gone. Our lives grow too short to keep up barriers."

Manny refused to answer.

"You idiot," she said. "Doris always has a smile for everyone, especially for you, but believe me, she's not happy. When's the last time you heard her sing? Can't you tell she's depressed? That's why she overeats, doesn't exercise, and sleeps so much."

"People have different ways to deal with impending death. I get depressed myself."

"She's depressed because you don't love her." Mariette snapped the last coupling on her head piece. "Joe's ready. I've got to go. Please. There's only the four of us on this whole world, and time is short. We all care for one another, but don't be a fool. Don't pass up something great because you daydream something else might be better. I guarantee it won't. Make Doris the most important person in your world, and make sure she knows."

DORIS LEANED OVER MANNY'S SHOULDER. HER EYES WERE RED, her cheeks tear-stained. He didn't point out the obvious. She could read the monitor as well as he could. No signal from the *Valhalla*.

"Where the hell did that dust storm come from?" Manny pushed away from the console and stood. "Why didn't Houston warn us?"

He paced to the window. A dusty haze, a red fog that rubbed against the windowpane and left visibility under two meters.

"Sunspots." Doris put her hand on his shoulder. "The *Valhalla* relay has been iffy for weeks, Manny. The storm just made it worse. Joe and Mariette are smart. They'll take cover and ride this out. As soon as the storm passes, we'll get the signal back."

"The horizon's only three kilometers away. We can't do line of sight at twelve kilometers or bounce radio waves off the missing ionosphere. Without the *Valhalla* to relay, we can't talk to them. They can't follow the signal to safety."

"They've still got a gyroscopic compass," Doris said. "Please, dear. Your face is red. Can I make you some coffee?"

"Plunge into a ditch a few times, hit a few hard bumps and the gyroscope can misalign." Manny paced to the far side of the room and clasped his hands behind his back. "Even with the re-breathers, they only had a fifteen hour air-supply."

"Always the pessimist. They have six hours of life support left, and I choose to believe the storm will let up soon."

"Martian dust storms can last a month, Doris. I've got to do something."

"Yes, Manny, perhaps that would be best. Something to keep you busy. How can I help?"

"If only we had another Mars Buggy—"

"We've got the two recumbent bicycles," Doris said. "They're still packed in tagalong seven, but without a beacon, you can't go far in this storm. Neither bicycle has a gyroscopic compass."

"No, but we've got a dozen radio repeaters still in the crate. They'll serve as beacons. We know the direction to the nearest crashed module relative to the shelter. I can drop them like the breadcrumbs in 'Hansel and Gretel.' A repeater every two kilometers while I travel should do the trick."

"Great idea." Gloria started for the storage module. "I'll unpack the repeaters and mounting tripods while you check our suits. Will the bikes have room for oxygen canisters? We may need some spares."

"Not with the repeaters and tripods onboard." Manny firmed his jaw. Won't she take the hint? "I'll have to make do with eight hours of life support."

"Help me assemble the bicycles when you finish the suit check."

"Just one bicycle." Manny glared at Doris. Why wouldn't she admit the problem? "You aren't going."

MANNY PLANTED THE FOURTH REPEATER ATOP THE TRIPOD AND extended the height to the maximum of a meter and a half. He had no doubt that he could follow the beacons home, but how much zig-zag error had crept into his path?

He looked in the direction from which he had come, but the wide bicycle tracks were already blown away. In the last few minutes, the storm had lessened so that visibility was up to four meters.

Manny wiped a film of dust from his face plate. Joe and Mariette had about three and a half hours of oxygen left. This was his chance to make up some time.

With the recumbent bike headed into the wind, the forty-centimeter-wide tread allowed the low- slung device to stand upright without extra support. Two repeaters and two tripods remained strapped to the bike. As he had done at the previous beacon sites, Manny activated one of the strapped beacons to broadcast before he mounted the bike.

He should be close now. Unless a substantial error had worked into his path, the errant tagalong should be less than five kilometers away. He hoped the moving signal from the onboard repeater would attract Mariette's attention, because without her response, he might pass within a hundred meters of the couple and never see them.

He gripped the handlebars and mounted the bike. With much of the fine surface dust airborne, the underlying, partially packed Martian surface yielded to his efforts, and he plowed the bicycle ahead.

"Manny?"

"Doris, please keep the channel clear for Mariette and Joe."
Manny upped his pedal rate.

"Beacon 5 went on line. I wondered how you're doing. Your
pulse rate is up."

"Visibility has improved, so I'm going faster." Why was he
angry with her? She was just doing her job by monitoring him,
but somehow it felt like an intrusion. He upped his pedal rate
again. "I'm shooting for twelve kilometers per hour."

"Manny, that's too fast."

"You worry—"

The front wheel caught in an unexpected erosion gulley,
twisted sideways, and tore the handlebars from Manny's grip.
In slow motion, the bike flipped up past the wedged wheel and
catapulted Manny over the handlebars. Old reflexes from his
days of diving competition on the three meter board surfaced,
and he attempted to tuck into a somersault. He was too stiff and
out of practice to control the rotation, and on landing, his left
leg jammed into a large rock at an awkward angle. His nose
slammed against his faceplate. The concussion left him
breathless.

After he hit the ground, the dust didn't get a chance to settle
—not with the storm blowing about. Strange. You expected the
dust to settle. Tears filled his eyes from the pain in his nose.
Why did his ears roar?

"Manny?"

"Uh…" Peculiar—his mouth wouldn't work properly.

"Manny."

Pain. Shouldn't move his leg. Really bad pain. "I think
I...broke..."

"Manny!"

Damn. He wished she wouldn't scream just when he was
passing out.

〜

WHEN MANNY WOKE, HE SAT UP AND SHIFTED HIS WEIGHT USING his arms for support. A bloody nose imprint smudged his face-plate. His left leg throbbed, and his head felt fuzzy. He was cold. Night would soon fall—in what, an hour or two?—and with so little activity, his suit already had difficulty keeping him warm. He sipped water from the nipple inside his helmet.

Summer on Mars. Whoop-te-do.

With slow, steady pressure he pulled back until his leg cleared the rock. The pressure suit made palpating the leg difficult. Was that a clean break of the fibula above the ankle? Damned osteo-porosis. He was brittle. Then the tibia could be cracked as well. His ankle felt stiff and swollen, even more painful than the leg.

Probably couldn't walk far, but could he ride? He swiveled about and located the bike. The front wheel was a twisted wreck. No bike ride for him.

He checked the time. He had about four hours of life-support left. Mariette and Joe had only two. He used his good leg and arms to pull himself across the sand. He unbuckled a tripod, attached the already active repeater, and stood the assembly up. He hadn't quite made a kilometer much less two from the last beacon, but he didn't think he could go farther with his leg broken. Returning to base was equally impossible.

"Manny?"

"Doris, honey." Manny worked to keep his voice even and matter-of-fact. "I've had an accident. I wrecked the bike, and my leg is broken. There's nothing you can do, baby. I'm so sorry."

"I'm on my...way."

"Doris, listen to me." Unbidden desperation crept into his voice. "Stay in the shelter. You can't help me. It would take a couple of hours to get here, and there's no way for you to carry me back."

"You are...clueless. I prepared...the other bike and my pressure suit...right after you left...I started out when we...lost contact. I'm already past beacon three... Forty-five minutes to an hour...I'll be there. You hang on, Manny...because I will not live on Mars alone."

"But..."

"Would you...shut up? I'm not in great...shape and pedaling this bike in...this tight suit is no picnic...I can't talk now. "

Manny shut up. They were both going to die. God, what a crazy woman. What a wonderful, magnificent, crazy woman.

He choked back a sudden thickness in his throat, and unbuckled the last tripod from the bike. A little flimsy, but it would have to do. He opened the storage basket under the bicycle seat. Beneath the pliers, he found a roll of all-purpose tape. Now, if he could keep the ambient dust from gumming up the tape when he strapped the tripod to his leg, he might get a decent splint.

THE BOULDER WAS LESS THAN A METER TALL, BUT MILLENNIA OF dust storms had worn it smooth. Clutching the last beacon, Manny pulled himself to the rock and rested against the leeward side to escape the worst of the wind. His ankle throbbed. He felt stiff and very cold but according to his suit, his core body temperature was just below 37?. Not too bad. Not yet.

Visibility varied, reaching ten meters at times and then dropping to five during strong wind gusts. He hoped the storm subsided before the evening spread out across the heavens, so that he could have a last glimpse of the Martian butterscotch sky turning blue at sunset. Would that small dying request disturb the universe?

"Manny?" Doris sounded exhausted. "Manny, I'm at the fifth beacon...I see your bike. Where are you?"

"Not far beyond my bike." Manny activated the last beacon. "Follow beacon six."

A few moments later, pushing her bicycle, Doris trudged into view through the dust. When Manny waved, she let her bike fall and staggered to him. She dropped to her knees and wiped the dust from his face plate.

At first, Manny attempted a smile, but then, suddenly concerned, he wiped the dust from Doris's faceplate. Despite the refraction of light through the dust that tinted everything red, she looked very pale. Her lips were cracked. Dried blood crusted her nose.

"I'm sorry, Manny." She sagged against him. "I tried. I tried so very hard, but I haven't any strength left."

"Not your fault." Manny wrapped both arms around her and pulled her close. "No one could have done better."

He checked the monitor on her suit. Blood pressure way too high. Pulse racing and erratic. Nothing he could do but comfort her. Damned pressure suits. How he wanted to kiss her forehead.

"We've had a hell of an adventure, Old Girl," he said. "And there's no one else on this planet or the entire universe that I would rather have shared it with. Thank you."

"I love you, Manny." Her whisper as almost too faint to hear. "I'm sorry that I couldn't be the one you wanted."

"You pegged me right, Doris, I'm a stubborn, senile old fossil. There are two important women in every man's life. The one he thought he wanted, and the one he thanks God he got. I love you, Doris, and I will cherish you for the rest of our lives."

Doris didn't answer. Manny pulled her face towards him.

"Doris. Doris? Did you hear me?"

"Yes, love." Her eyes opened slowly. "I hear you. You'll cherish me...for the rest of our lives...not a big promise in our current situation, but I love you for saying so. I'm so cold, could..."

She whimpered and her eyes fluttered shut.

Was this the way the world ends?

"Doris, please."

He checked her suit monitor. She was alive, pulse slowing slightly, blood pressure still too high. He sighed. Adjusting her head against his shoulder, he wrapped her in his arms and waited for the cold night to consume them.

THE VOICES THAT DRIFTED THROUGH THE COLD, RED HAZE sounded familiar.

"You folks need a ride?"

"Joe, can't you see they're in trouble? Unload the junk from the rear seat so that we can get them onboard."

Mariette! Joe! Manny struggled against the mind-numbing cold. "How did you find us?"

His eyes refocused. Mariette leaned over him. Beyond her, Joe worked at unloading the Mars Buggy.

"Oxygen got too low, so we started back blind," she said. "Gyro malfunction. Got lost. Been wandering about for an hour. Luckily, we picked up your beacon. Do you know where we are?"

Manny checked Doris's monitor. "Doris's core temperature is below 36?."

"She's not hypothermic yet," Joe said. He left the Buggy and took one of Doris's arms. "Mariette, help me get her inside the Buggy. We'll all be warmer inside."

Mariette took the other arm. Taking advantage of the light Martian gravity, she and Joe lifted Doris and dragged her to the Buggy. Manny could barely see them through a sudden swirl of dust. While they struggled to get her into the cab, Manny used his backrest rock to leverage himself to his feet. He tested his splinted leg and then settled his weight on his right foot.

Joe secured Doris inside the cab, and then climbed in after to check her vital signs.

"Don't you dare try to hop over here." Mariette pointed at Manny. "Wait until Joe can help you. Listen to me. Where are we?"

"About eight kilometers from base camp with beacons every two kilometers."

"Oh...I see. That would take an hour even with good visibility. Joe and I have only a half hour of oxygen left."

"Doris strapped two canisters of oxygen to her bike."

"I could kiss you." Instead, she ran to Doris's bike and busied herself unloading the cylinders.

Joe exited the Buggy and approached Manny. At the invitation, Manny draped his left arm over the doctor's shoulders. Thus supported, Manny limped to the Buggy.

Once Manny settled next to Doris in the rear seats, Joe nodded towards her. "She's stable, but we need to get her to the base and warm her up. I'll help Mariette with the oxygen canisters. Looks like we've got a chance to survive this."

"Chance?" Manny said. "More than a chance. We'll survive, and after the storm we'll salvage the supplies from all the resupply modules. I'll be damned if a little wind and dust will stop us."

Joe nodded and closed the cab door.

"Optimism, Manny?" Doris didn't open her eyes. Her voice was weak, but a faint smile flickered across her chapped lips.

"Doris, sweetheart." Manny embraced her. Cuddly. Why had he thought of her as overweight? "How do you feel?"

"Terrible." She shivered in his arms. "But stay cheery, love. I may be a fat lady, but I won't sing our swan song today. We've got too much to do, you and I."

# SUSPENDED ANIMATION

## MARTA TANRIKULU

**About the Author**

Marta Tanrikulu is an editor with a science background and a writer of stories in various genres, most often in comics format. Her work has appeared in *Mystery Weekly* and in magazines and anthologies published by Red Stylo Media, Aazurn Press, Stache Publishing, and others. In addition to comics miniseries and anthologies, she especially enjoys editing speculative fiction, mysteries, and historical fiction.

Slumbering through time
Dimmed awareness
Flickering shadows
Wheeling, distant stars

Elusive thoughts
Unbidden dreams
Glimpses of loved ones
All left behind

Untethered, unsynchronized
Intangible, impotent
Fading recollection of what was
And is no more

Trapped in stasis
Insulated, immobile
Alone
Accomplishing nothing

Dreading awakening
Dreading not awakening
The music of the spheres
A dirge not a dance.

# SUNRISE AT THE
# UNIVERSE'S END

## MARGE SIMON AND RODDY FOSBURG

**About the Authors**

Marge Simon lives in Ocala, Florida and serves on the HWA Board of Trustees. She has three Bram Stoker Awards, Rhysling Awards for Best Long and Best Short Fiction, the Elgin, Dwarf Stars and Strange Horizons Readers' Award. Marge's poems and stories have appeared in *Clannad, Pedestal Magazine, Asimov's, Silver Blade, Bete Noire, New Myths,* and *Daily Science Fiction.* Her stories also appear in anthologies such as *Tales of the Lake 5, Chiral Mad 4, You, Human* and *The Beauty of Death,* to name a few. She attends the ICFA annually as a guest poet/writer and is on the board of the Speculative Literary Foundation. Amazon Author Page: amazon.com/-/e/B006G29PL6

Roddy Fosburg lives in the Washington, D.C. Metro area. He has too many cats and needs to write more.

Their voyage spanned
a myriad of light years,
and then the rum ran dry.

Captain's voice turned stone,
"Put forth the Dyson sail,"
he said, lasering a crewman
who would not comply.

They gave his wasted body
to the vacuum, and heaved-to,
the starship's bones bemoaning
returning to the deep.

Perhaps they were the last
to brave the endless dark
in a ship built from the staves
of their determination.

Sailing on through space debris,
they searched for that blue globe
with diamonds in her sands—
a land the gods had prophesied.

As if answer to their prayers,
the coxswain cried "Land ho!"
and steered toward the farthest
galaxy along the rim.

Half mad, beset with scurvy,
the Captain spied a glittering,
a junction of the sand and sky,
and bade his sailors to attend

the sunrise of a new star rising,
making sparking diamonds
of an earth-type planet's shore,
at the universe's end.

# A CANVAS DARK AND DEEP

## ROBERT MITCHELL EVANS

**About the Author**

Robert Mitchell Evans has been a sailor, a dishwasher, a shipyard worker, and a cashier, and currently his day job is in the non-profit healthcare industry. He resides in San Diego, California and can frequently be found haunting southern California science fiction conventions. His science fiction/noir novel *Vulcan's Forge* will be available from Flame Tree Press in March 2020.

IN THIS ABSURDLY IMPOSSIBLE PLANETARY SYSTEM, WHILE THE REST of the exploratory expedition investigated doppelgangers of Mars, Venus, and Earth, Commodore Holt stuck me with its Kuiper Belt.

A duplicate of our home system, its stellar evolution utterly inexplicable, Dopple was the most spectacular discovery since the quickstream, and I did nothing but busy work. My little scouting vessel, the *Lovelock*, had taken three months to reach Dopple's Kuiper Belt. Three months cooped up with six scientists, three enlisted spacers, and a ship's network devoid of personality apps. I had little to do but compose weak poems and discover that, just like the theoretical speed of a quickstream, boredom has no limits.

I was in my cabin, little more than storage closet, working on an embarrassingly bad haiku, when someone signaled at my door.

Crew chief Dominguez and lead scientist Dr. Fitzgerald entered. Fitz quivered, on his face a grin that normally signaled the discovery of a particularly attractive snowball, but that wouldn't have interested Dominguez. Fitz started to speak, but the chief cut him off.

"This is big, Captain, really big." He waved towards my display and a local area space map appeared. "Fitz here found a new quickstream."

"It's not simply a quickstream entry event," Fitz said, his voice shaking with scientific excitement. His bald little head, with its tiny little nose, bobbed like a Ping-Pong ball in a storm. "This is unlike any quickstream seen."

He devolved into a stream of jargon, numbers, and other esoteric terms that the scientific types pass off as language. I held up a hand, but he barreled right over my attempts to regain control of the conversation.

"Fitz."

He ignored me, too deep down the rabbit hole to respond to

mere conversation. Dominguez, a head and a half taller than either of us, dropped a hand on his shoulder and the torrent stopped.

"No one here is a specialist," I said. "How about you give it to me in real simple terms, eh?"

"This quickstream, Ensign..."

"Captain."

Yeah, the *Lovelock* was a tiny ship, barely capable of riding a quickstream, and my orders as commanding officer terminated the moment we rejoined with the *Diogenes*, but she was mine and no matter my actual rank I was captain.

With a tone indicating that he was patronizing yet another mindless martinet, Fitz continued.

"Captain, this quickstream has the potential to be the fastest ever discovered, several orders of magnitude faster. That means thousands..."

"I know what 'orders of magnitude' mean, Fitz."

"Well, of course you do."

"Sir," Dominguez asked. "Are we going to see how far it goes?"

My stomach flipped and my throat dried up.

"It's hardly part of studying the Doppel system, is it?"

"Captain Newman, you can't seriously be considering not exploring this quickstream." Fitz's hand fluttered like horrified butterflies. "We have to transit this stream and record the events and..." He started going into a spasm of scientific tongues again, but Dominguez waved him silent.

"Sir, Dr. Fitzgerald here tells me that a short trip wouldn't impact their Kuiper Belt survey and it would be an opportunity for truly unique readings."

I started to reply, but Dominguez barreled on, leaving me with nothing to do but close my mouth.

"I took the liberty of reviewing the mission orders, sir. I think that this clearly falls under section thirteen, 'previously unknown phenomenon,' and you'd be well within your authority in ordering a brief survey to produce a complete report."

I seriously doubted that Commodore Holt would see my sudden excursion out of the planetary system as 'within my authority.'

I mumbled, "I suppose we could signal the *Diogenes* for instructions."

"Yes, sir, we could. The lag time from our current location is just a hair under seven hours, so nearly fourteen for round-trip communications." Fitz fidgeted as Dominguez spoke, desperately wanting, needing, to argue us to going down an unmapped quickstream. "And with teams scattered all over the system, who knows how long before they get back to us. I suspect our reports aren't exactly on the commodore's priority listings."

True enough, but it stung to be reminded what I did barely mattered.

"But if you confirm this finding, then that's something that even Explorer Command would take notice."

Oh, that was so easy for Dominguez to suggest. If this didn't pan out, it wouldn't be his butt de-orbiting. Still, he was right. It could be big, really big. They worked me over for another ten minutes, but the outcome never really wavered, and as usual Dominguez got his way.

Twelve hours later the *Lovelock*, her quickstream engines fully charged, prepared to slide out.

Going superluminal in a quickstream is both easy and frightening. These strange fractures in the fabric of space/time are sort of like faster-than-light water slides, some taller and steeper than others, letting ships slide from one place to another. Don't try to push the water slide analogy too far, as quickstreams flow both ways. The easy part was getting in position, engaging the drive, and letting the 'stream take you to the far end; the frightening part was how you felt.

If you took the sensation of goose bumps erupting over your whole body and combined it with fingernails scraping across a chalkboard, you'd be getting pretty close to what it is like to ride superluminal. Every moment of every hour of every day is a trial of nerves; people already given to outbursts and tantrums become unbearable in a quickstream.

We took our meds, reducing the worst of the effects and inducing a calmer state of mind, but I still dreaded entry. Dominguez, his blond hair military short and perfect, sat at the pilot-prime station while Takashi backed him up from the relief pilot and engineer's console. She struggled to sit still and project an air of calm professionalism.

"Chief," I said, trying to project command into my voice, "Take us into the 'stream."

With a sly and slightly insulting smile, Dominguez launched us out of the Doppel planetary system.

OUR NERVES TAUT AND TENSE, THE CREW OF THE *LOVELOCK* endured the quickstream. Scientists busied themselves with readings, computations, and heated arguments over interpretations while the crew sniped and insulted each other over endless games of chance.

I tried to relax, working on a report for Commodore Holt that didn't make this mission sound either foolish or entirely the brainchild of Chief Dominguez. Ship's night arrived and I went to my rack, my brain strained with an incipient migraine. My head hit my pillow, the lights went out, and sleep overtook me.

I fled a pack of predatory poetry critics armed with pruning shears to demonstrate to me the value of cutting. Every time I thought I had lost them by turning into some alley, I'd find my escape blocked by gigantic prints of my poems. Tearing through the poems let me escape, but gave the murderous critics a chance to close.

I awoke, covered in sweat, my heart beating so fast it was just a blur in my ears, and the migraine fully blossomed. I ordered medication from the *Lovelock's* network and fell into a drugged, dreamless sleep.

Night after night the nightmares returned, some variation of homicidal critics or fans, like a bad horror video, leaving me exhausted. After two days I noticed I wasn't the only person aboard with red eyes and a thousand A.U. stare.

Fitz sat at breakfast. His trembling hands made the fake food on his fork dance and drop before it reached his mouth. The other scientists fared no better, each lost in their own universe of sleep deprivation. I sipped fake coffee, the very real caffeine jolting my system but failing to budge my bone-deep exhaustion. We couldn't let this go on much longer; we'd be in no shape for any kind of survey. Finishing the coffee in one gulp, I went looking for Dominguez.

I found him on the bridge, his feet kicked up on a console, his eyes closed, apparently sleeping peacefully. I started to back out through the door, but he said, "Is there something I can do for you, sir?"

"Were you sleeping, Chief?"

"Naw." He sat up, bringing his feet flat on the deck. "Just checking for eyelid leaks."

"Nightmares?" I sat in the command chair, wondering if I were finally going to see a bit of humanity, or even humility, from the chief.

"Not much to speak of. Probably the same as everyone else."

"That's what's bothering me. I've looked through the files, and I can't find any instance of quickstream travel causing nightmares."

"Something for the smart boys to gnaw over. So we'll have at least one new thing to report. It's not every Explorer who can say that, sir."

"Maybe we should turn back." I sat back, letting my gaze wander around the tiny compartment, anywhere except his piercing, unsettling look.

"It's your call, sir." I swear his tone made me feel like a schoolboy failing a test. "But if you don't mind me offering a little service experience…"

He actually waited for me to nod permission, though we both knew that was a farce.

"This little mission is already promising big things; the kind of things that can help a fella get a jump on a stuck promotion list, but the service isn't going to promote an officer that they think has gone weak in the knees." He scanned the system read-outs, a lifetime of experience judging the systems status with a confidence I could only impersonate.

"It's more than that, Chief. Much more of this and no one is going to be in any shape for regular duties, much less if we have to face an emergency."

"Yes, sir, I can't argue that, but is it going to look that way back at Earth? I could see some tightly wound personnel officer reading your report and telling his bosses we turned back 'cause you got scared." He sighed. Dominguez missed his calling not being an actor. "It wouldn't hurt my career much, but I think it could cause you a whole mess of trouble, sir."

"But you can see what shape the crew is in. If we go on to disaster, that's going to leave a black mark on all our records, don't you think?"

He stood up, a towering figure with twenty years of spacer experience.

"You're the captain, sir, and I've seen tight and hard trouble before. Sir, I think this crew might surprise you. Why don't you give them the chance to prove themselves?"

"It's not that I don't have the utmost confidence…"

"I'm sure you do, sir, but they aren't likely to see it that way. It would be a bad shot to their morale, to be so close to going where no one has gone before and have it snatched away because the captain thought they couldn't cut it."

Somehow he turned the issue around, making me into the villain.

"The first sign that safety has been compromised, and we're turning back."

"I'll back you up if it comes to that, sir, but I think we'll all adjust faster than you might expect."

As you don't salute aboard a ship, he nodded in my direction and ambled off the bridge.

~

I WAS STRUGGLING WITH THE COMMODORE'S REPORT WHEN FITZ and one of his partners in science, Dr. Amanda Hollingston, arrived at my cabin, both wearing reality sets. Despite the wire mesh encircling their scalps, I could see both were fully interacting with reality. Fitz carried a third mesh.

"Not interested in any games right now, doctors." I tried to wave them away because the report was a black monster destroying any positive mood.

"As much as we enjoy your company, Captain, we're here with solutions, not pastimes." Fitz stalked over to my desk and dropped the mesh in front of me, wiping the report from my desktop.

I tried, and failed, to keep the irritation out of my voice. "This is not the time!"

"Put it on," Amanda said, her face lit with an infectious smile. A sucker for unsardonic scientists, I picked it up and slipped the mesh over my scalp. She nodded, her smile becoming a grin, for me to turn it on. Sighing, I activated the reality set, and with the swiftness of a well-executed landing, peace descended on my mood.

I grinned, and then I laughed. That moment Fitz became my best friend. I could have sworn that we had dropped out of the quickstream. Not one tingle of the 'stream's fingernail-grating, teeth-grinding influence remained, the scourge of superluminal flight reduced to a bad memory.

"What happened?" I asked. "I mean, this is fantastic!"

"Dr. Hollingston found the answer." Fitz waved to Amanda. "I'll spare you the math." In my ecstasy I even forgave his patronizing attitude. "But this quickstream event is so powerful that we succeeded in isolating the waveform patterns responsible for physiological and psychological aberrations from the background noise of superluminal flight. It's amazingly close to our reality-set carrier wave modulation. Dr. Hollingston theorized that we could use the sets to block the interference."

"Any trouble using the ship's fabricators to make enough for everyone?"

"Nope," Amanda said. "All we need is your authorization and we can have everyone sleeping peacefully tonight."

"You have it."

I authorized it through the ship's network and, good to their promise, we then slept soundly wearing our new reality sets.

Naturally, Dominguez managed to remind me that if we had turned back, none of that would have happened. You know what? I didn't care and I looked forward to reaching the end of the 'stream.

Then everything went pear-shaped.

Amanda had her place in history. The woman who made superluminal travel comfortable; people would be toasting her for decades, and I'd be among them. Still, no one would remember the lowly ensign who commanded the ship. How many people can name the captain of the *Beagle*?

Thirty-five hours later we reentered normal space, ditched

our reality sets, and started recharging the quickstream engines. While the engines powered through their twelve-hour recharge cycle, the crew got to work helping the scientists deploy telescopes in every conceivable wavelength, and I tasked Dominguez with completing our astrogation analysis. The sooner we knew where we had stopped, the sooner we'd have an idea just how fast that 'stream had been.

Not too much later, Dominguez reported that we were three thousand seven hundred and fifty-seven light years from Doppel; I was tempted to fabricate champagne. The fastest, longest quickstream and we discovered it. I ordered visible spectrum images of Doppel, just something to make our survey complete, and worked on the report, happy and optimistic. Once we learned what new quickstreams branched off from this system, we'd have a whole new network to explore, and I wanted to be out here on the bleeding edge of discovery. Things looked fantastic. Naturally, fate kicked me in the teeth.

Fitz barged into my stateroom with no door signal, not even a shouted warning. Like a ghastly apparition, he just appeared.

"This is an amazing discovery. We've got to stay more than just a dozen hours."

"Hello to you too, Fitz." Teaching him any courtesies, much less military ones, was as impossible as breathing vacuum. "If you have good leads on new quickstream entry points, we can stay long enough to map those." Visions of dozens of new quickstreams danced in my head, the sort of discovery that produced meritorious promotions.

"Oh, this is much more interesting than routine quickstream events."

A chill touched my heart and I imagined Commodore Holt's angry voice as he reprimanded me for wasting valuable resources. "What exactly are you talking about?" I managed while quelling a growing unease.

"A unique phenomenon, the sort of event we're out here to

find!" He waved at my display and a local-space map appeared, triggering a terrible déjà vu. What appeared had the same false-color coding for a quickstream, but instead of looking like branching rivers, this was like a dropped plate of spaghetti.

"What the hell is that?"

"We have no idea." I'd say he giggled like a schoolgirl, but I don't like insulting little girls. "We've never seen the energy structures associated with quickstream events display anything other than direct connection between planetary systems. Did you know that there has never been a quickstream discovered that failed to lead to a planetary system? There are several good theories on how the collapse of the accretion disk..."

"Fitz, what is that?" I pointed again at the display.

"I told you, we don't know. It's new."

"What about new quickstreams out of this system?"

"Oh." He waved his hands, casually dismissing my future. "There's no sign of any; it would appear that this is another terminus, but this—" he jabbed excitedly at the spaghetti tangle "—is worth a dozen new quickstream events."

I put my head in my hands while black despair closed in.

"Any chance that this might be a new kind of quickstream entry? Possibly leading to new systems?"

"Preposterous! Any fool could see that the energy density of these events is plainly far below the threshold for baryonic matter conversion; these threads aren't even..."

I tried to summarily dismiss him. "Then they are useless to us. We're leaving as soon as the engines are fully charged."

Fitz didn't take my dismissal. I bet the only reason that man doesn't get killed is that people are too afraid of the paperwork.

The intership communications suddenly beeped for my attention, and I activated it.

"Captain Newman," Amanda said, her voice strained, the words coming out with a pronounced deliberation. "Can you come to Analysis?"

"I'm in the middle of something. Why don't you tell me what's the trouble?"

"Well," she hesitated, and then blurted, "It's about Doppel. We might have figured out why it's so much like home and, well, it would be a lot easier to just show you."

Fitz stopped, stunned, like myself, into a brief silence.

"Fine, I'll be right there. I'm bringing Dr. Fitzgerald with me."

Her relief came through with the clarity of a laser.

"Oh, thank God!"

I hurried forward, calling for Dominguez to join us in the scientific spaces. He caught up with us just outside of the door to the four compartments that made up the labs, asking, "What's up, sir?"

"Apparently the solution to Doppel. Who knew it was four thousand light years away?" I doubted we'd found any real answers; more likely, the universe continued to joke with my career.

We stepped inside, and waiting for us was the entire scientific team.

Stepping between Amanda and me, Fitz demanded, "Give it to me first."

"Show all of us," I said, taking an open seat. Dominguez leaned back against a console and Fitz simply stood in the middle of the room, fuming.

Amanda turned to a large display unrolled and slapped up against a bulkhead and called up a stereo image of deep space.

"This is our visible light image of Doppel."

"Your telescopes got turned around," Dominguez said. "There aren't any nebulas near Doppel."

He was right, again. Centered in the display was a diffuse nebula, dark clouds visible as a shadow blocking out a swath of stars.

Amanda's voice wavered as she answered. "No, Chief, that

nebula *is* Doppel. Point the 'scope yourself if you want, we've done it four times."

Fitz shoved his way forward and began searching through their records, but I knew he'd find no mistakes. Like a macabre xylophone, cold shivers played along my spine and I realized the utterly inescapable conclusion; Doppel was artificial.

Under the influence of shock waves from supernovas, nebulas are compressed into stars and all the assorted bodies found in planetary systems, but that process takes billions of years, and Doppel was less than three thousand seven hundred and fifty-seven years old, the age of the light currently falling on our optical telescopes. No natural process can possibly take a nebula and turn it into a planetary system in four thousand years, none. Hell, it takes ten thousand years for the photons from the fusion events in a star's core to work their way to the photosphere, and yet three thousand light years away, Doppel shone bright, ignoring its own impossibility.

I sat there, silent and afraid while Dominguez confirmed the images, but I knew we had stumbled on the truth. Fitz, mumbling about gravitational lensing and imaging objects much further behind Doppel, still refused to accept it.

Finally he collapsed into a chair, muttering, "This is simply impossible."

"It's there." Dominguez pointed to the nebula. "There's no screw-up."

"A nebula can't form a planetary system in a few thousand years, it can't!"

"No, it can't," I said softly, amazed that Fitz failed to even consider the obvious solution. "Someone made it happen. They came along, took that nebula, and duplicated Earth and our entire solar system."

Momentarily, silence reigned, and then, like a bomb blast, everyone began shouting and wildly gesturing. I sat back, letting my thoughts just free-associate while everyone else argued and struggled for acceptance. Without any idea about what to do, I retreated to a quiet interior zone of my mind hoping for inspiration.

"Captain," Dominguez insistently pierced my reverie, "I suggest that we go 'dark' at once. Cease all signals, scans, and shut down anything not essential. Nothing more than life support, and keep charging the engines."

I thought it was a little late to be shutting the barn door, but before I could say anything, Fitz spoke up.

"There's no need to overreact. We've got valuable observations to make and there's no sign of any mega-structures in the immediate vicinity."

"Really?" I said.

"Is there something you'd like to add, Ensign?"

"Captain, and yes, you're missing that this is bigger than just Doppel. It's about the quickstream network too."

I turned to Amanda.

"Dr. Hollingston, that quickstream structure in this system, do those channels connect up with the 'stream we rode in on?"

She looked over at Fitz for approval and then to my surprise looked back at me before he could make up his mind. "Yes, sir, it does."

"So it's really a continuation of the quickstream?"

"Perhaps."

"Could it be that we've been wrong about the quickstreams? They are not natural and their purpose isn't FTL travel, but a galaxy-wide communication network?"

Fitz started to speak but then shocked us all by shutting his mouth, considering the suggestion.

"Sir?" Dominguez said. "Shall I start shutting down systems? We really need to go dark right now."

"It's too late for that, Chief. If they are going to notice us, they already have."

The scientists huddled around Amanda, debating some idea or theory while Dominguez moved up close to me.

"Sir, it's too damn dangerous to run that risk. Whoever built Doppel does not have our best interests at heart."

Fitz dismissed him with a word. "Preposterous."

He turned on Fitz like a hawk diving on a rabbit. "You think they went to all the trouble of duplicating our solar system for giggles? They did it for a reason and it can't be good."

"This is the product of a post-singularity civilization having as much in common with us as we do with bacteria. They are like gods, unconcerned with the messy chaos of our existence."

Dominguez stepped in close to Fitz. "I don't believe in coincidence. They chose us for a reason, and seeing how they didn't bother to say 'Hi' before putting their plan in motion, I don't think they give a damn about how we feel."

"Coincidence exists regardless of your belief, Chief. Any species that has transited through the singularity isn't part of our mental universe anymore, they…"

Dominguez snapped a finger towards the display. "Oh, they're still a part of our universe, and your pacifistic daydreams won't matter squat when they get rolling."

Amanda tapped me on the shoulder. "Sir, we've got an idea."

She took me over to the non-bickering scientists, and we spoke in hushed tones.

"We think you're right, it is a communications system and we can access it," Amanda said, her eyes nearly dancing with excitement. "It was the quickstream transit here that made all the difference. We had mistakenly assumed we were experiencing a naturally occurring effect, but it has a carrier wave. That is what creates the psychological aberrations experienced during superluminal travel. Instead of using the reality set to block it, we can integrate the carrier wave into the experienced reality transmission, submerging the recipient into the communications stream."

It struck me as an unlikely project. "Isn't it likely that anything being transmitted will be gibberish?"

Chuck Shirley jumped in. "Maybe, perhaps even likely, but the fact is that the quickstream effect has always affected the human mind, and we've just been blind to the idea it might have been a carrier wave at all. If it's already influencing us on a subconscious and emotional level, then with a direct connection, communication might be clear."

"Would this be two-way?"

Amanda shrugged. "No idea, this is wholly uncharted territory, sir."

"I had no idea you were a punster," I said.

With a sheepish smile she said, "Never on purpose." She looked over the other junior scientists and then back to me. "Are we going to do it?"

Fitz pulled his head back from his screaming match with Dominguez. "Absolutely not!"

He stormed to us, his hands dancing about like drunken dervishes.

"You have no idea what you are doing. We're talking about a species that has become fully transcendent. Their concerns will be totally alien to ours, communication will simply not be possible. All you could hope to achieve is to become an annoyance."

I said back at him, "If it's that impossible, I don't see what harm we could possibly cause."

"What your mind is capable of foreseeing is quite inconsequential. You are not going to contaminate this site with foolhardy and futile actions."

"Dr. Fitzgerald, I am in command of this mission and I alone will decide what actions are appropriate."

Fitz sputtered, his hands momentarily frozen in mid-air, before he rebooted his indignation. "This has stopped being an excursion investigating a particularly interesting quickstream event. This is now something far too big for you to have any input on, Ensign."

"Captain."

"Ensign! I refuse to play these 'bigger-ape' pecking-order games." He turned to Amanda and her group. "You will not do anything of the sort, do you understand?"

Before she could say anything I jumped in, "Dr. Hollingston, I am the commanding officer of the ship, the senior-most officer on the expedition, an expedition I might remind everyone is entirely under the umbrella of the Explorer Corps, and I will make the decisions on how we will proceed."

"Sir," Dominguez said, his voice level, but loaded with patronizing undertones. "Professor Fitzgerald might be right, but for the wrong reasons. He thinks that the aliens have gone all mystical and special, but I say anyone who copies our solar system has got a plan. If you try to communicate with them, well, sir, you're just tipping our hand when we haven't antied up yet."

I wanted to take his tone and those carefully measured words maneuvering me into his plan of action and shove it back down his throat. "Thank you, Chief, but when I want your advice, I'll ask for it."

"Of course, sir, but there is one thing I am obligated to remind you of."

"And what is that?"

"Standing Order number 1, sir, if any Explorer Team discovers indication of intelligent non-human life, that team is obligated to proceed at best possible speed back to the nearest Explorer Flag command and report the discovery for further investigation, sir." He gave me a sad little smile, perhaps intended to placate me with some faked sympathy, but I didn't fall for it. Not this time.

"And that's what we're going to do, Chief, in six hours. As soon as the engines are charged we'll take the quickstream back to Doppel and report our discovery to the commodore. Until then we'll collect all possible data about the situation as directed by our survey orders."

"Yes sir, but…"

"Until we depart I intend to do everything in our ability to establish who and what is going on here and why they created Doppel."

I looked at Amanda, signaled for her to follow me, and we strode out of the compartment.

We wasted an hour setting out parameters and specifications before she hurried back forward to get the scientists cracking on the software. I reviewed the mission orders, my hands shaking so badly that it took three attempts to get the system to recognize my gestures.

The safe thing, both personally and for my career, would be to do exactly what Dominguez suggested, fly back and leave it all to someone else, but for the first time I didn't want to be safe. I played it safe with my poems, afraid of offending someone, and I played it safe as an officer, never straying from the rules.

Out here, beyond our furthest port, I'd found courage. I didn't care if this burned my career, leaving me disgraced and broke; for once I wasn't going to stand aside. I thought about a drink, but resisted that foolish temptation. The odds were that I'd experience nothing intelligible, but if I did, I couldn't afford compromised judgment.

Alien intelligences. Just the concept felt unreal in my mind. For over a hundred years humanity had dreamt of finding a stellar family. We flew the first quickstreams with grand optimism and high hopes. That slowly degraded into pragmatic searching, before finally corroding into bitter and lonely cynicism.

Fitz and Dominguez sent streams of messages, pleading with me to reconsider, Fitz's concerned about my contamination and Dominguez's with alien butchers waiting for their moment to pounce. I couldn't shake the feeling that both were trapped in boxes of their own design. That something more fundamental lay at Doppel's purpose.

I had no illusion of solving the puzzle, but I was determined to make the attempt. How could we come four thousand light years and not even try? When Amanda informed me they were ready to start, my stomach cramped, and sweat beaded on my forehead. Our engines were nearly changed, and in just twenty minutes Dominguez would force my hand.

I walked slowly, on uncertain legs, to the science compartments. Everyone was there.

"I'm begging you, don't do this." Fitz's voice had no trace of his usual haughtiness. I nearly backed out and gave him what he wanted, but I shoved the fear aside, determined to see this through to the end.

Dominguez, cagier than Fitz, said nothing, his disappointed expression hitting me like a suddenly decompressed airlock. I stepped past him and sat in the prepared seat. Amanda, standing behind me, fitted the reality-set mesh to my scalp, and then bent over and on the cheek quickly kissed me.

"Are you ready?" she asked, standing by the terminal, her hands hovering, ready to gesture. Nodding, I barely saw her hands begin to move before a new reality shoved everything aside.

IN RETROSPECT, I CAN ONLY PARTIALLY DESCRIBE WHAT HAPPENED next. I ceased to be aware of self, experiencing emotion and sensory impressions without awareness riding interference.

I tasted blue, heard cinnamon, my skin flushed with the hot burn of a charcoal smell, and throughout this tumbling jumble of senses my mood became one of acute anticipation. Like locking in a troublesome digital signal, everything suddenly sharpened, my senses falling back into their familiar, but now cosmically enhanced, forms.

The galaxy lay before me, a vast tableau of stars, dust, gas, and countless bodies in ceaseless motion. With nothing more than a passing desire, I fell through time and space, light years as meaningless as yesterday's breaths, until Doppel's nebula hung before me.

The clouds roiled and boiled, centuries passing like seconds, the nebula's beauty entrancing in its transience. My awareness splintered, and our solar system spun before me while simultaneously I considered the nebula. Earth, blue and green, vibrant with life, commanded my attention, while the other planets in their orbits enriched the scene. No human had ever experienced what passed though my senses, the entirety of the solar system, perceived as a single whole thing, its vast scale comprehensible.

The nebula boiled and forces reached deep inside, pulling elements this way and that, sorting, compressing, and molding the cloud into a star and planets, guided by the dazzling jewel that was home.

The raw power and beauty of creation overpowered me, and had I a body, tears would have flowed, enough to flood worlds. Colors, only perceptible to myself, erupted from the newly forged planets, comets streaked across the scene, painting the new system with grace, and the very motion of their orbits pulled at my sense of heart.

Doppel swam in my mind, never a mere duplicate but an enhancement. Sol's ethereal beauty was captured, amplified, and displayed for those with the vision to understand. Humanity was far more lost than any blind man in Plato's Cave. Playing at thought, color, form, and sound as merely the finger paints of the universe, but perceiving Doppel through my new cosmic senses, I knew beauty as an Absolute.

My senses expanded again, perceiving dozens of planetary systems, the quickstreams tying them together, some created, some just admired, all inspiring in their natural glory. The collection was a gallery of Beauty within our spinning, exploding, and coalescing galaxy. My emotional being pulled apart, and inside me fear, love, hate, pride, joy, and nameless emotions collided, vying for dominance.

Cold deck plates pressed against my cheek, and tears flooded down to the deck as I sobbed. Amanda took me by the shoulders, helping me to my feet. Mustering a self-control I had never before realized, I stopped blubbering and looked around the compartment.

Chief Dominguez considered me with unconcealed contempt and Fitz's arrogant superiority had returned. Dominguez turned to Fitz and said, "We'll take care of him until…"

Easily I put fire in my voice. "No need to 'take care of me,' Chief Dominguez, I'm quite alright. Chief, please make ready for superluminal transit." I turned to Fitz. "Dr. Fitzgerald, please be sure your department is ready for departure."

"Something scared you out there?" Dominguez smirked, ready to guide me through an imagined crisis.

"Nothing like that, Chief." A few errant tears continued rolling down my cheeks, but I ignored them, still in the grips of the most liberating emotional experience of my life. "We've got lots to report, including what Doppel is."

They all spoke at once, scientists and technicians all consumed by the same insatiable curiosity that had propelled humanity from caves to the stars. That wasn't our only ineffable compulsion.

"It's art." I turned to Fitz. "You're wrong about the transcendent aliens. We have something in common; the need to create. To put our emotions out there for everyone to see and share."

They stood, silent and dumbfounded, and I said, "Chief, let's get moving. We've got a lot to report before we come back."

He hurried from the compartment and the science team started debating my revelation. I walked out, making my way to the small bridge while turning over and over in my mind the concept that even gods need to paint.

# SECTION III

## EVER EVOLVING, EVER REVOLVING

*If the human race were to vanish from the face of the earth save for one halfway talented child that had received no education, this child would rediscover the entire course of evolution, it would be capable of producing everything once more, gods and demons, paradises...*
—Herman Hesse, Demian

# A GREATER MOON

## GERALD WARFIELD

**About the Author**

Gerald Warfield's short stories have appeared in many online venues and print anthologies including *Perihelion*, *New Myths*, *Bewildering Stories*, *Every Day Fiction*, and *Metaphorosis*. "The Poly Islands," won second prize in the first quarter of the 2011 Writers of the Future contest. The same year, his humorous story "The Origin of Third Person in Paleolithic Epic Poetry" took first place in the Grammar Girl short story contest. Gerald published music textbooks and how-to books in investing before turning to fiction. He is currently finishing his third novel. He is a graduate of the Odyssey Writers Workshop (2010), Taos Toolbox, and a member of SFWA.

In the end, a final breath.
No sight or sound, I think,
but the universe contained
within a single ebb and flow.

That breath,
totem of a greater tide,
joins its kin within
a single cosmic sigh.

For each life, one season,
and from its farthest ebb, no return.
No call of moon nor sun nor stars may rouse it,
singly, from its last retreat.

Yet upon the sea there are many tides,
and on the tides many waves
in turn that rise and fall and
clamor to be heard and not to die.

I am told
of a universe that expands,
and of a last retreat
from which there is no escape.

But perhaps the breath of life, once drawn,
does not exhaust itself
but joins again a greater tide,
summoned by a greater moon.

A wave, once dashed upon the strand,
does not rise and fall again.
yet join it must the tide that brought it thus

to end upon unyielding shores.

The universe expands;
the universe contracts.
Who is to say it is not called
by a greater moon
that summons tides on endless shores
where endless waves exhaust themselves
though singly rise no more.

# A WORLD IN SEVEN FLAMES

## JAMEYANNE FULLER

**About the Author**

Jameyanne Fuller is a space lawyer by day, writer by night. Sometimes she sleeps. Her short story "Dissonance," which takes place in the same world as this poem, appeared in *Abyss and Apex* in 2016, and her other short fiction has been published in *Cast of Wonders*, the *2018 Young Explorer's Adventure Guide,* and *Andromeda Spaceways*. In her free time, Jameyanne enjoys inventing recipes, playing the clarinet, and plotting world domination with her team of black labs, retired Seeing Eye dog Mopsy and current Seeing Eye dog Neutron Star. She blogs regularly at jameyannefuller.com and tweets @JameyanneFuller.

LISTEN.

The beginning was silent, dark, cold.

Mother Flame and Father Song wove our world from music and fire—

A crackling, sparking melody.

Together, Mother Flame and Father Song cupped the world in their hands,

And wept for its beauty—

Their gem of blue and green and white waltzing with the sun.

MUSIC GAVE THE RUSH TO THE WATER, THE HUSH TO THE FALLING snow, the shush to the wind,

The tumble and roar to the mountains, rising, falling, rising.

Fire created heat and life, breath and passion,

The stars and moons and skies for dreaming.

Mother Flame and Father Song wept, and their tears were embers, beating hearts, beating drums,

Entire symphonies not yet dreamed.

And their tears burned and sang and grew into the first people.

MOTHER FLAME AND FATHER SONG DECREED THAT OF THESE first people would be born a child,

And before she became a woman, she would perish and rise again as the first Phoenix.

We would give her music for a heartbeat, and she would carry our world through her age—her flame bright and burning.

When her flame died, she would choose a second child to become the second Phoenix.

There would be seven Phoenixes—our world would rise and
fall with each—

A world in seven songs—

A world in seven flames.

THE FIRST FLAME BURNED FOR THE SINGERS.

We lived in caves, hunting, fishing, and gathering through
the days to sate our bodies,

Singing and dancing through the nights to sate the Phoenix.

We sculpted in red clay from riverbeds,

And painted upon walls with juices of fruit and flower,

To remember our songs, mother to son, father to daughter.

When we left the caves,

Built homes of wood and stone and sowed our first seeds,

The first Phoenix chose a second.

The second lifted our world onto her own back, and the first
cut her wing,

With her own claw, bleeding fire to make ink,

So we could write our music.

And the first Phoenix sang a simple melody,

With one voice, one story.

THE SECOND FLAME BURNED FOR THE WRITERS.

We wrote with the blood of our first Phoenix,

Our songs maps of fire across the world.

We shaped instruments of wood and brass, of strings, of
shell and stone,

Tinder for the fire in the Phoenix's heart.

Each child was born to an instrument,

To each melody a harmony.

And our Resonance made the second Phoenix stronger, brighter, faster, than the first.

Yet she depended upon the music more than her sister,

And when the music faltered, at the turning of the year,

She fell,

The world tumbling with her.

And the second Phoenix sang, in a voice like a symphony,

Of the beauty of creation and destruction, of music resounding and crashing through the world.

THE THIRD FLAME HAS BURNT OUR PAST TO ASHES.

The third Phoenix has carried a world desperate to fly, afraid to fall.

We have forgotten the singers were first,

Forgotten the first Phoenix gave her blood for our symphonies,

Forgotten that music is a journey,

Each note a step—together.

We remember only the fall of the second Phoenix, the darkness, the disaster, the despair.

We have fought to keep the third Phoenix flying,

But in our fight we have wounded.

And we remember, now, only as the flame rears high,

And those we have trodden underfoot rise with it,

The ashes of our past on their shoes, in their bones.

The third Phoenix has known this would come, but she has guided the flame, coaxed the flame.

Our world is falling again, but this time, we will not forget.

OUR WORLD IS FALLING,

Our fire snuffed by darkness,
Our music drowned by fear and pain,
Screaming, fighting, bleeding, falling.
It will worsen before we can recover.
But lift your head from the ashes.
Raise your eyes to the stars.

DO YOU HEAR HER?
Our third Phoenix is singing.
She is singing a rondo,
Of the past she knew as a girl,
Of the bright and bloody world she carried,
And of the burning future she dreams.
Listen.

THE FOURTH FLAME WILL BRING CHANGE.
Now no one will be denied music.
Those who make music with voice will mix with those who play with wood and brass, strings and bells.
The music will change; the Resonance will grow.
And we will reach for more—something more than music for our children.
We will explore other art, study history and science.
The stars and moons and worlds and suns, our own waters and lands and winds,
Will be a puzzle to be solved,
The pieces no longer simple steps in a dance—except in our poetry—
But elements, gravity, entropy.
We will still give the Phoenix our music, but now we will

question.

And as she flags in her flight, the fourth Phoenix will sing a lullaby,

Of a child growing up and stepping away from childhood,

Into a world of jarring, dissonant melodies.

THE FIFTH FLAME WILL SPARK SPEED AND KNOWLEDGE.

The fifth Phoenix will be born into a new world,

Where we have discovered we can use our music to power machines,

To create food and clothing, light and medicine,

To fly.

And when the fifth Phoenix bears our new world,

It will weigh upon her,

Racing and heavy with power.

Her body will ache with the strain,

Without the music to strengthen her,

And her heart will ache with sadness for the old world,

And wonder for the new.

The fifth Phoenix will sing, slowly,

An elegy.

AS THE SIXTH FLAME DIES, WE WILL LEAVE.

Our thirst for knowledge will carry us up,

Into the stars,

To soar as Phoenixes ourselves,

To build our own worlds.

We will forget we were carried.

We will forget we were guided.

We will not be afraid.

Mother Flame and Father Song will weep new worlds, stars, galaxies.

Their tears will burn and sing and grow with their pride,

And they will let our first world,

Their first world,

Burn.

The sixth Phoenix will sing alone.

THE SEVENTH PHOENIX WILL FLY ALONE, CARRYING AN EMPTY world;

The seventh flame only embers, darkening.

She will sing her own song, find her own strength,

And her sisters, reborn, will carry our new worlds, and sing their own songs,

Seven voices rising, falling, rising, together in harmony,

Singing of forgetting and fear and remembering again, of change and speed and knowledge, of leaving, dying.

Of bones of ashes and wings of fire and hearts of seven songs.

LISTEN, NOW, AS OUR THIRD PHOENIX FALLS, AS OUR THIRD FLAME dies,

Past the darkness, past the tumbling, past the pain and fear, listen.

We were born of flame and song. We wrote in Phoenix blood and shaped our own Harmonies.

We have fallen before, and we have broken.

But we can still heal.

We have new things to learn, new heights to reach, new songs to sing.

We have flames and flames before us.

So listen. Our third Phoenix is singing.
  She is singing a rondo,
  Of the past she knew as a girl,
  Of the bright and bloody world she carried,
  And of the burning future she dreams.
  Listen.
  Let us sing with her.

# THE WOLVES OF HORUS SYSTEM

## STEPHEN CASE

**About the Author**

Stephen Case teaches astronomy and pilots a digital universe on the campus of a Christian liberal arts college in Illinois. He has published over thirty short stories in places like *Orson Scott Card's Intergalactic Medicine Show*, *Shimmer*, and *Beneath Ceaseless Skies*. The results of his PhD dissertation in the history of science were published last year by the University of Pittsburgh Press as *Making Stars Physical: the Astronomy of Sir John Herschel*. His first novel, *First Fleet*, a military scifi thriller described as *Battlestar Galactica* meets H. P. Lovecraft, was published by Axiomatic Press. You can find him online at stephenrcase.com and tweeting at @StephenRCase.

MACKLE AND I ARCHED TOWARD THE TARGET. AS USUAL, WOLF was far ahead of us both. I could see his form small and dark against the belly of the ship we were aimed for. It was a good one, fat and slow and rich. We got a ship like this maybe once a Firstworld-year. If it was like the last, it would keep us stocked for weeks. But it would also mean there was a convoy passing through the stones somewhere nearby. The trick was to get in and get the good stuff before it was able to send a distress call.

Wolf was good at tricks.

I felt the cold at my joints and flexed my fingers. We could be in naked space for minutes before we felt pain or had any fear of damage. My lungs weren't even tight yet when Mackle and I reached the ship.

It had already gone dark. Wolf slipped the bolt-knives back into his belt. That meant I missed my favorite part: watching those electric blades lance out along the ship's skin. They scrambled sensors and usually fried a ship's ability to call for help. Wolf was on all fours now, pulling himself along the hull looking for an airlock.

*Maybe they'll have meat,* Mackle thought-spoke at me. The hope he felt made his words register bright and sharp in my mind.

I nodded curtly and shot out along the hull in the opposite direction, hoping to be the first to find a way in.

*There are seven convoy ships up here.* Job's thought-speak was muted with distance. *Not close yet.* He was back on the *Fenris,* hidden a little way off in the stones. Job's skin was soft and pink, so he couldn't come outside with us. Instead, he would keep watch and pick us up when we were finished.

Mackle found the hatch before either Wolf or me and waved his arm for Wolf to see. Him finding it saved us time, because Mackle could think-speak to computers to get doors opened. He had to be close to them though. I could do it sometimes, and Wolf and Job couldn't do it at all.

Inside the ship, the warm air felt like a blanket, heavy enough to burn my skin after the frost of space. Mackle made the airlock cycle, and I flexed my fingers again, feeling joints soften. I opened my nose and blinked my outlids up.

"Seven shifters, Job says," I told Wolf, pointing upward. Whatever direction you were inside a ship, pointing upward always meant outside. "Not close yet."

The first corridor ran toward the ship's center. Its lights were dark, which was a good sign. We separated at the first junction, Wolf in one direction and Mackle and me in the other. The plan was simple. There would be cargo bays along the hull. We would open as many hatches as possible, Mackle by think-speaking to them and me and Wolf by jimmying the controls, dumping bays into the vacuum as we went. Job would skim in with *Fenris*'s mouth wide open and scoop up as much as he could. Then he'd pick us up, and we'd be on our way.

*Maybe sausage*, Mackle was thinking. He peered into one of the doorways we passed, and I heard words I couldn't understand as he convinced the computer to open the exterior bay doors. This one was pressurized, which made it easier for the containers to drift loose.

"Air, Mackle," I whispered. "Talk."

*Safer to think.*

"You're afraid!"

*So are you, Lila.*

I pushed past him toward a terminal several doors away to show I wasn't and then stabbed at the buttons trying to get the bay beyond it open.

Spots of light appeared around the corridor's bend.

Wolf taught us when we were just cubs that surprise was the best defense. I pushed off toward the lights, aiming so I would skim the wall and offer the least exposed target. At the curve of the passageway I could see them, three crewmembers with lights and guns.

My first knife caught one of them in the leg, and the second got another in the chest. Then I was past them, and one was screaming and another was shooting. I heard Mackle yelling too, both in my ears and my thoughts. I reached for another knife and a handhold to reverse momentum, but something hit my arm. One of the guards tumbled by, and I saw a knife in his back, which meant Mackle was throwing too. But now there were more guards. A voice was speaking loudly, repeating the same word over and over again. After I second I realized it was "boarders" and that it was talking about us.

We were supposed to run. If there were too many to fight, that's what we did. Mackle was gone, which meant he had done what he was supposed to do. I tried to find a terminal so I could open a door and suck out the air. They hadn't had time to grab pressure suits, so that would hurt them a lot more than it would hurt me. But my arm burned, and someone grabbed my other arm. There were more screams, and thuds, and a low guttural roar.

Then there was Wolf.

~

"Two." I held up my fingers proudly. "I got two, and Mackle got one."

Job nodded. His fat, pink fingers were wrapping gauze around my arm. "And they got you, Lila."

I glanced down. "Just a little."

"You're going to have to stay inside until this heals. Your skin isn't a good seal against vacuum when it's torn."

Job was right. It had hurt like hell getting off that ship and into naked space. Mackle had slipped out an airlock, like I thought. Wolf had... Well, I hadn't seen very well what Wolf had done. But it had involved a lot of broken bodies and then hauling me out an airlock. Job was waiting beyond, and the mouth of *Fenris* was wide. Wolf had thrown me aboard.

"What did we get?" I was anxious to get back down to the *Fenris*'s main bay.

"Mackle and Wolf are securing everything now."

"Securing?"

"Convoy ships are getting close. We're going to have to run. Strap yourself in."

I hated running. Running meant dodging stones and dropping gas to confuse sensors and generally being miserable until either Job or Wolf thought we were safe or I got sick.

Or both.

"Don't tell me what's happening," I told Job. "Don't be like those pilots on the vids who are always cursing under their breath and explaining why the ship is about to come to pieces around them."

Job smiled and left.

I didn't care what he said; I wasn't going to stay behind, strap in, or stay put. He wasn't Wolf. He wasn't in charge.

I waited a minute and then followed him.

By the time I got up to the control deck (getting tossed against the curv-foam and canvas walls three or four times as Job kept throwing relative-up in different directions trying to shake pursuit), Wolf and Mackle were already there beside him. They didn't like staying below during a chase either.

"Did we get any good stuff?" I asked when I burst in. Wolf growled from where he clung to holds beside Job.

"Lots of food. No sausage though." Mackle shrugged. "But some clothes too, and some medical things I want Job to look at."

"Two, Wolf!" I said. I held up my fingers.

Wolf flashed a scowl and held up one hand, all fingers extended. He closed it and opened it again twice.

"Fifteen? That was probably everyone on the ship!"

The *Fenris* bucked and spun. Outside the window, stones careened by thick and fast. I watched Job's fingers (thick and soft but so much more flexible than my own) dance across the controls. He sat, strapped into a narrow chair against the shifting gravity, while the rest of us stood anchored to holds in the walls around him. My arm ached.

"There are a lot of ships, Wolf," Job said. His voice was tight with concentration.

Wolf snarled a question.

"Searchers, yeah. But..." The floor dropped away from underneath us as Job rolled us below a stone. "A few ship designations I haven't seen before."

The stones were a vast debris field surrounding Horus, stretching from the edge of the red star's radiation zone to where Firstworld floated a few days' journey outward. As long as I could remember, the stones had been our home and hunting ground. When people first came to Horus from the Hearthstar, they hoped there would be planets like Hearth close in to Horus. What they found instead were the stones, and the only places they could park their big crossing ships and build cities were on the moons of outer gas giants like Firstworld. But smaller ships passed through the stones all the time, either to travel from one side of Horus system to the other or to search for minerals. And when they did, we took what we could from some and tried to stay out of the way of the rest.

Job had explained this to me and Mackle when we were younger, but I only remembered it because of the glowing models he showed us: Horus sitting fat and red with a wide ring of fine golden powder around it and the big planets spinning out beyond its edge. I used to peer at the model as closely as I could, until my nose bit into the book's beam and cast a shadow across the system. It was unbelievable to me that those tiny bits of light were the immense stones we lived on and among.

We spun again and dove through a gap that closed behind us.

Mackle whistled. Job was definitely scared. He was pushing the *Fenris* harder than we had seen him before. Wolf caught it too and actually touched Job on the shoulder.

Job started. "I'm sorry, Wolf. I..." He licked his lips, his eyes never leaving the viewers in front of him. "One of the ships has an Admin crest."

Wolf bared his teeth.

We avoided convoys that contained Admin. Admin had controlled Horus system since a revolt gave them control of the original crossing-ships before Mackle, Job, or I were born. There had been some kind of war between the crews of those ships and the first Admin, which claimed to represent passengers and cargo. Admin won.

Wolf had taken a ship with an Admin crest just once, and it had been carrying lots of weird equipment and three frozen bodies: me, Mackle, and Job. Job said we were an experiment, created by Admin to be soldiers who could fly in vacuum and leap from stone to stone like Wolf, only that the experiment hadn't worked for Job.

The ship shuddered in a new way, a sort of stuttering cough. Wolf barked.

"I'm trying!" Job shouted. "They're too fast, and there's too many of them. One of them just fired a brace of bind-vine into *Fenris*'s ass."

Wolf flashed back down the throat of the ship before I had even loosened my grip on the holds. Then Mackle and I nearly collided in our haste to follow, racing down the length of the ship on all fours. I had never seen bind-vine, but I knew what it could do. If the seeds burst and their leaves unfurled toward Horus, roots would dig through the skin of the ship in minutes. If we didn't get outside and cut them out, we were done.

By the time we were out the airlock, Job had put the ship into a gentle spin and Wolf had both his bolt-knives out, raking

*Fenris*'s canvas skin. The spin meant we had to stay tethered, but it also meant everything Wolf mowed spiraled off the ship in writhing strands of green. He glared at us as we hurled out the airlock past him. Then our lines went taut and we spun back to the ship and began hacking at the carpet of spreading vines.

Job had been right. My arm was burning agony. I could feel blood bubbling under the wound.

Mackle and I cut at the plants wiggling and squirming like worms. It was nasty stuff, already pushing into the cracks between hull plates and canvas. When I pulled it, tiny roots wrapped my fingers, scraping like wire. I wondered what they would have done to Job's skin.

I glanced upward. We were in the middle of a mass of stones, but I could see a few golden hulls among them. The searching ships were close.

There was a lot of the bind-vine, but I think we could have pulled it all off before it did serious damage. We didn't get the chance. I felt a prickling sensation on my back and looked up to see the entire side of the *Fenris* bathed in light. I didn't know what a tension-beam felt like, so I wasn't sure what was happening.

Wolf knew. He arched toward us, slicing through our tethers and crashing into both of us like a rogue stone. I felt something in my side crack. But then his momentum was transferred and Mackle and I were spinning away. Looking back, the *Fenris* was cloaked in green with golden vessels around it. The light had Wolf now instead of us. It was pulling him into a hatch on the belly of one of the ships.

Mackle and I spiraled into emptiness.

*I can't hold my breath any longer.*

We were floating among the stones. The vacuum was starting to make my skin burn. Blood hissed from my wounded arm like air from a hole in hull canvas.

*Neither can I.* Mackle's eyes, double-lidded, were wide and touched with frost.

I couldn't see *Fenris.* Wolf was gone. Job was probably gone too, the ship torn to shreds by the digging green vines.

*What do we do?*

Our trajectory wasn't taking us close to any of the stones, and there was no way we would be able to find one of our nests without the *Fenris* or a whole lot more time than we had.

*Don't be afraid.*

*I'm not.*

Mackle took my hand. *Yes, you are. So am I.*

I sobbed once, and then there was nothing left. The cold gnawing at my limbs moved into my chest.

We died out there together, in a wilderness of stones.

WE WOKE BACK IN THE MAIN BAY OF THE *FENRIS.*

"I didn't know you could do that," Job was saying. He was bent over us, surrounded by the new medical equipment we had just liberated. Visuals danced on a screen beside me, a body outlined in greens and purples.

"Do what?" My head hurt and my tongue felt too cold to move.

"Go into stasis," Job explained. His eyes were wide with concern, and he blinked his single lids over them. "Go dormant. Your heart slowed way down and your body just sort of shut off. You were frozen solid when I found you."

"How long?" Mackle lay next to me. He didn't sit up, but his eyes were unlidded and open.

"Three days." Job frowned and looked back at his screens.

*Three days?* Mackle's thought-shout made us both wince. *They've had Wolf this entire time?*

I touched his arm to calm him. It felt like ice.

"It took me several hours just to get your body temperatures up to normal." Job chewed his lower lip, something I had never been able to do to my own. "I didn't want to wake you before then."

"What about you?" I asked. "What happened?"

"I ran. They didn't chase me. Maybe they just wanted Wolf. The bind-vine was pushing through the hull, so I dove into the radiation zone, as close to Horus as I could get." He shivered. "It fried the vines off the ship but it made me pretty sick too. There was medicine in this stuff for radiation poisoning."

"And then you came to find us?"

He nodded. "I tracked you. But it still took me a couple of days. And when I found you, you were completely frozen."

*What about Wolf?* Mackle thought-shouted at us again.

"He's right." Job sighed. "We've got to get him."

I knew Mackle was right, but I was annoyed he was the first to say it. "How?"

"The ships that took him left the stones," Job said. "They probably took him up to the planets, to some Admin base on one of the moons."

I pushed my fingers through my hair, which was nearly as thick and tangled as Wolf's and like his spilled down my neck and grew from my back and shoulders as well. It was still cold to the touch. "Why did they want him? Because of all the stuff we've stolen?"

Job crossed his arms. "I don't think so. There are a lot of pirates in the stones, and Admin doesn't bother taking them captive. I think they wanted Wolf because of what he is."

"What is he?" Mackle asked. His voice was as raw and raspy as mine.

"Like you guys," Job said. "He's like you." We waited. "Lila.

Mackle. You know you and Wolf aren't like me. Or like most people, in other ships and on the moons. Maybe they're looking for you because of what you are."

"They've left us alone so far," I muttered.

"Maybe they've been waiting."

"For what?" I asked.

Job looked from me to Mackle but just shook his head. I was trying to process this when Mackle interrupted again. "Fine. So they want to experiment on Wolf? They want to know how he works?"

"They let *Fenris* get away once they had Wolf," Job said slowly. "Maybe he's important to them. And if he's important, then you guys would be too."

"Then we offer them a trade." It was only the start of an idea, but I tried to make it sound like it was a lot more. "If they want people like us, they'd probably rather have two kids than one adult. Contact them. Tell them you'll trade us for Wolf."

Job shifted his hold beside the table and looked miserable. "I already have."

WE HELD OUR BREATH AND WATCHED THE VESSEL APPROACHING through the airlock windows. It was golden like the others had been, bloated like a huge balloon. I couldn't understand how something so ungainly maneuvered through the stones. *Fenris* seemed tiny and sleek in comparison, despite its canvas patches.

I was angry at Job. Part of me said we couldn't trust him now because he had been willing to trade us to get Wolf back. But he had thought we were dead. Could I blame him? If I were left alone in the stones, wouldn't I have done the same thing?

More than that though, I was frustrated with what he had said. I wasn't stupid. I knew we were different. We never saw other people like us on any of the ships we boarded. But the idea that Admin had gone after Wolf because of what he was, and that maybe they had actually been after me and Mackle instead, made me feel there was a new gulf between us and the rest of the universe.

And why now? We had been chased before. Had we just gotten unlucky this time, or had something happened that made Admin want to come into the stones to find us? I tried to recall anything out of the ordinary about the ship we looted. It seemed like one of any number of nameless cargo vessels we had stolen from before.

It didn't make sense.

I pushed the questions out of my mind and tried to wait, motionless beside Mackle in the tiny lock. His hair, longer and finer than mine, tickled my nose. We had no idea whether Wolf would be on the approaching ship. If the Admin officers Job contacted were lying, he wouldn't be there.

But we were lying too.

We had to look like two bodies in stasis. I tried to will myself back into hibernation, though I wasn't sure how it was supposed to work.

The other ship stopped within throwing distance of us. If they were lying, they might just take what they wanted. But we were gambling they would be too worried about damaging us, if we were as valuable to them as Job thought.

An airlock on the ship opposite popped open, and something tumbled out. It was Wolf, bound and kicking vigorously. An instant later, our own opened and Mackle and I fell into space. We had to float until we were close enough to Wolf. Job was supposed to grapple him into the *Fenris* while Admin took Mackle and me aboard their ship.

I let myself rotate backward and saw *Fenris* spin into view. It still had brown, withered vines clinging to its hull.

We weren't in stasis or dead. That was the trick. We would grab Wolf and use the propulsion belts we were wearing to jet back to the ship. When we did, Job would vent all the other airlocks, which we had filled with smear, cloaking the ship and providing cover to get back into the stones. Hopefully they wouldn't fire, because they wouldn't want to risk damaging all of us.

But maybe we were wrong. Maybe they didn't care.

Or maybe they could see we were lying.

We were almost to Wolf.

I was facing the wrong way, so I didn't see the tracers lance out from the Admin ship. Mackle's think-shriek was so loud I gasped, vacuum cutting into my lungs like knives. I felt the flare of heat on my skin and turned.

*Fenris* disappeared in a haze of light and flame.

Wolf snapped his bonds.

IN MY MIND, ALL I COULD SEE WAS JOB, OVER AND OVER AGAIN. The Admin ship banged its airlock shut and sent tracers after us, smaller ones that were probably meant to knock us out. But we reached Wolf and passed him the bolt-knives hidden under our belts. Wolf threw me toward the ship's engine and Mackle toward its control deck. Before the curve of the ship hid him from view, I could see Wolf carving a hole in its hull large enough to crawl through.

Once I had a grip on the hull myself, I started doing the same. I didn't want to think about what Wolf was doing to whomever he found inside, but then I thought about Job again and didn't really care. I was forcing open an access port when I felt an airlock farther down the deck open up. A moment later the door beneath me opened as well.

*We're in! It's open!* Mackle's thought-speak came faint with distance. Either Wolf had triggered something inside, or Mackle had thought open the ship's doors.

I climbed in, hoping someone would come out fighting. Instead, the few people I saw were choking on vacuum. One guy was struggling to get himself into a thinsuit, but I kicked the helmet out of his hands and then kicked him in the face and moved on down the corridor, opening every door I found.

*I'm turning you inside out*, I thought-spoke at them, though they probably couldn't hear me. *I'm letting the vacuum into your shitty little ship like you let it into mine. See if you can handle it any better than Job.*

In one room there were some crewmembers ready with guns and suits. I killed the lights, unreasonably proud of myself for a quick success with thought-speak to the computer. I could see better than they could, and I ricocheted between them, digging in with my heels and my blades. By the end of that, I was starting to get tired, and I grabbed a thinsuit helmet that had been ripped off in the melee and took a few deep breaths.

When I got to the main control room, Mackle and Wolf were waiting for me and there weren't many crewmembers still moving. I was starting to calm down, and I could tell they were too, but Wolf hadn't done all the damage up there by himself. There were several people on the ground gasping when Mackle finally cycled air back into the room.

"They might not all know what happened," I said, when the air was thick enough again to carry our voices. I leaned against one of the chairs in the room, suddenly sick. "Some of them might not have done anything."

I was trying to say that they all looked like Job to me. With their helmets off and again in the grip of air, it was hard to not see his wide, pale face on all of theirs.

Wolf had taken the controls and moved the ship until the wide viewports looked out into the wispy cloud of expanding debris that had been the *Fenris*.

He howled.

It was a sound we had never heard before, something that seemed to rise from his guts and rip outward, making the deck plates vibrate and the walls groan. In another moment Mackle added his voice, and then I did the same.

The space in front of the ship was empty.

Job was gone.

WE CARRIED THE BODIES INTO ONE CARGO HOLD AND MOVED THE crew who were still alive into another. Then we gathered up all the weapons and thinsuits and piled them in the command deck. There were about a dozen crewmembers still alive or wounded. There were about twice that many dead.

I didn't try to count how many had been mine this time.

Wolf took the controls. I had never seen him pilot a ship, though he must have been sailing *Fenris* for years before he found us. His long, stiff fingers were awkward, but he managed. We moved back into the stones, the wide Admin ship's bulk moving through them with less grace than our narrow, patched *Fenris*.

"What do we do now?" I asked.

The sounds of this new ship were hushed, not like the constant wheezing and snaps of the *Fenris*. In the silence I could hear Mackle's ragged breathing as he leaned over Wolf's shoulder.

"Job was right," he said suddenly, straightening. "Right about Admin. About them watching us."

"What do you mean?" I asked.

He was staring down at a holographic overlay of sensor data splayed out before Wolf. It showed a field strewn with stones, a god's-eye view from here to Horus.

"Their sensors." His eyes were wide. "They're stronger than

anything I've seen. Better than we had on the *Fenris*. They could find anything in here." He paused. "Which means ships like this could have found us a long time ago. Any time they wanted. They were watching us."

Wolf growled softly.

I stared down at the field of stones and tried to imagine what Job would say to that. He was always able to link things together into logical sequences until he reached a reasonable conclusion and could tell the rest of us, the rest of his pack, what to do.

"If they could see us," I said slowly, "but never caught us, it was because they didn't want to. They could watch us, but they left us alone."

"Why?" Mackle countered, his voice as sharp as his eyes. "And why let us take all those ships?"

"We always had enough," I said thoughtfully. I imagined Job standing beside me, nodding his head encouragingly at my train of thought. "And we learned. We were being trained. We were growing up." I trailed off, picturing the stones as a huge testing ground with unseen Admin observers pacing the parameter.

Wolf was watching me silently.

"But why kill Job?" Mackle asked softly.

Wolf turned back to the sensors with a searching expression, letting his fingers fly over the controls. The projected stones and the spaces between them shifted colors as he scanned the spectrum.

"I don't know." My vision of Job disappeared, but not before I saw his face swell and distend with the kiss of vacuum. I shook my head. "Maybe he wasn't part of their plan. Maybe he got in the way."

"What plan, Lila?" Mackle's voice had an edge of rising panic. "What do you mean?"

The sensor display stopped its dance and now held a new object. The flurry of stones around it had become muted and grey. Among them, like a beacon through signal noise, burned the luminous ghost of a ship, huge, at the very edge of Horus's radiation zone.

"What is that?" I asked, ignoring Mackle's question.

Mackle turned back to the display, his question forgotten. "A derelict." He leaned over Wolf's wide shoulder to look closer then glanced at Wolf's hands, which were now frozen at the controls. "Wolf's recalibrated the sensors." He shook his head. "Admin didn't see this. They might have been watching us, but they didn't see this. Wolf," he muttered wonderingly, "what did you do?"

Wolf made a small noise in his throat, somewhere between curiosity and fear.

I leaned over the display beside Mackle. "If that ship was hidden from Admin," I whispered, "we could go there to hide."

"Not if we take this ship with us," Mackle countered. "They'll come looking for it. For us."

Wolf cut us off with a bark and motioned for me to take the controls. I did, taking the seat as he slipped away and began prowling the control deck like a caged animal. Seated, I saw what he had noticed: there was another cluster of ships heading down from the orbit of Firstworld, almost certainly Admin.

"Whatever we do," I told Mackle, "we need to act fast."

"I've seen that kind of ship before," Mackle said, his attention still on the display. "In a book Job had. It's a crossing-ship."

"But Admin destroyed them all."

"The ones they could find. The ones parked at the moons."

Wolf stopped prowling and gestured toward the ship on the display.

"Go there?" I asked him. "Are you sure?" When he nodded, I shrugged and thought-spoke to Mackle, *You'd better strap in. That's in the thickest region of the stones, and I can't fly like Job.*

*You better learn,* he thought back.

I TOOK US THROUGH THE STONES TO WHERE HORUS BURNED HOT and fat like a bloated fusion coil. Every shudder of a stone that glanced off the ship's hull felt like Job was trying to shake me awake from a bad dream. What if he had been right? If Mackle and I were created by Admin to be like Wolf? And now they wanted us back?

By the time we got to the hidden ship, my fingers were cramped and aching from clutching the controls, which had been made for people like Job with short, fat, flexible fingers. My arms were sweaty in the ship's too-warm, too-moist air, and I was tired and cranky by the time we had a clear visual on our destination.

It looked ancient. It was huge, long and flat and larger than any ship we had taken before. The whole thing appeared little more than a particularly symmetrical stone, and if you weren't close and knew to look for it, you might pass it by without even knowing it was there. It bore no external markings.

"What is that?" Mackle asked Wolf, pointing at the screen. "That's not an Admin crest."

Wolf just shook his head. His wide face was drawn.

*What?* I thought-spoke to Mackle. *What crest?*

*That big blue eagle projected off the front of the ship.*

*I don't see anything, Mackle.*

He scowled. *Wolf sees it,* he insisted. *So do I. A holographic emblem, rotating, projected along the foredeck. It's got four faces and six wings.*

"I can't see anything," I muttered.

We would have to board it; that was clear. Whatever answers there might be, about our past or Wolf's, weren't going to be found out there on the moons. They were going to be found here in the stones, and this was the only thing that Admin apparently hadn't touched. And Wolf recognized it somehow, that was clear as well.

We worked with Wolf to pull out the central piloting and processing circuits on our ship. The Admin ship's brain was big and it fought back, but Mackle thought-spoke at it loud and long until we were able to carve out all the main controls into a box that fit on Wolf's back. We left only stabilizers and life support in the lobotomized control center. Then we went down to the prisoners in the cargo bay.

*Can any of you think-speak?* Mackle thought-yelled at them. Most of them stared blankly, but one woman near the rear flinched and raised her hand. Wolf grabbed her and pulled her into the corridor with us.

"You're captain now," I told her. I pointed at the box on Wolf's back. "We've got all the ship-brains with us. You think-speak to Mackle every fifteen minutes that you're all still here or we pop the ship open."

The woman nodded grimly. She had a uniform the color of our skin with a tiny blue Admin crest printed on the breast. "What if I can't think-speak loud enough for you to hear?"

"We're not going far."

"Where are you going?"

I shook my head and Wolf growled. "Every fifteen minutes. Wait on the command deck."

When she left, we went to an airlock. Since we didn't know how long it might take to get inside the crossing-ship and whether it would have any air when we did, Mackle and I brought thinsuits from the command deck and shrugged into them. Then we sliced long holes in the rest so the crew couldn't use any. Wolf refused to put one on.

"What is this ship, Wolf?" I asked him before we cycled out of the lock. "You've seen it before."

The airlock's suction kicked on, pulling our air back into the ship. It drowned out his growl, but what I heard sounded like *home*.

WE PITCHED DOWNWARD TOWARD THE DERELICT, ARCHING OUT using tiny vent-bursts from our suits. Wolf as usual was far ahead and didn't need any corrective propulsion to realign his perfectly coordinated leap. I half-expected tracers to lance out from the ship behind us, but it just sat there fat and stupid, stripped of any ability to act on its own.

The deck of the crossing-ship when we touched down was strange. It wasn't the cold metal of the vessels we had taken or the thick canvas of the *Fenris*. It was rough, almost like rock. We pulled ourselves along the exterior, looking for a door or a gap where the hull was marred by old impacts, but the scars were all sealed tight.

Eventually we were beneath where Mackle said the great eagle was suspended. He told me it hung over us like a blue cloud and even shielded his eyes against its glow, but I could see nothing.

I growled and pulled my helmet off, feeling the welcome chill hit my face and hair. Things looked too sharp through the glass of the helmet. They were better through the outlids I blinked over my eyes now. With them I could see what I hadn't before: seams of a portal directly below us. I touched Wolf's arm and pointed.

I thought he would draw his bolt-knives and carve open the doorway, but he didn't. Instead he went down on his knees against the hull, pressing his forehead to the base of the outlined entry. The plates beneath me vibrated as a door sluiced open.

Inside the ship, it smelled like death. But at least there was a smell, which meant there was air. I tried not to breathe it greedily, conscious that Wolf still showed no vacuum fatigue. The smell was strong. I tried not to think about the fact that it probably came from things that had been trapped inside for a long time.

*It's old, Lila,* Mackle thought-spoke at me. I could feel the fear under his words. *But Wolf knows this place. Look at him.*

I did, and I could see Mackle was right. Wolf had a searching look in his eyes, like he was remembering being here and playing out in his head something that had happened.

The doorway opened into a long, sloping corridor. It was wider than anything on the Admin ship and longer and straighter than anything had been on the *Fenris,* which had short tangled corridors where it had any corridors at all. The walls were of the same material as the outside: brown and pitted, more like rock than metal. The corridor burrowed into the ship. We drifted down it, following Wolf, to where it ended at a vast cavern bathed in a blue glow. The whole thing sloped down before us like a shallow bowl or auditorium.

"What is this place, Wolf?" I whispered.

Wolf ignored me. It was like he was in a trance, moving down into the depression where the blue light was the brightest, propelling himself loosely with his toes. When Wolf reached the center of the chamber, the blue light flared brighter. The upper portions of the space, which had been invisible before, became clear. The interior of the ship was even larger than I thought. If this had indeed been a crossing-ship, one of those that came from Hearth to Horus, then it had held room for thousands and thousands of cargo.

*We're still here.* The thought-speak was muffled by distance, but I knew Mackle could hear it clearly. The Admin woman was checking in.

*Stay there*, he thought back.

"Is she lying?" I whispered.

"She must still be close, or we couldn't hear her."

I nodded. But that didn't mean she hadn't released all the

prisoners and taken control of the ship again. This whole plan was starting to seem stupid. We should have taken the Admin ship to one of our nests in the stones and then blown it up.

No, I reminded myself, because that wouldn't have changed anything. Admin would still have been watching us. They would have just come after us again. This sleeping giant of a ship might be our only real means of escape.

Something was growing at the center of the bowl-shaped depression as Wolf approached it, something that looked like a blue fountain. Wolf stopped, and Mackle and I stared. The light shaped itself into a face, soft and round like Job's.

"Crewman?" it asked. The voice was soft and clear, belying its projected size. "What is your status?"

Wolf said something we couldn't understand, a low guttural clicking we had never heard from him before.

The face closed its eyes for a moment in response. "*Chesapeake* has been abandoned one-hundred fourteen standard years, according to internal chronometers. The mutiny was successful and Colonial Administration is in control?"

*Who is it?* Mackle thought-spoke.

I shook my head.

Wolf answered, and the face spoke again. "Who accompanies you? They are not crewmen."

The vague distaste visible in his vast expression bothered me, and I felt my hair bristle. "Who are you?" I asked it.

"I am the cognitive echo of *Chesapeake's* navigational officer, fifth generation intra-crossing. At the time of the mutiny, I took control of the ship's systems and archives. After that, I have no information."

"What's a crewman?" Mackle asked.

"Engineered centuries ago in Earth System for service on crossing missions." The face looked sad. "Only males were engineered. Proprietary Earth technology. None were cultivated outside Earth System. A female," and here his huge eyes locked on mine, "is a new variation and represents a difficulty. If a female variant has been engineered, sub-species could propagate outside Earth control."

"No one engineered me!" I told it.

"Then where did you come from? You are outlaw technology and indication that the Colonial Administration has been attempting to create their own crewmen."

Beside me, Mackle shifted uneasily.

"So what?" I said. "We don't work for Admin. We're running from them. You can help us!"

"I'm afraid I cannot." He closed his huge eyes. "My mandate is the protection of Earth System technology. You represent a breach in that protection."

*Run, Lila!* Mackle thought-spoke at me.

I turned, but the corridor closed behind us like a fist. Wolf and Mackle moved together, grasping my arms and pulling me away, but something I couldn't see was holding me, forcing a weight into my stomach and throat. I coughed blood into the dark corridor.

*Fire on the crosser!* Mackle thought-screamed outward.

*What's going on?* The response of the woman on the Admin ship was almost too faint to register. *You took our weapons systems, remember?*

Mackle fumbled for the box Wolf wore on his back. My chest and throat felt like they were filling with ice.

*You have control back*, he thought-shouted, stabbing the buttons that would release aspects of the ship-brain. *Fire on the ship now, or I pop yours open!*

The concussions were almost too faint to feel, but the luminous face blurred for a moment. Whatever grip it held me in loosened.

"The *Chesapeake* is under attack," it said.

Mackle and Wolf pulled me up the corridor, but the face followed. "You cannot leave," it said almost apologetically. "If there are viable female crewmen, there is the possibility of an independent breeding program."

Wolf shouted something in a low, guttural language I half understood.

"If you are the ranking crewman left in Horus system, that places you in command," the face acknowledged. "But my primary mandate—"

Wolf cut him off, louder and more insistent.

"Direct image downloading? Possible, but the results are variable. Only certain specimens are compatible. For an engineered crewman, it is doubtful—"

Wolf roared, and the face blinked.

"Commencing," it said.

Something flared behind my eyes and everything—the face, Mackle, Wolf, the strange walls of the corridor—dropped away. I saw seven ships like the *Chesapeake* coasting into Horus System after a voyage I knew had taken centuries. I could see within the ships, hollowed asteroids with entire cities hidden away inside. But out near their surfaces, in caverns like this that honeycombed the outer layers, were people like Wolf. People like Mackle.

But no one like me.

I understood.

I awoke to arguing. Someone was shouting at Wolf, and he was growling back. We were in a corridor outside an airlock. The woman we had left in charge of the ship was blocking Wolf's path back into the ship.

"He's hurt," she was yelling. "I can't understand what you're saying, but if you don't let me get him to Medical, we won't know how serious it is."

I admired her. She was standing up to Wolf. He seemed

taken aback as well, though he didn't want to let either of us out of his sight.

Wolf was carrying us both, as he used to when we were just pups learning to leap from stone to stone. Mackle was under his arm, his face a sickly yellow. Whatever Wolf had ordered the face on the ship to do, it hadn't worked for Mackle like it had for me. I pushed away from Wolf, woozy, and fell forward. The woman and the wall both caught me.

"You too," she said. "You both need medical attention."

I took a deep breath and tried to stand.

"Wolf, take Mackle to Medical with her." I nodded to the woman, which set my head spinning again.

"Janid," she said.

"With Janid."

Wolf growled a question.

"I'm going to the command deck. I think it worked. Whatever you asked the face on the ship to do. Downloading an image into my brain. It distracted it long enough that it stopped trying to kill me, and I think the memory thing worked."

He growled again.

"I'll figure it out. Take care of Mackle."

But there was nothing to figure out. I had the picture in my head. Wolf ordered the computer or the cognitive echo or communication officer to download enlightenment, and now I had it. I knew the schematics of the *Chesapeake*. I knew details of the mutiny, even though that data was itself a century out of date.

We didn't have much time. Admin hadn't been able to find the *Chesapeake* because it was an asteroid hidden among asteroids. But they would be able to find one of their own stolen ships. The vessel we were on now wouldn't be safe for long.

At the command deck I checked the status of our prisoners on board. They were still secure. I did a quick sweep of the space around us. There were Admin ships patrolling farther out, but none had ventured in toward the radiation zone yet. With surface flares, the boundary of that zone changed almost daily, but for now tolerances were all normal.

I started scanning through the ship's data system, wishing Job were here to help me figure out what to do. When Mackle lobotomized the ship-brain, he compromised all clearances, so I had access to all files. I looked for information about us. Job was right: Admin had been monitoring us for years. But I didn't find anything that actually told me why.

With what I knew now though, I could guess. Admin wanted to see how we would grow left to ourselves. They had made us from genetic material of surviving or prisoner crewmen from their mutiny. They wanted new crew, people who could do their work in space, take care of the outsides of their ships, maybe even build the orbital cities that were springing up in orbit around Firstworld. But maybe we would turn out to be too wild, too uncontrollable. So they wanted Wolf to train us. They wanted Job to show us what it meant to be human.

Lights flickered on the display. Admin ships were pushing into the stones, approaching our position. *Janid*, I thought-spoke.

*I'm here.* It was easier to hear her, on the same ship.

*How's Mackle?*

*He's going to be okay. I'm not sure what happened, but I've given him stims, and he's coming around.*

*Is Wolf with you?* She wouldn't have poisoned him with Wolf watching, and Mackle could hold his own against her, if need be, as soon as he was awake.

*Yes.*

*Send him up as soon as Mackle is awake.*

When Wolf arrived, I pointed at the long stone profile of the crossing-ship in front of us. "Can you control that from here?"

He grunted a question.

"Try. Open a channel with it and see. We've got a fleet of a dozen searchers coming up on us, and we need some tricks."

He looked at me.

"They want us," I explained. "They think we're their property —me and Mackle. They built us and then let you find us. But now they want us back. They didn't care about Job. I don't think they care about you either."

He didn't say anything in response. There was nothing to say. He had been running from Admin his entire life after the mutiny, a sole survivor hiding out in the stones until he found us. Now he sat and scrolled through a communications array, finally switching to a channel and barking out a string of the strange clicking he had used aboard the other ship. After a minute he turned back to me and nodded.

Admin wanted a race of servants, like crewmen on the original crossers. They didn't have the technology to clone a race of males like the original crossers from Hearth did.

It was easy to see what they wanted me for.

"Okay," I said. "This is it, Wolf." My anger had become cold and brilliant, like the light of Horus. I looked at the star's wide face, and I wondered suddenly about the cold beyond the stones, the cold of space between the stars. "We have to go. We have to leave."

When people left Hearth, they carved out into the emptiness in a dozen different directions. Every world they arrived at must have had a different story, and those stories were now separated by hundreds of years of darkness. That meant there were other worlds out there, maybe places where crewmen still lived at peace with cargo. We had no place here, in the story Admin had built around Horus star.

Maybe we could find a better one someplace else.

The ships were moving in, threading their way through the stones. We couldn't hide. But they still didn't know the crossing ship was here.

"Now, Wolf!" I said, when they were almost close enough to spin a net around us. He barked code into the grid before him, and a hundred tiny petals spun off the crosser. Four and then five of the Admin ships broke apart in the sudden flurry of projectiles. I wondered if the face that had tried to kill me was exulting, whether it knew these were the descendants of the rebels that had scuttled its fleet.

It wasn't enough. Even if we survived a fight with these ships that were now falling back to safer positions, they would send others. We couldn't hide on this stolen ship forever, and I couldn't hide on the crosser.

*Job could do this*, I thought and hadn't realized I had thought-spoke until I heard Mackle's faint answer from somewhere below.

*So can you, Lila.*

I pushed some numbers at Wolf and watched him stare at them, pulling his long stiff fingers along his chin. Finally he nodded and barked again at the huge crosser-ship. I heard it try to argue, but Wolf shouted it to silence.

It began to fall toward Horus, down through the stones toward the radiation zone. It was broad like a stone itself and rotated its wide side so we could fall behind it. This way, we could get closer to Horus than would have otherwise been possible, far closer than Job would have come when he burned the bind-weed from the *Fenris*'s hull. I let us fall, following the larger ship.

This close to Horus the stones thinned. I had never seen the star so close, red and bloodshot but eclipsed by the crosser. It was throwing off flares even as we watched.

The edges of the crosser were glowing from heat, but I knew that its surface would cool again. There was no one aboard now, though there would be, eventually, when we cleared this sling-shot approach and hurled upward.

Outward.

*Where are we going, Lila?* I heard Mackle think-speak at me, but I think maybe the woman's voice was in there as well.

*I don't know*, I said. *Away. Maybe, eventually, back to Hearth.*

We had a crosser. We had cargo to fill it with.

We would find a way.

Wolf and I glared at the angry eye of Horus and howled as we passed it in the night.

# FROND

## ANNE E. JOHNSON

**About the Author**

Anne E. Johnson lives in Brooklyn, New York, where she writes fiction, poetry, and music journalism. She has over a hundred published short stories and about a dozen poems. Her novels include the humorous science fiction series *The Webrid Chronicles* as well as two historical fiction novels for middle-grade readers. When she's not writing, she teaches music theory and plays and sings in the New York Irish traditional music scene.

Raindrop shiny as mercury
silver and deadly poison
splits the dead brown air
rips open Gloria's cheek
a trail of fire down her skin
scent of acid

"Stay inside, love!"
how many times has Tara said this?
Gloria's wife wise good woman
pulling her down
back into the bunker
Gloria's sadness burns deeper than her skin

She remembers outside life
the time before, a time of green
rain smelled of moss and growth
brought life not death
some days her longing is so bad
her blood aches

Tara gentle and patient
pressing gauze to the wound
"We're low on med supplies"
Gloria struggles from Tara's arms
choking on the dead air
needing—*needing*—sunlight.

"Wait!" but Gloria can't wait
she'll let the poison eat her flesh
it couldn't be worse than in here
"I love you, Tara"
but what she really means is

goodbye

Up the ladder, shoulders scraping stone
unlatch the concrete door
heavier than her spirit
a slit of hazy fuchsia sun hits green
green? green!
the first new frond
in a decade.

# BLISS

## DAVIAN AW

**About the Author**

Davian Aw is a Rhysling Award nominee whose short fiction and poetry have appeared in over 30 publications, including *Strange Horizons, Abyss & Apex, Anathema, Star\*Line* and *Diabolical Plots*. He lives in Singapore with his family.

by generation five, they have forgotten the earth
from their coffin of lead and concrete hallways
flooded with electric light; they know
no other existence. if the surface is green again
or distant cousins roam its ruins, they do not
think of them, nor know to grasp the fantasy
of a land above, for walls bound their world
in strict parameter. still, their philosophers
ponder the heresies of a place beyond
as their poets work in whispers, spinning dreams
out of old-world rumours weft with hope
and the innocent bliss of not knowing. they speak
of winds and sunlight, the mysteries of sky,
a world with no end.

# THE GREAT SADNESS

## JENNIFER LORING

**About the Author**

Jennifer Loring's short fiction has been published widely both online and in print, appearing alongside Graham Masterton, Joe R. Lansdale, Elizabeth Massie, Ramsey Campbell, Kealan Patrick Burke, Steve Rasnic Tem, and Clive Barker, among many others. Longer work includes the novel *Those of My Kind* from Omnium Gatherum and the novella *Conduits* from LVP Publications. She holds an MFA in Writing Popular Fiction with a concentration in horror fiction and teaches online in SNHU's College of Continuing Education. Jenn lives with her husband in Philadelphia, Pennsylvania, where they are owned by a turtle and two basset hounds.

FLUFFY SHIELDED HER EYES FROM THE CLOUD OF DUST AND SNOW that rolled toward her when the building a few blocks away collapsed in on itself. It happened more frequently as cold and water damage pried the city's towers and residences apart. With the snow, the wind carried the Howlers' mournful cries up to the window where she perched. One day, probably sooner than she'd prefer, her clan would have to move from the relative safety of their home high above the ground in one of the towers where the Howlers could not climb.

The young ones gathered around Greycat, the eldest of their clan and resident historian. Wide-eyed and mewling with enthusiasm, the children stared at him in anticipation of one of his stories. Greycat settled into a comfortable position and curled his tail around himself. He would tell the tale the little ones always wanted to hear, the disappearance of the Tall Ones, who had vanished from the world nearly twenty-five years ago. Greycat believed, as nearly every Cat did—there was little evidence for any other theory—that their race had risen up against the Tall Ones and stamped them out of existence in the great Cattyclysm. It seemed plausible enough; Cats now ruled the crumbling monuments where countless Tall Ones once carried out the business of their lives. Yet the idiot Howelers, once the Tall Ones' faithful companions, had survived along with the Cats. The story did not account for this anomaly.

"But no one walks on two legs!" protested the smallest, little more than two huge eyes set within a ball of silver fur.

"The Tall Ones did," said Greycat. "That's what made them tall. But tallness did not make them kind, for they kept their own cousins in cages for their entertainment, and performed terrible deeds on them. They looked down on everything, proclaimed themselves the rulers of all they saw, and wished to subjugate the whole world. And when the Cats realized that the world was on the brink of destruction, they knew there was only one way to prevent it. They would have to eliminate the creatures who had been their devoted slaves."

"But how?" Silver Ball asked. "You said they covered almost all the land in the world!"

"Like fleas!" a black-furred girl piped up.

"Well now, that's the question, isn't it? Some say the Cats stopped catching mice and rats, and those mice and rats carried a dreadful and previously unknown disease into the Tall Ones' communities. Some say the Cats deliberately infected themselves with the fleas. What we do know is that within a matter of months, half of the Tall Ones all over Earth had died, and in the next few months, the rest followed. The Cats declared them extinct, and none has been seen in the years since." Greycat dug his claws into the pocked floor and arched his back as he stretched and yawned. He was missing a canine tooth and appeared to wear a permanent sneer. "The Tall Ones left behind cities all over the world, like the one we live in. In fact, their entire history likely remains intact, but because of the Howlers, we have not been able to go to ground level."

Fluffy, who proudly bore the name of generations of her ancestors, lifted her brachycephalic face to meet Greycat's yellow gaze. "The cities are falling apart. We don't have much time to find out what really happened, if we want to. And someone needs to scout for a new home before this building falls, too."

"You'll scare the children," Greycat admonished. "Besides, the ground is crawling with Howlers who would kill you as soon as look at you. You spend all your time staring out that window—you ought to know."

Fluffy's short face gave her something of a scowl to begin with, but she scrunched it up further. She caught most of the mice and birds that kept the colony's collective bellies full herself; Greycat's fattened form could attest to her prowess. He had a point, though. Not a single Cat had deciphered the

Howlers' coarse and guttural speech, which in doing so may have allowed at the very least a promise against violence. They had always been mortal enemies, the Howlers and the Cats. This, Greycat had assured, was ineluctable fact. At the current impasse, however, only bravery would carry a Cat forward into destiny.

"But think of it, Greycat. You would be remembered as the great historian of our people."

Greycat licked his paw and smoothed the fur on his head. One needed only to appeal to ego to persuade most Cats of anything. "Well, I do want our history to be complete, and this is the great unanswered question. But who will we send? I am too old."

Fluffy's scowl deepened. "Me, obviously. I'm not afraid."

"You're barely more than a kitten yourself!"

"I can do it. I'm quicker than anyone here." And smarter, she thought, but kept that to herself. "I'll leave at sunset." Cats were nocturnal, after all. Only the stupidest of beasts moved about during the day.

Greycat shook his head, but he never argued anymore. "Very well. But *be careful.*"

*I'm more than just a hunter,* Fluffy thought, but kept that to herself, too.

Fluffy spent the next few hours catching what she could— mostly for the kittens, who had not yet learned to hunt. Not effectively, anyway; their prey tended to escape because they still liked playing too much.

She crept out of the large, open space with its columns and chipped tile floors and began her descent to the ground. She would be safe on the floors where the stairs had given way; the Howlers could climb intact ones but not when several were missing or broken, and their jumping skills paled in comparison to the Cats.

For several days, Fluffy stayed on the last floor with a

broken staircase—the third—and observed the Howlers from the shattered window where she pretended to sleep and swiped unsuspecting sparrows and starlings as they passed. The icy wind of eternal winter drifted in to cleanse, if only temporarily, the dust and rot of the old building. Fluffy sensed the memories imprinted here of the Tall Ones, that mythical race gone only two and a half decades, yet long enough that no living Cat remembered them.

Even Greycat knew them only secondhand, from his parents, and he was nearly eighteen. But things had been different in his parents' time. The Tall Ones took kittens from their mothers just weeks after birth, so that they never remembered their parents. Greycat had been among the first generation born after the Cattyclysm, and the first to stay with his parents until they died.

This, he'd said, was why he had formed the colony. So that no Cat would ever again forget its family.

One of the Howlers was staring at her. He sported large, erect ears, a square muzzle, and a bushy tail. Something in his quick brown eyes denoted intelligence uncommon to his kind.

"Ma'am, are you in need of assistance?"

Fluffy froze. She moved only her eyes as she searched for whomever he might be speaking to. She was not yet ready to contemplate why she could understand him.

"Ma'am?"

"Who...?"

"I'm trained to communicate with various creatures, ma'am. I'm a Marine."

Fluffy scanned her memory banks for any mention Greycat might have made of Marines but came up empty. "What's a Marine?"

"A member of the naval-based infantry force, ma'am. I'm a soldier. I was trained by my father, as his father trained him."

A soldier. The Tall Ones had used soldiers in their attempts to dominate the planet. The Howlers were too stupid to think for themselves; they'd have done anything the Tall Ones asked. Just pawns desperate for approval.

But soldiers also protected people, and that was exactly what she needed.

"I'm looking for something. Can you help me find it?"

"Depends, ma'am. What are you looking for?"

"First, stop calling me 'ma'am.' My name is Fluffy." She flicked her tail for emphasis. "Second, I'm looking for the Tall Ones' history. The part that says what happened during the Cattyclysm."

The Howler cocked his head in the idiotic way they had perfected. "The *what* now?"

"You know. What happened when they disappeared."

He bared his teeth. She thought he might be laughing. "Sorry. I've never heard it called the, er…Cattyclysm, is it?"

"That's right. What do you call it?" Of course, they'd never give Cats credit for saving the world.

The Howler looked away, toward the snow-capped buildings jutting from the earth like the broken ribs of some giant, dead beast. Love for the Tall Ones was ingrained in their ancestral memory. They'd never been able to view the Tall Ones with objectivity, but if they were lucky, time would dull those bright colors.

"The Great Sadness." He swished his tail once, twice, then it stilled.

Fluffy rolled her eyes. She should have expected something as maudlin and pathetic. "Can you help me or not?"

"Yes. Yes, I can." He let out a series of short, sharp barks. "The feline is descending. Do not engage. I repeat, do *not* engage."

She could have pounced on one, clawed its eyes out, and run away before they knew what hit them. But the Howlers, ever eager to obey orders, backed off as instructed.

Fluffy carefully jumped from ledge to ledge until she reached the first floor. "What's your name, anyway?"

"I took the name of my grandfather. Buddy." He nosed around her, sniffed under her tail to gauge her mood. If he knew anything, he understood that Cat was a mood unto itself. "I can show you where the history is. But are you sure you want to know it?"

"Of course I do. I want to complete our knowledge."

Buddy gave a little shake of his head. "Follow me."

"What are you not telling me?" Fluffy pranced alongside him. Patches of broken asphalt appeared within the large stretches of weeds and wildflowers. Rusted automobiles and trucks decayed on either side of what had been a wide road; Greycat had said that the Tall Ones used these to transport Cats to a terrible place—a torture facility, really—of cold metal tables, of needles and sharp instruments. He called the proprietor of this house of horrors The Vet.

"We don't always want answers, even when we're looking for them. Maybe it's not what you're expecting. That's all."

"Do you know?" Fluffy stopped and raised a paw as if to swipe her claws across his big, stupid black nose. "Is that what you're not telling me?"

Buddy gazed straight ahead. "Best see for yourself."

They were heading toward the other side of the city. Her short legs struggled to keep up with his smooth, elastic gait that covered so much ground in so few strides. The brambles here found her long, luxurious fur all too hospitable.

"Climb onto my back," Buddy said.

Fluffy was about to argue, but she swallowed her pride and leapt up. She hooked her claws into the thick fur at his nape as he trotted, the buildings bouncing closer and closer, ominously, dead things once the center of life.

*Maybe it's a trick. Maybe he'll lure us down here one by one and feed us to the Howler pack he's probably hiding out here. Fat old*

Greycat wouldn't last long without Fluffy; he couldn't hunt on his own anymore.

"We're here." Buddy came to a slow stop before a storefront with numerous faded signs in the windows and a tattered striped awning. Fluffy hopped down into the snow, and Buddy nudged the glass door, already stuck partly open, with his muzzle.

Darkness inside. The stink of urine and feces, of some kind of recently active life. She felt Buddy's protective presence behind her.

"She stays in the back," he said. "Most of the time."

Well, this was an intriguing wrinkle. "She who?"

He scampered around Fluffy and headed toward an open door from which light glowed so dully it seemed more a repellant than an invitation.

A mournful howl shattered the stillness. Fluffy peered around the corner at a long-limbed creature with dark, choppy hair sprouting from its skull. Its eyes were glazed white, its skin bluish and crystalline despite being wrapped in several blankets. It sat near a pile of blackened wood scraps and a cooking pot.

Buddy was still howling, pausing now and then to nose what could only be a Tall One, as if he might coax her back to life. "She was the last one we knew to exist. She was born with immunity to the disease."

"She was here all alone?"

"Yes." His head drooped. "She was cold, and hungry, but I thought... She had survived all this time..."

Fluffy felt a twinge of sympathy she didn't have time to indulge. "Did she tell you anything? About what really happened?"

"She kept records somewhere around here. You can reach places I can't. If you can find them, I'll translate them for you."

Fluffy narrowed her eyes. "What's in it for you?"

Buddy lay beside the Tall One and licked her frozen hand.

"She was my friend. She would be glad to know that she hadn't written it all down for nothing."

Fluffy pounced onto a metal desk. Two shelves were bolted above it into the wall; they each held a number of small books, each bearing a number on the spine. She swiped at them until they tumbled to the floor so Buddy could read them.

"Well?"

"You're really sure you want to hear this?" He whined softly, but she would not be discouraged.

Fluffy sighed. "I've told you already."

"'I was just a child, but old enough to understand what we'd done. To everything. Poisoned it all. It was a perfect opportunity for disease to breed. Bad weather, no clean water. Overcrowding. Garbage everywhere. We'd forgotten where we came from. Wanted to convince ourselves that we weren't animals, never had been. That we were separate from nature by destroying it.'"

Greycat had been right about that part. "What about the Cats? Did we stop them? Did we save the world?"

Buddy gazed at her with sad brown eyes, then returned his attention to the book. "'I don't have much left to eat, and I'm getting too weak to forage or find gas for the generator. My garden died a while back. Mostly, though, I'm lonely, even though a German shepherd found me and has been keeping me company. Humans are social creatures, though. Part of me wants to find out if there are others still alive.

"'But the truth is that we don't deserve to be, because we've left nothing worth saving.'"

BUDDY STOPPED OUTSIDE THE CATS' BUILDING, AND FLUFFY jumped from his back. "I can't tell them it isn't true. The story is all we have. Even Greycat wasn't alive to remember."

"Then don't tell them. Dogs were bred to love humans, but we know they were flawed. We didn't tell them. We just loved them. Sometimes they needed that more than anything."

Fluffy looked up at the fragmented windows. She could see Greycat's yellow eyes peering out.

"So tell them what they need to hear—because you love them. Because they're all you have, like humans were all we had."

Fluffy took a few faltering steps toward the lowest ledge, then looked back at her unexpected new friend. "Thank you, Buddy. Will I see you again?"

"I'll be around. A Marine's job is to protect, after all." Buddy swished his tail. "Until next time, Fluffy. You can tell me all about this 'Cattyclysm' of yours."

She scurried back to him and reached up to tap his big black nose. He nuzzled the side of her head. "See you around, Buddy."

As she hopped onto the ledge and made her way back to the colony, Fluffy formulated a story that would satisfy the Cats— but mostly, the one she would most enjoy telling.

*Yes, we saved the world, but we didn't do it alone. The Howlers— who the Tall Ones knew as Dogs—loved their masters so much that they could not bear to see them destroy themselves.*

*So they helped us do it.*

# REVIVAL

## SUSAN SHELL WINSTON

**About the Author**

Susan Shell Winston lives in a small Texas town, just west of Houston and two stars east of the moon. Trained in Anthropology and in medieval French and English literature, she lived four years under a Celtic hillfort in the forests of Germany where the Brothers Grimm once walked. As neighbors bought their teas and medicines in local hexestuben (witches' huts) and carted their morning milk cans into quaint half-timbered towns, her fantasy worlds sprang to life around her. Her novel, *Singer of Norgondy*, is available at Amazon. A member of the first Odyssey Writing Workshop and chosen by her class to lead its first TNEO workshop for returning grads, Susan is now busy editing for New Myths, preparing her other novels in the Colonium series for publication, and, oh yes, collecting and reproducing medieval and Renaissance puppet plays. For more about her fantasy world, visit holdenstone.com.

CLARIN STOOD ON HER TOES TRYING TO SEE THE QUETZAL through the crowd. A clear, not quite human voice carried through the revivalist tent.

"Grawk."

A child on his progenitor's shoulder asked, "What's grawk mean?"

Clarin shot the same disapproving glance at the child everyone around her did. She had grown too mature to admit she didn't know either.

"Hush! The quetzal is speaking again."

Clarin could just see a slight curve of the brilliant blue and yellow feathers—the shoulder and back of the bird, she imagined. She had camped three days in line for the chance to come inside the quetzal's temple and hear her speak; yet here she was crushed behind thirty others against the canvas wall of the small tent. Most people her age and younger were a good foot taller than Clarin, their progenitors having opted for a height gene.

The bird said something else.

"'Power is,' she said this time!" shouted one of the onlookers near the front.

"Ahh." A pilgrim nearby nodded his head wisely and looked around him for agreement that the quetzal had uttered a great truth. "Power is!" he repeated happily.

"Power is what, didi?" the annoying child asked. "Power is what?"

And the annoying child's voice inside Clarin that she should have quelled years ago wanted to ask 'what' too. But part of maturing in today's world was learning to become your own island, learning to search for any answer you lacked on your own down time, never intruding on someone else's privacy by asking what you could find out for yourself with a few mental clicks on your house mouse. As it was, Clarin, still too often driven by her inner child's voice, might ask more questions than most users did. Everyone she texted with sounded as if they'd long grown out of wondering anything off line. Down time to them was game time, or else time to send back and forth the week's newest joke.

"Power is. Grawk." Clarin heard the bird herself this time. "Grawk, grawk. Power is grawk."

She'd done a search on the quetzal weeks before it arrived in New Haven. A blue macaw, Rob Larents of the EcoInstitute called it. A bird as large as a sea gull and more colorful than the pigeons and crows that flew around the rooftops of New Haven. Diegozoo had old CG images of macaw parrots, all patterned on the last surviving one in captivity that had died out fifty-seven years ago. The last surviving one in captivity, that is, until the quetzal was brought out of the AmaZone last year by the EcoInstitute.

"Grawk," the quetzal said. It lifted its great bright blue wings and flapped them, and as the crowd shifted back, crushing her, Clarin caught a glimpse of the bird bobbing its head up and down. *The eyes of a goddess.* Those who were blessed would recognize them when she looked at you, it was said.

Rob Larents of the Institute disclaimed the idea. Parrots, he said, could live a hundred years, and had once been taught to mimic speech. That this one spoke in words did not make it a goddess with a divine message. It may have merely copied sounds it had heard from other birds, and they perhaps from other birds that had escaped to the jungles the AmaZone had once been.

But everywhere the quetzal toured, the people knew better, and her Word had spread across the webmind. Scientists like Larents were the ones who had killed faith, who had left the world without a mystery; you had only to turn off your implant to feel the emptiness in life now, to ask yourself, "Is this all we have left?" *Believe*, the disciples of the New Word texted to one another, *believe again! The quetzal herself has come to save us.*

"Power is!" the quetzal claimed. "Poly, poly, power! Grrawk."

The moment of Election had come, the Manager said. Those in the tent filed one by one past the bird on their way out. Clarin held her breath, wanting so to believe, to be chosen, to listen again to her inner child's voice. And when her turn came, she reached out a hand towards the brilliant blue and yellow bird. The quetzal bobbed her head down and bit her finger. Clarin was, oh yes! she was, one of the chosen.

Elation lifted her, teaching her how to fly as she walked. She left the tent to become a disciple of the New Word, holding in her heart to repeat over and over and maybe someday understand, the last mystery she heard the quetzal speak: "Grawk! Poly want a grawker."

Her inner child's voice was quelled and finally answered; and Clarin knew she would become the best grawker ever.

# SECTION IV

## ACCEPTING LOSS

*For after all, the best thing one can do when it is raining is let it rain.*
*—Henry Wadsworth Longfellow*

# WELLSPRING

## WINNER FIRST PLACE, NEWMYTHS READERS' CHOICE AWARD 2019

## ALY PARSONS

**About the Author**

Aly Parsons leads a writers' group she founded in 1980 that includes professional and unpublished writers. Her story, "Cold Hall," appeared in the DAW anthology *Sword of Chaos* (republished electronically by the Marion Zimmer Bradley Literary Trust). She wrote the Afterword to Catherine Asaro's collection *Aurora in Four Voices*. Aly's work is in anthologies and online in *Pen in Hand* and *Magnets and Ladders*. After co-directing programming for the 1981-89 Unicons, she hosted Green Rooms, critiqued for the Millennial Philcon writers' workshop, and co-directed programming for the 2003 World Fantasy Con. She loves reading speculative fiction, suspense, mysteries, and historical fiction. A graduate of the Odyssey Workshop for writers of fantasy, science fiction, and horror, Aly lives in Maryland.

THE ROCK GROUP'S DRIVING RHYTHMS BOOMED FROM THE BAND shell through the amphitheater and up into the summer night. Gia danced out of the sweet smoke into the darkness beyond the crowd's fringe. Flashing a wicked grin over her shoulder, she kicked off her sandals and broke into a run. Night and her long, denim skirt concealed her lower body's changes. She rose to tiptoe on her bare feet, reshaping nails, bones, and muscles to goat hooves.

Lee, cautiously stepping around couples sprawled on blankets to get past the last of the audience, called, "Gia, wait up."

She bounded upslope, away from the concert's electric atmosphere of cheers and claps, frenzied dancers, and amped guitars. Adding a shimmer made her golden hair a taunting flag for Lee to follow.

The scant moonlight lit the way as Lee chased her toward the crest of the sea bluffs. She frowned as he fell further behind. Unsure which of them was the tease, she shifted back to full human form, halted amid upthrust rocks, and stripped.

Lee laughed as Gia drew him into the rock's shelter. They kissed while he helped her undress him.

She stuffed their clothes between boulders and moved a stone to hide the chink. She grabbed his hand and yanked him onward.

He gave a tug. "Gia, here we're hidden—and we can still hear the music." But her exuberance was contagious.

She danced them across the summit, springing past clumps of poppies, grasses swishing against their legs. Clouds veiled and unveiled the fingernail paring of moon. Gleams slid over their bodies, revealing their similarities: Hair like spun gold, slenderness of face and arms, tapered bulkiness of torso and legs.

Gia inhaled the scents of salt, fish, and kelp. Below, waves slammed, transmitting vibrations through stone and her bones, increasing her wild joy. She was bursting with song. The band's music, now inaudible to them, would keep the audience from hearing her voice if she sang. But she wouldn't want to attract other strays on these heights.

"Let's have a swim, Lee."

"Are you crazy? There's no way down to the water from these cliffs."

"So we'll fly!"

Lee took a step back. "What are you on?"

Gia laughed at his joke and stretched out her arms, head flung back. Twirling, she caught him in an embrace. "Ah, my Leandros, my lion." She brought her lips to his.

Cupping her shoulders, he returned her kiss with warm enthusiasm. They parted, smiling. She pulled her head back, smile faltering.

"Leandros?" she whispered. Never before had he failed to respond with his own endearment of "My Ligeia, my siren, my love."

He had the listening look of one awaiting clarification. No. He was only feigning ignorance. He wanted the clash that always resulted in lovemaking.

Laughing, she raised strands of her hair into hissing snakes, narrowing her face to give them substance. Calling up the power of her eyes, she struck—

And met no defense.

He stood rigid, mouth open in terror, eyes lifeless as a statue's. She stubbed her fingers against his cheek. Stone hard, stone cold. With a sob, she toppled him backward, exerting her strength to lower him gently to the ground.

Cold spread out from her depths. Too soon. Much too soon. How hadn't he known? He should have felt the strong urge to return to the sea when his time to renew himself had come. And why hadn't she noticed he now believed in his humanness?

Last moon dark, he was on the East coast, repairing hurricane damage at animal preserves. Then they'd been working at separate beaches, helping after that oil slick. How long since they even spoke of past times, let alone reshaped in each other's presence?

With caresses, she restored his suppleness, restarting all the familiar functions throughout his human shape, tweaked chemicals and massaged facial muscles to produce calm. The shock of the changes she'd forced had rendered him unconscious. When he revived, instinct would adapt him to the existence in which he found himself. She should carry him to where they'd left their clothes. He'd rouse hearing human music.

Images flashed through her mind: Singing to the fog in sweet harmony with her sisters on rocks as Leandros finned up out of the ocean, flopping back, sending sheets of spray over them while more kin bobbed in the waves, grinning. Leandros, whose earlier antics created the legend of the sphinx, mocking the Great Sphinx by crouching in lion form, trying to maintain a human face expressive of wisdom, then rolling on his back, whooping with laughter. She and Leandros, shaped as bearded serpents, his gold mane ashine with sunlight, as they wormed off a cliff to swim across a river.

Never again.

She longed to stay with him in human form, transforming alone in secret. She could play human while that was all he knew, continuing their satisfying work.

But how long had it been since he forgot himself? The slow decay of his cells had begun. For his sake, she dared not wait.

Calling up all her inner strength, she murmured, "Farewell, my golden lion," and kissed his human nose, his cheek.

It felt odd to have control of his body's reshaping. She brought out gills, increased the fats beneath his skin, made all the adjustments for withstanding pressure changes. Formed webbing between his fingers. Fused his legs. Shaped flukes.

From hair and skin to fluke tips, she shaded him slate blue to gray-green.

Gia stood, aerating her bones. She slimmed as she pushed substance out into huge wings sprouting white feathers tipped with gold. Her hair retreated, replaced with white plumage close against her scalp. Glancing up and around, she flicked her skin and feathers to midnight blue.

She levered Lee upright and hugged him against her, his back to her front, and sprang out over the cliff. They plummeted, sea foam reaching for them. Her wings snapped out to full extension.

She skimmed low over the waves, veering south.

There. Sleek dolphins leaping. She pressed her cheek to the side of Lee's head, let him drop.

Dolphins dove to intercept him. The alliance held. The dolphins would protect him. He would wake at ease with the sea, his human life a fading dream.

The world ocean should welcome him home, nourish him, restore him, and, to some extent, it would. During early cycles, an unguessable span of years had stretched until he recalled himself, his entire life, and her. Past renewals included a period of seeking: Knowing names by which they called each other, long before the ability returned to recognize individuals of their kin, no matter the shape.

A rock isle protruded above the waves. She alighted, startled seals plopping into the sea around her. Only seals. She couldn't remember when she'd last met others of her kin. She resorbed her wings. No knowing how many lonely years before her own renewal time arrived. It hadn't always been so.

When they first mated, their cycles locked, giving them centuries together in each turn of life. Over the eons, their periods of renewal had lengthened and times aware of each other had shrunk. Last cycle, their time with freedom of the air and land had dwindled to just over a century, while her call to the sea had lagged behind his by several years. This time they'd had less than three decades together, living and giving as fully as they could.

Naked and chilled in her solitude, she found a sandy hollow between boulders. She raked stones into a circle, then flung together a nest of driftwood.

She wouldn't go back for the clothes, the house, or other appurtenances of human life. Sinking down, she reshaped into salamander form, flames roaring up from translucent orange skin flecked with emerald and sapphire.

Winged lions, winged serpents, eagle-headed humans... As part human, part animal beings or preternatural creatures, they had awed humans through the ages.

She extinguished her own fire. In pleasing spurts of color, flames consumed the driftwood.

Treading carefully to avoid smothering the fire, she clung with toepads to the warming rocks, inhaling and exhaling the wood smoke and sparks.

Coiling her long body, nose to hip, she tried to sink into the weighty exhaustion of grief, her restive tail keeping the rocks near. Another memory blazed up: A stone hearth, spacious enough for both of them to bask in, concealed in the flames from a roomful of sleeping men.

The flames died. The stones cooled too soon. She crawled over the boulders and reshaped. Seated on a tall rock above the spume of breaking waves, she clasped human arms about the scaled skin of what had been human knees.

Lee's time had crept up on him, unrecognized. She should enter the sea, too. If her own time came without warning, she would be safe in their original home, usual place of restoration. She could go to him, be with him so long as she retained self-awareness. That would fade. And, this time, no waking would follow.

Tears sliding down her cheeks, she tossed back her hair and

smiled, recalling their shared mirth whenever they discovered a new tale they and their kin had inspired. They might vanish, but they left behind a bountiful legacy for humans.

Last to live, last to love, she kicked her flukes against the rock and dove in a graceful arc into the sea.

# CHERRY BLOSSOM 2050

## MARY SOON LEE

**About the Author**

Mary Soon Lee was born and raised in London, but now lives in Pittsburgh. She writes both fiction and poetry, and has won the Rhysling Award and the Elgin Award. Her book *Elemental Haiku*, containing haiku for each element of the periodic table, has recently been published by Ten Speed Press. She has an antiquated website at marysoonlee.com and tweets at @MarySoonLee.

Ousted from her perfumed perch
by the miniature marvel
of synthetic insects:
the last wild honey bee.

# HOPE AND THE HR HOVERCRAFT

## SCOTT T. BARNES

**About the Author**

Native to Southern California, Scott T. Barnes grew up on a farm, lived, studied and worked in multiple countries, and now resides in Orange County, California as a proud husband and father of two girls. He studies samurai arts (Nami Ryu Aiki Kenjutsu) with James Williams and Russian Systema with Joseph Stoltman. In both the fantasy and science fiction genres Scott's short fiction has appeared in many magazines and anthologies, including *Passages*, *Pulse Pounders: Adrenaline*, *Gaia*, *Shadow and Breath volume 3*, *Space Opera Mashup*, *Shambles* (fiction bundle), and many others. His science fiction story "Insect Sculptor" won the Writers of the Future award. He also edits the magazine *New Myths*. You can find him at work in independent coffee houses all over the southland, or on the internet at scottbarnes.com.

IT WAS GIGGLE WEATHER. EYES WATERING, STERNUM PINCHED, barely keeping it together giggle weather. What else was one to do when Yellowstone was about to drop Old Faithful around your ears? The Yellowstone River flowed a muddy palette of yellows and oranges, a potpourri of sulfuric odors, as if it passed through Hades on its way to Billings, Montana. A fitting precursor of the inevitable blow.

The big kaboom. The supervolcano event of a gillion years.

And so when Mark from Human Resources summoned her to his office for an urgent meeting, Hope ate the last of her freeze-dried crickets.

*Keep it together. Keep it together.*

She licked the precious salt from her fingers and slipped the bag back in the vending machine, which sucked it inside greedily. Its screen displayed the depressing verdict:

**Hope Dempsey, credits: 0**

She turned her back on the vending machine, and on the auto dealership showroom. She climbed the stairs to Mark's office, picked her way over the skylight teeth which peppered the red carpeted stairs. The first earthquakes had done it, shattered most of the showroom's windows and skylights. Hope had been knocked to the ground, and was a little disappointed to have passed the event with nothing more serious than dust in her red hair and eyelashes.

Not that she wanted to die. Not exactly.

It's just that…she didn't feel like moving out of the way.

If the breeze shifting through the window frames wasn't enough reminder, a constant rumble warned of the Earth's agitation. Thunder from a distant storm. Hope had supposed all the *Apparecchiatura* types left on the first round of evacuations— or borrowed one of the faster models and tested its speed against the coming Armageddon. (Recalling her grandmother's native Italian, she smiled.)

She wished Dame Yellowstone would just get it over with. Hit the big red reset button.

Her loafer slipped on some broken glass; her ankle rolled painfully. God, her shoes really weren't built for this. She was a car salesman, not a junkyard rat. Despite being a young thirty-three, only slightly malnourished, the stairs to HR brought on panting. Probably a left-over adrenaline rush from when HR could actually do something to her.

As if.

With Yellowstone about to blow, only a lingering survival instinct could tingle Hope's spine.

What did HR want with her anyway? Maybe Mark was in a hurry to give her a raise.

That did it.

She giggled.

She needed to compose herself. Be dignified. From the top of the stairs she gazed over the Karma Romero showroom. God, she loved this place. Millionaire sports cars; out-of-reach SUVs; and Hope's favorite, the Hov-902, capable of traveling equally over land or water. A sleek, cerise hovercraft with mirror-shade windows graced the place of honor: directly in front of the dealership's grand entrance. The EPA particulate rating for the Hov-902 was such that only those with an astronomical Civic Tally could buy one. Way out of Hope's league. She could only admire from afar. And take it out to the wetlands for the occasional test drive.

It was enough.

Let other people aspire to politics or movie star fame. Hope's passion had been right here, on the showroom floor.

If she looked down the four lane King Avenue, past Dave's Bridal and Fuddruckers, down a wide strip of urban green that Billings had had the good sense to maintain, Hope could see a smudge on the horizon. God's thumbprint. *I painted it*, He seemed to be saying, *and it's time for a fresh canvas*. About 140 miles in a straight line to the nascent cinder cone, which the news said put them squarely in the blast radius.

She squinted at that distant smudge, but didn't detect any change.

~

MARK'S DOOR BLINKED INTO LIFE. IT SHOWED A RELAXING ZEN garden, stones raked into satisfying contours.

"Hello Hope," purred the door. "We care about you in Human Resources. Care to see your mood?"

"Sure. Why not?"

The image swirled. Golden sand cascaded into a shapely curve. Black boulders tumbled down. A volcanic mountain grew. Swaying palm trees sprouted.

Palm trees?

A tropical island.

Appeared a fathomless ocean. The palm trees whipped in hurricane winds. The fronds blurred. The ocean threw waves onto the sand, waves that surged past the sand, overwhelmed it, sought the beautiful vegetation, uprooted it, pulled it into the foam. It was astonishing and terrible and beautiful.

The AI allowed a few seconds for contemplation.

"We recommend postponing your meeting," said the throaty door.

"No time," Hope responded. "Appointment with Mark Watson. Urgent."

The door sprang open.

Mark Watson, black hair cut above the ears, double chin, fashionably overweight, with a black suit and matching enhanced reality goggles, spun his chair toward the door. His mouth registered surprise. The bio-marker tattoo on his neck pulsed 94—his Civic-T. Near perfect. He'd have extra food coupons on the weekends. He could buy shoes direct from the manufacturer. And a non-restricted driver's license. *Coglione!* as her grandmother would have said. He could "borrow" one of these beautiful Karma Romeros every evening. The open road. Tight turns. Seat-crushing acceleration.

A stuffed, electric blue bison rested on the corner of his desk.

Mark from HR removed his E.R. goggles. Rubbed the red lines they had left around his face.

"Hope, thank you for coming in," he said, and gestured to an empty chair.

"I'm used to standing. Stand all day, unless we're test driving."

"Did you enjoy your avocado toast?"

"Hum?"

"That's what you usually have in the break room. Avocado toast on wheat, I think it is."

She was surprised he'd noticed. They probably hadn't said a dozen words in the five years she'd worked here. Which suited her just fine. HR spelled trouble. And what was that stuffed bison, anyway? Too cheap to splurge for a life-size AI-Companion?

"Actually," she said, "they stopped shipping avocados from California days ago, what with the volcano and all. I used my food coupon on a bottle of gin. And you?"

"Ah, coffee, black, as usual. Trying to keep my weight down."

Suddenly he noticed the bison. He swept it into a side drawer and closed it. He looked embarrassed. "We could put this off, put down that you went home with the state of emergency and didn't—"

"No. No, I'm here."

"It seems so pointless."

"I insist," Hope said. Weak men annoyed her. That's probably why Mark went into human resources, to substitute free will for dictum. "We don't have a lot of time."

She had a brief mental glimpse of her dad astride his moped, his back toward his family. The letter 79 stitched across his leather jacket in bold yellow. His highest Civic Tally. The highest anyone in the family had ever achieved. A *thumbs up* and he motored off.

Two days later he swerved in front of a delivery truck.

The end.

A melancholy smile touched the red rims the E.R. goggles had left around Mark's face. "Yes, well, Hope, thank you again for coming in. I usually start with a discussion of the good news. A new start, finding your direction, the free time you're going to have, so forth."

"Let me guess. Did I clock too many hours again? Print an unnecessary receipt and pass my carbon allowance?" She waved her hand at the brown smudge outside Mark's still-unbroken window. "I promise never to do it again."

"For the record," Mark said, "this has nothing to do with your performance here at Karma Romero. Your performance here has been…"

He toggled some numbers. At some unseen command, the entire wall of the office flipped to an image of Hope in an ugly sales smock. Her neck tattoo flashed the embarrassing score of 19. Involuntarily, her hand reached up to scratch it.

"…well, never mind. The real problem comes from your behavior outside of the dealership. Your Civic Tally has dropped below twenty." A graph which could have depicted a spaceship reentry scrolled across the wall. "You've seen this, yes? Incidents here, here, and here." Each infraction brightened at Mark's verbal reference. His voice gained confidence. He was in his full, *politicamente corretto* element. "And the—what is this one? Treating an *Underrepresented* as if he were a normal customer."

"That wasn't my fault. The software glitched. It showed him as an *Unworthy Privileged*. I thought I was doing him a favor by quoting him a common price."

"A common price?" Mark hopped to his feet. His pressed slacks fit nicely against the back of his legs as he paced. He knew how to dress; Hope would give him that. His hands interlaced behind his back. "Miss Hope, haven't you been through Salesman 101? No one should ever get a common price. They either get a sale price, a reparations price, or a 'salesmen are having a party' price."

*That almost sounded like a joke*, thought Hope. *No way.*

"If you ever get into an official inquiry on the incident," Mark continued, "I advise you to stop at 'It was a software glitch' and let the authorities sort out what sort of price you gave."

"Is that your official HR recommendation?"

"Years of experience." He nodded.

The ground rumbled. They both dropped into crouches. The ripple rattled the desk drawers, passed through their feet, and continued on to visit Saskatchewan. They rose, sharing a look of relief.

Hope managed to swallow on her dry throat. "So, that's it, then? You're firing me?"

Mark turned again to his precious wall screen. "Banned words flagged eight times in the past week alone. Unsanctioned combinations of words twenty times."

"Cut it, HR. You're firing me."

"No, Hope. You are no longer eligible to work here. In fact, you are no longer eligible to work anywhere. You are due to check into Civic Rehab at—" he clicked a flashing icon "—three thirty tomorrow."

"Rehab that's going to be buried under six feet of ash," she growled. She turned heel and stalked out.

≈

THERE IT WAS. THE BEAUTIFUL HOV-902. THE BALCONY OFFERED
a God's-eye view. Sculpted headlamps. Clear rear hood to show
off its twin three hundred-horsepower electric engines.
Sweeping airfoil lines rising to the over-sized rear fan. Silver-
red skirt, glittery as scales on a rainbow trout, just waiting to
billow out. A bottle of gin under the passenger seat. Hope
breathed down at it in envy. The smell of synthetic oil and
rubber had her salivating.

How to get in?

Ineligible to work anywhere.

No test drives. No showing cars. Even the damn bottle of gin
was off limits.

She could find something to smash a window.

Mess up her Hov-902? Hell with that.

Mark would open it for her. He'd better open it for her. She
wouldn't be able to "test drive" it, but at least she'd have a cozy
place to watch the eruption.

What was that stupid bison, anyway?

Their little meeting had upset her more than she realized.
She itched to throw something. Scream and throw something.
"Here's what you can do with your damn Civic-T!" Adrenaline
coursed where antidepressants feared to tread. A string of
Italian cuss words vied for the use of her tongue.

Mark had done his duty; hadn't let the misfit off for a measly
volcanic eruption. In a few hours they would be buried under
several feet of ash, but his Civic-T would go down unblemished.
He could have evacuated with the rest of the brass but noooo,
he had to tick this off his to-dos.

At least he hadn't tried to escort her off the premises. That
would have seriously cramped her plans.

Why hadn't he done so?

For that matter, why was he still here?

Why?

HR had ruined a perfectly good ending. Mark and his stuffed bison.

She whirled. "Dempsey, Hope," she told the door. It still displayed the wind-whipped island. "I have an appointment."

Mark pulled off his goggles again and swore. He was seated.

"Forget to lock the door?"

"No, I—"

She stalked around his desk and planted a foot between his legs so he couldn't stand. "Why did you call me into your office?"

"I, ah, I figured you had been evacuated. I didn't want to fire you, really—"

"Your goggles would have told you who was in the showroom today. You're a hopeless boot licker, aren't you? Have to do your duty, even on the eve of Armageddon." She pushed down with her toe until he squawked.

"Okay, okay. I knew you were here."

"Then why? Why did you have to spoil my carefully thought-out ending?"

When he didn't answer, she shoved with her foot. Her glute gave a little twinge—nearly cramped. She'd have to drink more water! An absurd thought considering...

Mark's chair rolled back to hit the far wall. His head wobbled. His brown eyes crawled up toward his eyebrows.

She liked taking power from this measly HR punk. They'd been pushing her around with keystrokes her whole damn life. She felt powerful. Titillated. Thrilled. Hysterical.

Hysterical? Why not?

Without taking her eyes from Mark, with an exploratory left hand, she opened his desk drawer, removed the soft, fluffy bison. "You see that brown smudge on the horizon? It's getting bigger. Getting closer. They're calling it 'New Faithful.' Atoms split apart and reformed in interesting ways. New elements may even be formed. Our bodies shredded like Kleenex in a washing machine."

Mark's fingers twitched.

The wind picked that moment to snap the American flag on the corner of their building.

"Do you know what time it is, Mark from HR? It is a time when absolutely anything is permissible."

"I, ah, what do you mean?"

"I can call you any name I please. 'Figlio di puttana. Cretino. Idiota. Bastardo son of a nematode.' I can throw a tantrum, throw you through the window. I can smash up the vending machine and eat every chocolate bar I find, or light up these wasteful pieces of paper you've been doodling on and burn down the whole dealership. No one would ever know. Or care. Only you and me." She swept everything off Mark's desk. Paper, pencils, sharpener and clips, E.R. goggles and doodle-covered pieces of paper rained down. She sat on the edge of the desk demurely. Affected her best innocent librarian smile. "Or I could make passionate love to you right here, now, on this over-sized desk. And no consequences would ensue."

"You've, ah, obviously been drinking."

"Not. Enough."

He tripped out of his chair, his face full of fear and hope and awe.

God, this felt good! Her index finger stroked the bison's shaggy beard.

"Mark from HR, you are looking at a hopeless subversive with:

"Nothing.

"To.

"Lose."

She dropped the bison and grabbed his fancy chair, intending to make good on her promise and launch it through the window. She managed to roll it across the room, but couldn't pick it up. The danged thing was too heavy. Still bent over, she looked at him. "Well, come on, then," she said, "help me out."

"Hope Dempsey," Mark exclaimed, "where have you been all my life!"

He grabbed the back of the chair. "Not that way, here, inside." He steered the chair away from the window and together they heaved it into the screen making up the back wall. The glass cracked. There was a satisfying electrical pop from somewhere inside. The lights blinked.

"And this, too," Hope said, kicking the E.R. goggles where they'd fallen.

He gulped at them.

"Go on. No more Civic-Ts. No more anything but flesh and feeling and pain."

He raised a black-soled heel, heavy with hesitation, and dropped it.

"Not good enough."

He nodded. "I've always wanted to do this," he said. "I think I'm dependent on enhanced reality, you know? Like the world is just—"

"You're going to blow this."

He nodded, shut his trap. Raised the foot. Dropped it. Again and again until the goggles shorted out. "Wow, Hope. Just... Wow."

"I know. This isn't like me at all."

Mark held out his hand and she took it.

Mark said, "There is something I've always wanted to do. I think...I think you've given me permission to do it."

"Now wait," Hope said. Maybe he had taken her too literally. "I may have gone overboard about the desk."

"Not the desk. Come on!" He led the way to the door, through the door, to the grand balcony. He pointed. "There!"

"The Hov-902?"

"A skirt long enough to please a nun. Enough CO? emissions to grow succulents a mile high."

"I'm already there. I stashed a bottle of gin under the driver's seat. It already had the best view in the house, and now that most of the windows have been smashed, we'll get the full 4-D experience."

"Sit in it? Take it out."

"Take it round the world."

"Can we do that?" Mark asked.

"What can't we do? We're subversives."

The glowing Civic-T of Mark's neck tattoo had barely dropped. Still above 80. He must have really been a kiss-ass. She decided not to point that out.

"Wait." She ran back into his room, returned with the bison.

"That's, ah, embarrassing."

"So is this." She pulled him close for a kiss. His lips hardly responded—but his body did. It stiffened in red-eared panic.

"Ah, Hope, um. Wow. Just... Why embarrassing?"

"Because, I don't even find you attractive."

He blinked. Laughed. "Neither do I."

He leaned forward and she accepted a second kiss. This time his lips softened.

"Look." He pointed.

Dashed line by dashed line, King Avenue folded toward them, underground dominoes tumbling. An approaching earthquake tore through Billings. Trees shook in rapid succession. Streetlights swayed, jangled. Buildings wobbled one after another. Alarms shrieked. The AI door flickered out. Mark's neck tattoo expired.

They both shouted, "Run!"

They took the stairs down two at a time, too fast to hold hands. Two stairs down, now four, now six. An earthen tidal bore slammed into the building. The remaining windows billowed in, dragonfly wings. The chrome handrail became a thrumming piano string. Hope grabbed for it. It slapped her hand. *Get away! I'm playing music!* She hurdled over without meaning to, an Olympic leap. The new cars jitterbugged, bumper cars on a wild carnival ride. Mark barreled down the stairs sideways, spit flinging from open lips.

*Good God*, Hope thought, *do I look like that?*

The dragonfly wings shattered. Glass shards raced Hope to the floor. She spun again.

*Look, I'm walking on the ceiling.*

Wham!

Her spine erupted through her chest. Her elbows lay numb. Her hands were squashed spiders.

The floor shook still, bouncing her like an exploding popcorn kernel, mocking her with dust and ceiling tile hail. She could do nothing but shake. It took great force of will to keep her tongue from between her chattering teeth.

Mark arrived before the trembling stopped. Scratches adorned one side of his face. His bangs covered one eye. His collar was askew. He might have been in a gentlemanly scuffle for all the damage he'd taken.

"Are you? Are you?"

"Gin," she croaked.

"All right."

More glass tinkled, what she assumed was Mark breaking into the hovercraft. Moments later alcohol stung her lips. She swallowed as fast as her prone position would allow, though all too much leaked from the sides of her mouth. Pain radiated from the back of her hands, crawling through the damaged elbows like a line of stinging ants.

Pain was what it felt like to be alive, she realized, and wished she could feel the same from her feet. So far, nothing.

"How do I look?" she managed, after her third sputtering swallow.

His eyes roved. He shrugged into a sort of half smile.

"That bad?"

"After an 8.7 earthquake, I'd say you look fine."

"Is that what it was?"

"We can claim anything we want, can't we? Nine point three. Nine point seven."

"Make it a perfect ten," she said, noting the play on words after the fact. "Help me into the hovercraft."

"I will have to drive it on manual," he apologized. He picked her up—Mark from HR was surprisingly strong and gentle— and set her down in the passenger seat. "GPS will be down. The earthquake killed the autopilot."

Looking at her now-useless hands, she didn't argue. She wondered if the bones would set on their own, if they'd have to be re-broken, if any doctors would be left to do it. She wondered if she were paralyzed, and if it mattered anymore.

Would Mark still care about her if she were paralyzed?

He added, "I can fly over anything above about three feet. Beyond that, I've done lots of sims."

The car allowed them to start it. Maybe Mark's Civic-T was still high enough. Maybe the hovercraft's on-board computer had a survival instinct. The car floated with an air-conditioner hum through the broken doors and into the street. The vibration was even and soothing, in contrast with the black cloud rushing to swallow the entire horizon.

"She must have blown," Hope noted.

"Which way? Onward toward the paint pots, geysers and sulfur springs? Or do we turn tail and run like cowards? That cloud will be expanding at three, four hundred miles per hour. No way to outrun it."

Hope inhaled deeply, considering. "God, this leather. If I wanted any smell to be the last one to touch my nostrils, it would be leather seats in a Hov-902."

Mark placed the blue bison on the dash. It reflected in the tinted window, giving the eye of the storm an electric blue tint.

"It might be poison gas, turn our insides to jelly. Or superheated air, peel the skin from our faces like getting stuffed inside a Traeger. Or maybe it's that six feet of ash they keep talking about—"

"What's with that bison?" Hope interrupted.

"I named it Compassion. Whenever I have a meeting like...well, like today's, I hide it in a drawer before the start. It's like knowing that deep down inside I have Compassion but not letting anyone else see it. This time I forgot to put it away. You think that was a sign?"

He floated over the cement barriers, down a steep bank, onto the surface of the river. The aroma had degenerated further, now a deep bitumen, as though the volcano had already digested a good-sized city and burped it out of the Yellowstone. Mark turned south, straight toward New Faithful.

Hope didn't see fit to correct him. Wind whipped through the broken window to tangle her red hair. The cold air crept down her neck. Her skin replied with goosebumps.

It felt glorious.

"Is it a sign?" Hope smiled over at her new companion. "Yes. A sign that you are an idiot, Mark from HR."

Mark pushed a black lever forward, kicking the propulsion fan into high.

"That's good enough for me," he replied.

# UNDER LAND AND SEA

## DAVIAN AW

**About the Author**

Davian Aw is a Rhysling Award nominee whose short fiction and poetry have appeared in over 30 publications, including *Strange Horizons*, *Abyss & Apex*, *Anathema*, *Star\*Line* and *Diabolical Plots.* He lives in Singapore with his family.

when the storms begin, we flee into the earth
digging on through basements of malls and
    stations
from an era slipping into the past; the drowned
    streets
paving the bed of a new sea.

adventurers swim up through airlocks
to explore the old city. washed-out buildings rise
through the sodden blue of prolonged twilight,
cars rusting quietly beside them.

the roads are flanked with dead trees.
in the gardens, pale flowers trail limply
from the ends of tendrils, reaching with us
for a distant memory of sky.

# LIVING ON THE SOUNDS OF STATIC

## BARUCH NOVEMBER

**About the Author**

Baruch November is the author of the recently published book of poems entitled *Bar Mitzvah Dreams.* His works have been found in *Paterson Literary Review, Lumina,* and *The Forward.* He teaches literature and writing at Touro College.

We wear metal-plated pajamas
for business, for pleasure.

This is the future, we sleep
standing up,

but wake up to sit down,
while enjoying sounds
of static with cohorts.

We later orate in small tin
echoing voices.

We cast votes for towering
electromagnets.

We do not love anyone but ourselves
and even that
is not recommended.

We cannot pick tulips because we cannot
fall in love,
and there are no more tulips.

This is the future—no one dares
grow a beard, unless
it is a fiber-optic beard.

No one dares kill ants or bacteria
without specific license.

No one fears any version of darkness

for our bodies
manufacture light.

# PAUSE

## DAVIAN AW

**About the Author**

Davian Aw is a Rhysling Award nominee whose short fiction and poetry have appeared in over 30 publications, including *Strange Horizons, Abyss & Apex, Anathema, Star\*Line* and *Diabolical Plots*. He lives in Singapore with his family.

we walk down empty streets with naught
but inanimate life, driverless cars flashing
headlights to warn and uncover and glint
momentarily off the wet sheen on the side
of a robotic trash can, turning round and round
in the perverse solo dance of malfunction
with grasping claws that catch only air
all around it rains the dream rain, slowing
to a glowing suspension of water threads
before hideaway alleyways, dark open portals
that might still have people within them,
mere ghosts of consciousness that flit and worry
a plane apart, unreachable
in this forever night, time has run its course
to leave us be with noontime stars
and echoing images of our pasts;
the reckless youths we used to be
speed out an alley, laughing—
wheels crush newspapers, crackling leaves
outriding the stars and searching streetlights
to corners where darkness still reigns
and no one will find them
for they are the only ones left.
remember that time when there was time
unravelling in persistent linearity
and we thought we could lose ourselves
and still find our way back home;
we are the only ones left.

# BONE READING

## JOANNE STEINWACHS

**About the Author**

Joanne lives and writes in Colorado with her husband and Great Dane. When not writing, she spends a great deal of time in the mountains—mostly in places with no cellphone coverage. Her writing focus is on people's transformations and growth.

THE LAST STARS OF THE NIGHT REFLECT ON THE SMOOTH HUTS OF the Gibraltar camp and make the Rock squatting offshore a blurred, dark presence. The sea sounds lonely and inhuman. I like it. A nanosphalt trail leads down to the water, a perfect dry line in the sand. I walk beside it to the cave where the bones are. Sand gets in my shoes. The damn archeologists can all sleep; I need to get to work the faster to get out of here.

Lights come on automatically when I pass through the gate at the cave mouth. Geometric trenches and squares are dug into the ground, bones lying in them like skeletal bathers. One of the Neanderthal skulls tilts face up, eyeholes shadowed by the lights above. Sound begins in the back of my head, near the place my memories stay, but not the same. I wonder if it's one of the bad ones sneaking into my attention.

Christine, you know what to do. Take a deep breath in. Hold it. Count to eight. Let it go. Shield up. I feel the nanites moving around in my brain, shuffling the neurotransmitters.

When I got my prosthetic, Dr. Demarest told me I didn't really feel anything because the brain had no sensation. She said the headaches and the feeling of the shield working were imaginative constructs. I loved her so much then that she didn't need to be right. I was a kid.

The shield mobilizes and cool distance descends, but the sound still floats there. I can almost make it out; the sound of singing. I tell myself I'm just manufacturing it out of the sound of the sea, jetlag and the early morning wind. It feels like I'm working; but I've never scanned a subject without touching at least one of the artifacts. Dirty bones, the scraps of clothing, tarnished wedding rings—the pathetic debris a dead person leaves behind. Artifacts.

When I walk deeper into the cave, I check the floor to make sure no one's left any stuff laying around to trap me in an invol. I don't want to take any chances. No involuntary scans right now. No picking up dirty secrets from someone's forgotten glove. I check for traps; the floor is bare.

"Off," I say, "turn the lights off." There's a slight hesitation—billions of lighting nanites whispering to each other; "Did she say off?" and then the lights fade down to a subtle glow.

"Completely off." But the lights don't dim any more. Frustrated, I turn to the mouth of the cave, to check if those lights are still on. The dim light is the sea reflecting the rising sun into the cave, a gentle green wavering on the rock walls.

At the mouth of the cave, barely inside the entrance, lies a Neanderthal skeleton. Just excavated, it sprawls across the floor. I hadn't noticed it when I walked in. Unlike the rest of the bones, it's alone. The skull lies on the floor, a little distance from the rest of the body, turned towards the light, shadows under the big brows and cheekbones.

The singing noise gets louder, a rhythmic chanting like the sea. I can't tell myself I'm making it up anymore. For a moment, I see myself race back into that stupid perfect hut and call my agent, Tony. Tell him to break the damn contract and get me the hell out of here. But I don't.

My shield is still. The sea breathes its green seaweedy breath. I sit down next to the skull in the dirt. The ground is damp under my butt. A fine layer of moisture, sand, and salt accumulates on my face from the early breeze. My hand brushes the skull and a vibration moves up my arm to resonate in my chest. It's like a slow electrocution, without the violence.

A howl works its way from the back of my head. Far away, I wonder if my shield has malfunctioned. My throat tenses in preparation, muscles long unused leaping into action, old soldiers who haven't laid down their arms. Back when I was a little girl who wanted to be a dog, therapists on the ward said I only let out the pain when I howled.

Face to the morning wind, my hand flat on the ground next to the skull, a whisper howl escapes me. Not a mournful dog howl, but the singing howl of a wolf. The first note of a melody sung back and forth with pack mates. Low at first, the howl rises and gets louder; my throat opens and my chest fills with wet salt air to give it life. The wind from the sea pulls it from my mouth and whips it away and I sit empty.

Damn. I haven't howled in twenty years.

Hand close to that skull, I look out at the sea, resonating with the howl like one of those old bells that vibrate silently long after they've been struck. After a time, I hear footsteps. Get it together. You are Christine. You are a thirty-year-old woman. You are not a dog. But I don't move.

I know it's Whitnand before he turns the corner. Andy, he told me to call him, late last night when I got to the dig—not Andrew, not Dr. Whitnand. The lead archeologist. I don't have to see his clever bearded face to sense his surprise at finding me there. I'll give him credit though, he picks up something is going on. Maybe he thinks I've begun the scan. I guess I have.

Turning my head to him feels like it takes all day. Everything is moving so slowly. It's what happens when I move into a scan, the now world slows down and the subject's world is regular speed. But I don't think I'm working yet. I can see his girlish lips begin to move; he's going to say something. So slow, I can almost see his neurons firing.

"This one." The words flow out of my mouth like cool honey. I lower my hand and release my shield.

Just before my hand makes contact, he touches my shoulder, saying something. "What…" I feel a thick, hot wave of yearning from him, but the pull from the skull is strong. I slip away.

Down, down fast. Faster than ever before, a smile on my face. Down and back, back so many years. No Child has ever gone back this far. A distant part of me cries out in fear. The sea beneath me advances and retreats; the rocks become less weathered. Shadows move in the cave, cast by a bright sun. Rockslides move up the cliff. Then the shadows on the cave wall become the shadows of people.

Smells fill my nose, dirt, sweat, and smoke. I am in a body. Just like all the other times. It's asleep. I relax. This is one of the times I haven't entered at the moment of death. I make myself a quiet rider—the perfect anthropologist who observes and doesn't interact.

The person rises towards wakefulness, eyelids fluttering. Then the eyes open, the body moves. A hand reaches down, scratching. Male. He stretches, muscles sliding over heavy bones, his skin roughened by the cold damp air coming in the mouth of the cave. He turns and sniffs; a rush of scent comes in through that nose, pouring information and knowledge. Peace washes over me—his peace.

A young girl, maybe nine or ten, comes from further inside the cave and squats next to him. Her face is heavy, her eyes shadowed under heavy brows. In the now she would be ugly, but she is so all of one piece, so well made. Her body is thick, muscled; tiny shells intertwine her curly gold hair, her dark tanned skin is covered with black lines of tattoo. She turns and I can see the lines travel down her back below a pelt of thick-haired reddish fur. Fox?

She is beautiful. A low mutter comes from her, an extended arm, a quick movement of her hand slips across the air between them. He shifts his stance and hums a note in response. Her eyes dart towards the cave entrance. Another shift of his body; he moves his weight to his left leg. They are communicating, but I can't figure out what they are saying.

She smiles and waves out toward the sea. I feel his face stretch in an answering grin. Just barely taller than her, I realize he's young, too. Grabbing his hand, she pulls him out of the cave and races down the slope to a wide flat beach. When she touches him, I think, this is why I do this. In the distance, the sea glitters. As he runs, a fine sheen of salt spray builds on his face.

They spend the day digging for clams, gathering seaweed and eating crabs. I taste a clean salt in his mouth, mixed with the sweet taste of crabmeat. The sun washes down on them, warming his neck and shoulders.

Even when the wind blows sound away, they communicate. The smallest movements—the flicker of a hand, all have meaning. I don't understand, but the time on the beach soothes me. Towards noon, she leads him back into the dunes, looking for berries and plants.

As the day goes on, I begin to get a sense of how they are connected. Each tilt of the head, each set of the shoulders, each blink means something. It's hard; I keep trying to make words, but there are none.

Near sunset, they sit on the crest of a big dune and watch the sea. She makes a soft trill deep in her throat. He smiles, and answers, the exact sound. She gives him a note, he matches it. I can tell this is an old game with them. He catches her by mutating the note just slightly. I am closer than I have ever been to a subject. If I'm honest, I know I am closer than I have ever been to anyone. I can tell when he will move, and move with him. Until I came to him, I hadn't realized how hard I hold my chest. His ribs and lungs expand and contract, easy and full.

Once, he tosses his head back and gives an ululating cry, loud and long. She laughs and gives it back to him, exact, but one octave higher. In the distance, the call echoes from the cliff walls, wordless. They move close to each other and he rests his head on her shoulder. The familiar ache rises in me. Only when I'm in a subject's body is touch safe. Sometimes, getting what you want brings up the hundred million times you wanted it, and couldn't have it. I push the pain away. Pay attention, you're getting paid for this.

Ocean and seaweed scent the hard breeze. Her stiffened hair brushes against his cheek as he rests against her. I feel his peace.

She shifts under him and they rise and walk together back towards the cliff. I twist, a fluid water movement in my mind, and disengage from him. As I recede, I feel a notice, an attention. He senses I was there and now I'm gone. I feel a goodbye; then an image, white shredding across a sky. A name. Cloud? I throw back to him my howl. That's never happened before.

When I come into the now, Whitnand's bright blue eyes are on me, his hand is on my arm. His sick charge of need slithers into me and I jerk away. I'm lying on the floor of the cave. My hand, still poised above the skull, vibrates in a tiny furious tremor, millimeters above the brown bone curve. I make another mental twist and release the connection. Time speeds up again, back to normal. My stomach sours from Whitnand's touch.

"Are you OK?" Whitnand sits back on his heels. It takes me a moment to make meaning of the strange noise coming out of his mouth. Even when I do, there is a slight unfamiliarity to the sounds.

I lick my lips, expecting them to be dry. It was so long in the then, only moments in the now. Staring up at him, I try to speak. Nothing comes out but a strange husking noise. I feel fear trickle into my gut; I've never had this reaction to a scan before.

Whitnand looks worried. "What happened, did you have a seizure?"

Like a lock tumbler falling into place, the sounds become words and it feels natural to communicate like this.

I bet he wonders if he can get another Child if I'm messed up. Then I see understanding break across his face like a chain reaction.

"You got through," he says. "What did you see?" He doesn't even see me—just the object of his desire. Now the shield starts to work, furiously. The peace I learned from the boy and girl leaches away, leaving in its place the numbness I had once mistaken for peace.

Words come back to me. Whitnand's still too close. "Get away from me," I snarl.

He rocks back on his heels again, then reaches out and puts his hand on my shoulder. Even with the shield working, his angry desperate wanting charges through his arm and into me. Give it to me, give it to me. Give. It. To. Me. It takes the last of my energy, but I push his hand away.

"Don't touch me." My voice shakes. I feel tears in my throat.

"What..." He stops and just stares at me. His face gets the kind of blank the normals use to cover their righteous indignation. "I'm not..." Then he remembers. Never touch a Child.

"Ms. Tenaya, I'm sorry. I didn't think—"

I stand up, wave him quiet. The shield is working so hard now, I have to concentrate to feel the ground under my feet.

I know what Whitnand saw; I watched other Children work when I was in training. We sit or lie collapsed for seconds, minutes or hours, hands on or near the artifact. The bones, clothing, watches, and rings. Our hands hover above the thing, as if attached by an electrical current, unable to let go. All Whitnand saw was me collapse, my hand, if he noticed, hovered above the skull, my eyes flickered behind closed lids. Maybe it scared him.

Tony's voice whispers in my head, "Be a professional. Tell him something, Christine."

Long breath out. The coldness recedes just a bit. He stands and waits, not too close. He's not my mother—he can't hurt me.

"I don't know if it's the age of the subject..." I begin.

"This is the oldest subject you've scanned?" He cocks his head to the side. Now he's doing that irritating thing normals do. They ask questions they know the answer to. They don't like surprise answers, the normals. That's probably why they don't like us.

"It's the oldest subject any Child has scanned, Dr. Whitnand. You know that." We usually do forensics. This archeological stuff is new—Tony's idea.

Anger flickers like heat lightning across his face. I wonder how long we would live if normals understood how transparent they are to us. Enough. He's used up all the break I'm willing to give.

"I'm having a strange reaction. I'm going to my hut, I'll tell you what I saw when I feel better." I look at him, dare him to stop me. He doesn't. Probably knows I'll never tell him anything if he doesn't back off. Under the coldness of my shield, anger mutters and snarls.

On the way back, I stay on the nanosphalt and let it buoy my feet back to the hut. Inside, I close off the window to shut out the noise of the waking camp. Sunlight has just begun to pour into the beach below the cliffs; shadows fall away from the translucent skin of the hut. Inside, it's warm and dry and quiet. Inside it's perfect. I want my old house in Denver. I want that cave.

I pull out the clothes from my bag, to look for a Three Musketeers. I brought about twenty, but I can't find them. My hands shake as they rummage through my clothes. It must be from hunger, I tell myself. Tony's always good when I get strung out on a job. I'll call him and make him earn the twenty percent he gets for being my agent.

He picks up on the second ring. "Hey, Christine, you all right? Whitnand called me."

The phone projects the image of his pointed face and wild black curls onto the wall of the hut. His head is tilted to the side, a half smile on his face.

"I'm just dandy. Remember what you told me about this job, Tony? No murder, no forensics, just who wants to know more about some people who have been dead for about thirty thousand years. Top fee, you said I wouldn't have to work again for six months."

"That's what Whitnand contracted for." His smile falters.

"If it was so goddamn wonderful, why didn't you take it?" I ask him. His smile disappears completely.

I don't know why I said it. Tony's getting worse, pretty soon he won't be able to even use view—we'll just be able to talk, like on those old-fashioned telephones.

All of us Children, we use Tony as our agent. He's great with contracts and negotiating since it's just emailing back and forth.

"I'm sorry." God, I hate saying that.

The silence stretches on. Again I see the boy and the girl on the beach, and feel the effort of communicating. Tears slide down my face.

"Christine? What's wrong?"

"I howled."

For a moment, Tony says nothing. I stare through the projection at the smooth wall behind. The nanites are making swirling artistic patterns in the skin of the wall.

"Like you did on the ward? When things got bad?"

"Just like." I keep my eyes on the swirls.

"That's never happened before." He purses his lips, thinking.

"No lie."

"Tell me what happened."

"I went into the cave with the bones, and just before I picked my subject, I heard this singing sound and I howled."

Another pause. I can tell from his expression he's looking for the exact right thing to say.

"How did the scan go?"

That isn't it. "Okay."

"Okay how?"

"Just okay, I don't want to talk about it."

"A bad one?"

"Yeah, kind of." What can I say? I spent the day on the beach with some cave people and it freaked me out?

"So then what, Christine?"

"I had a hard time talking when I came out."

He pulls his eyebrows together and taps his index finger against his lips. The end of it is bitten off. Tony did that before he got his shield. His chart said, "Trauma-induced self-mutilation."

My chest aches and my stomach feels hollow. "I had an invol when Whitnand touched me after the scan."

"He what?" Tony's voice snaps. What are you going to do, I think, send him a bad-ass email?

"It's okay, he's a research dork. You know scientist curiosity, it's like a bad drug habit."

From out of nowhere a memory comes. Once Diane got really mad at one of the research dorks that came to observe when he called us "the subjects." Tony and I were there when he did it. Diane's face got blank and hard and she hissed at the guy, "They're children, god damn it." Diane called us children, so that's what we call ourselves.

"Christine?" Tony's voice jerks me back. "Do you need to come home? If he did that, I can break this contract."

"I'm okay."

"It's a new thing you're doing here, Whitnand knows this. We can pull you out, just tell him it didn't work."

"He was there when I came out, he knows I got something."

"So what? Screw him. Come back."

"I said I was okay."

He puts up both hands, a gesture of defeat. The bitten finger catches my attention again.

"Tony?"

He gets a wary look. "Yeah?"

"When are you going to go see Diane?"

His face gets heavy. "Dr. Demarest can't help me, Christine, we've been through all that."

"You can't just spend the rest of your life in that house in Florida."

"It's not the same shield, Christine."

I know he's right. It's been fifteen years, so it's changed; we think it's become weaker. Selective bioengineering of nanocyte neurotransmitter pumps and relays, resulting in a higher correspondence to nondeviant behavioral norms. Which, in English, means the newer Children are closer to normal. I guess that's good. It also means the new Children don't have what Diane calls hypersensitivity to neuro-emotional stimuli and the rest of the world calls psi powers. They can't scan.

Tony shakes his head. A black curl near his left eye rocks back and forth. "They're scared," he says. "Demarest and the Institute are maiming the new ones so they can't do what we can."

"I don't know. I can't believe she would screw up the new Children just to keep the normals on top."

Tony just looks at me. "Christine, she's a normal," he says, really quiet and sad. "She doesn't love us, we're research subjects."

"Yeah." This is an old argument between us.

"Call me if anything else happens?"

"I will."

"Promise you'll leave if I ask you to?"

It's my turn to tilt my head and smile. "Maybe."

"You're such a control freak, Christine." He's got that shit-eating grin on his skinny chops.

"That's what you love about me."

Before he can say anything else, I cut the connection. I hate it when he thinks he knows what I need. I hate it worse when he's right. Sometimes, like right now, I wish I could reach out and touch that wild mop of hair. I wonder how it would be to have him rest his head on my shoulder.

The door chimes. Even though I hate talking to a building, I ask the hut who it is.

"It is the honorable Dr. Andrew Whitnand, lead archeologist for the Gibraltar Neanderthal excavation." the hut replies in a stupid British Indian voice. Some idiot programmed it like that. I keep the default female machine voice on anything I have to talk to.

"Ask him what he wants."

"The memsahib is otherwise engaged, sir, but she is wondering what it is you are wanting." This is ridiculous; I open the door and the hard wind from the sea buffets my face.

Whitnand startles when he sees me.

"Ms. Tenaya, I just wanted to apologize for this morning."

I nod, unsure what to say. Tony says when you're not sure with a normal, do an inscrutable. I learned mine from old movies—Garbo. I make my face a mask and pull up my shield. Icy now, both inside and out, I wait.

"I'm really glad you're here." His voice stumbles. My inscrutable often does that to them. "We, the team, were having breakfast and I, we, well, we wondered if you were…"

Behind my shield, I watch microbursts of embarrassment, confusion, curiosity, and anxiety flicker across his face. Nothing dangerous. To give him a break, I had been forgetting to do all those normal things, like eye contact and acting like you care.

I catch his eye and smile. "I'd be glad to join you. Let me grab my stuff." I go back in the tent and get my eating gear.

He gives the silverware in my hand a look. "We've got that in the tent."

"When I use other people's stuff, I pick up too much. It's tiring." I keep my voice neutral.

"I didn't think about that."

Big surprise.

He goes on. "You can reprogram my hut if you need to. It'll take about a couple of hours to collapse and rebuild. Just save the settings."

"So you programmed the voice?"

A proud smile slides across his face. "Oh, yes, that's one of my touches." I keep my mouth shut and look out at the sea.

"We're over here." He gestures to a big nanohut, made to look like an old canvas tent. Why do the normals have to disguise everything? It's a nanohut, for god's sake. As we approach, I can see the other archeologists sitting at long tables, eating and talking.

Entering the tent, I'm busy scanning for traps and adjusting my shield. Whitnand, oblivious, is introducing me to the other scientists. I only catch one name. She's pretty and young, maybe in her twenties. Whitnand introduces her as Dr. Lail Metari. His tone tells me to pay attention to her.

Inside, the cold wind has disappeared. A light breeze, devoid of sand to ruin their eggs and pancakes, wafts in from the sea. Nanites inside the gauze tent curtains scrub the moisture, scent the air, clean it of particulates, remove the aerosol toxins and lower the velocity. Yeah, these people are really roughing it. I wonder why they don't just nanotent the whole damn site.

Irritation wins out over my desire to make this easy. "So what do you really want, Andy-the-lead-archeologist?" To avoid his eyes, I lay out my silver and plate. The pattern on the handles of the fork and knife soothes me. This silver once belonged to a happy old lady who lived in my neighborhood. When I touch the fork, I get the faint pleasant invol.

"I thought I could talk to you about the job." I glance at his face—hurt and anger. Oh well.

I hold up my hand. "It might influence the results." I don't believe that, but all of us say it. Tony says it gives the job a more scientific air. Whatever.

Whitnand is talking again. "I won't tell you any details, I just want to tell you what we know about the Neanderthals."

"Why?"

"To give you some background."

Does he think I'm going to come to a job without doing my homework? So I say in a snotty voice I've practiced for about ten years: "Like the fact they weren't the savage brutes we thought they were? Like the DNA macrosimulations at Stanford? Like the digs in Vindija Cave and at Altamura? Like the Chatelperronian technology?"

"I'm sorry," he says. He's not really, but if things don't ease up here, this job is going to be hell.

So I do something I usually never do. I begin to gather his emotions and smooth the waters between us. It usually makes me sick to do this because I feel so fake, but Diane said normals do this almost unconsciously and women are usually better at it than men. That's hard to believe because Tony's so good at it; I can't always tell when he's doing it to me.

Whitnand calms down and it becomes easier to talk to him. It's not hard—I just listen. He's all caught up in it, and a couple of other archeologists at the table begin to chime in. I don't say much because I'm maintaining my shield.

Then Lail Metari turns to me with a smile. "So what's it like, you know, to do what you do?" The whole table turns to look at me.

My shield rumbles around in my synapses. It's harder to pay attention to the feelings of more than one person, but I do okay.

There isn't a whole lot of the Frankenstein stuff going on with them. Mostly they're just curious. Except for Whitnand, and he's jealous. He really wants to do what I do. I scan him some more. This Neanderthal stuff is a real passion for him and he would do anything to get closer to it.

I give my stock answer. "It depends on the job. It's like

watching a movie, sometimes the movie is really scary, but you never know what you're going to see." All of a sudden, I feel really closed in, so I go to the head. I spend about ten minutes in there, humming to myself, letting the shield work. Once I asked Diane what it's like for the nanites, dealing with the tidal waves of my brain. She said they were made to do it, like an artist is made to paint, or I guess the way Whitnand is made to dig up Neanderthals.

When I come out, Whitnand and Lail and another two guys are all bent over a net projection of the cave, jabbering away. When I pick up my knife, I feel a faint residue on it that wasn't there before, like a sheen of grease.

Whitnand shoots me a glance when I put it down. "That's a really old silver pattern, Ms. Tenaya. If you've got more of them, they're worth something."

He's touched the knife. I take a breath, nod and push it away with my finger. The fork is okay, but I can't use the set again.

We spend about three hours in the tent. Whitnand asks me everything; I tell about the singing, the movements, the silent communication.

"I had no idea you were so efficient," Whitnand says. Like I'm a machine. I guess to him I am.

Lail speaks up. "I have a question."

Now what?

She tosses her hair back over her shoulder. I give her an inscrutable. "Yes?"

"The skeleton, the one you scanned?" She pauses and looks at Whitnand. He gives her a nod so small, most people wouldn't even notice it. Do they think I'd miss it? Probably. I wait to hear what she has to say.

"It's not an adolescent skeleton, it's a full-grown male, about thirty."

I rearrange my Garbo face to show a bit of polite interest, but don't say anything. She shoots Whitnand another glance and he takes over. Perhaps he thinks she's outgunned here. He's right.

"I think Dr. Metari is saying the information doesn't quite match."

The Garbo face doesn't seem to have the same chilling effect on him. "So the information you've given us on the vocal patterns is…" Time to nip this.

"How much research did you put in when you hired me, Dr. Whitnand?" He looks at me, puzzled. Right, I think, how much do you need to know to buy a toaster?

I sigh. "I can see not enough." His face gets all red. Obviously, he's not used to being talked to this way. Well, I guess he'll have to learn.

"We have been compiling forensic data from our work for ten years." His pupils dilate. Data. He likes that word. "Each investigation has certain commonalities." I hold up my hand and tick them off on my fingers. "One, the resonance from the artifacts is usually strongest at the moment of death. But—" I raise my second finger "—in about thirty percent of the cases, there are multiple memory traces." Give him percentages, he'll like that.

"What are the characteristics of this subpopulation?"

Oh god, now we have to speak scientist. "The characteristics are, in order of statistical frequency: crisis-free life events, secure relationships with significant others, death by natural causes…" This causes him to frown. I wonder why? "And a premorbid psychological profile of stability."

He nods. "So the thirty percent had a nice life and died in their sleep?"

"Not all of the subjects have all of these characteristics, but many do."

A guy on his right leans forward. "Too bad, Andy."

Whitnand laughs. "Yeah, it looks like the old man and the sea lived long and prospered." Screw you, I think, his name was

Cloud. The shield's up and Garbo face is on, so there's no way he could pick this up.

Then Lail pipes up, "None of what she's saying contradicts a mass die-off, Andy."

"A what?" I ask her.

"A mass die—"

Whitnand puts his hand on her arm to stop her and looks at me with a half smile. "Let's not influence the results, shall we?" Even a normal could see he really enjoyed that crack. I give him more Garbo.

Whitnand puts his fork down. "When you go back in, this is what I want you to look for," he begins.

"No."

"You won't look for what I tell you?" He's incredulous.

"No, I can't look for what you want."

"Why not?" His voice is getting louder. "Do you have any idea how much you're costing me to eat and sleep? If you can't do it, I'll get another treated person."

"Listen, Andy-the-lead-archeologist. There aren't any other Children who will take this job if you fire me." He tries to break in. "Shut up and listen. What I'm trying to tell you is no Child can search for specifics; we can just get what's available. I'll remember everything I see and experience, and hopefully it'll be useful to you. If you'd done some research before you hired me you'd know that." Even a normal could see I enjoyed that.

Whitnand's face is red and tight. He knows I have the upper hand.

"Just get what you can." He stands and stomps off.

Lail looks at me; amusement, anger and contempt flicker across her face. "I don't think you understand how important this is."

"So tell me."

"Well, Andy's been working on two hypotheses. The first is the Neanderthals spoke and were more advanced than is pres-

ently assumed. All of our research really hinges on the findings
of the hyoid bones, bones that indicate..."

"Indicate the Neanderthals had the same or similar vocal
structures as we do." I wave her on.

"Yes, and our donors are getting impatient."

"Yeah. Fine. I don't care about Whitnand and his hypothesis,
and I'm just going to do what I need to do to get this job done,
and go home."

"Good." It slips out, but once it's out, at least she doesn't try
to take it back. I don't remember until I'm in the hut and it's too
late to ask what the second hypothesis is.

I lie on the bed and watch the nanites make the swirling
artistic pattern in the skin of the ceiling.

"Off. Stop. Make it dark." The hut obeys without speaking.
Warmth slides down my face. I'm crying and I don't know why.
The world tilts into darkness. All night I dream of running
down the beach with Tony and those kids, howling like a pack
of wolves.

For just a second, when I swim up out of the dream, I don't
know where I am. Then I see the perfect darkness and silence of
the hut.

"Light." The lights come on, not too bright. Rather than ask
the time and listen to that ridiculous voice, I fumble around in
my pack looking for my watch. It's an old wind-up Rolex Tony
gave me. I don't wear it very much; I'm terrified something will
happen to it. It's stopped. I sit on the edge of the bed and wind
it, concentrating on the slow slide of my fingers over its stubby
little stem.

"Time."

"At this very moment it is five forty-six a.m., the wind
speed is..."

"Shut up." It does.

Outside, the sound and smell of the sea brings back the
dream. The sun is just rising. I feel a tiny howl rise up in me. No

one is around, so I tilt my head back and let it loose. The wind picks it up and hurries away.

When I round the corner into the cave, the wind stops. As I get closer to Cloud's skull, a wisp of singing and peace comes to me, like a hint of a song learned in childhood. Not my childhood. Sitting, I drop my hand to the cool brown bony curve. Connection is instantaneous.

Once I saw a film of a tidal wave, the sea sucked away from the land by a huge invisible force. It felt like that. Shadows again, and then I feel him. Cloud. It's dark this time; the sound of the sea fills my ears, pounding on the rocks below. Fire lights the faces of the people around him. His body hurts, a raw aching comes from his left arm, his right eye is closed. No, blind. What happened to him?

Sounds of a storm fill the cave, echoing and hissing above the roaring sea. It's cold. Tears cover his face, his chest hurts. He looks at someone lying on the floor, blood-matted hair. It's the girl, she's dead. Grief comes, his, mine, I don't know. A howl sings in my bones, hidden inside of him, I can feel it gathering force. Cloud's head raises, he shifts, to his left is a woman, old, old, holding a child, his and the girl's. The woman looks at him, head tilted, the age-old gesture of questioning. He reaches out for the child, and it comes to him, a little girl. She sits on his lap and nestles against him. I'm ashamed right now, their touch feels like another gift to me. He puts his arms around her and I see one ends in a barely healed stump. Rocking her, his chest opens and fills with my howl. I can't stop it. As it rises up in us, I know he knows I am there. His head tilts back, throat opening and the howl pours out long and full, piercing the sound of sea and song in the cave.

Their song stops in mid-beat. Cloud knew I was there before, and now they all know. Faces turn to him in the firelight, they are as known to me as my own. They see me in him. There is no fear.

I can feel him reaching around for me. The others watch him. Waiting. Silent, his daughter rises and goes back to the old woman's lap. The storm is a hissing backdrop; lightning flashes a harsh white light into the cave. No one moves.

I'm busted. Some anthropologist I am. I feel Cloud's boy muscles tighten against his bones. No, not a boy, he is a man now, an old man maybe. A crippled man certainly. His muscles are so tight my ghost bones hum.

His hand lofts, flutters in the smoke and firelight. An image appears in my head. A bird. The others lift their hands and flutter. The bird image becomes a flock. Sea birds. Something big and white that surfs the hard breeze off the coast. Gulls? In unison, they all put their hands down and watch me in him. Waiting again. I sit inside and watch them. He lifts his hand again and the tribe makes the same gesture.

They are naming themselves. They wait for me to name myself, but I have no voice in their language. A howl itches again in the back of my mind and tears itself free. In his wide chest it builds power, his throat forms and passes it into the world as it should be. Loud, wide, free. I now have a name.

I can feel the muscles, still tight as he rocks, a low bass hum coming out of him, taken up by the others. I can't see but it sounds like only the men. A low muttered hum, seeping out of many thick chests.

I stop, feeling his resistance, a slowing of my thoughts and tumbling images. He rocks, finding a rhythm. The humming grows louder. Suddenly, all in one motion, he rises. How can a body so savagely torn move with such grace? He steps, elegant, into the circle of firelight and sweeps out his arm in a slow spin. Through his eye, I see the lambent reflections of the fire in their eyes. The cadence shifts, becoming faster and at the same time heavier, deeper, darker. Voices move into a familiar flow, backing his rhythmic motion. Long shadows flash across the wall of the cave, lightning scratches my eyes. Far, far away I feel the shield tumbling. It's nothing. Safe inside, I watch him dance a story.

First, the beginning of the world, a break in the vast dark and endless silence, illustrated by the sinuous glide of his one arm into motion out of stillness. Stamping, he shows the storms of the early earth, then the sweetness of life arising, a lilt of the women's song weaving into the bass rumbling. The first people, the Ancient Ones, danced by two aged people. The woman so old her breasts were flaps of skin against her ribs, the man's haunches thin, his chest flabby.

Holding the space, Cloud shuffles around them as they shift and slide. Then the People, danced by a young woman, fat and beautiful, belly full of child. Then this tribe, this clan, the People Who Are Here. Their journey to the sea from the cold north-lands, over many years and many generations. The children born to live and the children born to die too soon; all have a gesture or note or movement that is their memorial. Cloud moves slower now, his chest grows heavy as the dance goes on. Each member of the Tribe comes forward to dance his or her song. Each song different, expressing the individual, but blended into a whole. A sleepy child, maybe two or three, stumbles into the circle to stamp once, spin once and toss his head back with a perfect imitation of a gull's cry. No one smiles that condescending smile adults inflict on children. Solemn, he goes back to his mother's lap, breast, and sleep. The circle closes again and whirls through another cycle. At last all have danced their own dance. I feel I know these people better than I have known anyone.

Cloud steps forward. A tightness rises, mine, not his. He is utterly relaxed around the leaden pain in his chest. Vision blurs as his eye fills with tears. His movements slow, dispirited, he dances the beach, sings the song he and the girl sang together. I ache to hear it, so lonely without her reply. He dances their love, his pelvis thrusting in the sacred movement. His hand slides through the air in the life gesture, sliding towards the little girl, her eyes wide in the dark. Her dark, heavy-browed face shines with tears. His shoulders are pulled forward to shelter his chest; his hand slides through the air, again the gesture of life. And stops. At the same time, a thrumming sound from the tribe. In the back of the circle in the dark, someone pounds rocks together, then someone else and someone else—making the sounds of a rockslide. A woman screams. I feel my heart beat sideways. Cloud gestures toward the body of the woman who had been the girl on the beach. A groaning, tearing cry comes, mine, his, I can't say. It is echoed by the others.

Cloud sits, breath heaving in and out of his chest. Stillness enters the cave, all eyes turning to me in him. They wait again. This time I know what they want. Pulling inside myself, I give it all, the shield, my mother, Diane, Tony, my house. Wordless images, imageless feelings, I send them all to him. He closes his eye at my deluge.

He turns his body over to me, slipping away from his bones and muscles, leaving me room to move. I stand and walk into the center of the circle, stiff and awkward, feeling the pain in his body.

A wash of pity comes from them. In just one movement, they can see I can't dance, can't sing, can't speak. So gently, he nudges me and takes his body back. He tilts his head back and I let out my howl. It comes from my ghost body, and is flat and tight, so unlike the howl he gifted me with earlier. He moves again, sliding his feet across the dust. A low hum comes from the old woman holding his daughter, he echoes it, and another woman picks it up. I release the last shreds of my hold, and float.

Cloud dances my life. He gets it all, my mother, the shield, Diane, Tony. He dances my loneliness, my anger, my shame. And as he dances the tight bands of scar tissue rip inside of me, a wrenching freedom. Tears come down, my lungs expand to fill his barrel chest. Pulling in a breath, I let loose my howl into the cave. It echoes off the rock ceiling and shudders in the air. In answer, thunder growls in the distance. I begin to dance with him and together we dance the story of the People to Come. Caught up in the power and dark beauty of the dance, I don't think of what I am telling them. I dance the wasting of the world, the fouling of the seas; I dance loneliness and isolation and the faceless, meaningless violence. I dance life as I know it. When I stop, they have turned their faces from him and from me. Muffled weeping fills the cave.

I feel a pushing away, a dismissal, the adult sending the child out of the room. I am sent away. When I float up through layers of time, iron grief lodges in my throat.

Coming into the now, my teeth are clamped together, and a strangled sob escapes. I can still hear the sound of thunder but it isn't raining. I am lying under a blanket. From the light on the wall of the cave it looks like day.

Whitnand is talking off to my left. "No sign of trauma on any of the other bones, I'll have to ask her if she knows."

I think about just lying here for the rest of the day, staring at the reflected light on the ceiling of the cave. I can still see those faces turned away from me. I can still feel him pushing me away. The thought of sharing any of this with Whitnand is disgusting, but I know he will ask.

My legs are shaky but I make it up. A hand pulls aside the hanging they've rigged for me. I wonder who the hanging is supposed to shield.

This time Whitnand doesn't make any motion toward me. "Back to the hut?" His voice is dry, no emotion. That's good, I don't want the shield to rob me again.

I can only nod. "I'll talk to you when I get up," and stumble out of the cave, the taste of iron still in my throat.

The hut is again perfect. I fall onto the cot and sleep. I don't think I dream. When I wake up I can't tell if it's night or day because of the stupid perfectly dark hut.

"Time."

"At this exact time it is three twenty-six a.m., memsahib."

I wonder if Andy is waiting up for me.

"Messages?"

"At this very moment there are no messages for your attention, memsahib." I'm too exhausted to be annoyed.

Lying in bed, I feel my body move with Cloud's slow stately grace. I see the faces turning away. Tears rush down my face, I pull my knees up to my chest and cry, hard wracking sobs that sound like I'm puking. The shield is strangely still. I cry until I am dry and light, like an old bone.

Tony, I'll call Tony. All I get is his recording. I don't know what time it is in Florida; maybe it's late—he sleeps like the dead.

"Hi this is Tony can't answer now either I'm out or I'm busy please leave—"

I can't help it and I start to cry into the phone. "Tony, it's me. I'm in trouble…" Then I run out of words. I have to get back to the cave, so I hit disconnect and walk out of the hut.

It's dark. The stupid hut turns an outside light on when I open the door. I have to hiss at it to shut off. Tonight, I take the path. The nanosphalt nudges my feet towards the middle when I get too close to the side.

It's instantaneous this time. Inside the cave, Cloud stands, slowly, as if he's been waiting for me. I feel his sickness, the smell of death on him. He's almost blind, but as he looks out, I can see in the gray distance the great rock rising out of the sea. The wind shifts and I am choked by the smell of rot. He rocks, a faint memory of his powerful dance. He knows I am here. A movement of his hand. A shift of his still massive shoulders. He is speaking to me and I am too stupid to understand.

I nudge, sending waves of question. What's happened, where

are they? Where is your daughter? Nothing. I bring the vision of his child to my mind, her dark face, her eyes liquid with tears, peering out of the dark. He turns, faces the cave; the smell is overpowering. He lifts his hand, making the life gesture and stops. Tears slide down his face, he sighs. Throwing back his head he fills his chest with salt-laden air and lets go a howl.

They are all dead. He begins the dance, shuffling through the movements for each. My heart beats a knifeslice beat when he dances his daughter. He goes through all of them and then begins a new dance, the dancing of the end of his people. He dances the New People coming out of the south, he dances them tall and thin and dark, moving quickly, without the massive grace he knows so well. He dances the end and the beginning.

In his dance, I feel movements from my dance to his people, the dancing of the People to Come. I feel him tiring, I can tell it's been a long time since he's eaten, but he goes on. He dances his people as they assimilate my dance, the consideration over years. He dances the coming of the New People. Deep in his chest he makes a noise like the harsh call of crows. He dances the sickness that came over his people, the fevers, the dying. His dance winds down. I can only watch in despair. He lies down on the sandy ground just inside the cave, he closes his eye. I feel him drifting; the great whirl of death approaching. His chest fills again, a howl floats out into the air, so small only I can hear it, mine, his, I don't know.

I can't help it; I give the twist, the fluid water movement that breaks our connection. As I recede, I feel him sending after me, a gift, the memory of his dance.

When I come out this time, Whitnand's looking at a palmtop in his hand, avoiding my eyes.

"Next time, I want you to check out some bones in the back. We've found a child, we think it's female." He points to Cloud with his foot. "I'm not satisfied with what you're getting from this one." Now he looks up. "I'll need your report this evening."

A smile that doesn't reach his eyes. "After you get your beauty rest, of course."

This time I can't bear to go back to that hut, so I walk down the beach. To the east, hotels are lined like soldiers, but this part of the beach is empty. Images of Cloud and the girl overlay my vision, but the sea has moved the sand and it's not the same. Still, I find a dune like the one Cloud and the girl sat on, and watch the sea.

The taste of iron is still lodged in my throat. I can't feel my shield. I can't feel anything. Exhaustion ambushes me, and I fall asleep, my back against the dune. Sea and salt and wind infect my dreams. I run forever down the beach, hearing the gulls, alone. When I wake, it's late afternoon. Above, gulls surf the wind. One dips towards the beach and I follow it with my eyes. Someone is coming towards me—a man in a business suit with wild black hair, carrying a backpack.

A glimmer of curiosity swims up through the heaviness. It's Tony. He climbs up the dune to me.

"Christine, do you know what day it is?" It's hard for me to make sense of the sounds coming out of his mouth. I shake my head. The glimmer of curiosity fades. How can this matter?

"It's Friday. You've been here since Monday."

A slow current of interest moves in my gut. "Friday?" My brain moves slowly. "I must have been under each time longer than I thought."

"When's the last time you ate?"

Tony pulls a water bottle out of his pack and makes me drink. The water tastes so good, I drink it all. The daze begins to recede.

Tony pulls Three Musketeers, beef jerky and another water bottle out of his pack. He opens a candy bar and hands it to me. "Eat."

The water was wonderful, but nothing like this—salt and sugar in my mouth. I eat five candy bars and three pieces of jerky, drain the water bottle, then sit back against the dune. My brain feels like it works again, but it feels different. Something's missing.

"Why didn't you call me back?" Tony's voice is soft and flat.

For a moment I don't understand his words. "I didn't get your message. Did you come to talk to me about the contract?"

"Screw the contract, I voided it. That idiot admitted to touching you." Tony's voice is hard.

I don't respond. This doesn't matter.

Tony shifts in the sand. "I saw my record the other day."

The trickle of interest is back.

"Online?"

"No, I went to DC." He gets up and stares out at the ocean.

He sits back down next to me, closer than we've ever been. "That's where I was when you called. When I picked up your message, I caught a flight." He smiles at me. I know I'm not supposed to notice his shaking hands, the sweat glistening on his ashy face.

"Diane showed you your record?"

He nods.

"All of it?"

I can feel him vibrating away in that suit.

"I let her check out my shield."

I don't say anything. The sound of chanting hovers in the back of my head.

"She said it was okay—I needed to push myself harder to get out." He squats in the sand, takes a handful and lets it fall. "In my record there was a bunch of stuff about my father. He was a real whack job. When he got older he never left his house."

"So was he..."

"Diane didn't think so; she said he was just anxious."

"Anxious."

"Yeah."

I start to laugh; Tony hunches his shoulders and peers at me.

His brown eyes look like the eyes of Cloud's daughter. My laughter turns to tears. "Why did you really come?"

Tony cocks his head at me. "Because you were crying."

My left hand makes a truncated life gesture and a howl tickles the back of my throat again.

"Okay, tell me." His voice is soft. I try, but it's like the squawking sound Cloud made in his deep chest. My throat pulls tight and my eyes sting.

Then Cloud's body memory descends on me, my chest opens up and the late afternoon air floods in. Standing, I dance the freedom of my howls. I dance Whitnand's lust and his greed; I dance how I can't surrender Cloud to that. I dance Diane Demarest. I dance my mother—Tony draws a deep breath and lets it out slow and ragged. I dance being a Child in a sea of normals. I dance all the Children. I dance Tony and I dance me. At the very end, I dance my terrible gift to them.

After, Tony just sits on the sand, looking at me. His face is open, he looks young. Muscles fail again and I collapse next to him, unable to meet his eyes.

"What else, Christine?"

This time, I have no tears. "I think I killed them." Between us, I see him draw a circle in the sand with his mutilated forefinger. He nods, listening.

"When I told them about now, this…" I sweep a gesture out at the world. "They cried. Tony, they sent me away."

He nods again, draws another circle. "Who were they crying for?"

Cloud's voice rumbles in my ears, I feel his massive lungs in my chest, the howl that's been tickling my throat rushes out of me. The wind picks it up and lofts it into the sky.

"They were crying for me, Tony. They were crying for us. They sent me away because they didn't know what to do to help. Cloud gave me the only thing he had."

Tony stands, looks in my eyes, then lifts his hand and makes a clumsy life gesture. When his hand descends, I catch it in mine. His eyes grow wide with fear and we both freeze, waiting for the shock of the invol. This time, I don't hold it off. I let Tony wash over me and into me. It's hard, but it's not bad. He's letting me do the same. The sharp lines on his face soften, tears fill his eyes and he puts his arms around me, clumsy at first, but then, when his muscles relax, we move closer. Tony and I dance together in the late afternoon sun and wind. My face is wet with tears and the taste of iron has disappeared.

All the way back on the suborbital, Tony holds my hand. Several times, I reach out and touch his hair. Each time, he smiles.

# ONE THOUSAND STEPS
# BEFORE DAWN

## RUSSELL HEMMELL

**About the Author**

Russell Hemmell is a French-Italian transplant in Scotland, passionate about astrophysics, history, and speculative fiction. Winner of the Canopus Awards for Excellence in Interstellar Writing. Recent stories in *Aurealis, Flame Tree Press, The Grievous Angel,* and others. HWA and Codexian. Find them online at their blog earthianhivemind.net and on Twitter @SPBianchini.

THE PETROGLYPH WAS SLEEK AND COLD UNDER HER FINGERS, THE rampant lionesses on the rock of the cliff snarling with their red fangs, in depictions larger than life. Larger than Kilda's life, too: for it was going to end in 24 hours.

She turned her head towards the village, standing still in the sweeping breeze of the morning. Kernag's view didn't fail to impress her, not even today when those millenary stones were going to become the site of her immolation.

For aeons of time, on a twelve-year cycle, a girl of the village had been sacrificed to the spirits of the air. The brightest, the most intelligent among them. Now it was her turn; Kernag's menhirs were going to be nourished by her innocence to keep bestowing good fortune and fair weather on the crops and the land. Every stone a miracle, every miracle a wound on her body, for a thousand cuts of which only the latest was mortal but all were invariably painful. Wasn't that what the druids had said?

Kilda washed her face in the crystal water of the pond, chasing scattered clouds on its clear surface. They glittered and fluttered and almost disappeared in the waves her hand created. Kernag was the passage between two worlds, connecting the world of the living beings with the one where the dead whispered. A passage she was going to take at nightfall.

Only one day to live, she whispered, one day to say goodbye to my mortal existence.

As all other Kernag's martyr girls, Kilda toured the village, hugging toddlers and letting the elders touch her tunic, as a token of good luck. She consoled her mother in tears, drank fermented milk with her brothers, and bowed in front of her father's burial ground.

"Only girls are offered in sacrifice," she had said once. "Why do the gods only want girls?"

"Because men created the universe in their image, including the gods they have chosen for themselves," he had replied.

When it had come out she was the girl offered to the gods in that occasion, Kilda had for a moment thought about rebellion. But somebody else would have had to take her place. Who else but Terzh, the girl she loved?

Kilda had kissed Terzh goodbye the night before without telling her the truth, but she couldn't force herself to pet her hound again: the puppy would've felt her sadness and made her mourning worse. And when a reddish sun larger than the giant menhir at the village's border eventually disappeared behind the birch trees, she cut her waist-long golden hair and shed off her tunic. Then, nude and pale like a spirit of the forest, almost as incorporeal as the white crescent up there, she walked, one step after another, in between the axial alignment of the menhirs, away from the village, heading to the passage.

The air became silent, while the stars populated the darkening sky.

The chirping of the birds stopped as suddenly as the singing of the crickets and, in the desolation of the stones, Kilda trembled with fear and cold, waiting for the invisible hand of a malignant god to plunder her of flesh and life. She was going to become a satchel of bones, despoiled of flesh, devoid of air—

The breeze, the stars, the moonlight.

Menhir's shadows growing in size and darkness.

Butterflies of the night dancing into a circle, twinkling dark lanterns in the mist.

She pushed herself against the wind, deeper and deeper into the no man's land, one thousand steps for one thousand famished stones, awaiting the ordeal.

It was not before dawn that Kilda reached the other side, the fabled other world of the druids and the dead. Have I passed away without realising it, she thought, looking at her hands, long and thin, opalescent in the orange luminosity of the sky.

She wondered if any of the priests and the savants of the village had ever glimpsed at what lay beyond, about which they were so assertive in enunciating the rules and exacting sacrifices.

Then she turned around, gazing at the valley she had left behind.

And gasped.

A frozen blanket covered the ground, an immense white sea with no ship on its surface.

The luminescence coming from the terrain was so glaring that the sky looked black in comparison, like a world in reverse.

Where the thousand and more menhirs had been, there were only gaping holes in the grass, reminding her of giant footprints left by prehistoric animals. The mist surrounding the vale had a fairy quality, as the gelid hand of a ghost or the contour of a mythical land lost in time.

Kilda walked away from the now-invisible stones and reached a clearing on the borders of a forest. As if it were on a magic mirror, she glanced at the same constructions of her village, with their conic shapes, their wooden huts, the birch trees moving their branches under the northern gust. But instead of persons, only man-sized silhouettes of wax populated the scene. Fixed in their immobility, they reflected humanity made hollow and vain by untested beliefs and cruel decisions, and whose gods were not more real than the statuettes of marble she had been taught to worship.

As her father had said.

I call the Earth as a witness, she said, kneeling on the icy ground, for one thing was sure: Kernag's alignment was indeed the passage between the world of the living and the land of the dead, but the dead belonged to the village she had come from. Somewhere, in the land opening in front of her astonished eyes, her sisters of martyrdom were well and alive, already building a brave new world.

Unfettered, unchained, unbound, Kilda headed to Broceliande's whispering woods, without looking back.

# PAN'S DESCENT

## BRUCE BOSTON

**About the Author**

Bruce Boston's poems have appeared in *Asimov's SF, Analog, Weird Tales, Amazing Stories, Daily Science Fiction, Pedestal, Strange Horizons, the Nebula Awards Showcase* and *Year's Best Fantasy and Horror*. His poetry has received the Bram Stoker Award, the *Asimov's* Readers Award, and the Rhysling and Grand Master Awards of the SFPA. His fortieth poetry collection, *Artifacts*, is available at Amazon and other online booksellers. His fiction has received a Pushcart Prize and twice been a finalist for the Bram Stoker Award (novel, short story).

Beneath an ever cloudy sky
that never rains a drop,
Arcadia is slowly dying.
Dead limbs fall to the ground.
Blackened leaves flutter down
in a constant whispering rush.
Bare trees assume postures
grotesque and startling.
Beneath this dark hemisphere
where pastures once thrived,
fields are filled with weeds.
Nettles and thorns abound.
Beast and fowl have fled,
all humans long before.

Only the God Pan remains,
once King of Arcadia when
it flourished with life.

He strolls the abandoned
glens and desiccated fields,
playing his wooden flute
to harsh and mournful songs,
feeding on that darkness
as once he fed on life.

He has grown in stature
to twice his normal size.
He is now Pan Furioso
and his fur has taken
on a far darker shade,
his hooves are sharper,
his thoughts are tinged

with holocaust clouds.

And once Pan ventures
into the world beyond,
he discovers threads
of darkness have spread
from Arcadia and all
has become infested.

He sees the torrent
cities and the faces
of the tangled crowds,
the trash landscapes.
Arcadia is long dead,
the idyll lost forever.
And Pan understands
his tunes must always
be stained with reality.

# ONCE AND FUTURE

## DAN MICKLETHWAITE

**About the Author**

Dan Micklethwaite writes stories in a shed in the north of England. Along with other pieces in New Myths, his recent short fiction has featured in *Beneath Ceaseless Skies*, *Thrilling Words*, and Flame Tree Press' *Urban Crime* anthology. His debut novel, *The Less Than Perfect Legend of Donna Creosote*, was published by the award-winning UK publisher Bluemoose Books, and shortlisted for the Guardian's Not the Booker Prize. He is currently at work on his second book. Follow him on twitter @Dan_M_writer for further updates and info.

EARLY MORNINGS, BEFORE THE TOURISTS SHOW UP, GORDON Barrow likes to lean against the hotel roof and watch the trains. There are two of them, the engines no bigger than his size eight shoes. They circle the village at a leisurely speed, with a buffer space of about three or four metres between them. On some of the colder mornings, like today, the steam wreathes the track in its entirety, and the engines race onwards through each other's ghost.

He takes out his hipflask—the one with "Teeside" engraved on it—and has a little swig of the whisky it carries, telling himself it's to keep out the chill.

He thinks about his father, of what his father might have said.

There are hundreds of reminders of his childhood around here, in the brickwork of this village. The stonework, rather. All of it actual sandstone, fashioned by actual masons, set down by schoolchildren, from his time and after. He'd personally placed and cemented many of the blocks in the hotel—formerly the manor house—which is why he often stands beside it. He feels quietly confident that it won't collapse beneath his weight.

Some of the cars as well, they're his. Had been. The older, tin-chassis ones. A Rolls-Royce Silver Phantom that had been the pride of his collection now rests in the local Councillor's parking space. A couple of first-run MINI Coopers, one red, one blue, sit parked half on the pavement on one of the streets. A rust-afflicted E-Type, another former favourite, is laid up on a driveway, a figurine placed cunningly near its passenger door, disguising the void where it should have a wheel.

There's an old cream and brown bus, double-decker, which had been his as well. Idling forever by the village's only bus stop; never driving its appointed route, but never late either.

Timing is important. Gordon keeps track of everything, due-dates for bills, for bank statements, electricity readings, in a series of notebooks on the desk beside his bed.

Routine is important.

Another thing he does is push off from the hotel roof and parade along each street in turn. The daily inspection, he calls it. Though, in truth, it's twice-daily. Before the tourists arrive, he pauses at each and every house and peers down at the finely kept lawns, the pristinely pruned hedgerows; savours the saccharine glint of the dew on the grass. Bends to reach and rectify any gardening resident or stray lawnmower that might have been toppled by the wind overnight; clears any cobwebs from between the branches of the bonsai trees that are rooted in each small strip of turf. Little beeches, birches, a couple of Japanese maples. There's even a laburnum, bare at the minute, but which in summer trails flowers like a floating field of baby corn.

After the tourists leave he makes another parade, stopping before the gates of each house and each building to check that nothing is missing, no persons abducted, no family pets stolen, that no branches have been broken on any of the trees. He inspects the windows for cracks; paying particular attention to those in the hotel, and the stained-glass arches that cap three of the four sides of the cruciform church.

Lately, he's been inspecting the windows for signs as well.

"Sale!" signs.

"Half-price!"

"Everything must go!"

The village proper has always been of the type that might be considered idyllic. Traditional. Full of old, well-established families and businesses; not a single chain-store nor a super-market anywhere in sight. Not within miles. But still, for all that, it hadn't been without the occasional criminal element. And it hadn't been immune to the financial crash.

Whatever minor misdemeanours had occurred there, however, none have been replicated here. Not on his watch. Not really. The signs are something different—he doesn't know what to call them. But at least this version isn't afflicted by the road-works he witnessed the last time he was out in the actual centre. At least nothing ever gets nicked or tagged with graffiti.

People, even the tourists, seem to respect the things they're bigger than; albeit in a different way than they respect those that are bigger than them.

There is, he imagines, in each of them a lurking, latent notion that they could all too easily run amok and level buildings, entire streets. Perhaps especially in any locals that come to visit. That they could raze the abode of the next-door neighbour who often annoys them, or the primary school, or even the replica of their own house, if the stress of the mortgage payments and the extensions and general maintenance has all become too much.

Yet they exercise mercy, and feel better for it.

They become saviours here. They are in control.

Away on the fringe of the settlement, unobtrusive but omniscient, Gordon feels himself to be in control, too. Sometimes. He feels special. No, maybe not special, but useful. He wouldn't ever say he feels Godlike—brought up as he was, that still rings sacrilegious—though there is a sense in which he feels almost priestly; a guardian of some ancient, faraway faith.

Indeed, when he takes it into his head that the village is a kind of temple, suitable for contemplating mankind's place within the grander universal scheme, that's often when he thinks most about the days of his youth. Not the long Sunday mornings spent warming the front pew, neck sore and stiff from staring up at the lectern, jaw aching from trying to stifle a yawn. But the summers and evenings of being six and seven, exploring the small copse of trees beyond the back garden fence.

∾

SOMETIMES, THERE WERE CIRCLES OF WILD MUSHROOMS. Toadstools. In the shelter of larger flora, the taller, more lumbering ashes and elms.

It was his older sister, Jemima, who'd pointed them out. She delighted in escorting Gordon along the more shadowy paths in that body of trees. And as he gripped her hand tightly and hurried after her, only an inch or two behind her heels, that's when she would tell him stories.

Most often, those tales would be of the age when that wood was joined to the forest that covered the whole of the country. The Olden Days, she called them. History, she said.

She told him how ancient, magnificent knights once roamed throughout that forest, from the top of the land to the bottom, and back again, protecting it, guarding it from evil spirits and malevolent wizards, and great flocks of dragons, and legions of wolves. At the mention of which she would always go quiet and stop walking, as though waiting to hear the sound of such an animal howling or otherwise licking its slobbering jaws.

He shivered at those moments, and clung to her hand even tighter, and she'd turn and look down at him and ask, "What's the matter with you, Gordon? Don't tell me you're scared?"

But he always shook his head, composing himself, pushing his shoulders back and his chin up, the way he'd seen his father do whenever his mother used a similar tone; and so Jemima always carried on.

She told him how, in the Olden Days, one of these knights decided that he would no longer patrol through the forest, from the top of the land to the bottom, because, besides anything else, the forest had started to shrink. The knight saw that the woodland was going because there was too much ill magic, and too many trees had been burnt down by dragons, and he decided that it was unfair of him to risk the lives of so many men by riding out across the open country.

Instead, he felt the best way to keep his people safe was to build a castle. It took six years to assemble—"That's how old I am!" said Gordon, awe-struck and beaming—but it was worth the time and the effort, because, when it was finished, it was the finest, strongest, most astonishingly powerful and beautiful castle there ever had been or ever would be. This knight, she said to him, had called the castle Camelot, and when they saw what he had made, his people crowned him King.

"Was Camelot near here?" he asked her, and grinned in further bewilderment when she'd simply turned to him and nodded. "Yes."

A few steps later, he became confused. He stopped walking of his own accord—maybe-wolves be buggered!—and peered into the dim. Then he turned back to Jemima and asked, "Well, where is it now?"

And she'd looked down at him again and said, "I'll tell you tomorrow."

WHEN GORDON WAS SIX OF COURSE, HE'D BELIEVED ALMOST anything. Now that he's going on sixty-seven, there's the fear he's heading back towards such depths of gullibility. Or, worse still, that his faculties are failing; that his eyes or his mind, or both, are giving up.

If that's not the case, then where have the signs come from? And how have they got there? Actually inside, behind the glass. The doors do not open; the roofs cannot simply be unhinged and lifted off.

He's tried.

Also, those posters aren't around all the time. That's the thing. There wouldn't be so much room for doubt if they were.

Maybe he'd only started spotting them after he got back from the funeral—that's something he worries. That he's been seeing things that aren't real because he can't stand the coldness of anything that is. That he's been drinking more than he should.

Exceeding his weekly limit, as his doctor would have cautioned.

Though, he doesn't go to see his doctor any more.

He doesn't really go to see anybody in particular. And even the people he can't avoid, the ones who come here, he keeps at a distance, as much as he can.

He should probably make more of an effort to remember their faces, on the off-chance that they ever visit again, if only so as he can keep a tally of such regulars; it might show the Council he's being proactive, doing market research, which he knows that they like. But it's easier, he's discovered, to let the visitors largely blend together into a single entity, a unified mass.

Tourists, is how he thinks of them. Even the locals that sometimes come down.

Besides, whenever he has made eye-contact lately, the expression he's been met with hasn't set him at ease. Particularly when someone's gone out of their way to be noticed. Only the troublemakers stray from the herd, he remembers his father saying. Or was it "only the troubled"?

Occasionally, a tourist, or more often a few, will stop and loiter around a certain point in the village, as if something untoward or obscene has occurred, though they can't say for certain that this is the case. Maybe those "Sale!" signs, that whitewash, maybe it's meant to be there? They look towards Gordon to confirm or deny.

Yes, that's how it should be, he nods to reassure them.

Admitting that something is askew or off-kilter would break the calm they've come here seeking. The peace they obviously need.

No sooner had they pushed through the treeline than he'd pulled her to a stop and demanded, "If Camelot's so near here then how come I can't see it?"

She turned around to shush him, and then carried on walking, over slick, dead leaves and breaking twigs, her eyes fixed noticeably upon those autumnal phenomena, upon the ground they covered. He hadn't followed her gaze, had kept watching her face, biting his tongue, eager to repeat his unanswered question but not to disturb her evident focus. She did have a temper on her, after all, as their father had often remarked.

A minute or so later, she brought them to a stop, and looked back towards him. He took this as a signal to ask again. "Where's Camelot now?" he said, and stood there abuzz with expectation.

"It's right there," she told him. "It's just difficult to see."

"Why?" he asked, far less than satisfied with such an elusive response.

"Well," she said, "that's just how King Arthur wanted it."

"It is?"

"Yes."

A pause.

"But why?"

She actually seemed stumped by this for a moment, and looked down again, then up again, and then at him. "Because the wolves kept on getting hungrier and wilder, and the dragons kept on getting bigger and breathing more and more fire, and the forest kept on shrinking, and so finally Arthur told his magician, Merlin, to shrink the castle down as well. Because that was the only way that he could keep his people safe."

Gordon had stared up at her, he remembers, and felt utterly entranced. By that image. By the idea of a magic capable of such an otherwise impossible thing.

"So, how can I see it?" he asked.

Jem looked down and he followed her stare.

"This is a fairy ring," she said. "It holds a tiny, tiny version of Camelot, and it's guarded by fairies."

Gordon crouched down to inspect it, peering hard at the small, slightly wonky mushrooms and their reddish, yellow-dotted caps. A woodlouse or something similar climbed one of the stems. Leaves were in between them, halfway rotted to their bones.

"I can't see the castle," he said, looking up.

"Of course you can't. You can't even see the fairies. They're too small. That's how they stay so well hidden. But there is a way to see it full-size…"

"How?" he all but shouted.

"You put one foot inside the ring, and then you close your eyes and say 'Camelot' three times. And if the fairies think that you want to see it badly enough, they'll let you."

She'd sounded so convincing back then. So authoritative. He did exactly as she said, and on the second attempt he saw it. He saw the vastness of its pale and crenelated walls, the banners streaming down along them, the trumpets raised and catching light; he saw the cloud-wreathed peaks of its towers; the draw-bridge, larger and more impressive by far than the old wrought-iron gates of his school.

He felt honoured to see this. He felt in control, a part of some huge and antique and mystical secret, but felt as well like there were things in this world that were far more powerful and more special than him at the self-same time. Hadn't perhaps known that was what he was feeling—hadn't wanted to step out of the moment and try and put a form to it with words—but he can remember it and pin that description to it now.

He developed a habit of going there, to that circuit of fungi, every few days—Jemima had warned him not to do it any more often than that, in case the fairies became tired and spiteful, and decided he was being greedy, and hid the castle away even further—and he kept up that routine for the best part of a year.

The more he went, the more he saw. The better he became at putting himself in the scene, at travelling around the hallowed grounds. He would squeeze between the bars of the portcullis, take a tour of all the stalls and happenings that filled the court-yard, from the stables to the blacksmiths, from the public well to the archery range. Medieval strangers would smile at him and ruffle his hair—behaviour that seldom passed muster in his parents' house—and maybe even throw him crumbs of food; which he could taste, he swore, as he made his way back through the woods, through the shrinking copse of trees. He would burp, in the isolation of the field, and marvel at the flavours that returned to him.

Once or twice, he even snuck past guards and found himself in the great hall, with the round table, with the shields and swords of all the knights laid out upon it, though none of those knights were in attendance themselves.

And from there on down into the cellar, a great subter-ranean cavern through the ceiling of which he could see the roots of trees like loose, stripped wires intruding, almost sparking in the darkness, flashing in the damp. He nearly opened his eyes, nearly ran, wanting the light through the canopy, the open field, the fence. But carried on, bravely, boldly, stepping between pillars, tearing through cobwebs, until at last he reached the resting place.

The cold blue chamber in which the King lay sleeping, on a slab, with Excalibur upon his chest. Ready to be woken—so Jemima had said—should his people ever have a need of him again.

It was the building of this place that disillusioned him, he thinks, that went most of the way toward breaking that spell.

He had thought, upon looking at the tiny, fingernail-sized

bricks, that no building could be smaller than these, magic castle or otherwise. But that hadn't saddened him. The reverse, in fact. In the absence of actual magic, he found himself fascinated with the world of miniature craftsmanship, which, at the age of seven and three-quarters, had seemed more or less the next best thing.

That fascination had, before he scarcely knew it, become a lifelong passion. He'd never gotten too much into the actual manufacture, besides contributing a new bus shelter when the original had succumbed to rain-damage and rust, but his real talent, his real calling lay in curation. In keeping it safe and cared for. In taking note of any subtle alterations—those figurines and scaled-down lawnmowers sent scattered by an overzealous breeze—and doing what he could to set them right. It was the way he had found to be useful, which is all that he'd ever really wanted to be. Ever since that first time he'd been brought here.

Seeing these signs—the little posters behind the glass reading "Sale!," reading "Half-price!," reading, most recently, "Everything must go!"—it makes him feel shaky. Instils in him a fear of Viking raids upon this, his monastic seclusion.

He's come to prize that early morning stillness all the more each day. Those moments when he can knock back a dram or two of whisky, can lose himself in the silent salutes that he levels at the trains. Can lean against the hotel roof and feel its security, its solidity behind him.

It is only when the gates open that he begins to think it possible that some malevolence might wend its way in. The first group of tourists, striding across the patch of bare grass before the village outskirts—the no-man's land between the village proper and the village that he, more than anyone else, can claim for his own—they seem sinister and ghostly, increasingly, behind the veil of steam.

They step through that ring without acknowledgment, as

though it isn't even there. They walk up and down the streets, only missing cars, sometimes, by an inch or so. Missing miniature pedestrians by even less.

He has to turn away. He has to look towards the small church, its small graveyard. Has to look beyond, towards the distant brown stalks of winter-struck trees, in another field, three over from this. Takes deep breaths, tries and then fails and then tries better not to think too much about her. About how things are ending up.

He can tell himself as much as he wants to what the tourists come here for—all that peace and control and contemplative sanctuary—but that doesn't make it true. When he sees them all walking the streets without caution, without passion, he just doesn't know. He doesn't pay attention to their faces, really, at least not as much as he watches their feet. Is entranced—or incensed—by the footprints they leave. The mud that they trail onto the thin strips of tarmac.

On the days when it has rained, when the surrounding field is churned up like a rugby pitch, he goes to his shed, his gatehouse, and fetches the broom. He doesn't follow them around, sweeping up as they go. As much as he might want to. He saves it all up until his post-tour inspection. He waits and looks about himself to be sure the coast is clear, and then swallows most of what's left in his hipflask and sets out along the streets, brushing the mud into the gutters as he goes. Picking up any small scrap of litter that's tumbled out of pockets, whenever tourists reached for their chewing gum or their cigarettes or mobile phones.

When the roads are clean he makes another pass through the village, checking for any damage, for any changes. It is during that pass that he's most likely to see the signs. More of them lately than even last week, last month. And now one of the windows gone whitewashed; through the gaps in the paint, the insides look empty. Another with its shutters drawn down. Though he wasn't even aware that they had any shutters.

In twenty or so years, he's barely taken a holiday. Has only rarely called in sick. One time when he fractured a finger after slipping on some ice; another when he caught a vomiting virus, and was laid up in hospital for a week, the December before last. Most days, he's here before opening time, and stays until well after closing. So he isn't sure when anything like that would have been fitted. Or why he's never noticed them before.

The Council should have notified him, surely, if anything had been done. They'd always assured him they would. It was in his contract.

He'd received a letter from them a couple of weeks ago, but he hadn't bothered to open it. It'd be his annual pension statement, early though it was, and he rarely checked those these days. He was always plenty aware what the numbers would be. He kept track of them all on a grid-paper pad that he kept on his bedside desk with the others. He kept track of everything. He was always reliable like that, his father had said.

JEMIMA, THOUGH.

She'd been through a lot of jobs, and had moved away to do some of them. Her last one, in fact, had been all the way up north. It was something an old boyfriend had managed to find her—out of pity, Gordon suspected—and which she only ever explained in the vaguest of terms. Something to do with importing products. Logistics, she called it. Even if he had found the words to ask, she probably wouldn't have told him exactly what the products were. Or she would have lied outright, and he'd have known she was lying, and still would have been none the wiser.

When he and his classmates were brought out here, one

early summer morning, and he'd been confronted with the sight of these miniscule bricks, he'd felt something twist and rearrange itself inside him. Not just in relation to his ideas about magic, but in relation to his idea of her as well.

Before that point, whenever his parents had been arguing about her, had been debating how much of what she'd just told them was a falsehood, he'd always found himself jumping without pause to her defence.

That was to change.

He didn't condemn her straight away—he didn't understand what was happening inside of him straight away—but, despite being distracted by bricklaying, and the fact that, if he turned his head to the left and squinted a little, he could see the roof of the hotel proper poking up in the distance, he resolved to question her about it as soon as he got home.

He couldn't do it at school, because her class hadn't come to help out, and besides she'd started making more friends her own age and didn't always want her younger brother around. She'd shooed him away on more than a few occasions, but he had taken it, because he knew she must have her reasons and would tell him in good time.

At home, he managed to catch her before any of her new friends came calling, and asked her, cautiously, if she'd like to come with him for a quick walk in the woods. She nodded yes, and they set off. Both of them clambered over the fence at the same school-wearied pace. His hands hurt a little as he made the vault, from the work he'd done earlier, but he didn't let on. He didn't mention anything, not until they were safely behind the treeline.

Then all he said was, "You lied to me, Jem."

They no longer held hands on their walks but, had they been, he got the sudden feeling she would have let him go. She turned to face him, her temper simmering quite clearly under her skin; her cheeks and forehead flushing red. She stepped closer, bending down so that her face was only an inch or so from his.

"Lied to you about what?" she said.

"About Camelot," he said, doing his best not to blink.

"Oh."

"You told me it was so tiny I couldn't see it, but I don't think there's any building that size. I don't think it's possible."

"Well, you won't see it again," she said, "if you think things like that. The fairies won't let you. I told you that as well, didn't I?" He couldn't be sure, as she said that, whether she was about to cry, or hit out at him, or both. As it turned out, she did neither. She simply walked back the way they'd come, not bothering to check if he was following.

He watched her, the sharp silhouette, as she broke out through the treeline; which already seemed thinner, sparser, more open. He made his way along the lightening path towards where the fairy ring stood, or squatted rather, in the shadow of an ageing, mouldy-barked ash.

He set his left foot down, slowly, within the circle, and closed his eyes. He didn't see the drawbridge any longer. Or the high, pale walls, and the banners that fluttered along them. Or the cloud-spearing towers. Just the fading stripes of the trees that he'd been looking at in the moments before, and was looking at again when he got tired of waiting.

He kept them like that, staring straight ahead, as he withdrew his foot from the circle.

He kept them like that as he pulled his foot back, and then let it swing forwards in a swift little kick.

Only risked looking down again once it had landed, to see the wreckage of those small, crooked mushrooms, their caps and stems splintered and ripped from the earth. Bits of them clinging to the tip of his school shoe as well, which he wiped clean on the grass when he was back in the field.

Gordon takes another sip of whisky, but doesn't like the lightness of the flask upon his palm. He reaches out and scratches at the whitewashed window, but no paint comes away beneath his nail. He ruffles the shutters on the shop next door and they feel real enough, but then when he looks again the shutters are gone. So is the paint. The "Closing Down Sale" sign in the shop after that, also.

He rises, a tad unsteadily, but doesn't topple, and knows by heart the places on the street where it is safe for him to stand. He walks out of the village via the main road, and then steps out over the railway line, directly above one of the trains that has come to a stop.

It is not, and has never been, his job to deal with the engines. They are running, more often than not, by the time he arrives, seen to by the steam enthusiast who built them. He's just about the only other employee who comes out here. But he's a doddery old bugger, these days, and so there's no reason for the finger of blame to fall on him. He couldn't have set up anything so elaborate as whatever's going on here. It's not his style. When they've talked in the past—that is, when they've traded a few words here and there—the older man has confided that, for him, it is "trains, always trains." And Gordon, tending to the housing and street repair as he does, believes that. Respects it.

But the Council, he doesn't respect them. Lately, he's been getting the sense that the feeling is mutual. No matter how many times he asked them what would happen, and what was happening in his absence, when he went up north for the week of her funeral, he had always been met with the same response.

"Don't worry, it's being taken care of."

A whole week of being three hundred miles away from this, his village, and that was all he was told. He couldn't fathom why. They'd been mostly alright on that front before, when he'd been sick, or taken a weekend off here and there, but not recently. There had been subtle alterations. Their timing had grown increasingly off. The posting of his annual pension statement was just another example to add to the list.

Feeling the lightness, the rattle of his flask in the inside pocket of his coat, he begins to worry that maybe someone has told them about his drinking. But that doesn't make sense. He's always so very careful. Always checks, is always vigilant, making sure that there's no-one else around if and when he has a snifter. He doesn't even go down to the local for a pint anymore.

Besides, he only started drinking like this after Jem had passed away. He only bought this hipflask—the first one he's ever had—up there, the day after the funeral, as a kind of morbid souvenir. It says "Teeside" on it. That's where she's buried. Not in the churchyard of the village proper, in the plot beside their parents.

SHE HADN'T BEEN BACK HOME, BACK HERE, FOR ABOUT EIGHTEEN months. Not even for Christmas, despite his repeated invitations. Not even for his birthday. For either of the birthdays he'd had since he saw her last.

He hadn't travelled up to see her either, but she'd never invited him, and it was such a long trip, and it would have meant leaving his village behind, taking holiday time that he might, he kidded himself, need to save up for later.

He asked her to visit, again and again, but all she ever said on the matter was, "I don't feel welcome there anymore." She'd fallen out with their parents many times over the years, but had more or less patched things up with them, by the end, when they both caught some kind of hospital bug, and went within six weeks of each other.

After that, she started trying for more and more distance,

more and more space. Whenever he did see her, she had a hounded look about her, as though all the temper of her youth had steadily been redirected inwards. Instead of seeming flushed, she seemed to grow paler whenever anyone said something that might have upset or enraged her. Whenever he said anything like that.

Since she left, he doesn't go out much. He takes the shortest way here and the shortest way back to his house—the house their parents left him. He's never been one for having too many acquaintances, not since his school days, and so nobody really seems to miss him at the pub. Nobody who cares enough to call him up and ask him where he's got to, anyway.

Tonight, however, he takes the turning that leads towards the village proper. It's thinking about their parents that's done it. Whenever he stops to realise they're no longer around, he feels the need to at least walk by the churchyard. To make that realisation more concrete, or to fight against it, he isn't really sure.

He can't help but notice how poorly the roads are kept in some places. And how much work is obviously going on in others. The cones and temporary traffic lights standing as an indication that Council funds are being put to at least some other use. He's heard the drilling and digging, sometimes, from his house in a morning, and from his village, but has never yet been tempted to come and have a closer look. He doesn't like the smell of tar.

They seem to be constructing another roundabout, to complement the smaller one at the other end of the street, and diverting the traffic in another direction; but it is even colder at night than in the mornings, and so he doesn't pause to read the laminated notice that's been taped against a lamppost, doesn't ask the workmen who sit idling in their van.

On the high street, he is reminded further just how little attention he's been paying to this version of the village. It's partly been a conscious effort to minimise his daily commute. But still he didn't realise quite how much has been changing. How many of the small shops—the cobblers, the greeting cards place, the bookshop—are now closed. Even the grocer's—whom he has arranged to have his weekly shop delivered by, early on Sunday mornings—doesn't seem in the healthiest state.

A lone cabbage wilts in the window tray, joined only by a half-dozen irregular spuds.

GORDON LEANS AGAINST THE CHURCHYARD WALL, PEERING through the long grass towards where his parents' headstones stand, a little crooked, in the shadow of the church's east wing. The smell of the turf seems to prognosticate rainfall. He wipes his nose. He reaches inside of his coat for the flask.

He likes the seclusion, the quiet, the peace of the model village. He likes to take his time surveying the stillness of the dawn, when his heart and the trains on their tracks are the only things moving. And maybe a pigeon or a blackbird, as tall as a house.

But he knows for certain, right at this moment, that he doesn't like being alone.

Even the tourists, even they are comforting, after a fashion. Watching them, he knows that his own problems are not so big. He can put himself in their shoes—the shoes that he keeps track of, fastidiously—and look down at the houses, and then up at the other people, all of them giants in comparison, and know that none of their problems are such big ones, really.

Here, though, on the pavement below the raised ground of the churchyard, he doesn't feel safe in that knowledge. He feels small. Wretched. The stones tower over him. The walls are cold to the touch. Clammy. It is not as welcoming, as helpful, this church, as the one inside the other village. It doesn't do its job the same.

Another swig, and his eyes are closed against the threat of weeping.

It takes a few seconds, but he sees himself, even smaller, slipping inside through a gap between stones. Into the mud, pushing down through the topsoil. The clumped roots of weeds, the tendrils of fungi like cold iron chains; the bulbs of latent snowdrops and bluebells like torches.

Follow them, carry on, deeper and deeper. Past the spent shells of woodlice, like discarded saddles; past the still lengths of worms, like dragons slain in the dark. Onwards and onwards, as though pulled, as though guided. Until the cold and the blue of an underground chamber, and his breath steams and circles his head like a halo. And in the middle are two slabs, and on them two bodies. And his father bears a cross on his chest like a sword.

BACK AT HIS HOUSE, HE'S HALFWAY THROUGH THE FIDDLY BUSINESS of refilling his hipflask before it dawns on him that in here he can just use a glass. He empties it out into a tumbler he's taken, not fully clean, from the draining board. Bids the cheap blended whisky godspeed to his gut.

Then downs another.

Finds his way, cradling the third glass, through the living room to his armchair. Which was his father's before him.

Finds his way, after the sixth glass, upstairs to his bed.

THIS EARLY MORNING, HE IS RUNNING A BIT LATE. HIS HEAD ACHES a little, and he had a bad stomach until he took an antacid with his first cup of tea.

But that isn't why he feels so sluggish, so lethargic. He doesn't think so, anyway. He barely knows if he's slept. He thinks he was probably awake most of the night, tossing and turning, but cannot now be sure.

He feels, besides the ruin the whisky wrought, a twisting, a rearrangement taking place inside him.

On impulse, because he noticed it on the kitchen worktop, beneath another empty bottle, he'd picked up the Council's letter. Torn it open with a butter knife—unwashed and greasy—and squinted at the flickering words, trying hard to comprehend. It became clear, after a minute or two, that it wasn't his pension statement. Their timing wasn't as off as he'd thought.

It is scrunched up in his pocket now, that letter. Balled up inside his fist inside his pocket. He feels as though he wants to kick out at something, but has not yet found anything suitable to kick. Not yet. But here he stands at the gates.

He unlocks them, passes through, and then locks them again behind him. His feet sink just a little bit into the mud of the field; the aftermath of the heavy rain overnight. He walks across the grass, squelching, leaving indistinct footprints. The trains are out there ahead of him, three or four metres apart. Steam billows from their engines, roiling behind them, forming a wreath around most of the track.

A couple of yards short of that track, he stops. Looks down towards the ground, as though in contemplation. As though he's his own older sister, readying himself to make something up.

Even though, today, he doesn't need to.

Doesn't have to close his eyes to see the wide, white bulk of that building, the one that is coming, that will be here within months. Even without setting one foot inside the ring of that track, he can see it. The bright, antiseptic lights that stream out through its windows the size of regular houses. The "Special Offer" signs behind that glass. The promise to give people whatever they need. The masses of tourists, milling inside it. The shopping trolleys. The car park, three or four or five times the size of this village. His village.

Even without closing his eyes, without saying its name three times, he can see it. Even without setting one foot over the track, breaking the chain. He doesn't have to do that, not to know what's coming.

## ABOUT NEW MYTHS PUBLISHING

Publishing the finest in science fiction and fantasy. See our entire collection at NewMythsPublishing.com.

## ABOUT THE COVER ARTIST
### "SUNSET MUSIC" BY JUNE

June is an artist and game developer from South Korea. You can find more of her work at deviantart.com/hongryu.

## ABOUT THE COVER LAYOUT ARTIST

### COVER LAYOUT BY ARIELLE ROHAN-NEWSOM

Arielle is a graphic artist living in Texas. She loves to tinker and craft in her spare time.

Made in the USA
Middletown, DE
20 June 2022

67451008R00249